LEAGUE OF THE GRATEFUL DEAD

And Other Stories

Day Keene in the Detective Pulps
Volume #1

LEAGUE OF THE GRATEFUL DEAD

AND OTHER STORIES

Day Keene

RAMBLE HOUSE

League of the Grateful Dead, *Dime Mystery Magazine,* February 1941
As Deep As the Grave, *Detective Tales,* January 1946
Fry Away, Kentucky Babe, *Detective Tales,* December 1947
Crawl Out of That Coffin, *Detective Tales,* September 1947
Marry the Sixth for Murder, *Detective Tales,* May 1948
Nothing to Worry About, *Detective Tales,* August 1945
Dance with The Death House Doll, *Detective Tales,* May 1945
Dead As in Mackerel, *Detective Tales,* February 1945

ISBN 13: 978-1-60543-479-7

ISBN 10: 1-60543-479-5

Cover Art: Gavin L. O'Keefe
Preparation: Fender Tucker

Dancing Tuatara Press
Special Edition

TABLE OF CONTENTS

DAY KEENE IN THE DETECTIVE PULPS

Introduction by John Pelan

The 1950's are generally thought of as the golden age of the *noir* or hardboiled novels. Publishers such as Lion Library and Gold Medal flooded the shelves with action-packed and suspenseful novels by the likes of Jim Thompson, David Goodis, Gil Brewer, Harry Whittington and others. Another name that stood out from the crowd due to the exceptional quality of his work and the sheer volume of novelettes and short stories he turned out was Day Keene. However, like most of his contemporaries, Day Keene went from apprentice to journeyman to master craftsman in the preceding decade, where seldom a month went by without a Day Keene novelette or short story featuring *somewhere* in the myriad detective and general fiction magazines being published.

Keene made his debut under his real name of Gunard Hjerstedt in 1931 with "Pure and Simple" in *Detective Fiction Weekly* following up with a handful of detective tales and a couple of western yarns in *West* during 1932. After the appearance of "Case of the Bearded Bride" in *Clues Detective Stories* in May, 1935 Gunard Hjerstedt seemingly disappeared, perhaps one of the many, many writers frustrated with the low pay of the pulps.

What actually happened was far more interesting. Hjerstedt moved into radio regularly scripting shows for *The First Nighter* and *Kitty Keene, Inc.*; the former an anthology series and the latter a soap-opera about a female detective who runs her own agency. Hjerstedt also worked on the popular *Little Orphan Annie* and produced scripts for at least a couple of other shows including *Behind the Camera Lines*. Old radio is not exactly my forte, so it's quite possible that he has additional script-writing credits yet to be unearthed.

What we do know for certain is that once WWII broke out, he returned to the pulps only to be told that a Teutonic-sounding name was not ever going to get cover billing. As related by Talmage Powell in an interview conducted by Al Tonik in *Pulp Vault #5*: "When Day began writing for the magazines, he went up to the office of the editor who told him: "This name is absolutely impossible. I would like to cover-mention this story, but I am not going to put that name on the cover of the magazine. Why don't you pick out a good pen name to work under?" On the spur of the moment, Day remembered that his mother's maiden name was Daisy Keeney. Day thought to himself, "If I can't use my father's name, I will use my mother's." He contracted her name to Day Keene. That became his legal name." Many thanks for this information to Bill Crider, who has an excellent webpage discussing Day Keene and many of the other great crime writers who worked for Gold Medal in the 1950s and 1960s.

The writer that emerged in 1940 was different in manner as well as name. Almost as if the new name had reinvigorated him, the man now known as Day Keene launched into a frenzy of production that would not only get him cover billing, but would make him a household name among aficionados of the detective story. For the next dozen years Keene would seemingly have a story a month appearing somewhere. His mainstay was Popular Publications where he featured frequently in *Dime Mystery* and *Detective Tales*. Keene also branched out into some of their other publications such as *Ace G-Men*, *Short Stories*, *Strange Detective*, and even one appearance in the venerable *Weird Tales*.

When the pulp magazines began to fade away at the end of the 1940's, they were replaced by the digest magazines and paperback houses. Some of these paperback publishers such as Gold Medal, Lion, and Graphic picked up right where *Detective Tales* and *Dime Mystery* had left off and pulpsters like Keene, Bruno Fischer, and John D. MacDonald made the transition without missing a beat. By my count (and again, the bibliography is a work in progress), there are nearly fifty novels written by Keene between 1949 and 1970. With the viability of the paperback market Keene's short fiction slowed to a trickle after 1951. He did author a handful of stories up until his final appearance in the detective magazines in 1964 with a tale fittingly titled "For Old Crimes Sake".

This is the initial volume in what proposes to be the longest series devoted to a single mystery author since Dennis McMillan collected the bulk of Fredric Brown's mystery stories starting over twenty years ago and running to nineteen volumes. As Mr. Keene specialized in the novelette and our as-yet-incomplete bibliography numbers nearly one hundred tales, it's to be expected that this series will run to at least ten volumes.

Our intent is to produce affordable hardcovers along with a less expensive trade paperback edition. There will also be a signed, limited edition of each volume featuring guest introducers whenever possible. Rather than present stories in chronological order, I have endeavored to make each book a representative sampler of Keene's work. Thus, you will see series characters such as Doc Egg appearing throughout the series rather than collected in one place. I feel this approach gives the reader more of a sense of variety, as was of course the case when these tales originally appeared in the magazines.

This initial volume opens with one of the last "weird menace" tales to feature in *Dime Mystery*, wherein the formula of implied supernatural forces is gradually revealed to have a rational explanation. This story is particularly noteworthy in that it inspired the lead guitar player of the San Francisco-based band The Warlocks to change the band's name to one which is much more familiar today . . . The Grateful Dead. Jerry Garcia mentioned in an interview that he took the name from "an old pulp magazine". However, the interviewer neglected to ask him whether or not he read the story, and if so, whether or not he enjoyed it.

It's my hope that you enjoy not only "The League of the Grateful Dead" but also the half-dozen novelettes which accompany it . . .

John Pelan
Midnight House
Tohatchi, NM
2010

LEAGUE OF THE
GRATEFUL DEAD

AND OTHER STORIES

Day Keene in the Detective Pulps
Volume #1

LEAGUE OF THE GRATEFUL DEAD

CHAPTER ONE

WANTED—CORPSES

IT HAPPENED IN CHICAGO. The first of the mummified corpses, its tight, parchment skin stretched across its bony features, and a lighted cigarette still burning in one corner of its shriveled lips, was found sitting on a Help-Keep-The-City-Clean box leering through its hollow sockets at the busy traffic on the corners of La Salle Street and Monroe.

The second corpse was found huddled in the doorway of the West North Avenue Station by desk sergeant Phil Regan of the 30th District Police when he went off duty in the morning.

One man had been a multi-millionaire. The other had been on W.P.A. They had only one thing in common. Despite the fact that reputable witnesses swore that both had been alive and seemingly in the best of health five minutes before their mummified bodies were found, both men were listed on the records of the Department of Health as "dead" and should have been rotting in their graves for weeks.

The third mummified corpse was a woman of the streets. But she wasn't found. Tim Murphy of the *Morning Reformer* and a bartender named Thompson watched her die. She mummified right before their eyes as she sat on a high legged stool in a dingy North Clark Street bar. One minute she had been a red-lipped, hard-eyed wanton, smoke curling from a cigarette clenched between white teeth as she talked with crisp, staccato bitterness. Within the next five minutes she was dead. Her soft, white flesh had shrunk upon her bones to leave her a withered mummy whose dried brown skin stretched tight across her straining skull and whose empty eye sockets stared down vacantly at the thin brown sticks that had been her legs, and on which her sheer hose hung in folds.

At least so Thompson, the bartender, testified before they led him away, a shrieking maniac, to an asylum.

Tim Murphy couldn't testify. His was the fourth of the mummified corpses to be found. But before he died he told the incredible
truth of what, acting on the dead woman's tip, he had witnessed in
a lonely, snow-blanketed cemetery on the outskirts of Chicago. He
told it to drunken Doc Meredith, who in turn used the ladder of
eerie tragedy and fantastic horror to climb back to the personal and
professional heights from which he had fallen. But that comes
later in our story—much later.

Night, cold winter night, had begun to creep up Clark Street from
the tall spires of the Loop in swirls of icy pellets that battered
against the frosted, lighted window of the bar like so many frozen
finger-tips that were anxious to be warm. From where he sat on
the high, leather-cushioned bar stool, a paper spread on the bar
before him, Tim Murphy raised his eyes to the window. Ghost-like
figures flitted past it, eager to be home—those who had homes.
The reporter poured himself another drink from the bottle at his
elbow, sighed deeply.

"Tough on a guy who hasn't got some place to crawl into on a
night like this, eh?"

But for himself and the bartender, the bar was deserted. The
bartender paused in his toweling to fleck a bit of lint from a
brandy glass with his thumb.

"It sure must be," he agreed. He nodded at the headline of the
paper on the bar. It read: FIND SECOND MUMMIFIED
CORPSE.

"But them guys," he continued after a moment, "won't worry
about where they're going to sleep tonight. Were you in on that,
Tim?"

"I saw both corpses," Murphy admitted.

"What did they look like?" the bartender wanted to know.

The reporter shrugged.

"Just like the mummies you see over in the Field Museum.
Only—" he hesitated for a word—"well, fresher."

"How do you explain it, Tim?" the bartender asked.

"I don't," Murphy told him. "The thing is impossible. Somebody's screwy. Witnesses have testified that they saw both guys
alive five or ten minutes before they were found. And down on the
records at the City Hall, both guys are listed as dead. One died
four weeks ago. And the other, that broker, died two months ago."

The bartender eyed the brandy glass with a critical eye.

"Then supposin' the witnesses are mistaken, could guys turn into mummies in that time?"

Murphy sipped his drink, glanced up at the clock on the back bar.

"Don't ask me. That's why I'm waiting for Doc. I thought perhaps he'd know."

The bartender opened a cigar box on the back bar and took out a small, clipped bundle of tabs.

"Four-twenty you owe me for his tabs," he told Murphy. "He was in here last night until I closed."

The reporter laid a five dollar bill on the bar and tore the tabs into pieces.

"Yeah. I know. He came back to the apartment last night as stiff as an owl."

"Why be a sucker for that rum hound, Murphy? What if he was a big shot doctor once? Why I'll bet he wouldn't even have talked to you when he was a big shot."

"So what?" Murphy bristled. "When he was a big shot he didn't need a friend, now that he's down on his luck, he does. Why? You want to make something of it?"

"Certainly not, certainly not," the bartender soothed. "Just keep your shirt on, Murph. So you want to support him, that's your business. But you don't have to keep him lushed up, do you?"

The reporter toyed with his glass.

"Booze is about the only thing that he's got left. It keeps him from remembering. I've got faith in that guy. Doc'll make a comeback some day. Besides, I like him."

In that one last statement Tim Murphy summed up his philosophy of life. If he liked a man, he'd go to hell for him. If he didn't, the man could go to hell, and the back of his hand from Tim Murphy.

The door to the street banged open and shut. Both men looked up instinctively. Neither of them recognized the girl who stood in the doorway shaking the snow and sleet from a cheap, white fur jacket. Her hair was a bleached and frowsy yellow. Her profession was obvious.

"Sorry, sister," the bartender waved her out.

The girl's smile faded. She glowered at him with cat green eyes. Her lips were two crimson slashes across a dead white face that had once been pretty.

"Who's talking to you?" she demanded. She walked slowly down the bar to where Murphy sat and climbed up on the stool beside him. "You're Tim Murphy, the hot-shot reporter of the *Morning Reformer,* aren't you?" she accused.

"My name is Murphy," he admitted.

She smiled at the bartender.

"A double brandy, please. The gentleman is paying."

He looked at Murphy.

"Give her a drink," the reporter told him.

The girl sipped at her drink in silence, then turned back to Murphy.

"You're a good guy, Murphy. Everybody says so. That's why I've come to you. They told me in the restaurant next door that I'd probably find you in here."

"Yes?" Murphy said. His tone was noncommittal. The girl, he decided, for all her attempt at nonchalance, was on the verge of panic. Her lips were quivering and the muscles of her neck stood out like cords. "Yes—?" he asked once again.

Fear fought with avarice in the girl's green eyes.

"How much will your paper pay for the biggest story that it ever printed, Murphy?"

Murphy lit a cigarette. "Concerning what?" he asked.

The girl tapped the headline of the paper on the bar.

"Concerning the devil," she told him. "I don't know how he did it, but I know who killed those fellows."

"A cigarette?" Murphy offered.

"No, thanks. I've some of my own," she refused. She opened a shoddy handbag, extracted a package of cigarettes, lit one from the match he held, then fished in her bag again. She found what she was looking for and laid it on the bar. It was a small red card printed in flamboyant gold. "You seen one of these yet, Murphy?"

Murphy picked up the card, sat looking at it.

"Yes. I have," he told her.

There was small doubt the man was a charlatan, but his advertisement was tempting. Too strong for any of the daily papers, it was printed in gold on scarlet cards and passed out discreetly on the corners. It was simple and to the point. It read—

WANTED—CORPSES: Have you a loved one who has died? Would you like to bring them back to life, know again the thrill of their caresses? You can. Would you like to assure yourself of everlasting life, know youth again and all the pleasures it once held? You can. See Satan—Suite 21A, Braddock Building.

They had flocked, still flocked to Suite 21A by the dozens: the rich, the poor, the young, the old, the halt, the maimed. And they went away seemingly satisfied. But what Satan promised, or what Satan did, the general public didn't know. For Satan wouldn't talk to anyone but a legitimate applicant—and his consultants wouldn't talk at all.

The hands of the police were tied, had been tied for six months. That it was a racket, they knew. But until someone filed a complaint they were helpless.

So were the papers. Murphy, with every other leg man in town, had tried to crack the story since the printed cards had first appeared. But they couldn't. Satan could smell printer's ink through the closed inner door of his expensively furnished suite of offices. All that any reporter or sob sister had ever gotten was a bland smile from Satan's smug-faced Oriental secretary and a courteous, "So sorry. Satan no can see." There were even a dozen descriptions of what the man himself looked like.

Murphy laid the card down on the headline of the paper.

"You mean the two are connected?"

The girl nodded. Her face seemed suddenly lined and haggard. She had difficulty in breathing.

"That's right." She turned to the bartender, smiled. "Give me a glass of water, will you, Jack? I guess I'm scared," she admitted. "I feel like I'm burning up."

She gulped the water greedily, sucked deeply at her cigarette and spoke through a wreath of smoke as she tapped the card on the bar with a too long, crimson, fingernail.

"I went to him two months ago. He told me he could bring Bill back to life." She paused, added bitterly. "But he never. That's why I'm talking."

Murphy studied the girl's face, puzzled. In the indirect, fluorescent lighting of the barroom she seemed much older than he first had judged her to be.

"You aren't sick, are you, sister?"

"No," she shook her head. "Just a little scared, that's all." She glanced at the clock on the back bar. The hands stood at three minutes to eight. She laughed, nervously defiant. "He told me I'd die by eight o'clock. But I'm still alive, aren't I?"

"Who told you that you'd die?" Murphy asked.

She tapped the card on the bar impatiently.

"He did. The devil. He told me I'd dry up and burn in hell flames if I talked so much as a word."

"And just who is the devil?" Murphy probed.

"Why, Satan," she told him unsmiling. "Didn't you know? He came up from hell to organize the League of the Grateful Dead."

The bartender grinned and went back to toweling glasses.

"You're out the price of a double brandy, Murphy. She's hopped to the eyes."

"Go on," the reporter told her patiently. "You said you went to him two months ago to bring Bill back to life. Who's Bill?"

"My baby," she said simply. The flesh had grown strangely taut across her cheeks. "He died six months ago. And Satan told me if I gave him all my earnings for two months, he'd bring Bill back to life. That's why I went on the street. But he never. I guess we were such small fry he wouldn't mess with us."

Murphy stared at her, hard. The girl's lips were twisted as though she was crying but there were no tears in her eyes. Her cat-green eyes, themselves, had lost their hardness and their glitter and were sunk deep in her head. He had to rap sharply on the bar to recall her wandering attention.

"You say that Satan murdered these two men?"

She nodded, with an effort.

"That's right. First he brought them back to life, and then he let them die again because they threatened that they'd talk just like I'm doing."

"Brought them back to life?" the bartender scoffed.

"Yes," the girl told him slowly. "He could empty all the graves in town if he wanted to. He's bringing Max Boderman, the rich banker, back to life tonight at Maplewood Cemetery. They say at the Club that his widow is paying half a million dollars for the resurrection." Her voice trailed off in a whisper.

The bartender reached for the phone.

"Better let me call a squad, Murph. The dame is not only hopped, she's nuts."

The reporter stopped him. He pointed to the girl but made no attempt to touch her.

"Turn on those ceiling lights, Jerry," he ordered curtly.

The bartender switched on the brighter lights and stood staring at the girl, his eyes bulging from his head.

The girl still perched on the stool, one arm on the bar. But in the glare of the full light her whole figure seemed shrunken and shriveled. Her dress gaped loosely from her body. Her skin had turned a sickly brown. As they watched, it tightened across her cheekbones until it cracked like parchment. With an effort she turned her shrunken, faded eyes up to the clock and shuddered. Her voice was faint and seemed to come from far away.

"He said I'd die by eight o'clock if I talked. Satan said—"

Accustomed as he was to scenes of violence and sudden death, the reporter turned away briefly, gagged. The girl was dying, drying up as she sat there. Her words had stuck in her throat as the flesh of her neck contracted visibly to a taut, dried thickness no larger than a small man's wrist. Then, as he watched, her eyes dissolved, dropped back inside her skull and disappeared. But the burning cigarette still dangled from her grinning teeth and smoke began to issue from the empty sockets where her eyes had been.

The bartender, staring wide-eyed, began to whimper and make strange noises in his throat. Murphy leaned across the bar and shook him.

"Snap out of it, Jerry. This is murder."

"But she's dead," the bartender whimpered. "She's dead. She turned into a mummy right before our eyes."

The reporter stood up on the rail and slapped him sharply.

"Snap out of it, Jerry!" he ordered. "You'll go nuts if you don't!" He discovered that he himself was shouting and fought hard for self-control.

His stomach retching, he backed off his stool, his eyes still on the girl and fumbled for his overcoat.

"You call the police. I'll phone the paper from the cab stand." He paused, fought his queasy stomach. "Then I'm going out to Maplewood Cemetery to watch Satan resurrect Max Boderman." One searching hand swept the bottle from which he had been drinking from the bar. The glass neck chattered against his teeth, briefly. Then he corked the bottle and dropped it in his pocket. His face was white but determined. "This is more than a story. Hell's loose in this man's town!"

The reporter forced himself to check the contents of the dead girl's purse. It held nothing but a motley assortment of make-up and odds and ends that gave no clue to her identity. Then he turned up the collar of his coat and strode out of the bar.

But the bartender didn't even see him go. He was still staring at the grinning mummy on the stool. A big man, his plump, smooth shaven jowls shook like jelly. Then, as the still contracting skin of what five minutes before had been a living woman caused a bony, brown, mummified arm to slide along the polished bar, its outstretched fingers pointing toward him, he screamed. He was still screaming and smashing at the "thing" with bottles from the back bar when the police from the Chicago Avenue Station arrived.

CHAPTER TWO

THE DEVIL LAUGHS

T TWENTY-FOUR HUNDRED NORTH, the western limits of Chicago are 72nd Street or Harlem Avenue. That's where the car line stops. Beyond that stretch, there are only a few cheap real estate developments, a few small suburban towns, then prairie. In between, several cemeteries blossom white and pink with their old-fashioned tombstones, stark white crosses, and squat, expensive mausoleums. Of these cemeteries, the largest and oldest is Maplewood.

Bounded on one side by the Chicago, Milwaukee and St. Paul tracks, on the others by two highways and the little unincorporated town of Prairie Grove, Maplewood slept—its dead wrapped warm under fragrant evergreen grave coverings and a three foot blanket of snow.

Two yellow eyes that groped through the blinding snow and sleet grew to be a cab that skidded to a stop before the heavy wrought iron gates that separate the living from the dead.

"Four-sixty, Bud," the driver pulled his flag.

Murphy passed a five up through the glass partition, changed his mind and made it ten.

"Wait for me," Murphy repeated to the cabby.

The cab driver scrubbed at a side window with his glove, peered through the snow at the gates.

"You can't get in there no more tonight, Bud. They lock them gates at five o'clock."

"Wait for me," Murphy repeated.

He turned up the collar of his coat, pulled his hat down over his eyes, and stepped out of the cab, slamming the door behind him. The snow came to his knees and ten steps away, the cab had vanished behind a stinging curtain of white.

"But it's nice to know it's there," Murphy smiled wryly to himself. "If I have gone nuts he can drive me right on out to Elgin. If I haven't—" He shrugged and shook the wrought iron gates.

The gates clanked eerily but didn't give. Murphy ran his gloved fingers down the center bars and found they were looped with a chain, in turn fastened by a stout steel padlock. There was, however, if he remembered correctly, a second, smaller gate that opened directly from the platform of the now obsolete and seldom used Maplewood Station. There was a chance it might be open.

The reporter braced himself against the wind and plowed through the snow along the fence. At the corner of the fence he stopped and looked back. Loud on the rushing wind, the cemetery bell had begun to toll a requiem for the dead. Yet there was no light inside the lodge house or the office. Murphy stood, irresolute, listening to the bell while the short hairs on his neckline stiffened.

"What the hell," he reassured himself, "it's just the wind, that's all. Every phenomenon has got to have some natural explanation."

Still, it seemed strange that the bell should have started to toll. He turned the corner grimly. The wind was stronger here and he had to pull himself along the fence hand over hand. The gate he had remembered was both unlocked and open. And the snow on the path that led inside had been freshly trampled by many feet.

"So," Murphy said.

He crouched in the shelter of the ancient station and finished the whiskey in the bottle in his pocket. It tasted good but failed to warm him. When he had phoned the office regarding the girl on the stool, they had claimed that he was drunk. He almost wished he was.

Far inside the cemetery a yellow light showed through the curtain of snow, went out, then showed again. Murphy moved toward it cautiously, wading from tombstone to tombstone where the bare shrubbery and trees failed to hide his progress from any possible outposts whom Satan might have stationed. The bell still tolled.

"Three mummified corpses and a resurrection," he muttered to himself. "What the hell? No wonder the office thought I had an edge on."

The yellow light grew brighter, turned out to be a pressure lantern standing in the low, stone doorway of a mausoleum. Its intermittent periods of darkness were caused by the passage of a score or more of heavily muffled figures who tramped a narrow circle around the mausoleum.

The reporter edged as close to the circle as he dared, stopped finally behind a huge stone cross. In the light from the lantern he studied the faces of the figures as they passed, and was surprised to find he knew as many of them as he did. Most of them were prominent businessmen and women whom he had interviewed at one time or another. But all had a strange unearthiness about their faces; an eager rapture he had never seen before. They seemed to be waiting for something—or for someone.

He tabulated their names mentally as they circled the expensive white marble Boderman mausoleum, stamping their feet and beating their arms against their bodies in an effort to be warm.

There was Boderman's widow wrapped in a sable coat that brushed her heels. She looked frightened. There was Judge Taggart, the retired Federal judge. And Marc Long, the merchant. Sam Green, the banker. Pete Harris the labor leader. Grenfal the lawyer. There was Petey Nichols, the gunman who had dropped suddenly of a heart attack in the lobby of the—

Murphy's mind stopped short in its tabulation. The grim, cold hand of fear clutched at his heart until he gasped for breath. He knew with a sudden, sickening sense of horror what had made their faces seem so strange. But for Max Boderman's widow, they were dead—had been dead, some of them, for half a year. He, Tim Murphy, himself, had written the obit on most of them, had seen them lowered into the ground and had heard the thump of clods of earth upon their coffins. He leaned back on the cross and fought for sanity. He was mad. This thing couldn't be. Or could it? He had seen a living woman turn into a mummy right before his eyes—was seeing living dead tramp in a circle around the mausoleum of a man whom the girl had said that Satan meant to resurrect. He forced his eyes back to the circle.

As he watched, a puff of smoke rose from the snow before the mausoleum, turned into a red, blinding glare that forced his eyes to blink. When he opened them the flare had faded and a man stood where the smoke and flame had been. He was a man of medium size, well built, with a jet black mustache and a small goatee that looked like they were painted on the ivory pallor of his face.

Murphy realized he was breathing in huge, labored gasps.

"Satan, I'll bet you." He grinned involuntarily.

"That's right," a bland voice whispered in his ear. "That's right. He Satan. Supposing you come meet."

The reporter felt something prod him sharply in the back and knew without looking that it was a gun. He turned to see the usually smug, now evil and distorted face of Satan's Oriental secretary not six inches from his eyes.

"Why—" he hesitated.

The snout of the gun dug viciously in his spine.

"You come meet," the Oriental hissed. "Satan not like spies."

The gun insistent in his back, Murphy plowed in silence through the snow toward the circle of men and women clustered around the man who had appeared in smoke and flame. Satan was laughing. Murphy could hear him laugh, an unpleasant, tinkling little laugh that cut at his nerves with icy razor blades of fear.

Doctor Meredith was sober. There were three reasons for that. The first was that he had no money. The second was that in the only bar in which Tim Murphy had guaranteed his credit, a burly Irish cop had replaced the slavering bartender who claimed the dried and fragile mummy he had been discovered pounding into dust with whiskey bottles had walked into his bar alive. The third and most substantial reason he was sober was that Tim had not as yet come home to be imposed upon.

A tall, gaunt man with sad smiling eyes, Meredith had once been the top man in his line. His skill and his fees had been fabulous. And then the post-operative deaths had started. One, two, three, four, five, in orderly succession. Then there had been a lapse of almost two months before they began again. After the tenth death, Doctor Meredith had laid down his scalpel and vowed he had scrubbed for his last operation. And he had. A highly sensitive, cultured man, he had gone to hell fast.

It had taken him fifteen years to climb to the pinnacle of his fame as a surgeon. Ten months from the day he had laid down his scalpel, Doctor Agnew, who had been his assistant, had cut him dead on the street. Two months following that, Tim Murphy had picked him out of a Clark Street gutter and given him a home. For that Jim Meredith was grateful.

His long white fingers beat a tattoo on the frosted window of the apartment as the Doctor stared out at the night. His eyes were bloodshot and his nerves were screaming for a drink. Then the clock on the mantle struck twelve.

Meredith stared at it reflectively. If he could find a hock shop open he could hock it and perhaps buy half a pint. That the clock belonged to Murphy didn't even enter his consideration. He had fallen too low for that.

He picked up the clock and was weighing it in his hand when Murphy's key turned in the door. Murphy closed the door behind him and stood leaning up against it. His face was lined and haggard, his eyes deep pools of puzzled horror.

"You look," Jim Meredith told him, unabashed, "as though you'd seen the devil."

"I did," Murphy answered briefly. "And no need to hock the clock. I've brought you a quart of whiskey."

He tugged an unopened bottle from the pocket of his overcoat and set it on the table. The derelict reached for it, stopped, came around the table.

"You look all in, boy. Let me help you off with that coat."

"No," Murphy backed away. "Don't touch me, Doc. I don't know what the devil's done to me. But he did tell me I'd die if I talked. And I've got to talk to someone before I phone the paper."

As he talked he stripped off his snow-sodden overcoat and tossed it in a corner. Then followed it with his hat and shoes. He took his money, cigarettes, and notes from his pocket, piled them on the table and stripped to his shorts and shirt.

"You can't—catch—death, can you, Doc?" he asked.

"N-no," the once-great surgeon smiled. "I wouldn't say that death was catching. Why?"

"Because I've been rubbing shoulders with it for the last two hours," Murphy told him curtly. "I've been interviewing men and women I saw buried. I've been talking to the devil."

Meredith smiled politely.

"And damn it, don't smile at me." Murphy rapped. "Crack open that bottle and pour us both a drink—a big one. I'll be back as soon as I wash."

The surgeon did as he was told. His fingers were trembling so he could hardly hold the glass but he waited for his drink until Murphy had finished splashing in the bathroom.

"How long," the reporter asked him as he sat down at the table, still dressed in only shirt and shorts, "would it take to turn a guy into a mummy, Doc?"

The surgeon sniffed at his drink, savored the bouquet reflectively, then gulped it.

"Perhaps," he coughed, "two years. Perhaps two thousand, dependent on the condition of the soil. Why?"

"Then you haven't read the papers?" Murphy asked,

"No," Meredith admitted, not the last few days, "I haven't."

"The devil can do it in no time at all," Murphy told him. "I saw a woman turned into a mummy in five minutes by the clock. I saw her dry up and die right before my eyes as if by magic. Now look, Doc. Pour us both another drink and listen to me."

Impelled by the urgency in his voice the older man obeyed.
"Yes—?"

Swiftly, graphically, Murphy told him what had happened in
the bar.

"Impossible," the surgeon said.

"I saw it happen," Murphy shook his head. "And I saw more. I
saw the devil bring a dead man back to life tonight." He sorted
through the papers on the table. "I've written down the names of a
dozen dead men and women whom I talked to. And if anything
happens to me—"

Meredith smiled.

"It won't. Nothing more than a headache. But you certainly
have gotten yourself a peach on, boy, I envy you."

"That's what my city editor told me," the reporter said dryly.
He tossed Satan's red card on the table. "But if anything happens
to me, that's the guy. He told me tonight I was going to die. And
somehow I believe him."

Meredith sat staring at the scarlet card printed in gold that began, "WANTED—CORPSES."

"I met him tonight out at Maplewood Cemetery," Murphy told
him. "His secretary, a slant-eyed chap by the name of Yoshama,
prodded me up to Max Boderman's tomb with a gun."

As he talked the air in the room grew electric.

"I saw the devil lay his hands on Max, saw Max sit up in his
coffin." The reporter's voice rose shrilly and broke. "So help me
God, I did."

"Steady, boy," the surgeon told him. He poured a water glass
half full of Scotch. "Drink that."

The reporter gulped it, stretched his forearms on the table and
cradled his head for a moment. When he looked up his eyes were
calmer.

"I'm letting it get me, Doc. And I mustn't. I've got to make
someone believe me. The devil's come up from hell and he's right
here in Chicago."

The derelict surgeon regarded the man who had befriended
him. He wasn't drunk. And he wasn't mad. Jim Meredith would
stake what little honor he had left on that.

"Go on, boy," he said quietly.

The reporter fished a cigarette from the crumpled pack on the
table, lit it, and drew the smoke deep into his lungs.

"I don't know just exactly what his game is," he began. "But he's making millions at it. He charged Max Boderman's widow a half a million dollars tonight for bringing Max back to life."

"And it *was* Boderman you saw?" the surgeon asked.

"I thought of that." Murphy looked up at him sharply. "But it wasn't a switch as far as I could tell. His widow recognized him and after a few hysterical shrieks she fell into his arms."

"But not even the devil could bring a dead man back to life." The surgeon shook his head. "The thing is mad."

"Or I am," Murphy said grimly. "I tell you I saw it, Doc. And I talked with Judge Taggart, and Sam Green, and Grenfal."

"But they've been dead for weeks, months."

"So have the two men whose mummies were found on the streets today," Murphy said grimly. "I—" he hesitated. "Would you mind getting me a drink of water, Doc? I guess I must have caught cold out there. I feel like I'm burning up." He gulped the glass of water greedily, sucked deeply at his cigarette, continued. "They were brought back to life, then allowed to die again because they threatened to talk, just like the girl did, just like I'm talking now."

The surgeon sat eyeing him sharply. His friend seemed somehow older, more haggard than he had ever seen him.

"Did he give you anything out there, Murph, make you drink anything, or inject anything subtravenously?"

"No. Not a thing," Murphy told him. He grinned wryly through lips the skin of which seemed taut. "All I had to do was kneel in the snow with dead men and women all around me while Satan said Black Mass." His voice seemed faint and far away. "He promised us everything here on earth our hearts desire. And in return all those living dead men and women had to promise him—" His voice trailed off inaudible.

Meredith got slowly to his feet, stared with clinically professional eyes at the other man's face.

"You're not well, Tim."

"No," the reporter admitted frankly. "No. I'm not." Revulsion filled his face. "I don't feel any pain, but I'm dying. I—I can feel my insides dissolving, drying up. I—I don't know how the hell he's done it, but he has."

He spoke dispassionately, calmly, drugged by the sleepy torpor of death. He was a dead man and he faced the fact. He had watched another die as he himself was dying.

Meredith stood in silence, his eyes on the other man's face. There was nothing he could do. There was nothing that anyone could do. He had watched death's stealthy approach too many times not to know. But this death was obscene.

The reporter's shrinking lips framed a word. But he never spoke it. The word evaporated in his throat as the liquid and the tissue of his glands and organs dissolved and shrunk into atomic matter in the painless hell flame that was eating at his vitals.

Then Murphy's eyes began to run, dripped down, a gelatinous mass, inside his skull. He was dead. Only the smoke-plumed cigarette stuck to his withered upper lip was still alive. What once had been a man was but a leering mummy with cracked, dried parchment for a face.

Meredith slopped some whiskey in his glass with shaking fingers, raised it to his lips, then set it down untouched.

"No," he shook his head. "I don't need that. Murphy was my friend." He picked up Murphy's notes from the table and stared at them through blood-shot eyes. There was something vaguely familiar that the names of the living dead had in common—but what it was, his drink-sodden mind was unable to recall. "Murphy was my friend," he repeated. "I'll find the devil who killed him."

The dead man shifted slightly in his chair as the flesh on his bones contracted. The night wind howled cold and mocking at the window like a laugh—a devil's laugh straight out of hell.

CHAPTER THREE

PLEASE TO MEET SATAN

THE GIRL AT THE SWITCHBOARD was new. She stared dubiously at the unshined shoes, the unpressed suit, and the beard-stubbled chin of the man before the desk. "Yes—?"

"Doctor James Meredith," he told her. "To see Doctor Agnew."

She raised an eyebrow slightly. "You have an appointment?"

"No," he admitted. "I haven't. But I know he always operates on Thursdays and I had hoped I'd find him here."

The girl had been about to order him out of the lobby, but the obviously cultured voice emanating from the derelict's bearded lips gave her pause. She consulted a list on her desk.

"Doctor Agnew will be here today," she admitted. "He's scheduled to operate at eight."

Meredith looked at the clock on the wall. It was seven.

"Thank you," he told her. "I'll wait."

His worn shoes scuffing on the tile, he crossed the corridor of the hospital foyer and seated himself in a large, over-stuffed chair just to the right of a door that bore a small brass plate announcing that it was for Doctors only.

From time to time a surgeon with an early morning schedule passed him. Most of them didn't even recognize him. The few who did merely nodded.

He opened the paper he had brought and stared thoughtfully at the headline. It was terse and grim with understatement. It read: TERROR GRIPS CITY.

The sub-head read in almost as many points: Tim Murphy Ace Reporter of Morning *Reformer* is fourth mummified body to be found!

There followed a description of the finding of the reporter's underwear-clad mummy following an anonymous phone call. There had been no one else in the apartment but there had been a whiskey bottle on the table with two glasses. The whiskey was being analyzed. A homeless derelict known to have been be-

friended by Murphy was being sought for questioning. It was believed, however, that he could throw little light on the situation.
The best medical minds in the City after an exhaustive examina-
tion of the three mummified bodies previously found admitted
themselves to be baffled.

A new and insidious terror had grown up overnight. Nor was
that terror modified by the fact that two of the mummies found,
while listed by the department of health as "deceased" some weeks
previously, were said by sworn testimony to have been seen alive
but a few minutes before their dried and mummified bodies had
been discovered. As yet, their families had not been located for
questioning.

This was contradicted, in turn, by an A.P. dispatch from Los
Angeles. The widow of one of the men had been located there and
swore there must be some mistake in the identity of the body. For,
despite the fact that she and her multimillionaire husband had been
estranged for some time over another woman, she had been with
her husband on the night that he had died in Mercy Hospital. The
death certificate had been signed by Doctor Agnew.

Meredith folded his paper neatly and slipped it back into his
pocket. He wondered grimly if it might not have been best for him
to take Tim Murphy's scribbled notes directly to his paper first,
decided that it wouldn't. Tim's notes consisted mainly of a dozen
scrawled names of men and women known to be dead. He, Jim
Meredith had the story, he believed, but he wanted to be certain of
his facts before he talked.

He sat rubbing the worn welts of his shoes together and listening to the conversation in the doctor's lounge. It was, as was natural, mainly of the gruesome terror and tragedy headlined by the
morning papers.

A voice he recognized as Ben Winton's, the noted pathologist,
scoffed at the whole affair.

"But damn it, you know as well as I do," Winton snorted, "the
thing's impossible. It's mad. Certainly. Some chemicals can burn
up flesh and tissue like that." He snapped his fingers. "After all, in
the chemical composition of the body we find sixty-six percent
water, three percent nitrogen, two percent hydrogen, six and
seven-tenths percent oxygen—all vulnerable elements easily done
away with by an opposing chemical process. But the papers claim
that two of those men were dead, climbed back up out of their

graves and walked around for several weeks before they dropped dead—mummies.''

"But not Murphy, the reporter," Glendive the genealogist protested. "Nor the mummy of the girl they picked up in that North Clark Street bar. Both of them were known to be alive at eight o'clock last night."

Someone else said something that Meredith couldn't catch. Then he saw Agnew coming in the front door of the hospital and got slowly to his feet as the other surgeon who had once been his assistant paused at the desk for his mail.

Prosperity, he decided, agreed with Bill Agnew. His former assistant, who had taken over his practice when the series of unexplainable deaths had driven him to drink, was plumper, less ferret-like about the features. He wore an expensive broadcloth overcoat lined with fur. His silver mounted bag was of pin seal.

Jim Meredith ran his hands down the sides of his own greasy top-coat. Despite his own fall, he didn't envy Agnew. The man was a fair surgeon, but he was money-mad. And not even his prosperity could conceal nor heal the twisted and deformed right leg that had left its indelible stamp of bitterness on the mind of the man. Agnew was always conscious of it, thrusting himself forward as if to hide it by making it all the more obvious.

"Hello, Bill," Meredith greeted him.

Doctor Agnew paused, pretended to wipe the steam from the Oxford glasses he affected, although Meredith knew that he had seen him when he first came in the door.

"Oh. Oh it's you, Meredith," he said finally.

"Yes," Meredith admitted. "It's me."

Agnew cleared his throat impatiently, frowned, and reached for his wallet.

"Well? How much this time?"

"This isn't a touch," his former superior assured him. "You've read the morning papers?"

"I have."

"Well, Murphy was my friend."

The other man looked puzzled, then his thin lips twisted. "What am I supposed to do, cry?"

"No," Meredith said quietly. "I just wish that you'd make it possible, Bill, for me to look at the hospital records."

"I don't understand."

"Judge Taggart died here at Mercy, didn't he?" Meredith asked him. "And Grenfal the lawyer? And Marc Long? And Pete Harris?"

Agnew puzzled his brow in thought.

"Some of those names are familiar," he admitted. "Perhaps they did. What about it? Mercy is one of the largest hospitals in the city. A lot of people die here. A lot of people die in every hospital. Just what is it that you want?"

"To have you make it possible for me to look at the records." Meredith smiled wryly. "I believe I've been dropped from the staff."

"Yes," Agnew nodded, "you have. And you can't blame the board, Jim. Frankly, the way you've let yourself go to pieces—"

"I know, I know," the older man interrupted wearily. "But if you'll just okay me to the girl at the desk and see that I have access to the death records for half an hour, that's all I ask."

For a moment the other man seemed about to refuse, then he shrugged.

"All right. But it sounds as insane to me as some of the other things that you've done." He stepped across the corridor to the desk. "This is Doctor Meredith," he introduced him. "He formerly was on the staff here and I'll appreciate it as a personal favor if you give him access to any of the hospital records he may care to see."

The girl behind the counter beamed. Her smile alone was proof of the former assistant's standing.

"Yes, Doctor Agnew. Just as you say, sir."

Agnew smiled in his superior fashion, turned to Meredith.

"Certain a few dollars wouldn't help you?"

The night before Meredith would have taken them and been grateful. Now he shook his head, flushed slightly.

"No. Thank you." He paused, eyed the other man intently. "But you might tell me this, Bill. What did you ever do with that saline anesthetic that we were working on?"

Agnew looked puzzled.

"I don't recall it, Jim. Why?"

"No reason," Meredith told him. "Just wondered." He turned his back abruptly, faced the desk. "And now if I may, Miss, I'd like to look at those records. The case records and death certificates of certain names I'll give you. Men and women who have died here."

For a moment the ferret-faced surgeon glared at the threadbare back of the man who had once been his superior, then he turned on his heel and stamped across the corridor into the door that was marked—For Doctors Only.

When she found out that he had been *the* Doctor Meredith, the record clerk couldn't do enough for the shabby man, who for the best part of an hour had sat poring over the case records of men and women long since supposed to be dead.

"You saved my mother's life," she told him. "You trepanned for a blood clot."

Jim Meredith smiled wearily.

"That was a long time ago, before I lost my skill." He folded up the papers on which he had been writing and put them in his pocket. "But thank you. You've been kind."

He slipped into his top-coat as a fresh-faced young intern banged into the office.

"Four-sixteen just died," he told the clerk.

"Mrs. Boderman?" she asked.

"That's right." The intern grinned. "And boy. Would I like to inherit those millions."

Meredith frowned, puzzled.

"You don't by any chance mean Max Boderman's widow?"

"That's the one," the intern told him. "She came in an emergency last night. It seems she smashed that big imported car of hers right smack into a culvert out on the Maplewood road."

Meredith closed his eyes. In his day he had been considered an over-conscientious surgeon who refused to cut until every detail of the diagnosis checked with all known facts. And in the case on which he was working, Max Boderman's widow had worried him. Her death had clarified a lot. He was ready now to face Tim Murphy's editor. If he wasn't locked up as insane, he believed he could point out the devil. Proving it would be up to the police.

He bowed, thanked the record clerk again, and left the office. Through the thin partition he could hear the intern ask—

"And who was that bum?"

"Why that," the record clerk told him, "was Doctor Meredith. *The* Doctor Meredith."

The intern's muffled, "Gee!" was solace to his soul. Perhaps Tim Murphy had been right. Perhaps he could come back. Perhaps he hadn't been responsible for those ten deaths. Perhaps—

The bite of the icy wind that rushed up Michigan Avenue to greet him as the door of the hospital closed behind him cut short his thoughts. It sank its icy fingers through his threadbare clothes and tore at his tortured nerves. What he needed, he decided, was a drink.

He counted the change in his pocket. He had exactly fifteen cents and he had picked that off the table on which Tim Murphy had died. He braced his body against the wind and walked out to the curb. The traffic light was against him. He stood huddled against a lamp post waiting for it to change.

"Taxi, mister?"

A cab drew up beside him and he shook his head.

"Better get in and ride, mister," the driver insisted.

"No thank you," Meredith refused. "I—"

He looked up to find himself staring into the muzzle of a gun held by the slim yellow fingers of a smiling Oriental who sat on the rear seat of the cab.

"I think perhaps you had better ride," the Oriental smiled. "Satan would like to see you."

Meredith licked his lips. The smiling Oriental was a killer. It showed in the glittering pin points of his iris, in the cruel, thin lips.

"But I don't know Satan," he protested.

The Oriental's yellow fingers whitened on the trigger of his gun.

"That is an oversight we mean to remedy. Step into the cab. You will please to meet Satan."

Meredith did as he was told. There was nothing else he could do.

CHAPTER FOUR

DEAD MEN DON'T TALK

THE ROOM WAS AS IMPRESSIVE as the man. Semi-dark, it was lighted by four red flares, one in each corner. Each flare gave off an insidious, yet somehow pleasant, smell of sulfur. The walls were draped in thick black folds of heavy silk. The only furniture was the chair and desk at which Satan sat and a chair for the consultant. A fifth red beam of light shone through the glass-topped desk and etched Satan's ivory face in bas-relief against the gloom behind him.

"So," Satan smiled, "you are Doctor Meredith."

"I am," Meredith admitted.

Satan waved the waiting Oriental from the office.

"You may leave us, Yoshama. I hardly think that Doctor Meredith will attempt any violence."

The Oriental backed to the door, bowed from the room.

Meredith sat studying the face of the man before him. It was vaguely familiar. It once had been a strong face but both the eyes and the ivory pallor of the skin gave evidence to trained eyes that the man was addicted to drugs.

"You wanted to see me?" Meredith asked finally.

Satan smiled.

"Yes. It has been brought to my attention that you have developed an overwhelming curiosity concerning certain of my subjects who belong to the League of the Grateful Dead."

"Can't we drop the fol-de-rol?" Meredith asked. "You're not impressing me at all. I know you're a fake. And I believe I know the man who is behind you."

Satan merely smiled his languid smile.

"No one is behind the devil. I have chosen this means and form of returning to earth for certain reasons of my own." He paused. "But we digress. I want those notes and names that your friend Mr. Murphy so unfortunately wrote down last night at Maplewood

Cemetery while I was resurrecting a certain Mr. Max Boderman from the dead."

Meredith took the notes from his pocket and laid them on the desk.

"Also what data you collected at Mercy Hospital this morning," Satan insisted.

Meredith added his own notes to the small pile of papers on the desk.

"I can remember the names," he smiled. "And when I leave here I'm going to the Morning *Reformer* first, and then to the police."

"The police?" Satan smiled. "I see you are still laboring under a grave misapprehension, Doctor Meredith. You still believe I am a fake, a charlatan."

"I know you are."

Satan shook his head.

"I am sorry, for your sake, but I am real. And when you leave this office, you won't talk. The police will merely be more mystified when a fifth mummified corpse is found." He chuckled. "You have no idea of the disciplinary effect of those four corpses on the members of my League of the Grateful Dead."

"They aren't dead. It's a racket," Meredith said grimly.

Satan smiled.

"There have been complaints?"

"No," Meredith admitted. "Dead men can't talk. You kill them before they can—kill them as you killed Tim Murphy, killed that woman in that Clark Street bar."

"That's right," Satan agreed. "As I am going to kill you in just a moment." He paused, opened a humidor on his desk, selected a cigarette and lighted it. As an afterthought, he waved his long thin fingers to the box.

Meredith took one.

"Thank you."

Satan extended the still burning lighter in his hand, an amused smile on his face. Meredith leaned forward, the cigarette between his lips. But before he could light it, the door to the office opened.

"Is the police again," the Oriental hissed. "They will not believe you are not here."

A frown of annoyance crossed Satan's face. He gathered the scattered papers on his desk into a mound.

"Burn these in one of the flares," he ordered. "I had hoped we could postpone this, but it seems we can't." Ignoring Meredith completely, he sat stroking his small black goatee. Then he smiled at the heavy, impatient rapping on the door. "So the police want to question Satan. All right. But I am afraid they will be surprised."

The corridors of the South State Street Central Bureau swarmed with camera men and leg men. A palpable fake though he was, they were covering the biggest story Chicago had ever known. Satan had been arrested.

Inside the commissioner's office, Commissioner Craig sighed wearily.

"Why will you persist that you are Satan? You're a faker and you know it."

The man who claimed that he was Satan smiled.

"Yes?"

The commissioner spat out his cigar.

"All right. We'll wait until your fingerprints come back from Washington. Until then we'll hold you on an open charge."

Satan shrugged.

"And now you." The commissioner turned to Meredith. "What were you doing there inside this charlatan's office."

"I was forced there at the point of a gun," Meredith told him truthfully.

"By whom?"

Meredith pointed to the sober-faced Oriental. "By that man there. I believe Yoshama is his name."

"Is that right?" the commissioner asked the oriental.

"No, sir," Yoshama lied. He pointed to Meredith. "He come in answer to advertisement. He say he lose good friend named Murphy, would much like to meet his spirit."

The commissioner covered his face with his hands for a moment, then exploded.

"Now look here, damn it," he stormed. "I'm getting tired of all this run-a-round." He leveled a finger at Satan. "Just what kind of a racket are you running?"

"No racket," Satan told him. "If you would ever care to consult me professionally, I'll be pleased to talk to you. But under the circumstances I am afraid I must refuse. As you yourself suggested, why don't we wait until my fingerprints come back from Washington?"

The commissioner looked around the grim, stern faces in his office. Most of the more influential civic leaders had gathered there at his request.

"Is the editor of the Morning *Reformer* here?"

A wiry little white-haired man stepped forward.

"Here I am, sir."

"Murphy, the fourth mummified corpse that we found, worked for you. Is that right?"

"That's right."

"And you say that he phoned you last night that he saw the dame in that Clark Street bar turned into a mummy?"

"He did."

"And that he was on his way out to Maplewood Cemetery to watch Satan here resurrect the body of Max Boderman?"

"That's what he said. I figured he was high."

The commissioner nodded.

"I still do. But we can tell better on that score when the squad I've sent out to Maplewood call in their report. If Boderman's body is still in his tomb, then Murphy was drunk."

"But he wasn't drunk," Meredith protested. "I talked to him when he came back." He pointed a finger at Satan. "And as I've already told you, Tim said that he not only saw Satan there resurrect Max Boderman but he had talked to at least a dozen men and women whom you have listed on your files as dead."

The commissioner smiled skeptically.

"I believe you were once quite a well-known surgeon, Doctor. Can you explain a dead man coming back to life?"

"In this instance, yes, I think I can," Meredith admitted. He scribbled a phone number and a name on a piece of paper. "But before I begin my explanation I'd like to have you call that number and ask that man to be here."

The commissioner pursed his lips.

"Why not?" he decided finally. "The more the merrier. The whole town is going to have hysterics unless we crack this case." He handed the paper to an assistant. "Send out a squad car and bring this fellow in."

The assistant left the office.

"Might I ask the name of the man for whom you're sending?" the white-haired editor of the Morning *Reformer* asked.

"Doctor Agnew of Mercy Hospital," the commissioner told him. He stared hard at Meredith. "But just where does Doctor Agnew come in?"

Meredith smiled grimly.

"If I'm right, he's the devil."

The man who claimed to be Satan laughed thinly.

"How amusing. I seem to have a competitor."

"You, shut up," the commissioner ordered. He turned back to Meredith. "And you say you know how those guys and that dame were turned into mummies, Doctor Meredith?"

"I think I do."

The commissioner wiped the perspiration from his forehead.

"Thank God for that. Another of them mummified corpses popping up, and I'll have hysterics myself." He looked at the man who claimed to be Satan. "I was beginning to believe you were the devil."

"I am," the other told him smiling.

A lieutenant fought his way into the office through a mob of howling reporters. His eyes were puzzled. His face was pale. He looked at the man who claimed to be Satan and then looked away.

"Washington has just reported on those fingerprints, sir," he saluted.

"Yes—?" the commissioner looked up.

The lieutenant stared hard at the man who claimed to be Satan, huge drops of perspiration beading his forehead. He forced his eyes back to his chief.

"And Washington wants to know what the joke is, sir. They say that according to the fingerprints we sent them, he's ten men—and that all ten of those men are dead!"

The silence grew inside the office until the beating of their hearts pounded in the eardrums of the straining men like strange and somehow obscene tom-toms.

White-faced, the lieutenant laid a sheaf of telephoto pictures on the desk.

"According to the whorls of his left thumb, he is Mace Manders the magician who was electrocuted at Stateville two years ago for the murder of his wife. According to the whorls of his right thumb, he's Johnny Green, the bandit, who was shot last year by a squad from the Woodlawn station. According to the whorls of his left forefinger—"

The man who claimed that he was Satan laughed an unpleasant, tinkling little laugh.

"Perhaps now you will believe me." He picked up his hat from the commissioner's desk and shaped it on his head. "Satan is not one, but many people." He stretched out his hand and a belch of smoke and crimson flame flared in the doorway. "If you want me for any further questioning, gentlemen, I'd suggest that you go to hell!"

He had the door already open when the commissioner came to his senses.

'Stop him! Shoot him! Stop that man!" he bellowed.

The lieutenant leveled his gun. "Stop!" he ordered. Satan smiled, turned his back deliberately and walked out of the door into the hall.

"Stop!" the lieutenant ordered—then fired.

Six steel-jacketed bullets picked curiously at the cloth of Satan's well-tailored and departing back. But that was all they did do—that, and scatter the reporters scrambled cursing for safety. Satan didn't even turn his head, just kept on walking down the hall.

"So sorry," Yoshama beamed. He closed the door behind them.

For a moment there was only silence in the room and the pungent smell of gun smoke. The commissioner broke it with an oath. His superstitious, Irish face was florid.

"By God!" he swore. "By God! *He was the Devil!*"

CHAPTER FIVE

LEAGUE OF THE GRATEFUL DEAD!

DESPITE THE FACT that it was three o'clock in the morning and bitter cold, the corners of State and Madison were as crowded as they had ever been at noon. Men and women avoided each other's eyes as they milled in a mass for safety. The thing was mad, impossible—still, there was no explanation but the fact that it was so. Hell was loose in the streets of Chicago and the devil roamed the by-ways.

Twelve blocks down the street, past VanBuren, in a cheap South State Street bar, Doctor Meredith stared with solemn eyes at the headlines of the paper in which he had just invested the last three cents he had. A glass of five cent beer sat on the bar in front of him—untouched.

The paper made no exaggerations. It merely stated fact. Since disappearing from the police commissioner's office in a harmless fusillade of lead, Satan had not been seen . . . Contradictory witnesses testified he had disappeared into the ground—stepped into a cab—walked briskly north on State Street . . . A mysterious fire had developed in the suite of offices that he had used in the Braddock Building . . . The corpse of Max Boderman, said to be resurrected was not in its tomb . . . According to the infallible fingerprint department of the F.B.I., the prints sent them by the C.P.D. were those of ten men who had been executed in the State of Illinois within the last two years . . . A ragged derelict, once one of the city's most respected surgeons, had made wild and unsupported accusations against a prominent citizen whom the paper allowed to remain unnamed . . . The derelict, believed to be insane from drink, had disappeared . . . It was known to be a racket of some kind . . . It was known to be the truth . . . Several noted clergymen were holding special services in an effort to re-establish the city on a normal spiritual keel . . . The thing couldn't be . . . It could be . . . Responsible citizens were beginning to report to the police that they had recently seen men and women on the streets who were known to that department to be dead . . . The grief-stricken families of the men and women specified had sworn that it wasn't so.

"And it all boils down," Meredith told his glass of flat, stale beer, "to the fact that no one knows a damn. No one even suspects the truth but me, and they say I'm mad."

"You say something?" the barkeep demanded.

"No, just thinking aloud," Meredith shook his head.

"Then drink your beer and get out," the barkeep ordered. "You bums make me sick. You come in here and soak up a night's warm lodging on a nickel beer."

Meredith walked to the door and stood staring out into the night. It had begun to snow again and the curbs had piled high with the drift. He wondered what he ought to do. Perhaps he was crazy. Perhaps the man was Satan.

He fished in his pockets for a cigarette, found one in his coat pocket, put it between his lips and fumbled for a match.

His hand stopped halfway to his pocket. He took the cigarette from between his lips and stared at it. It was an expensive Turkish brand. It was the one that Satan had given him in his office. His eyes grew suddenly cold.

"Well, I'll be damned," he said. "I will be damned."

He put the cigarette carefully back into his pocket. Then he strode out into the night, his shoulders squared. He knew where he was going—and he knew what he had to do.

The building itself was attractive and comparatively new. It had been built in the boom of '29 as a hotel, sold in the slump of the early '30's to Doctor Meredith for a private hospital, and at his mental collapse had been absorbed in the general debris of his estate. Later, an undisclosed syndicate had bought it as a residence club house, and as such it was now used.

A liveried doorman stood at the door, but few members came or went. Those who did went out the back way and at night. The neighbors were normally curious, but no more. It was obviously a rich man's club and as such held little place or interest in their own busy, narrow lives.

Outside the heavily curtained first floor windows, a lone watcher crouched behind a tree for meager shelter from the wind and snow. From time to time he raised his eyes to contemplate the bright white light that shone through the skylight window on the top and seventh floor in what once had been an operating room.

Inside the heavily curtained windows of the club house, the air was thick with smoke and conversation. The lounge was filled with old men, young men, rich men, poor men; colorful with red-lipped youthful girls whose eyes were too bright; drab with pursed-lipped, prim old ladies; tempered with well-dressed matrons, and all had one bond in common.

Most of them were living dead. Most of them had died, been buried, and were resurrected. All were in debt to Satan. All had sold him their souls for life. All belonged to the League of the Grateful Dead.

The League rules themselves were simple. There were only three of them. They were:

1: Thou shall Eat, Drink, and be Merry for thou hast been dead and buried and now thou shalt live forever.

2: Thou shalt converse with no one but a fellow member of the League concerning thy resurrection under penalty of returning to the grave.

3: Thou shalt remember thou hast sold thy soul to thy master who is Satan. When he speaks *thou shalt obey.*

On the second floor of the club house Yoshama the oriental rapped softly on a paneled office door.

"Come in," the voice of Satan called. Yoshama turned the door knob then stepped politely to one side. "Please to proceed," he bowed. The florid-faced, white-haired man in the doorway nodded curtly, took his younger, golden-haired companion by the arm and walked into the office.

It was similar to the office where Satan had held his consultations in the Loop but even more elaborate. Purported hell flames flared against the entire background of the wall. The air was heavy with incense.

"Yes, Mr. Green—?" Satan asked. "Yoshama says you want to see me."

The dead banker nodded glumly.

"I do."

Satan indicated two snow white chairs with legs of gleaming human thigh bones, seats of interlaced human ribs, and backs of tibias webbed with human clavicles, each corner tibia posted with a human skull.

The resurrected banker sat down heavily.

"I want to get out of here," he said grimly.

Satan raised his neatly arched black eyebrows.

"That is possible—for a price."

"But we've given you almost everything we have," the golden haired girl protested. She began to cry. "Oh, if I'd only known that it was going to be like this I never would have come to you the night Sam died. I'd have let him stay in his grave."

Satan shrugged.

"If it is Mr. Green's desire it can be arranged that he return to his grave." He smoothed out the pages of an early morning extra that featured a picture of the four mummified corpses. "I have sent three of our League members who grew garrulous down to hell within the last two days."

"No. Not like that," the banker shuddered. "I don't want to die. I want to live. But I want to leave this awful place—this club-house. How much for Gwendolyn and me to leave here?"

"Money," Satan mused, "is the root of all evil, and I am evil." He considered. "Suppose we say the customary plastic surgical operation that I insist upon whenever a member leaves, your promise to report to me once every month, and five hundred—" He stopped short in the middle of his sentence, listening.

"Yes, Master—?" Yoshama asked him tersely.

Satan pointed to the wall. "I thought I heard something just outside the window there, something that sounded like leather scraping on rungs of steel."

"Is perhaps somebody climbing up fire escape." The Oriental smiled evilly. A long, thin, glittering knife appeared in his hand. "You please to excuse me, Master."

Satan listened thoughtfully for a moment, then shook his head.

"No, Yoshama." He rose from the chair behind his desk, nodded curtly to the man and girl in front of it. "You two will leave now. We will discuss the matter later."

The elderly man got up wearily from the gruesome chair on which he sat and helped his still weeping companion to the door.

"Yes, Master," he said quietly. Yoshama closed the door behind them, pulled a switch that killed the crimson hell flame, and parting an asbestos curtain on the wall, looked out and up through a window.

"Is man," he announced in a whisper. "One man. Is almost up to fourth floor now and climbing higher."

Satan lighted a cigarette, smiled thinly.

"He is welcome, Yoshama. Being Satan, I am intuitive. It must be the one man in all this city whom we might have reason to expect." He placed one long ivory finger to his forehead in mock psychic thought. "Yes. I should say it is the once-great Doctor Meredith who has grown over-anxious to become a member of the League of the Grateful Dead."

He chuckled evilly, without mirth. Yoshama ran his thumbnail the length of his glittering knife blade, chuckled with him.

From where he clung to the last steel rungs of the spidery fire escape, slippery with ice and sleet, the crawling lights of cars on the street below looked like toys. And the wind was stronger here. Jim Meredith braced his weight against the ladder and blew on the tips of his gloveless fingers to warm them.

It would, he thought, be so easy to just let go. He put the thought from his mind. He was the one man in Chicago who knew who the devil really was. It was up to him, for Tim Murphy's sake, if nothing else, to prove it—kill him if he could. He clutched at the icy steel rungs with his bleeding fingers. "Up we go," he grunted. With the last of his strength he pulled himself over the bulge of the roof. He lay there in the snow for minutes, breathing hard.

The skylight window, only feet away, lighted the snow around it. Too tired to stand, he crawled across the flat roof through the snow to where he could look inside. It once had been his own private operating room. It was as he remembered it with no new equipment added. Only the scrub nurse, the third nurse busily picking bloody sponges from the floor, and the anesthetist were new. They were, he decided grimly, probably members of the League of the Grateful Dead.

The corners of the room, lighted only by the powerful dome light over the operating table, lay in shadows. He stared long at the operating surgeon's back. He was performing a difficult operation on an elderly white-haired patient, and was bungling every move. The devil was attempting, probably had attempted hundreds of operations, that only six or seven surgeons in the world were qualified to do.

Meredith got slowly to his feet and peered through the blinding snow to locate the kiosk of the trap door that he remembered led down through the roof. It was piled high with the icy drift but was unlocked. Painfully, with bleeding fingertips, the once-great surgeon picked the ice and snow away. It was then he found the bar. It was of steel, thumb thick, and two feet long. A pry bar, forgotten by some worker, it was a murderous bludgeon in the hands of a determined man.

The surgeon laid it down again where he could find it and tugged gently at the door. It opened slowly, outward. Then he picked up the bar again, stepped into the darkened stair well and closed the door behind him.

The familiar odor of antiseptics filled his nostrils. He smiled wryly. He was only a few steps from his own operating room. He had come back as Tim Murphy had prophesied. But not in the manner Tim had meant. He had come to take life, not to save it.

"For God's sake hand me that adrenalin syringe," he heard a thin voice say. "Quick. The old goat's dying on the table."

"He's gone," a male voice Meredith decided must be the anesthetist's answered. "I can't feel any pulse at all."

"Well, take him away, then," the thin voice said impatiently. "And send up another case," Meredith could visualize the thin lips smacking.

Meredith waited where he was until he heard a swinging door sway shut and the soft suck of the rubber tires of a stretcher on tile fade down the hall. Then he stepped out of the stairwell, stared with cold eyes at the door of the operating room presided over by the bloody butcher who posed as a human being.

"Wish me luck, Tim," he said quietly.

Grasping the bar firmly he strode across hall and in through the swinging doors.

The surgeon looked up, smiled.

"Well, so you got here," he said thinly. "You're just in time. I'll take you next. I guess I'll do a trephine on you in an attempt to find your brains."

Meredith stood where he was, the bar in his hands, his muscles poised to spring. Then two figures stepped out of the shadowy corners of the room.

"Drop that bar!" a sibilant Oriental voice hissed in his ear. "Drop that bar or else you are a dead man!"

Meredith gritted his teeth against the pain as the sharp point of an eager knife sank experimentally for a good half-inch into the thin flesh between his ribs.

Then the soft voice of Satan chuckled.

"Your English composition is very poor, Yoshama. Doctor Meredith is a dead man whether or not he drops that bar."

CHAPTER SIX

THE DEAD DIE ONCE

MEREDITH HADN'T A CHANCE, and he knew it. But he resolved to die hard. With a surgeon's knowledge of anatomy, he knew that the slanting thrust of the knife blade where it was started would be painful, but not necessarily fatal. At least not immediately. The Oriental was expecting him to draw away. But he didn't.

Meredith literally spitted himself on the knife as he lunged, sideways, felt the blade slip into his flesh and twist from Yoshama's hand. Then the swinging steel bar in his own right hand curved in a vicious arc and he heard a satisfying crunch of bone as the Oriental's skull caved in.

"Stop him! Stop him!" the white-faced surgeon behind the operating table screamed.

Panting on one knee in the corner where the force of his blow had sent him, Meredith thought desperately. A wire ran around the baseboard of the operating room. If he could break that wire, plunge the room into darkness—he hooked the curved end of his bar in the wire and yanked. The wire snapped in two, its insulation frazzled. But the lights still burned.

"Ripping out the outside telephone wire won't do you any good," Satan smiled. "We don't need to call for help."

He walked slowly, warily, an automatic in his hand, toward the panting figure crouching on one knee. He didn't dare to fire for fear of hitting his compatriot in evil. Before he could, Meredith again did the unexpected. He ducked in under Satan's guard and swung the short steel bar at the terror-stricken surgeon's head.

It missed its mark by a hair's breadth as the screaming surgeon jerked back his head and the bar slid off his shoulder to fracture his upper arm just above the elbow.

That was the last that Meredith remembered. The whole back of his skull exploded and Yoshama's dead face came up from the floor to meet him.

When he recovered consciousness he was surprised that he wasn't dead. He hadn't expected to open his eyes again. He looked around him blearily.

He was still in the operating room, lying in the shadows in one corner. In the full glare of the dome light Bill Agnew sat on the operating table on which he had but recently killed a man while the anesthetist set his fractured arm, arranged it in a splint, and bound it to his body.

Jim Meredith smiled grimly. It was at least a compound fracture. He'd done that much. Bill Agnew wouldn't operate for months, if ever.

The man who claimed to be Satan was the first to notice that the man on the floor had come to. He walked over and kicked him in the teeth.

"You die hard, don't you?" he said.

Meredith spit out a mouthful of blood.

"Yes," he admitted, "I do. Perhaps," he added quietly, "it's because I've been dying for the last two years." He looked at the man on the table. "You did that to me, Bill."

His former assistant scowled.

"Just you wait until Breen, here, finishes fixing my arm. Then I'll fix you." He toyed with the scalpel in his hand.

"No," the man on the floor shook his head. "You can't do anything more to me than you already have."

But for the dome light over the operating table the rest of the room was in darkness. Meredith moved uneasily. He seemed to be lying on something sharp. He found it was the ripped end of the phone wire and hunched himself up to a sitting position against the wall. The knife was still in his wound. He drew it out and mopped ineffectually at the oozing blood with his hand.

"Knowing what I know now, though," he continued, "if I had that phone at your unfractured elbow for just five minutes, and could talk to the Commissioner of Police, I believe I could send both you and Satan, there, back to hell where you belong—via the electric chair!"

Doctor Agnew slashed viciously at the cord of the useless phone with the scalpel in his hand, then hurled the heavy instrument at the man who had been his superior. It struck Meredith on the temple, fell, the mouth-piece one way and the receiver another while the severed cord lashed across his eyes like a whip.

"Certainly you may have it," he taunted. "Go on and call the police. They wouldn't believe you if you could." He chuckled obscenely despite the pain of his fractured arm. "The great Doctor Meredith." His face sobered. "But what caused you to suspect me? That new saline anesthesia on which we were working when your patients started to die?"

"That's right," Meredith agreed. He hunched himself back to a sitting position, his hands behind him. "I dropped it as too dangerous. But you added several new ingredients, didn't you, broke it down into a powerful gas, piped the gas into tiny vials and put them into cigarettes? All your victims had to do was light them. The heat dissolved the gelatine and they sucked the gas down into their lungs with the smoke. In five minutes they were dead . . . mummies, all the juices in their bodies burned into atomic matter."

"It was really very simple," his former assistant boasted. "That is, once you know the ingredients and principle." He warmed to his subject. "I went back to the early Egyptians, took—"

"If you please, Doctor Agnew," the anesthetist protested. "Sit still. I want to be certain that this splint is supporting your fracture correctly."

"It had better," Satan warned. "Doctor Agnew is a very important member of our League of the Grateful Dead." He chuckled. "He makes young men out of old men—sometimes."

"That one tonight was too old," Agnew shrugged. "He died on the table." He looked over at Meredith in the corner. "But just you wait until I start on you. You'll wish you died two years ago—" He stopped abruptly. "What was that?"

"What was what?" Satan asked.

"I thought I heard a woman's voice," the thin-lipped surgeon told him. "Probably one of our little coryphées down stairs that's drunker than usual."

"Probably," Meredith agreed coldly. "And if I had one last dying wish," he spoke distinctly, "it would be that the police could only know the type of place that you're running in my old hospital."

"Wistful thinking," Agnew chortled.

"Perhaps," Meredith agreed. "But I do wish that Commissioner Craig could be listening in on this little conversation here before you kill me." He looked at the man who claimed he was Satan. "The Commissioner actually half believes you are the devil—after that shooting in his office this afternoon."

"Merely a bulletproof vest and a lot of nerve," Satan chuckled. He nudged Doctor Agnew. "You should have seen them when the fingerprint report came back from Washington. It was worth the pain I suffered when you grafted on those fingertips just to see the expression on their faces."

Meredith sat up more erect.

"Who are you, really?"

"Mace Manders the magician," Satan boasted. "Sure, they electrocuted me. But Doc here brought me back to life with methylene blue, gave me a nice new devilish face, and nine dead men's fingertips."

"You figured out this racket?"

"He did not," Agnew boasted. "I did."

"No, Bill," Meredith shook his head. "You're not smart enough to figure out a deal as big as this is."

"No?" Agnew jeered. "I was smart enough to kill ten patients of yours by always managing to leave a sponge inside the wound and fishing it out before you found it when we did an exploratory or a post."

"So," the gaunt man on the floor breathed quietly. He closed his eyes, a wave of relief sweeping over him. "So that was how it was done." He raised his voice. "And some of them died right here in my old operating room where we are now."

Satan kicked him again.

"We can hear you. You don't need to shout."

Meredith sat doubled in pain for a moment, then managed to sit back erect, the wound in his side throbbing madly, the pain stabbing deep into him.

"I—I suppose," he said, "you two have made millions."

"Millions," his former assistant boasted. "And I've had all the experimental material that I needed. It's been a surgeon's dream."

"But how in hell, Bill," Meredith demanded, "do you bring the dead to life?"

Both Doctor Agnew and Satan chuckled like school boys. Then Doctor Agnew grinned his twisted smile.

"You compliment me, Doctor. I don't. They merely think they've been dead, that's all."

"It is simple," Satan boasted. "When a patient worthy of our attention goes to Mercy Hospital, Doctor Agnew merely drugs them into a cataleptic state and signs their death certificate. Then before the undertaker goes to work, Yoshama calls on the dead man's sweetheart or his wife, and tells her I can bring the dead to life—and I do."

"But all your members of the League of the Grateful Dead aren't rich," the man on the floor protested.

"That," Agnew told him, "is where we are smart. We take in an assortment of various types to staff our place and to entertain our paying guests. Some of them believe they have been dead—the others have sold their souls to Satan, here, to bring their loved ones back." Doctor Agnew's thin face was sharp with triumph. "And you are the man who said I was a fool, Jim—said I was money mad. Well, I have it. And I'll have more. I've got a perfect racket."

Meredith shook his head.

"No, Bill. No racket is ever perfect. No matter how smart you are, there's always someone who out-thinks you." His battered lips formed the semblance of a grin. "You don't know it, Bill, but you're going to burn for murder. That's a promise."

"Kick him," Agnew ordered.

Satan did. In the mouth.

Meredith spit out a mouthful of blood, continued calmly.

"For example. You think you're so secure. What would you do if the police should raid this place and find two dozen men and women who they believe are dead?"

"They wouldn't find them," Agnew boasted. "Our doorman is a lookout. And at the first sign of the police, our 'guests' know what to do. They merely file into the cellar and from there into an unused portion of the little known merchandise tunnel that has honey-combed the ground beneath the streets of downtown Chicago for years."

"But we won't be raided," Satan stated with assurance. "Our 'guests' are afraid to talk. They believe I can send them to hell—and I can."

The anesthetist stepped back from the table.

"There. I think that will do it, Doctor Agnew."

The thin-faced surgeon slid down from the operating table.

"Pour me a drink, a stiff one," he ordered.

His younger assistant did so. The surgeon lifted the glass in a toast.

"To your long and lingering death, Doctor Meredith." He gulped his drink and threw the glass on the floor. "All right, put him on the table," he ordered. He smiled thinly. "I won't bother to scrub. I don't *think* that he'll die of infection."

The other two men laughed as they lifted the limp and unresisting figure of the bloody, once-great surgeon from his corner to the table.

"First—" Agnew probed none too gently with his dirty scalpel at the bleeding wound in Meredith's ribs—"we'll see how his reflexes are."

He turned the scalpel in his hand.

"Next, we'll see—"

The sharp bark of a service revolver spat at him from the swinging doors and the scalpel flew from his hand.

"What the hell!" he demanded, stopped short, his thin face blanching as the swinging doors swung open simultaneously with the frantic flashing of a red light on the wall—and a squad of grim-faced Chicago plainclothesmen walked into the room, guns in hand.

"Up with them. And up with them fast!" the lieutenant who had fired the first shot ordered. "The whole building is surrounded and you haven't got a chance."

Satan chose to disbelieve him. His arm jerked up and down, his gun spitting in his hand.

The big lieutenant staggered—then fired again.

Satan tried to raise his gun, but couldn't. He was dead, shot through the heart. He toppled to the floor, a crumpled, motionless heap.

The anesthetist chose to run. The phone cord tangled in his feet and tripped him. He lay where he fell, whimpering for mercy.

Doctor Agnew stood staring at the corner where Doctor Meredith had been lying. The phone he had flung from him in anger was connected roughly to the outgoing end of the severed wire along the baseboard.

The big lieutenant grinned, felt of his shoulder where one of Satan's wild bullets had burned a flesh wound. He nodded toward the phone on the floor.

"Clever, eh? The big Doc on the table there out-thought you. I don't know how he got you to throw him the phone, but you did. So he connects it to the outgoing line and we've been on our way ever since."

Doctor Agnew didn't answer. And they saw then why he didn't. One of Satan's wild bullets was embedded in his temple. His nervous system was completely paralyzed, and Dr. Bill Agnew was dying on his feet.

Eager hands lifted Jim Meredith from the table.

"We come up the outside fire escape," a red-faced detective explained. "And mighty glad to get here when we got here, Doctor."

"The relief was mutual," Meredith smiled. His eyes were on the face of his former assistant.

"He's going to die, Doc?" the lieutenant asked, plugging a wad of cotton packing against the wound in his own shoulder.

"No. Not just yet," Doctor Meredith told him. He seemed another man. Despite his bleeding wound, his unshaven, battered features, and his bloody, ragged clothes, he fully looked the great and famous surgeon that he was. They all looked at him with respect in their eyes.

"No. Not just yet," he repeated. "There are several little items like the pretended resurrection of Max Boderman and the murder of his widow still to be explained. Besides, we'll want him to go to trial, spread the whole story in the papers, so that the countless men and women upon whom he has imposed will know the truth. I'll see to it that he's able to take the stand."

The lieutenant looked dubiously at the once great surgeon's battered lips and trembling hands.

"But can you save him, Doc?" he asked.

"Why of course," Doctor Meredith said simply. He held out a shaking hand and it ceased to tremble. "Of course I can save him. Tim would want me to. I'll save him for the chair. I promise you that, Lieutenant."

And he did. Tim Murphy had been right. For Doctor James Meredith did come back.

AS DEEP
AS THE GRAVE

CHAPTER ONE

DYING ENEMY NO. 1

OKAY. SO I SHOULD HAVE KNOWN BETTER. In every man's life some rain must fall—he must walk into some spider's parlor. And I not only walked into Red Faber's parlor, brother, I got drenched!

The day had been run-of-the-mill. I had spent most of it at H.Q. trying to get a line on an elderly "alleged" Army colonel who had married a blowsy blonde from Wisconsin via the lonely-heart-club-route, only to leave her stranded in Chicago with little but a hotel bill and two nights of flaming memories in lieu of her life savings.

Feeling it an unfair exchange, she had come to me. But I hadn't been able to find any previous record on the man. I had called it a day and was locking my desk when the phone rang. The woman's voice was pleasant and well-modulated. But either she was trying to disguise it or she was laboring under a strain,

"I am speaking to Tom Doyle?" she demanded.

I said she was. Her next line was a lulu.

"How much," she wanted to know, "would you charge to kill a man?"

I told her I thought she must have the wrong Doyle since, after all, as a private investigator with a license issued by the State I was, in a sense, an officer of the law.

She said, "I know who you are and what you are. I also know that since opening your own agency you have killed a number of men. In fact, State's Attorney Beamer refers to you openly as a 'kill-crazy veteran.' "

I told her not to take Beamer seriously as he was a little man in a big job and had to make a lot of noise to cover up his own inability.

She seemed on the verge of hysteria as she told me she knew that, but she was desperate. "I can assure you," she pleaded, "you would only be anticipating justice."

I was beginning to enjoy the conversation. "I could say that about a lot of men," I told her. "By the way, to whom am I speaking, please?"

She said that was none of my business and wanted to know, "If you were given proof that this man deserved to die, would you kill him for ten thousand dollars?"

"Not for ten times that," I told her. She wanted to know why.

I told her, "Because the last time I looked at the State statutes the penalty for murder in the first degree was still burning until death—or a reasonable facsimile thereof—ensues."

She said something that sounded like, "Oh, dear God, what am I going to do," but she was sobbing so hard by then I couldn't hear her clearly. I asked her to speak up but she hung up instead.

I debated trying to trace the call, and didn't bother. The whole thing had left a bad taste in my mouth. One thing was obvious. Beamer's eternal yapping about my being a kill-crazy veteran wasn't doing my reputation any good when a total stranger would call my office to inquire my fee for killing a man. True, since opening my agency, I had killed quite a few men. Their deaths had been forced on me. That was justifiable homicide, an entirely different matter from premeditated murder.

There was the usual five-o'clock-crowd in the bar downstairs. I ordered a double rye and was staring in the back bar mirror trying to decide whether I looked like a killer when I felt the hard barrel of a gun bore into the small of my back. The voice was meant for my ears only.

"Drink your drink as though nothing was happening. When you've finished, walk out to the tan sedan parked in front."

I looked over my shoulder at the lad and felt my spine begin to tingle. It was Gimpy Saulk, one of Red Faber's boys. He was so hot it was a wonder that his mere walking in hadn't set the bar on fire. The last I had heard of him was that noon when Captain Gleason of the bank detail told me gleefully that a sheriff's posse had Red and Gimpy and Cal Shields holed up in a swamp near Benton Harbor, Michigan.

"We bust through the posse and came back," Gimpy read my mind. "Drink your drink and let's go."

He had his gun in the left-hand pocket of his topcoat and was leaning his right elbow on the bar. To any casual observer we were merely two friends talking. But his throwing a gun on me didn't make sense. There was a four-state alarm out on Faber, but I had never tangled with him. "Sure you got the right guy?" I asked him.

"Unless you're Dick Tracy in disguise," he told me. "Get going, Doyle."

There were two more hoods in the sedan. The driver was a young punk I didn't know. The other was Cal Shields. He was so nervous, a fine film of perspiration beaded his cheeks and forehead, but he grinned, "Hello, Tom. Long time no see."

I balked. "Look. I never tangled with you guys. What—?"

Shields opened the door. "Get in."

Saulk dug his gun into my spine. "You heard what Cal said." He was as nervous as Shields and talking between clenched teeth. "Get in or I'll blow your spine in two."

He meant it. I got into the car and the punk at the wheel let out his clutch so fast the big sedan jumped like a jack rabbit.

"Watch your driving, you fool," Saulk warned him. "If just one cop spots us, it's curtains."

I was in a bad spot. I knew it. But for the life of me, I couldn't figure why. As we crossed State there was a prowl car waiting for the light. "And just what would happen," I asked, "if I were to stick my head out and yell cop?"

Shields looked at me thoughtfully. "I think you have more sense." He slipped an automatic from a shoulder holster. "But just in case—"

I saw the blow start but couldn't duck it. It caught me flush on the left temple. There was a blinding flash of light. Then he hit me again to make sure and nothing mattered.

The car was stopped when I came to again. I hadn't the least idea where we were. Shields and the driver were gone, but Saulk still had a gun in my ribs and we were parked in front of a rundown looking office building.

"Nice nap?" Saulk inquired.

"Fine," I assured him.

I bent down and looked up at the office building, trying to orient myself. Only one office, a dentist's, was lighted. As I looked up, someone pulled the shade.

"That's us," Saulk told me. "Out of the car, across the walk, and up the stairs."

I didn't like the set-up. I said, "To hell with that heifer dust!", grabbed his gun wrist with one hand, forced it back so his gun would blast into the cushion and streaked my free hand for my own gun. The holster was there but the gun wasn't. I felt like a damn fool.

Shields opened the door of the car. "You should have known better than to think we'd let you keep a gun," he chuckled. He motioned me out of the car with his gun barrel. "You're a kill-crazy veteran. The State's Attorney says so."

I told him where he could put the State's Attorney and walked up the stairs of the office building, both of them hard on my heels.

A tall man, thin to the point of emaciation, Faber was waiting in the dentist's office. His once flaming red hair was a pale carrot color. His skin had an unhealthy look. His hands were blotched and spotted. As I walked in he was coughing and there was blood on his handkerchief.

"Hello, Doyle," he greeted me cordially. "Long time no see. In fact I think the last time we met you were investigating a hijacking for Inter-Ocean way back in the good old prohibition days."

I ignored his hand. "And to hell with you, too," I told him. "So you're hot as a firecracker. What's the idea of having your boys put the arm on me? I'm not working on the case."

"That's why I sent for you," he told me.

I told him he wasn't making sense.

He took a pint of Scotch from his pocket, took a drink and offered me one. When I refused, he continued, "You know what I think of policemen, Doyle, private or otherwise. But you've always been a right John. That's why I had the boys put the arm on you. I'm in a spot where I have to have a private shamus I can trust."

I said that all the private agency men in the United States couldn't get him out of the jam he was in. He said he knew that. The commission he had in mind, he admitted had nothing to do with his being wanted by the law.

"It's an entirely personal matter," he told me. "You know how hot I am. Maybe the cops get me an hour from now. Maybe I stay clear for a few more weeks. But when they get me. I burn." He coughed into his handkerchief again. "Not that it matters a hell of a lot, catch?"

He took another drink. "And once they get me, the only guy they'll let me talk to is some sharp-shooting mouthpiece. It just so happens there's a little personal matter I'd like to attend to before I'm picked up."

I didn't say a thing. It was his party.

Faber added, "And you don't need to worry about losing your license for not reporting that you've seen me. Five minutes after I walk out of here, you can tell Harry Nobby and Beamer and the whole damn Force if you want."

I couldn't get what he was driving at, but said it looked fair enough on the surface. It was quite a story. He told it well . . .

Some twenty years before, only a punk himself, he had gone up to Eagle River as the bodyguard of Big Joe Wolinski to wait out a period of heat occasioned by a slight difference of opinion with the Capone mob. During the six weeks he was there, a local girl by the name of Mable Sloan caught his eye. She was swept off her feet by Faber, and they were married in Eagle River.

On his return to town, he was picked up in the Murell case and sent up for five years. His wife was a sweet, country kid. She didn't even know he was a hood. Rather than have her find out, he merely stopped writing to her.

She continued to write for several years. She even came to Chicago to look for him—sent him a picture of her and the baby taken while they were in Chicago.

Faber had trouble lighting a cigarette. "But I never answer, see? She's a sweet, simple kid. I'm a hood. I know it will break her heart if she finds out I'm in pokey. I send her a couple of grand through Joe and tell her to forget me."

He took a picture from his wallet and handed it to me. It was the picture of a young girl and a baby so blurred with handling I couldn't distinguish the features. I thought I had the set-up then. The girl had been the one decent thing in his life. Now that the noose was closing, it was natural for him to think of her. "What do you want me to do about it, Red?" I asked.

"I want you to find Mable and her kid," he told me. He laid ten hundred-dollar bills on top of the picture. "I've got a little property the law can't touch, worth maybe fifty grand. And I want the kid to have it."

I asked him why he didn't have his lawyer handle the deal. He smiled wryly. "You know how a lawyer would handle it. He'd put an ad in the paper: "If the heirs of Red Faber, Public Enemy No. 1, will contact this office, blah, blah—" Then what happens? Some smart reporter spots the ad and smears the whole thing in headlines.

"Maybe Mable and the kid don't want it known they ever even knew me, see? I don't want to play 'em no dirty trick. I just want the kid to get the property. And you could handle it on the hush.

What do you say, Doyle? One grand now and I'll give you another grand if you can find Mable and the kid."

I turned the whole thing over in my mind. Red Faber was a killer and a rat. But as far as I could see, it was a perfectly legitimate commission. Even rats had paternal instincts. It was a natural gesture from a man with only a few months to live. And I was in no position to argue. "Okay. I'll take it," I told him.

CHAPTER TWO

FIRST BLOOD

BOTH NOBBY AND THE FEDERAL BOYS WERE FINE. They took my word and let it go at that. But sad-sack Beamer went as far as he dared.

"Are you going to talk or not?" he demanded.

I told him I had said all I intended to.

He shook his fist in my face. "Then you'll not only lose your license, I'll see that you do at least five years as an accessory after the fact."

"After what fact?" I asked him. "The fact that I was kidnapped by a hood—at the point of a gun?"

He wanted to know if I could prove I had been kidnapped. I was forced to admit I could not.

The little man frothed, "They were here. Right here in this office—Faber, Shields and Saulk. And you let them go."

For the fifth time I told him that they had taken my gun during the ride from the bar to the building and that just as soon after their departure as I could, I had called his office, H.Q., and the F.B.I.

"But you won't tell us what Faber commissioned you to do?"

I said I would not. I knew what was eating on the little man. He was up for re-election. Despite all the bobbles he had made during his four years in office, the capture of the Faber mob would have set him solid with the voting public.

"Don't let Beamer get you, Tom," Harry Gold of the local F.B.I. office told me. "You're perfectly clean with us. Under the circumstances, I don't see how you could have done anything else but what you did."

Beamer sneered. "You're not so tough, are you, Doyle, when you're up against a real killer? You kill-crazy veterans are all alike. There's a yellow streak a yard wide up—"

I put my palm in his face and pushed. He went down screaming that he'd get my license. I went looking for Lieutenant Nobby. I had some phone calls to make. But I couldn't make them from there. The building, in fact the whole neighborhood, was swarming with federal men and cops.

Charlie Harris of the Morning Record tagged me in the hall outside the office and wanted to know if it was true that Red Faber had paid me a fee to do something for him. I told him that was correct. Then he wanted to know what it was. I told him to go ask Beamer.

I found Nobby talking to Hanson of the tech squad. Nobby had taken my word that the commission I had accepted from Faber had nothing to do with Red being wanted by the law. But he wasn't over-friendly about it. He wanted Red Faber too badly.

"You want to go where?" he asked me when I asked if it was all right for me to leave.

I told him, "Home."

He said that was okay with him. But from the way he said it, I knew that I'd have a tail. And that was all right with me. Now I'd had time to think it over, I wished I had told Red Faber where he could put his thousand-dollars. But having taken the case, I meant to see it through.

The building was on the near south side in the heart of the old levee. The tan sedan had obviously turned off the Outer Drive onto 22nd Street right after Shields had sapped me with his gun barrel. I flagged a cab and rode on down to the office to make my calls and pick up a spare gun before I went on home.

In the office I put through a long distance call to Eagle River, then called Sue while I was waiting. She said it was a fine time for me to be calling, the pork loin had dried up, the mashed potatoes were soggy, the twins were screaming their heads off, and who did I think I was. She added that some woman had called me three times, wanting to know if I had located Colonel Cramer and saying it was vitally important that she see me at once.

That would be the blowsy blonde from Wisconsin. I told Sue if she called again to tell her that I could stop in at her hotel on my way home.

"And that will be when?" Sue sniffed.

I told her I didn't know as I had been kidnapped into a case.

"Hmm. A likely story," she threw at me, and hung up.

The sheriff at Eagle River turned out to be a friendly old duffer named Swanson of no help at all, as far as I was concerned. He said he knew the Sloan family well. Rather he *had* known them well. Both the elder Sloans were dead and to the best of his recollection, their only daughter, Mable, had left town some twenty years before, after an unfortunate marriage. As far as he knew she had never returned, not even for a visit. There were no near relatives living. That was all he could tell me. I thanked him and hung up.

It began to look as if I were on the well-known spot. I had a thousand dollars of Red Faber's money. With nothing but a faded picture of a girl and a child, I was supposed to find her after twenty years. Red expected me to make good. And if I didn't, he hadn't a thing to lose by adding me to his daisy-chain of murder.

I studied the back of the picture under the light. The photographer's name was as worn as the features but I could decipher the three words "Clark Street" and "Chicago." It wasn't much to go on. But it was a start. I could begin there in the morning.

Pat Grogan of Nobby's squad was holding up a post in the foyer when I came down again. I pretended I didn't see him, got into my own car that the garage attendant had left around the corner on Dearborn and drove to the Osbourne Hotel.

The "Colonel's" wife was waiting in her room. She looked even more blowsy than she had in the office, and her breath was heavy with gin. I broke the sad news to her as gently as I could. As far as I had been able to ascertain, both the Colonel and her life savings were gone. I told her the best thing she could do was to swear out a warrant for his arrest, in the hope that when he was picked up, he might still have some of her money on his person.

She said she couldn't do that because the story would reach her home-town paper and I knew how small towns were. Tears rolling down her cheeks, she told me, "I guess the best thing I can do is to go back home to Eagle River and try to forget what a fool I've been."

It was the first time she had mentioned her home-town. All ears, I asked her if she had known the Sloan family.

"Very well," she told me. "The old folks died some years ago, but the last I heard of Mable Sloan, she was living right here in Chicago."

It was a break I hadn't expected. I made the most of it by asking if she happened to know her address or knew anyone who might know it.

The aging blonde thought a moment, brushed an untidy wisp of hair out of her eyes and told me, "No. I don't know where she lives." She brightened. "But Cora Hart might know. They were

like that when they were girls." She added. "Her name isn't Hart
now, though; it's Wren."

"Not Mrs. Michael Wren by any chance?"

"That's just who she is," the blonde beamed. "I tell you that
Cora is a girl that Eagle River is proud of."

It had reason to be. Mike Wren was running for Governor and a
cinch to be elected. I knew him well. A brilliant, outspoken lawyer
with an envious legal, civil and military record behind him, he had
the coming election in the bag and the bag in his back pants
pocket. We had worked on several cases together when I had been
with Inter-Ocean, but I had never met Mrs. Wren. Since she was
now society with a capital S, I doubted if she had kept up the girl-
hood friendship. But it was worth a try.

I didn't need to look up the address. Wren, when he was in
town, lived in a swank apartment hotel on the Gold Coast, a half-
mile closer to the Loop and five-hundred a month closer to the sky
than I did I gave my card to a butler in an entrance hall the size of
my living room and asked to see either Mr. or Mrs. Wren.

While I was waiting a boy and girl in evening clothes came in.
Both nodded pleasantly and said, "Good evening."

I decided the girl was Mike's daughter. I knew the boy by sight.
He was the youngest Potter boy, heir to God knew how many millions, and recently a much-decorated lieutenant of infantry. As
soon as I saw them, it came back. Several nights before Sue had
seen the announcement of their engagement in the society column,
and had remarked what a fine-looking pair they were.

The butler returned to tow me through ankle-deep beige broad-
loom into a beamed living-room, saying that Mr. Wren would be
right out. Mike's daughter had shed her fur coat and was curled up
in a chair. The Potter boy, a rolled newspaper in his hand, was
speaking earnestly to a slim brunette in a low-cut black evening
gown. I decided that she was Mrs. Wren although she and her
daughter could have passed for sisters.

The brunette stared at me as though I were something that had
crawled out from tinder a stone. "You are Mr. Doyle." It was an
accusation not a statement.

I pleaded guilty. There was something familiar about her, but I
couldn't place it.

She said, "Oh, I see," and we looked at each other.

I felt like a damn fool. I had a feeling that we were fencing but
I didn't know what about. To the best of my sober knowledge, I

had never annoyed her before by intruding my seemingly obnoxious presence.

Young Potter said he guessed he'd run along and the girl in the chair said, "Oh, damn your Aunt Sofia. I don't see why you couldn't have remembered it was her birthday before we made our date."

He kissed the tip of her nose. "I'll be back in an hour, puss."

He left and the girl complained to her mother that they had no sooner reached the street when he had remembered that it was his Aunt's birthday and he'd have to postpone their dinner to a supper date. And that meant she would have to change again because she simply couldn't wear such a stodgy dinner gown to a night-club.

I stood listening in, feeling more like a fool than ever and trying to get up nerve enough to ask the swank Mrs. Wren if she knew the present address of her former friend, Mable Sloan. Then Mike came into the room.

A big man physically, with a booming voice to match, he shook hands cordially. "Glad to see you, Tom. And sorry to keep you waiting."

I said I was sorry I had disturbed him.

He said, "Not at all," and introduced his wife and daughter.

The girl smiled, "Good evening," for the second time. His wife merely looked coldly at me.

Then Wren offered me a drink and wanted to know what he could do for me. I refused the drink but told him I was looking for a Mable Sloan, whom I believed Mrs. Wren had known in Eagle River, and I would appreciate it very much if she could give me her present address.

"Mable Sloan," Wren rolled the name on his tongue as if it were distasteful.

"Mable is dead," Mrs. Wren told me coldly.

I said I was sorry to hear it. "Now I wonder if you could tell me this," I persisted. "Is her child still living?"

"Her child died also," Mrs. Wren informed me in the same icy voice. And that seemed to be that.

"Mable Sloan. I place the name now," Wren said. He turned to his wife. "That's the girl, isn't it, Cora, who you told me was so unfortunate as to become involved with the notorious Red Faber?"

She nodded, thin-lipped, and Wren swung back to me. "Sorry we aren't able to be of more help to you, Tom. You working on the Faber case?"

Mrs. Wren handed him the rolled newspaper that young Potter had tossed on the sofa. "So it would seem," she said.

Wren unrolled the paper and chuckled at the headline. It was a so-called Extra and Charlie Harris hadn't wasted any time rushing into print. My picture was plastered next to a rogue's-gallery "mug" of Faber's and over them was the streamer:

TOM DOYLE SUSPECTED AS CONTACT MAN
FOR KILLER

"That's Beamer's fine hand," I told Wren. "I merely agreed to try and find Faber's wife and daughter for a fee of two thousand dollars."

He repeated that he was sorry they weren't able to help me, then changed the subject to ask what I thought his chances were in the coming election.

I told him he looked like a cinch from where I stood. Then Mrs. Wren reminded him he was due at his club at nine and looked pointedly at me. I picked my hat from the table, went through the usual mumbo-jumbo about being pleased to meet her and hoping we would meet again.

Her nod was hardly enthusiastic. Mike walked with me to the door. He was a good politician and shook hands cordially in parting, telling me not to be a stranger but to drop in any time and to bring Mrs. Doyle with me.

Out in the hall I turned back to look at the door. There was something screwy in the apartment but I was damned if I could place it. Mrs. Wren had been too quick in telling me that both Mable Sloan and Faber's child were dead. It was far more likely that she was covering for her friend—that Mable had made a good marriage and didn't want to be "found." That was all right, except that it left me on the well-known spot marked X.

The only thing left to do was to try to trace the picture in the morning. But before I did, I meant to check the death records. If Mable Sloan was dead, both a doctor and an undertaker would have had to sign her death certificate.

A cold, wet wind was blowing off the lake. If Grogan was still tailing me, he was in out of the cold somewhere. I walked up the street toward my car, started across the parkway and stopped as a man loomed out of the darkness. His hat was pulled over his eyes. His coat collar was turned up.

"Oh-oh," I thought. "A stick-up."

And that was the last thinking I did for awhile. Before my hand was halfway to my gun, he had knocked me off my feet and he belted me twice more before I hit the ground. The last thing I heard was him saying:

"I'm sorry. Believe me. I wish I didn't have to do this."

The joker was, he sounded like he meant it.

CHAPTER THREE

AND SUDDEN DEATH!

I HAD NO WAY OF KNOWING how long I had been out, or where I was. All I knew was that the room was dark, I was lying on a cot of some kind, and my head was a sore boil.

I tried to raise my hand to my jaw and couldn't. I was lying on my side, my hands tied behind my back. The same rope extended to form a loop around my ankles. The lad who had slugged me knew his business. But he didn't fit into the picture. He wasn't a hood. Hoods didn't apologize for slugging you.

I tried to straighten up and almost choked. It was a three way hook-up, ankles to wrists to throat. The harder I struggled, the tighter I drew the noose. I lay still, cursing Red Faber for getting me into this mess. It had to be tied in with him. A lot of guys don't like me. But there was no one I could think of who would slug me. The hoods I had cuffed around in the line of business were more apt to use machine guns.

Mike's wife's coolness could be the tip-off. It could be that Mable Sloan was very much alive, but didn't want to be found. That was okay with me. I had taken the commission under duress. And I had had all I wanted of the results of the youthful love-life of Public Enemy No. 1.

With an effort I turned on my other side without choking. On the far side of the room, a door was outlined in light. A radio was playing softly but above it I could catch a faint murmur of voices.

The man who had slugged me was saying, "A filthy shame it had to come up at this time. Otherwise, it wouldn't matter so much."

The woman's voice was vaguely familiar but I couldn't catch the words. He laughed bitterly at whatever it was she said.

"Now you are being utterly ridiculous. Doyle isn't an unknown. We can't hold him here trussed up like a fowl forever." He was matter of fact about it. "Why don't you let me kill him?"

I could feel the cold sweat start. It didn't make sense. But there it was. The woman's voice rose sharply in protest. But she wasn't thinking of me.

"No, you can't," she cried shrilly. "I won't allow you to ruin your life."

One thing was clear. I knew the voice. She was the woman who had phoned me a ten-thousand dollar offer to kill an unnamed man. Then the wheels in my brain began to turn. I knew two more things. She was also Mable Sloan and the man whom she had wanted me to kill was Faber. I had been a fool not to spot it in the first place.

Faber didn't want to leave his former wife any money. With all of the heat he already had on him, he was working a blackmail angle and I was merely additional pressure. Small wonder that Mrs. Wren had been so cool! She thought I was hounding her friend.

I eased my feet down until the rope was taut around my neck. The rope refused to give but I had found out what I wanted to know. It was a simple turn not a slip noose around my throat. By being careful, I could put pressure on the rope without tightening it to the point where it could strangle me.

I lowered my feet to the floor and stood up gingerly, my body bent in a bow. Half shuffling, half hopping, I got to the window without falling. The window was open and unscreened. What was more important—it was on the first floor. Beyond it was a line of trees, and I could see water shimmering in the moonlight. As closely as I could figure, the place was a summer cottage on one of the hundreds of lakes within a few hours drive of Chicago.

I lowered myself to the floor, braced my toes against the baseboard and bent backwards in an arc until the top and bottom section of the rope hung free and my fingers were touching the knot in the rope around my ankles. After that it was fairly easy. My ankles free, I stood, slipped the rope from around my neck and went to work on my hands. My wrists were raw flesh when I finished, but my hands were free.

I slipped out of the window, swore as Faber's tan sedan rolled up the drive, its headlights barely missing spotlighting me against the clapboard.

Red got out, followed by Shields and Saulk and another man whose face I couldn't see. Three of them walked toward the front door. Saulk walked toward the rear of the cottage, passing *so* close to where I huddled back of a snowball bush that I could have reached out and touched him.

Red rapped sharply on the door and as he did a shaft of moonlight struck the face of the man beside him. It was Phil Carver, the criminal lawyer who boasted that he had never lost a client to the chair. I tried to figure his angle and couldn't.

There were two things I could do. I could scram while the scramming was good or I could get myself a gun and stick around. My name being Doyle, I inched along the wall toward the rear of the cottage.

Gimpy was watching the rear door, his right hand in his topcoat pocket and his back to me. I tiptoed across the flower bed, cupped a palm over his mouth, braced my other forearm against his neck—and pulled.

There was a sharp, cracking sound. I took the gun out of his pocket and walked back to the front of the cottage. The door was wide open. Red Faber, his face twisted in a snarl, was ordering young Potter away from a door he was blocking with his shoulders.

"Don't make me hurt you, kid. I don't want to. But I will if I have to."

Phil Carver lighted a cigarette. "You're being very foolish, Potter. All we want to do is talk to Mable." He shrugged. "And after all, this *is* really none of your affair."

"I'm making it my affair," Potter said grimly. "She's told me the whole story. And you can't prove a thing."

"No?" Carver chuckled. "Wake up and learn the facts of life, son. We have one of the best private agency men in the city, a hard-boiled Irishman by the name of Doyle, backtrailing on Mable now. And if Mable makes us shoot the works, we will, with Tom Doyle as our witness."

Potter shot a quick glance at the door of the room I had been in. I walked in holding Saulk's gun on my hip. "Doyle doesn't live there anymore, Potter," I told him. "And as for you, Red, I'd stand very still. Mable offered me ten thousand dollars this afternoon to kill you. And who am I to turn down good, clean money?"

I didn't expect Shield's next move. He turned, cursing and shooting at the same time. His slug plowed a furrow across my ribs. Mine caught him in the wishbone. He hiccoughed solemnly, took two quick steps toward me, caught at Carver for support, then slid down him to the floor.

"Well, you saved him from the chair," I told Carver. "How about it, Phil? You want more of the same? Or would you rather take your hand out of your pocket?" He raised his palms shoulder high.

"And you?" I asked Red. He hesitated and I flipped a slug into the floor a half-inch from his foot. He dropped his gun and whined, "You have me all wrong, Doyle."

I took the bills he had given me from my pocket wadded them into a ball and threw it in his face. "I don't want any part of you," I told him. "I don't like guys who lie to me."

Young Potter started to say something and changed his mind. I said, "You took a pretty big chance in slugging me, didn't you, son, just to help out the girl friend of your fiancée's mother?"

Faber began, "Now, look here, Doyle—"

"You stay shut," I told him. "When I want you to talk, I'll say so. But right now I'm up to here with you. In fact, I'm practically trigger-happy."

"I'm afraid," young Potter said, grimly, "that you still don't understand the situation, Doyle."

I was plenty sore at him, too. "No. I don't know your part in this," I admitted. "But I do know that I heard you ask Mable why she didn't let you kill me."

He grinned, "Don't be dumb. I wasn't talking about you. I wanted to shoot Faber." He scowled at the hood. "I still think it's a swell idea."

I checked back mentally. He could be leveling. I nodded at the door behind him. "If Mable Sloan, Red Faber's former wife is in there, son trot her out."

He hesitated briefly, shrugged, "Why not. Just give me a few minutes, Doyle, to convince her that it will be best for all concerned for everyone to come out in the open with this."

As the door closed behind him, Carver cleared his throat uneasily. "Just what do you intend to do, Doyle?"

I admitted, "I don't know, shyster. But my natural inclination is to shoot you both and drop your bodies—" I stopped short as someone ground the starter of the car standing in the drive.

"Mable and the punk slipped out a window," Faber swore. "They're taking a powder."

I swung toward the door shouting, "No. Hold it!" But the tan sedan, Potter driving, was already half-way to the highway. And turning my back on Faber was a bad mistake.

He snatched up the gun he had dropped and brought the barrel down in a hard, raking, blow that almost tore off one of my ears. Blind with pain, I swung back, pegged a shot at the spot where he had been, then dove out the door into the blackness of the night.

Lead whistled through my hair. Then a slug knocked me flat on my face. Still crawling, I heard Carver call: "I think I got him that time."

"In a pig's britches," I grunted. Then I was on my feet again and zig-zagging for the screen of trees, hot blood spurting down my side. There were still plenty of angles that I didn't know. I'd had the whole case in my hand and blown it—and only myself to blame. Six months before, I wouldn't have let young Potter leave the room and I wouldn't have turned my back on Faber. But things had been going too well. I was too cocky. Fat fees had softened me up. I was living by my name instead of my brains.

I reached the screen of trees and raced on. Behind me Carver was screaming: "Find him! Kill him! If Doyle gets back to town you're a cooked goose, Red."

It didn't make sense at the time. But it did—soon.

CHAPTER FOUR

FRAME FOR MURDER

THE DRUGGIST WAS SMALL AND BALD and wore thick-lensed glasses that made his eyes look like a pair of frightened blueberries.

"Look, Mister," he protested. "Believe me. I'm not an M.D. I'm only a pharmacist. You want I should lose my license, for treating a wounded man?"

I was in no mood to argue. I showed him Gimpy's gun. "Now shut up and produce. For all you know, I might be Red Faber."

He gulped and went to work with the sulfa powder and the gauze. The blow on my head hurt more than the hole in my shoulder did. But it had cleaned away some of the cobwebs. I knew why young Potter had slugged me. I knew why he wanted to kill Faber. The whole thing had been as obvious as Betty Grable's gams right from the start. But I couldn't see what the hell I could do about it. I had no proof of anything. Potter would deny having been at the cottage. So would Mable Sloan. So would Phil Carver for that matter. I couldn't even prove that I had killed Saulk and Shields. And if I even mentioned having seen Red Faber again, the State's Attorney's distorted little mind would undoubtedly accuse me of collusion.

The bald little druggist did a good job, then told me shyly, "You aren't Red Faber." He ran a finger across a red scar on my belly. "Your name I wouldn't know. But speaking as a former medical corpsman, only a piece of mortar shell can leave a scar like that."

I grinned and showed him my shield to lift him off his mental hot spot. Leave it to a medic to know. They should. They were out in front of the lines enough.

When he had finished strapping me up, I used his phone. "This is Tom Doyle," I told the feminine voice that answered. "Are you still willing to pay ten thousand dollars to have me kill a certain man?"

There was a gasp at the other end. "I don't know what you're talking about."

"I bet you don't," I told her, and hung up.

There was a restaurant next to the drug store. Since it was some time after midnight, I had the place to myself with the exception of a cabbie who was eating breakfast and telling the Greek counter-man between bites—

"It all just goes to show you, Nick. You can't trust none of them private dicks. Just like in the movies, they're all the time hand-in-glove with the crooks."

I ordered coffee and wheat cakes and refolded a morning paper lying on the counter from the sporting to the front page. My picture was still on the front page. But either as a favor to me or in fear of a libel suit, the city desk had cut Charlie's lurid account of me as Red Faber's contact man down to a stick of type. It played down the fact that I had admitted accepting a thousand dollars to execute a commission for Faber, and played up the fact that he had emerged from hiding briefly, only to disappear again, evading capture. But the intimation that my fingers were sticky was still there. A lot of potential clients would reason that where there was smoke there was fire. And as far as I could see at the moment the only way to convince them differently would be to deliver Red Faber's corpse to H.Q. and tell Beamer where he could put it.

On a hunch I asked the Greek if he had a magnifying glass. He said he had, and I used it to study the Clark Street address on the back of the picture that Faber had given me. It was either 305 or 505 N. Clark.

"I use it to spot counterfeits," the Greek explained.

"This seems to be real," I told him. Then I spent a nickel for a slug, dialed the Osbourne Hotel and asked for the "Colonel's" wife, Mrs. Cramer, I expected to be told she had checked out. But she hadn't. She picked up her phone too fast.

"Yes—?" she demanded.

"This is Tom Doyle again, Mrs. Cramer," I told her. "And while I hate to bother you so late at night, I wonder if you would do me a favor?"

There was a moment's pause, then she wanted to know what it was.

I said, "As I told you earlier this evening, I'm trying to locate a Mable Sloan. Mrs. Wren wasn't able to give me her address. In fact, she seems to be under the impression that she's dead."

I waited for her to say something. When she didn't, I continued, "But I have reason to think differently. And I think I know how I can find her."

I explained about the picture, saying it wasn't very clear but the photographer's address was on the back and I was on my way to see if he had another print in his files or could make one from the negative. I concluded, "And if I can get a fresh print I wonder if you would be so kind as to look at it and tell me if the girl is the Mable Sloan you knew?"

She said she would be pleased to and wanted to know where in the city I was calling from.

"A long way from the photographer's," I told her. "It may take me almost an hour to get there."

She was still talking when I hung up. I paid for my cakes and coffee, walked out of the joint, and flagged a cab. "Just drive for an hour," I told the hacker.

I still had two more phone calls to make. But if I was right, I had baited a trap. Faber had tried to play me for a sucker. I had been. But my eyes were wide open now. And everything depended on just how dumb he and Phil Carver thought I was.

The hour-hand was pushing two when I paid off the cab on N. Clark and Chicago, but the cabarets and honky-tonks were still going full blast.

I walked south slowly. 505 wasn't the place. 305 was. The name on the sign was Tonelli and the window was filled with dusty pictures of brides and grooms, service men and children. An old Italian with a scraggly moustache was standing in the door-way.

"Take your picture for a dollar, Mister?" he asked hopefully.

I told him that I wasn't that proud of my looks and handed him the picture. "You're Tonelli? You took that picture?"

He turned it over and looked at the back. "Could be," he admitted. "That's my name." He stared at me shrewdly through bushy white eyebrows. "Why you give me this? What you want from Tonelli, Mister?"

I told him the picture was too worn for me to distinguish the features and I wondered if he could check his records and negatives for the year 1920 and sell me a reprint.

He grumbled that it was late, he had been about to close up, that finding the negative would involve a lot of work, and that it would be better if I came back in the morning.

"For twenty dollars?" I said.

He shrugged his thin shoulders. "For twenty dollars, how can I turn you down?" He closed and locked the door behind us, saying that it might take him some time and that I had better come back in the studio to wait.

He switched out the front lights and shuffled through a pair of green baize curtains. I followed him with my hand on the gun in my pocket. I hadn't missed.

Phil Carver was sitting on a filthy day bed, a twisted smile on his lips. The blowsy blonde was sitting beside him. Red Faber was standing to her left, a sub-machine gun in his hand. As I came in he said, "Surprise!"

It wasn't. But I pretended it was.

"Your trouble, Doyle," Carver said, "is that you're only half-smart. After what happened at the cottage, you might have known that Bessie, here, was phony. She called me as soon as you called her."

"I was good though, wasn't I?" the blonde asked. She blew the same untidy wisp out of her eyes. "All my friends always told me I should have been an actress."

I asked Faber, "Supposing I told you I knew that your blonde girlfriend was a phony but calling her was the only way I knew to get in touch with you?"

He swore softly under his breath. Carver sat up straighter. "I will be damned. So you're crooked as hell after all, Doyle. You've got the whole set-up figured out, but instead of burping it to the law you're coming whining around for a hand-out."

Faber snarled, "You lousy copper." He lifted the submachine gun and I pointed my pocket at him.

"Sure. You can take me, Red," I told him. "But I'll have time for at least one shot. That's all I need."

"Want to play along?" he hesitated.

"You couldn't give me a dime," I told him.

Sudden suspicion punching his eyes, Carver got up from the day bed. "What the hell are you talking about?"

"Wrecking a man's career and a kid's life," I told him. "It was a clever idea, shyster. But you've played your string too thin."

He repeated, "What the hell are you talking about?"

"A blind dame named Justice," I said. "You're going up the river, Phil. And unless sudden death catches up with him first, you've lost your first client to the chair."

Faber's voice wasn't as strong as his words, "You're crazy. They won't dare burn me!"

The blonde was the first to get the set-up. She staggered to the back of the studio, looked out of the window and screamed, "Kill him! He burped to the law after all. The alley is lousy with cops !"

Then everything happened at once. Red triggered a burst at me as I threw myself to one side. Glass crashed in the front and back of the studio. An axe began to whittle at the door. From somewhere in front, Nobby called, "Don't try it, Red. We have the building surrounded!"

Frothing like a cornered rat, Faber shot a burst through the green baize curtains, then swung the gun back on me. "Damn you to hell, Doyle!" he screamed. "At least I'll take you with me."

I said, "Boasting again," and nailed a pink rosebud on his forehead that blossomed into a bloody veil. But all of his slugs didn't miss me. I took two through the thigh before the sub-machine gun flew out of his hands to thud at Carver's feet.

"See what I mean, Phil?" I needled. "Red's dead, but it's twenty years for you!"

"The hell you say," he babbled, and snatched up the gun from the floor.

It all I was waiting for. The blonde and Tonelli were small-fry. Their word wouldn't mean a thing. But Carver's would. He could still lift the lid on Mable Sloan's coffin and drag her out of her grave. So I pinned a second rosebud on him just as Harry Nobby followed by Gleason, of the bank detail, and State's Attorney Beamer burst through the green baize curtains.

Nobby and Gleason helped me to my feet. The little sad-sack shook his fist in my face. "You didn't even order him to drop his gun," he bellowed. "I saw that with my own eyes. You—"

"Sure. I'm a kill-crazy veteran," I forestalled him.

Nobby tightened his grip around my waist and wanted to know how badly I was shot. I told him I didn't know, but that things were blacking out and I thought they had better get me down to County and notify Sue.

He barked an order for a stretcher. My knees had turned to rubber. If it hadn't been for him and Gleason, I couldn't have managed to stand.

Beamer continued to annoy me. "Phil Carver was a respectable attorney," he insisted. "What was he doing mixed up with a rat like Faber? And why were you so eager to kill him?"

"It's a long story, sad-sack," I began. "Maybe your mother told it to you. Or did you have one? You see once upon a time there was a pretty little blossom, minding her own business, when along came a handsome bee. Then what do you think happened?"

But that was as far as I got. Before I could go into details, the floor and ceiling came together . . .

CHAPTER FIVE

STAY DEAD, MABLE

BEAMER, WEARING A SURGEON'S GOWN AND MASK, was trying to burn out my eyes with a blow-torch. I tried to lift an arm to sock him and someone said: "Okay. Switch off the light. He's coming to."

Suddenly the room was blessedly cool. I opened one eye cautiously. Her face as white as the operating-table sheet on which I was lying, Sue was standing beside me holding like death to my right hand. Doc Hartzig was standing beside her admiring his fancy hemstitching.

"He'll be all right?" Sue asked.

His eyes twinkling the old Dutchman told her, "Jawohl, Frau Doyle. Yah. Sure. Ach Gott! Such an Irisher I couldn't kill mit a scalpel."

He shook a rubber cased finger in my face. "Young man, someday yet, one chance too many you will take und into you will some lead gedt that old Hartzig can't oudt gedt!"

"Remind me to increase my insurance," I told him.

He strode off to wash up, leaving the air blue behind him. Sue kissed me hard, her tears wet on my face. "Oh, Tom."

That was all. But it made me feel swell the way she said it. A nurse began to clean up the table preparatory to rolling me onto a stretcher and carting me up to a room. "Nobby is here?" I asked Sue.

"I'm right here behind you, Tom," he said. He walked around where I could see him. "How about it?" he asked the nurse. "Is it all right for him to talk?"

She gathered up a bundle of soiled linen. "You heard what Doctor Hartzig said. Durable Doyle seems to be about as good a name for him as any."

As she pushed through the swinging doors I could see that the waiting room was crowded with police and reporters. A big black cigar tilted until it almost touched his hat brim, sad-sack Beamer was wearing a hole in the floor. "How does the score stand?" I asked Nobby,

He said, "Both Faber and Carver are dead. So are Gimpy and Shields. And I've tucked the blonde and Tonelli away until you could straighten things out. You remember telling me to have young Potter and Mrs. Wren handy when you came to?"

I didn't. But it had been the last thought in my mind. "They're here?" I asked.

He nodded. "But strictly on the q.t." He opened the door of the doctor's lounge and called, "Mrs. Wren," softly.

She came in dragging her feet as if she were walking the last mile. She wasn't icy now. Her eyes were red and swollen with crying. I doubted if she could walk, if it hadn't been for young Potter's arm.

"Who knows they're here?" I asked Nobby.

He shook his head. "No one. I wasn't sticking my neck out until I found out the score."

Young Potter said hesitantly, "We shouldn't have run out on you, Doyle. But I thought you had the situation well in hand and—"

"Forget it," I cut him short. I looked at the woman beside him. "Hello, Mable." She spread her hands in a futile gesture. I could see the worry lines in her face now. She had been kicked around plenty. She expected me to kick her some more.

"What's this Mable business?" Nobby asked.

"She's Mable Sloan, Red Faber's former wife. And her daughter is Mable's kid," I told him.

He said that he still didn't get it.

"It is involved," I admitted. I told the story as I saw it, hoping the nurse would stay out until I had finished. "Some twenty years ago," I told Nobby, "Cora Wren, here, lost her head over Red Faber."

Nobby scowled. "I thought you said her name was Mable."

I told him, "There was a Mable Sloan, Every small town has a Mable. But she had left Eagle River some time before. Cora lost her head over Faber, but she made him marry her. She married him under the name of Mable Sloan. I wouldn't know why unless it was a secret marriage and she didn't want her parents to know about it. Was that the angle, Cora?"

Crying too hard to talk, she nodded that it was.

I continued, "She knew she'd made a mistake—right from the start. But the damage had been done. How long did you live with Faber?" I asked her.

"A week," she sobbed.

"Then you got an annulment, came to Chicago and married Mike Wren with whom you had been in love before you lost your head over Faber. That right?" She nodded.

"But you neglected to tell him about Faber, and he thinks your daughter is his child."

"Stop torturing her," young Potter told me hotly.

"You keep your shirt on," I told him. "What with assault and kidnapping, I've got enough on you to send you up for twenty years.

The skin on his cheek bones grew taut but he didn't answer. He knew I was telling the truth,

Mrs. Wren sobbed. "He was only trying to help me, help Constance."

Nobody wanted to know who Constance was. I told him she was Red Faber's daughter but had been raised to believe Mike was her father.

"It didn't matter to me," young Potter said. "But the truth would have broken her heart. She would have felt that she could never hold up her head again."

"It was a blackmail angle then?" Nobby asked.

"In a way," I told him. "As I see my part in the picture, Phil Carver, as Red's lawyer, was in possession of the facts. He knew the truth but he couldn't prove it. Too much water had flown under the bridge. It was Red's word against Cora's. Mike wouldn't have listened to him. So they sucked me in as a clincher. My word is known as my bond. Whatever other sins I may have, I don't lie. They knew that Mike would believe me. So Red had Gimpy and Cal pick me up. The general idea as I see it was that I would backtrail the picture, find out it was really Cora Wren, and when I had confronted her with the fact, she would break down and do what they wanted her to. To make certain I didn't slip up, they planted the blonde on me to point directly at Cora. But things didn't work out that way. In the first place, Cora was fighting back. She phoned me and offered to lay ten grand on the line if I would kill a certain man whom I know now to be Faber. When I turned her down, she confided in the only person she could trust, her daughter's fiancé. And young Sir Galahad here leaped on his horse by smacking me in the bugle and bundling me out to that summer cottage to keep me from finding out any more than I knew.

Meanwhile, Red and Carver came to the cottage for Cora's final answer. And you know what happened there."

The nurse came back with an interne and a stretcher.

"And that's that," I summed up the case.

"But I still don't see," Nobby puzzled, "what Carver and Faber hoped to gain."

"Who is going to be our next governor?" I asked him.

"Mike Wren," he said promptly.

"And if you were Public Enemy No. 1, with the electric chair staring you in the face, who would be the man with the power to commute your sentence, even to pardon you openly?"

"The Governor," Nobby answered thoughtfully.

I tied it all together, "And if you were the governor of a state and such a mess was dropped in your lap, what would you do? You'd do the same thing Mike would have done. If he *knew* the facts were as stated, he would have pardoned Red and probably Cal and Gimpy. It would have washed him up politically, sure. But it would have saved his wife's reputation, and the happiness of a sweet, innocent kid whom for twenty years he had believed to be his own daughter."

Nobby swore softly.

I concluded, "As I see it, Red was tired of dodging the law. He wanted to give up. But before he did, he wanted to *know* the fix was in. But it had to be done hush-hush. Once the story broke, he'd lose his lever. That was where I came in. Once I had established the facts he claimed were so, he could lay his cards in front of Mike and collect the promise he wanted, under the threat of exposure." I looked at the crying woman. "But all the time, Cora, was fighting them—more Mike's sake, I imagine, than for her That right, Cora?"

Her eyes brimming with tears, she told me, "I couldn't let them do that to Mike. He's too fine—too good."

I nodded. "Then stay dead, Mable."

She stared at me, puzzled. "I beg your pardon?"

"You heard me," I told her.

Young Potter got it before she did and squeezed my hand hard. "You're okay, Doyle," he said warmly.

I said, "In your hat. Now go on. Get her out of here before I climb off this table and pay you back the punch in the bugle I owe you."

Cora spilled tears all over my face while she kissed me as hard as Potter had squeezed my hand. When they had gone out the back door, I asked Nobby, "Can do?"

The big lug cleared a frog from his throat. "Can do."

Sue scrubbed the alien lipstick off my face and replaced it with some of her own. Her eyes were as wet as Cora's. "I'm glad I'm married to you," she whispered. "You're really something pretty fine."

His hand on the door, Nobby hesitated, briefly. "But look. What do you get out of this, Tom?"

"I've got mine," I told him, grinning foolishly.

One of the swinging doors stuck as he went out and I saw Beamer hurry up to him. "No one tells me a thing," the little sad-sack complained. "What is this all about? What's going on here?"

"Well, I'll tell you," Nobby began, "It's a long story, Mr. State's Attorney. It would seem that once upon a time there was a pretty little blossom, minding her own business, when—"

Then the door swung shut and the nurse said sharply, "Stop laughing, Mr. Doyle."

I tried to—but I couldn't. So help me, I laughed so hard I damn near busted my stitches.

FRY AWAY, KENTUCKY BABE!

CHAPTER ONE

SO HELP ME, MURDER!

IT WAS STRICTLY A CHARITY CASE. Or so I thought at the time. So, if some of the bread that I cast on the water came back chocolate éclairs, who am I to complain?

It began with the girl in the grey squirrel coat. She was young and moderately pretty, mostly eyes, legs, hips and other feminine equipment. She walked into my office one noon, sat down in the chair I indicated, and tears rolled down her cheeks as she told me: "He didn't do it, Mr. Doyle."

I said I was pleased to hear that but suggested it might aid in the meeting of our minds if I knew *who* hadn't done *what.*

She was annoyed at my stupidity. "Why, Larry didn't kill that awful man. And he didn't make love to—to that girl. He didn't have anything to do with her."

Now we were getting places. Someone named Larry hadn't made love to some girl, and he hadn't killed some man, identity still unknown. I asked my caller if she could be a trifle more specific.

Ignoring me, she continued, "But I want to be fair, Mr. Doyle. I haven't a dime to pay you. It took all our money for the lawyer and the appeal. But Larry didn't do it. Honestly, he didn't. He's fine. And he's good. And he loves me."

That was her story. By clever deduction, and finally asking her outright, I learned that her name was Mrs. Reagan. You may, or may not, have read of the case in your local paper. Some of the papers played it up. Some didn't. The Chicago papers gave it quite a spread.

It wasn't a very savory mess. A young reporter and war veteran from downstate, Reagan was accused and convicted of killing his city editor in a drunken quarrel over the purchasable affections of one Ruby Thiel. There was also a money angle, the State of Illinois alleging the two men had entered into a conspiracy with unknown and unnamed parties to run Cobb Junction as a wide-open town for a percentage of the profits. The dead man had been found in the girl's apartment, killed by two slugs from a gun registered in the name of the accused. Reagan, his pockets stuffed with hundred-dollar bills, had been found in a cheap hotel nearby, so intoxicated he couldn't tell the arresting officers his name. The girl, Ruby Thiel, was neutral, claiming she had been elsewhere at the time. From what I had read in the papers it looked like an open-and-shut case.

I asked the girl why she had come to me.

Still crying, she said she had gone to the American Legion Hall to see if the Legion might be willing to help Reagan finance another appeal, and some man there, she didn't know his name, had told her that while I charged enormous fees I was always willing to give a former service man a break and I almost always got results.

I pointed out that I was a private detective, not a lawyer. She said she realized that, but the lawyer in the case hadn't been able to help her husband and possibly I could.

Still stalling, I wanted to know what had happened to the large sum of money that had been found on her husband. She said he had disclaimed any knowledge or ownership and the state had impounded the money, some four thousand dollars. "Please help us, Mr. Doyle," she begged. "Don't let them do this to Larry. He didn't kill Mr. Jackson. He didn't make love to that awful girl." She had trouble with the word "executed". "You wouldn't want to see an innocent man . . . executed, would you?"

She had me there. Being in the racket, I know the law isn't infallible. Mistakes are made. And if Reagan was innocent the state would play hell trying to rectify this mistake after the accused was dead. I asked her how long it was to the deadline.

She sobbed, "Six days."

"And how do you know he's innocent?"

She looked at me wide-eyed, wondering how I could be such an awful fool. "Why, he told me so."

And there it was. He'd *told* her so. The smart thing for me to have done would have been to tell her that while I sympathized with both of them deeply there didn't seem to be a thing that I could do. But I didn't. She was nothing but a kid and scared. He was a former service man. I liked her frankness in admitting they were broke. The least I could do was talk to Reagan. So, instead of playing it smart, I chumped off. I made it clear I was promising nothing, but I would drive down to Joliet and talk to her man that afternoon.

It was mid-November. A heavy snow had fallen the day before. My heater wasn't working properly. The trip down from Chicago was both long and cold. I was glad to see Stateville rising, squat and grey, out of the snow. Nasty places, prisons. But at least the warden's office would be warm.

The warden was away at some convention but Sam Kane, his chief deputy, wrote me a pass to see Reagan. "Not that you or anyone else can do him any good," he told me dourly. "Reagan seems to be a nice kid. I like him. But—" He shrugged and left it there.

"He did it, huh?"

Kane said that would seem to be obvious.

A dozen prisoners working under one guard, not counting the boys with rifles on the walls and those with machine guns in the towers, were shoveling snow from the exercise yard as I crossed the prison grounds to the death house. The driver of the dump truck, Porky Bauer, a former Chicago racketeer and night club owner whom I had helped pry loose from the election rolls, ignored a sharp warning from the guard to ask what I was doing at Stateville. I told him I was there to see Reagan and, talking fast before the guard could shut him up, Bauer offered to trade me information pertinent to the case if I wouldn't rap him when he had his hearing before the parole board.

Most lads in prison are the same. They'd ship their mothers to Rio for a five-day reduction of sentence. But it could be that Porky had something. I told him I'd think it over and walked on into the death house.

A good-looking punk about twenty-five, with jet-black hair and the kind of hazel eyes the girls go ga-ga over, Reagan was sitting on his bunk with his face buried in his hands. He looked up as the guard unlocked his cell door, then buried his face in his hands again. I don't know who he thought I was.

"Feeling kind of rocky, eh?" I broke the ice.

He said he was.

"My name is Doyle, Tom Doyle," I introduced myself. "I have my own private agency in Chicago. Your wife asked me to come down and see you."

He showed his first glimmer of interest.

I lighted a cigarette and tossed the package to him. "I'm here for just one reason. Maybe you're guilty, maybe you're not. I wouldn't know. But despite the preponderance of evidence to the contrary, your wife seems to feel you are getting a raw deal."

He took a cigarette from the pack with fingers that shook slightly. "I am." I liked the way he said it. He was in a tough spot but he wasn't whining. He was merely stating a fact. "I'm in a damn tough spot. I don't care what the state proved. I burn in six more days for something I didn't do."

"You didn't kill Jackson, eh?"

"So help me, God," he swore. He scowled at me suspiciously. "But just a minute—Doyle, you say your name is. Neither Jessie nor I have a dime. What did she offer you to stick your nose in this?"

I said if he was thinking what I thought he was thinking he was insulting his wife. I liked the way he apologized.

"I'm sorry, Doyle." He waved his cigarette around the cell. "But when a man is cooped up in a place like this he gets to thinking lots of things he shouldn't. I remember once as a cub reporter I wrote a hell of a yarn surmising what a man in the death house thought about. But I was wrong. Mostly all I think about is Jessie."

A trusty came in with the supper tray. Reagan told me his side of the story while he pecked at his food.

Cobb Junction, it seemed, was one of the few war-boomed towns in Illinois that had continued to grow with reconversion. Located in the soft-coal district, not far from St. Louis, with excellent transportation facilities, its former airplane, chemical, munitions and ordinance plants had been taken over by a prefabricated house concern, a big insecticide outfit, a farm implement manufacturer and a nationally known plumbing company. A textile mill, a drop forge and a structural steel plant were employing even more men and women in civilian production than they had during the war.

Never a Sunday-school town, Cobb Junction had grown progressively more rotten.

"Fun is fun," Reagan told me. "I'm no blue-nose. I like my fun as well as the next man, but there is a limit."

He continued. Four of the seven big plants in town were working a full three shifts. So were the bars and gambling hells and ladies of light morals. Murders became commonplace. Workers were fleeced right and left. The police, while nominally honest, were handicapped by an antiquated budget, the temptation of easy money and the fact that the merchants liked the town as it was. So he and his city editor had started out to see if they could clean up the town.

I said, "That wasn't the way I heard it."

"I know," he said sourly. "The state alleged that Ernie and I conspired to run a wide-open town. But not even two screwball newspaper men can conspire to bring about something that already exists. I wish to God we'd let bad enough alone. Now Ernie's dead and I'm here accused of killing him."

It was a plausible story as he told it. "At first we thought the rackets in the Junction were like Topsy—they just grew. Now I'm beginning to wonder."

"You think you got too close and stepped on someone's toes, eh?"

He pulled Sam Kane's line on me. "That would seem to be obvious. On the night the state says I killed Ernie we had a call front Ruby Thiel, a local tart, saying she had a story for us that would break the town wide open, and she was willing to sell it for five hundred dollars. I had met her, casually, several times but she insisted on talking to Ernie. So he went up to her apartment. I dropped into a nearby bar to wait for him. I had two drinks. And the next thing I knew I was in a room upstairs with two plain-clothes men trying to shake me awake."

I asked him about the money that was found on him.

He scoffed, "Hell, I never had four thousand dollars all at one time in my life."

I asked him the names of the two plain-clothes men and wrote them down with the name of the hotel in which he had been picked up. "Now, about the *gun.*"

His smile was wry. "That was a bobble on my part. Sure, the bullets that killed Ernie were fired from a gun registered in my name. But I hadn't seen it in two years. I lost my week's pay in a crap game about three months after I got out of the Army and I hocked the gun for eating money. But the state had only my word I'd hocked it. The pawnbroker claimed he had no record of my hocking it and couldn't even remember the incident."

I wrote down the name and address of the pawn shop and the date on which he claimed he'd hocked the gun. "And the gun was found on you?"

He laughed, almost hysterically. "No. The gun was never found. But it was the only gun I'd ever owned. I *knew* I hadn't

killed Ernie. So on the night I was arrested I begged Chief LaRue
to send officers to my dad's basement, tear open a small display
bale of cotton they would find there, and compare the slugs in it to
the ones they found in Ernie."

"And they matched."

"And they matched. They were what really convicted me because I had signed a statement saying I had emptied a clip into the
bale to test the gun on the night before I hocked it."

I said I would be damned.

He continued, surprising me by saying, "My trial was both fair
and impartial as far as the state was concerned. Old John Manners,
the judge, leaned over backwards to be fair. The prosecution
wasn't vindictive. And I think they were both surprised when the
jury brought in a verdict of 'Guilty of murder in the first degree'—
with no recommendation of mercy."

In answer to my question he said he did not have the names of
the jurymen, but his lawyer, a lad by the name of Degano, had a
list.

His voice was bitter. "Someone wanted me to die. The witnesses against me lied like hell. Ruby swore both Ernie and I had
been intimate with her for months and I had threatened time and
time again to kill him if I caught him in her apartment Simpson the
pawnbroker lied. The barman lied. The clerk at the hotel lied. He
was the worst witness against me. He swore I had staggered in
boasting I had just killed Ernie and I would do the same to any
man who tried to take Ruby from me."

I added the clerk and barman's name to my list. Reagan wanted
to know what I intended doing with the names that I had written
down. I thought it over a moment, then said I intended to grab a
train for Cobb Junction and talk to the parties involved.

He was incredulous. "Then you believe me?"

I didn't know if I did or not. I said so frankly, adding, however,
that he had convinced me of the possibility he had been convicted
wrongly and I was willing to investigate—and would.

His knuckles white on the bars, he watched me out of the death
house.

There was some commotion in the mess hall as I passed it. Four
lads with rifles were posted at the door. When I reached Kane's
office he was raising hell with perhaps a half a dozen guards. As I
opened the door, he shouted, "I don't give a damn whose fault it
was or how it happened. I am responsible for the prison while the
warden is away. I am the one who will be blamed. Now get back

into the mess hall and find that knife and the man who used it if you have to tear down the mess hall stone by stone."

The guards filed out red-faced. I gave Kane a minute to cool down, then asked him what had happened. He made an impatient gesture and told me, "A prisoner was just killed in the mess hall. It *would* happen while I'm in charge."

It didn't matter a damn to me, but I sympathized with Kane to sooth his ruffled hackles. Then I asked if I could talk to Porky Bauer.

He wanted to know what about.

I told him the Reagan case, explaining how Porky had called out to me in the yard, offering to trade information pertinent to the Reagan case if I would promise not to rap him when he came up for parole.

Kane made with the jutting eyebrows. Then he said, "I see. And you'd like to talk to Porky, eh?"

I said I would consider it a favor.

"A favor, hell!" he exploded. "It would be a miracle. Porky Bauer was the con who was killed."

CHAPTER TWO

MR. BIG

I DIDN'T LIKE WHAT I COULD SEE of Cobb Junction from the window of the Pullman. It wasn't to grow on me. It looked cheap and dirty and tawdry, a typical small manufacturing town that had mushroomed overnight into near city size.

It was almost nine the next night when I reached it. I gave the porter a buck for brushing an imaginary speck off of my new camels hair top coat and followed my seat companion, a fat man who said his name was Adler, down the aisle.

I didn't like him any better than I liked the town. He was, or so he claimed, a local undertaker and he had been up to Chicago to have himself a time in the big city fleshpots. His curiosity was as big as his belly. He wanted to know my racket so bad his kidneys hurt him. He stopped in the vestibule for one last try. "You'll like Cobb Junction, mister. What did you say your line was?"

I told him I hadn't said.

He looked hurt and wheezed down the Pullman steps. I followed at his heels, then turned and reached up for my bag.

The two shots were almost simultaneous. The first one grazed the porter's hand and thudded into my bag. The second slug whipped the skirt of my top coat and ricocheted, screaming off the steel steps to smack soddenly into flesh.

I whirled, my own gun in my hand, just in time to see Adler take two uncertain steps, point an accusing finger at no one in particular, then collapse on the station platform.

Behind me the porter moaned, "Oh, Lawd."

No more shots were fired. I couldn't see anyone to shoot at. The platform was well lighted. There was a fair-sized crowd. But no one was waving any gun. No one was even moving. It was like looking at a movie still.

A few feet from the spot where Adler had collapsed, two young girls, overdressed and over-rouged, were fascinated by the gun in my hand. Beside them, a well-dressed matron stood looking at

Adler. Behind her, a blind pencil seller, his white cane immobilized a few inches from the pavement, stood seemingly frozen in fear. Over his shoulder I could see a flashily dressed lad who looked as if he might be a gambler and who was greatly amused about something. The crowd was typical. They were young. They were old. Some were well-dressed. Some were wearing overalls.

The blind man broke the silence by shrilling, "What were those shots? Why doesn't someone tell me what has happened? Why doesn't someone speak?"

The well dressed matron obliged him by screaming, "Murder! Murder! Murder! Someone call the police! Mr. Adler has been murdered!'

That broke the tension. There was a surge of movement as the crowd pried their feet loose from the pavement and began to tell each other what had happened.

A chunky, red-faced lad wearing a salt-and-pepper top coat pushed through the crowd and tried to take my gun out of my hand. I wasn't having any.

"Burny-burn," I warned him. "I have a license to carry the rod."

He gulped and looked from me to Adler and wanted to know why I had shot him. Before I could inform him I hadn't, one of the over-rouged young girls protested, "He wasn't the one who fired the shots." Her pointing was as vague as the dead man's had been. "There were two shots. They came from over there somewhere."

The blind man chipped in his two cents' worth. "I heard them sing right past my ear." Behind him was the taxi rank and the white-toothed lad who looked as if he might be a gambler. "Did someone say it was Mr. Adler who was murdered?"

"Mr. Adler, the undertaker," the overstuffed matron informed him.

Several other folks claimed to have heard the shots go by then. They had them coming from all points of the compass. A youngish man knelt beside Adler, glued his ear to his chest a moment, felt his pulse, poked back the fat man's right eyelid, then stood up dusting at the knee of his trousers. "He's dead all right, Benson," he showed off his medical school knowledge. "He's caught a slug smack through the old ticker."

It transpired Benson was the lad in the salt-and-pepper top coat. "In that case," he told me sourly, "gun permit or no permit, you'll have to come to the station with me, mister, until we get this straightened out."

I lied that was fine with me and slid my gun back in its holster. It wasn't the arrival I had planned. I had hoped to tiptoe into town, not arrive in a blaze of cordite.

Benson asked if I had seen who had fired the two shots at Adler. I said I had not. I could have added that the shots hadn't been fired at Adler, but I didn't. I was beginning to think more of Reagan's story by the minute. Someone in the crowd on the platform had a dirty nose. That someone knew who I was and why I had come to Cobb Junction.

The police station was old and wooden, on a side street not far from the railroad station. The chief of police was a companion museum piece. His name, it would seem, was LaRue. A clean-shaven, petulant little man bloated by his imagined self-importance, he looked as if he would be hell on chicken thieves. His looks weren't deceiving.

He adjusted his gold-rimmed glasses and deduced from the printing on my operative's license, "So your name is Thomas Doyle and you are a private detective from Chicago."

I pleaded guilty as charged. He scowled at me over his glasses.

"And just what brought you to Cobb Junction?"

There were two ways I could play it. I could stand on my constitutional rights, tell him it was none of his business, and antagonize the local force. I chose to lay my cards on his desk. Crime fiction and B-pictures notwithstanding, it isn't the wise-cracking private eye having the crime of his life making chumps of the lads on civil service who pays taxes in the upper brackets. Unless you stand in with the boys in blue you can make more money hawking herring.

"I'm making a last-minute check on the Reagan case," I told him. I explained how Reagan's wife had come into my office the day before and how both she and Reagan insisted his conviction had been a mistake, although Reagan himself admitted his trial had been fair and impartial.

Some of the ice in the office thawed.

I melted it some more by putting words in Reagan's mouth. "And Reagan himself told me he doesn't blame you or your boys. He says you merely did your duty as a law enforcement officer. All I am doing is checking up on his story to make certain no mistake was made."

LaRue and I were suddenly pals. "I felt like hell about Larry," he admitted. "His old man and I used to play cribbage down at the fire house together before this danged town got so large. But like he says, there was nothing I could do but have him picked up."

I asked if he thought the right man had been convicted for Jackson's murder and the old man surprised me by saying he didn't know.

"I was certain at the time,"' he told me. "Now I'm not so certain. This town is plain rotten, Doyle. I need thirty more uniformed men and half that number of plainclothes men to police it properly. Now take Adler's murder for example. It probably never will be solved."

I doubted that but didn't say so. No one throws lead at Mrs. Doyle's little boy Thomas with impunity.

LaRue deduced, "You'd think if Reagan and Jackson had been back of everything as the state claimed and proved, that things would have tapered off. But they haven't. The saloons and gambling joints are running twenty-four hours a day. And there are more painted women on our streets than there were in Sodom and Gomorrah."

I asked if he felt that way about it why he didn't run them all out of town.

The old man confided, "The merchants won't let me. They are all making more money than they ever made in their lives. They *want* the town to run wide open. They claim that it attracts business." He seemed disgusted with his own position. "On the other hand, they expect me to run a wide-open town without any shootings or murders."

I described the lad I had seen standing back of the blind man.

"That was Tony Cass," Benson told me. "He is a stick man at the Golden Wheel. Why? What about him?"

I remarked that Adler's death had seemed to amuse him greatly. Then, on a hunch, I asked if Adler had been a member of the Reagan Jury.

"Why, yes," LaRue said. "Come to think of it, he was." He didn't seem to think it important so I let it pass.

Neither Mason nor Carter, the two plainclothes men who had picked up Reagan, were in the station at the time, but LaRue promised to send them to my hotel as soon as they came off their tour. He also suggested a hotel.

"Not that one is much better than the other," he admitted.

Benson ran me over to the hotel in a squad car. As he opened the door in front of the marquee he hesitated, asked what I thought of LaRue.

I said I liked him.

"Yeah. I do, too," he said dryly. "But just because the old man popped off the way he did, don't get the idea, Doyle, that we want Cobb Junction any different than it is. In plain English, a word to the wise is sufficient. You should have seen this town before. Hell, we all practically starved to death."

I said I wasn't interested in cleaning up Cobb Junction, that all I had come to town for was to assure myself that Reagan was guilty as charged.

He offered to shake hands. "Then I'm with you all the way."

I'd met his type before. As long as the icing on his cake was thick he didn't care if the chef's hands were a little dirty. I asked if he knew a lad from Cobb Junction by the name of Jaferey, now residing in Stateville for an indefinite period. He said the name was familiar but either couldn't or wouldn't tell me anything about him.

The hotel was new and modern. It was also broad-minded. The bell boy who carried my bag to my room assured me he could get me anything I wanted.

He stressed the word, *anything.*

I thought a moment, told him to send up an elephant. He gave me a dirty look and slammed the door.

Without even taking off my hat, I put through a long distance call to Stateville. Kane sounded tired. He said they had questioned Jaferey for hours but were no nearer a solution of Bauer's murder than they had been. Jaferey admitted he had been sent up from Cobb Junction but insisted he had never discussed the Reagan case with Porky and hadn't the least idea who had stabbed him. Kane wanted to know if I was certain I was on the right track. I said I thought I was and for him to keep after Jaferey and wire any developments to me in care of the Bonanza Hotel in Cobb Junction.

My call complete, I started to hang up and the girl on the hotel switchboard asked me if I was interested in the Reagan case. I said I was. She told me, "Larry Reagan didn't kill Ernie Jackson, mister. They are electrocuting an innocent man. If you're working for Reagan, you get to Ruby Thiel. She's the one who can tell you the truth."

I asked if she'd care to tell me more after hours. She said she would not and broke the connection. The knock on my door was almost furtive. So was the lad who had rapped. He looked from me to the revolver in my hand, then gulped, "Put it away, Doyle. Put it away. You're in no danger from me. My name is Degano. I was Reagan's lawyer."

I laid the gun handy to my hand and said I was pleased to meet him. He answered my question before I could ask it.

"A phone call informed me you were in town and at what hotel I could reach you." His face white, he added, "I was told to give you a message."

I said I was listening.

"You are to get out of town, Doyle," he told me. "You're taking the next train back to Chicago and forgetting about the Reagan case."

"That's interesting if true," I told him. "But this is the first time I've heard about it. Tell me more."

He said he was merely repeating the message given him, verbatim.

"And if I don't?"

"He says he won't miss next time."

"He?"

The lawyer sat down on the bed, took off his hat, and ran his fingers through his hair. "I don't know. I've heard the voice before, but I can't remember where. Whoever he is, he's determined that Reagan will burn. And Larry didn't kill Jackson, you know."

I said it was the second time I had been so informed within four minutes but if he felt so strongly as he seemed to feel about it, why hadn't he gone to the governor with his information?

He said it wasn't a matter of information. He had no new evidence to present. It was just something he knew in his heart and so far as he was concerned his recent phone call had confirmed it.

"There's something radically wrong in this town, Doyle," he told me, "a sinister someone back of everything that's going on. The town is running wide open you know but all the boys and girls are paying tribute."

I said I hadn't known that. "To whom? LaRue?"

"That fuddy-duddy," Degano dismissed the chief of police. "He doesn't know he's alive. No. He isn't Mr. Big. I don't know who he is. But I do know that Ruby Thiel is one of his chief collectors."

I slid my gun hack in its holster and suggested we call on her.

Degano shook his head. "Not me. I'm in bad enough as it is for having defended Reagan. My practice has dropped away to practically nothing. And I know why. People are afraid to come to me." His voice was bitter. "Just as the jury was afraid to bring in any other verdict than the one they did. It isn't nice. It isn't something you talk about. But the whole damn town, including LaRue, is scared to death. He says the merchants want an open town. They don't. But they are afraid to open their mouths."

"If they did, just what would happen?" I asked him.

"Stink bombs, broken windows, whispering campaigns, bullets fired through their windows in the night, ancient indiscretions turned over to the newspapers, any of a dozen things. One of the boys, a hardware man, tried to buck them. He was found hanging in his store the other morning. Worried over business reverses, the papers said."

"And you haven't the least idea who this Mr. Big is?"

He raised his right palm. "I swear it." Sweat stood out on his forehead in beads. "And while it's a rotten thing for me to say, if I were you, I wouldn't try to buck him, Doyle. It would be a different thing if you could help Larry, but he has only five days left and I don't see how you can do a thing for him. Even to get a stay or a reprieve, we'd have to have new evidence, and the devil back of this is clever."

I said he would seem to be, shaped my hat to my head and stood up. Degano wanted to know where I was going. I said I was on my way to talk to Ruby Thiel. Before I could reach the door, the phone rang.

"This, is a friend, Mr. Doyle," a faintly familiar voice informed me. "Mr. Degano is with you?"

I said he was.

"He gave you my message?"

"He did."

"And you are leaving town—when?"

I asked him who he thought he was scaring.

There was sincere regret in his voice as he told me, "I was afraid you were that type of person the minute I laid my eyes on you. Money wouldn't interest you, I suppose?"

I said that under the circumstances I was afraid it would not.

My caller sighed. "I think you are being very foolish, Mr. Doyle. And I resent your interference exceedingly. You are forcing me to do something I dislike doing very much."

So saying, he hung up. I joggled the fork on the phone. "Trace that call, operator."

"I am sorry, sir," she informed me, "but it came in on an outside line and I have already broken the connection."

CHAPTER THREE

SNAKE EYES

THE BUILDING WAS NEW, four-storied and flanked by a night club on one side and a beauty parlor on the other. A quarter of a block down the street I could see the sign of the Regal Hotel, in a room of which Reagan said he had recovered consciousness.

There was no desk and no house phone in the apartment building, but a gum-chewing blonde elevator operator informed me Miss Thiel was not at home but had left word with her to tell any callers she would be home at midnight. I looked at my watch. It was eleven-thirty. I said I would be back.

The blonde turned coy. "And whom shall I tell Miss Thiel to expect?"

She was a cute little trick. My right hand never did get married. I patted a convenient bulge. "Let's not tell her, sweetheart. Let's surprise her."

Her look was more amorous than outraged. I was lucky to get out of the lobby with my marriage vows still intact. Cobb Junction was some town. If the little blonde was any criterion, it was a wonder the professionals made a living.

The bar at the Regal Hotel was much like all the others I had seen along Main Street. Men, with a good smattering of B-girls among them, were standing three deep to the wood. A row of one-armed bandits lined one wall. Through an open arch in the rear I could see a roulette wheel and a crap table, both well patronized. Well-dressed men and women out to have themselves a time rubbed shoulders with workers in overalls and girls in low-cut evening gowns. The joint smelled of stale beer, cheap perfume and people. On the opposite wall from the slot machines a cadaverous piano player was making merry with the keys and perhaps a half-dozen couples were dancing.

I elbowed my way up to the bar and ordered a double rye. It wasn't bad for watered stock. I was considering ordering a triple to get enough whiskey to feel it when a redhead built like Jane Russell turned a toothy smile on me and wanted to know if I was lonely.

I bought her a drink in self-defense and asked her which of the barmen was Marty Shannon. She said that none of them were, that Shannon had been promoted to manager and pointed out a hard-faced lad standing near the edge of the postage-stamp size dance floor.

He looked out of place in a dinner jacket, and the bulge under his left arm wasn't muscle. I walked over to the dance floor. "Your name Shannon?" I inquired.

Turning a pair of fishy eyes on me he said it was. "Why? What's it to you, chum?"

I said my name was Doyle and I was making a last-minute investigation of the Reagan case on behalf of the accused's wife.

"So what's that to me?" he asked. "Am I supposed to be interested."

"Reagan get drunk in here?" I asked him. "That is on the night of the alleged murder."

He said, "You mean the night he killed Jackson? Yeah. He had a couple of drinks in here. But he was staggering when he come in. I sold him two drinks, no more. I didn't want him to pass out on my hands."

"And he boasted to you that he had just killed Jackson."

Shannon shook his head. "Naw. He didn't say nothing to me, or if he did I didn't hear him." He motioned at the bar. "You can see for yourself we're usually pretty busy around this time of night." He nodded at the door leading into the lobby of the hotel. "But he did spill the whole thing to Sammy and Sammy came busting in and wanted to know what he should do. I told him I thought he ought to call the cops."

It was a good story and I could see how it would register with a jury. I shrugged and walked on into the lobby of the hotel. Crime had paid Shannon and Sammy Ricardo well. One had risen to be manager of the bar, the other the manager of the hotel. It all just goes to show what a lie at the right time can do. It was to put both of them into their graves, but of course they had no way of knowing that at the time.

Ricardo was Latin and suave. He regarded me over the glass of his desk for a full minute before he said, "I heard there was an investigator in town probing into the Reagan affair. I forget who told me. Bill Benson, I believe. You say your name is Doyle?"

I reached across the desk and grabbed me a handful of shirt front. "Yeah, the name is Doyle," I told him. "And for your edification, entertainment and amusement I am in Cobb Junction to prove that Reagan didn't kill Jackson and it was your dirty lie, among other lies, that convicted him. Now try telling the truth for a change. Who is this Mr. Big who wanted Reagan out of his hair and how much did he pay you to tell the story that you did?"

He tried to squirm free and I slapped him so hard I almost broke my own grip on his shirt front.

He spat out a two-toothed bridge that I had dislocated. "No one paid me a dime. Every word that I said was the truth. Reagan swaggered up to the desk boasting he'd just killed Jackson and he would do the same to any other man who tried to take Ruby away from him."

I slapped him again without much hope. If what Degano had told me was gospel, none of the parties involved would dare to change their stories.

"You let me go," he insisted. "If you don't I'll yell copper."

I hit him again just to show what I thought of the Cobb Junction police force. And that was a mistake on my part. He did yell copper and a big square-head with plainclothes man written all over him stuck his head in the office door and wanted to know what was going on.

"This dirty private eye from Chicago is trying to kill me," Ricardo sobbed. "He wants me to change my story. He wants me to lie about what Larry Reagan told me on the night that he shot Ernie Jackson."

The big detective turned his eyes on me. Just from the looks of his face, I was willing to bet he was honest but a trifle thick between the ears. Such proved to be the case. "Your name is Doyle, isn't it?" he accused. "The chief told me you were in town the last time we called in. He said you wanted to talk to me and Carl. So went to your hotel but they said you'd just gone out."

I asked him if he was Mason or Carter.

He said his name was Carter.

Ricardo, fingering his broken bridge, screamed that he wanted me arrested for assault and battery. "I was sitting here in my own office, minding my own business," he spluttered, "when this big white-haired lug walked in and punched me in the face three times."

Carter said judiciously. "You shouldn't have ought to have done that, Doyle." He seemed undecided. "The chief said we should co-operate with you, but that don't give you no license to go around punching guys in the jaw."

I was about ready to punch him. I didn't. Instead I asked just what the set-up had been on the morning that he and his partner had arrested Reagan.

"Why, we get a call on the two-way to come here," he told me. "But we don't make it all the way at first. We are passing the building where Miss Thiel lives when she opens one of her front windows and screams down at us that Jackson has been killed in her apartment."

"So you made an investigation?"

He nodded. "So we made an investigation. And we found Jackson lying on the floor of her bedroom with two slugs in his back. That counted as much as anything against Reagan at his trial. Most guys don't like fellows who shoot other guys in the back."

"And the Thiel dame was in the clear?"

"Absolutely," he assured me. "We find the body at 4:10 A.M. But the coroner set the time of death at not later than 2 A.M. And from midnight until after 3:30 A.M. Miss Thiel was entertaining at the Kit Kat with maybe two hundred folks to swear she never left the room."

Ricardo offered, "It was about 2:10 or maybe 2:15 when Reagan showed up here."

I ignored him to ask Carter, "Did Miss Thiel suggest to you that Reagan had killed Jackson?"

He thought a moment, shook his head. "No. She didn't exactly suggest it. But she did tell us that he was very jealous of Jackson and that he had a key to her apartment." He shrugged. "Then, after we'd called the station for the Homicide boys to take over, we came on down here and Sammy tells us that Reagan is dead-drunk in one of the rooms upstairs but that before passing out he boasted he killed Jackson. So we went up to his room and made the arrest." His face brightened at the memory. "Boy, I never saw so much dough as Reagan had in his clothes. He was positively filthy."

I lighted a cigarette. "You say, Ricardo, that Reagan showed up here between 2:10 and 2:15?"

"That's right."

"But you didn't report what he had told you to the police until after four o'clock. Why?"

He spread his hands in a Latin gesture. "I didn't know what to do. How did I know the guy was telling truth? Maybe he was just talking like drunks do. I thought it over for a while then went into the bar and asked Marty Shannon what he thought I ought to do. He said if it was him he thought he would report it. So, after thinking about it some more, I did."

It was a good story and a tough one to crack. I could see where Degano had had trouble at the trial trying to disprove it. But what I couldn't see was why, with his fences holding as well as they were, Mr. Big had pulled the kid trick of calling Degano and myself and trying to warn me out of town. Guys in the private eye racket don't scare easy. We don't eat if we do. And by phoning me in person, offering me a bribe, and then threatening me, he had not only admitted there was a Mr. Big but he had proven, at least to me, that Reagan's conviction was a phony.

I asked Carter how Reagan had acted when he and his partner had arrested him.

"He acted dopey-like," he told me. "He wouldn't believe us when we told him that Jackson was dead."

"You made a paraffin test of his hand and tested his stomach content for chloral?"

"We didn't test him for anything," he told me. "We just pinched him. Why?"

I told him to skip it, thanked him for his information, made a mental note if I ever wanted to commit murder to bring my victim to Cobb Junction, then asked Ricardo if he still wanted to prefer assault charges against me.

Suspicious, he wanted to know why.

I told him seriously, "Because if you do, I intend to knock out the rest of your teeth to make certain I get my fine's worth."

He told Carter there were no charges.

Back on the street the night was cold but the honky-tonks were still going full blast and both sidewalks were crowded. I wanted to talk to Ruby Thiel, but I still had five minutes to kill. I killed them leaning up against a building watching the passersby and trying to put a mental finger on Mr. Big.

His, *"I was afraid you were that type of person as soon as I laid eyes on you,"* would seem to indicate he had been on the station platform when my train had pulled into Cobb station.

It was a two-to-one bet that he himself had shot Adler in a try for me. Smart men seldom delegate murder.

His voice, over the phone, had been faintly familiar. It was definitely male. But there was nothing distinctive to stamp it. It could have been Chief LaRue. It could have been Benson. It could have been Shannon or Ricardo. I mentally scratched the last two out. I hadn't heard them speak when Mr. Big had phoned me. But it could have been the young doctor. He had been on the station platform.

Thinking of him made me think of the amused lad whom Benson had identified as Tony Cass, a stick man at the Golden Wheel. The Golden Wheel was just up the street and across from Ruby's apartment building.

I walked on up to the corner and crossed the street. Walkers were crossing in both directions, but no one paid any attention to the blind pencil seller who was waiting patiently on the curb, tapping his white cane on the walk from time to time as if trying to screw up nerve to cross the street alone.

I asked if he wanted to cross the street. His voice was husky with cold. "Please."

I walked back to the curb that I'd just left with him, scowling as I did so at the ruptured duck in his button hole and cursing a parsimonious government that would force a blind veteran to sell pencils.

His suit was fair, but he didn't have an overcoat and his lips were blue with cold. He was young, not more than thirty, but his cheeks were hollow and there were dark circles under his black glasses. On impulse I slipped out of my two-hundred-buck camels hair and slipped it around his shoulders. "Wear it in health, Mac," I told him. "I went through the mill myself."

I left him feeling the cloth with his free hand, a puzzled expression on his lips, and crossed back to the Golden Wheel thinking what a lousy break it must be for a guy as young as he was to be blind.

The Wheel was strictly a gambling joint with a small bar in connection. There was a good crowd around the tables, but the bar wasn't getting much of a play. I built a fire with a double rye and asked the barman if Tony was around.

"He was here just a minute ago," he told me. "And you should see the roll he was sporting." He put his two index fingers and thumbs together. "So help me, it was that big."

I was skeptical.

"I seen it with my own eyes," the barman told me. "What's more, he's quit his job." He became very confidential. "He said he's shaking the dust of this rube Las Vegas from his feet, stopping in St. Louis to pick up a tasty dish, and heading for the Coast."

I was properly surprised. "No! Where did he get the dough?"

The barman mopped morosely at the bar. "I wish to God I knew. I wish *I* could make a killing. I get so tired of listening to drunks and guys that should have bet on the red instead of the black that I damn near wish I was back mining coal."

I told him not to let John L. Lewis hear him say that, paid for my drink and began to circulate between the tables, hoping to spot Tony before he left town. If I could find him my problem would be simplified. No wonder he'd been so amused. He'd known a killing when he had seen one and someone had paid him off—but plenty.

He wasn't at any of the tables although a couple of lads said they had seen him a minute before. By the time I got to the back of the place the only spot left to look in was the men's room. I shoved through the door, but there was no Tony.

I turned to go, turned back, as the widening pool at the base of a door that opened into what looked to be a broom closet registered on my brain. It was a broom closet, all right. But there was more than brooms in it—plenty more.

Tony Cass wasn't going to Saint Louis. He wasn't going to pick up a tasty dish. He wasn't going to the Coast. He wasn't going anywhere except, possibly, on a short ride to Adler's successor. His lips skinned back from his white teeth in agony, he was hanging by his necktie from a hook, the wooden handle of a common kitchen butcher knife protruding from his back.

CHAPTER FOUR

RUBY'S REWARD

LARUE WASN'T AS CORDIAL as he had been before. They had
disinterred him from bed for one thing. Twin pale lavender
pajama legs dangled under the cuffs of his trousers. For another he had gone to bed pretty high. His breath smelled like an
interrupted stupor.

"Don't give me that, Doyle," he told me, pounding on his desk.
"Of all the guys in Cobb Junction, you were the one who just *happened* to go in that men's room, open the broom closet door and
find Tony Cass."

I said that was correct.

"In a pig's eye," he scoffed. He waved a Western Union blank
under my nose. "I'm not entirely a fool. I wired Chicago and
checked on you as soon as you left the station. And what kind of a
report do you think I got?"

I said that would depend on whom he wired. Benson polished a
lieutenant's badge by thumping my shoulder lightly and telling
me, "Nix, now, Doyle. Don't try to get tough with the chief."

There was no use playing friendly. It wasn't that kind of a
gathering. "You lay your hand on me again," I told him, "and I'll
push your teeth so far down your throat that it will take an appen-
dectomy to find them."

Benson didn't touch me again.

The pot-bellied little chief of police waggled his index finger at
me. "You acting as you are just confirms what this telegram says."
He read it aloud:

Re your request for information on one Thomas Doyle licensed as a private detective by the State of Illinois stop there
are no charges pending against Doyle in this office at the present time but would advise you to deal cautiously with this man
stop his ego inflated by numerous highly newspaper publicized
successes Doyle has come to believe he is above the law and

will stop at nothing to assist his client particularly if that client is a former service man stop it is my considered opinion that Doyle is a money mad kill crazy veteran and that his license should be revoked but to date have been unable to bring this to pass stop would appreciate if you would inform me of any infractions of the law he may commit in Cobb Junction that would assist in this matter stop signed . . .

"Sad sack State's Attorney Beamer," I beat LaRue to the signature. "We the people of Chicago certainly left our brains behind the door when we elected him queen of our mayhem. Why didn't you wire Captain Nobby of Homicide, or Burns of Narcotics, or Inspector Shale?"

"The state's attorney is jealous of you, I suppose?" Benson sneered.

"No. He's just a sad sack," I told him, "who sits on his head and thinks with his opposite end. But that's neither here nor there. Let me get this straight. Am I here to report a homicide as required by the rules and regulations under which a private operative is licensed, or am I being charged with murder?"

Neither man was willing to go that far.

LaRue admitted he wasn't charging me with anything. "As yet," he added. "But it seems damn funny to me that you no sooner get off the train than one of our most respected and respectable citizens is killed. You aren't in town two hours before you punch another citizen in the face because he refuses to change honest testimony that happened to send your client to the chair."

Someone had gotten to someone. Tony Cass wasn't the only one who had been paid off. That much was obvious.

I said, "You used to play cribbage with Reagan's old man down at the fire house, remember? You don't like the town as it is. It's the merchants who want it to run wide open."

Color crept into Benson's jowls. LaRue told me not to be impertinent. "What I want to know," he said, "is what happened to the roll of money Cass was known to be carrying when he was killed."

I said I was sorry but I couldn't help him out on that one. I hadn't touched the body. And if he and Benson hadn't found a roll on it, either the roll had only existed in the barman's mind or someone, probably the killer, had beaten them to the take.

Red-faced, his fingers itching around his lapel over the gun in his shoulder holster, Benson would have given a month's pay to have had me handcuffed and back in the local squad room. But he swallowed his bile long enough to ask what LaRue wanted done with me.

"Run him out of the station," the old man snapped. "And watch him. If he breaks the law just once, however slightly, run him out of town."

I rubbed it in. "You mean I can't buy a drink after midnight or play a friendly hand of cards?"

So mad he could hardly speak, Benson said, "You heard the chief. Get out!"

It seemed like good advice. I did. In the outer foyer in front of the sergeant's desk, Carter was frisking the blind lad. I stopped to ask what he'd done and Carter beat me to the draw.

"Hey, I got back your coat that this guy stole," he told me, pleased as Punch. "And he had the nerve to try and tell me that you gave it to him."

I'd had about all I could stand of Cobb Junction. "I did, you dumb moron," I snapped.

His lower jaw gaped open. "You gave a blind man that good camels hair?"

I picked it up from the bench and draped it over the blind lad's shoulders again. "Now scram before you get crumby in this joint."

He thanked me in his husky voice and tapped off across the tile. No fool, I apologized to Carter. He was the only honest cop I had met in Cobb Junction so far and if it should come to a showdown I wanted him on my side. I said I was sorry I'd blown up, that bringing in the lad on suspicion had been good police work on his part, and I supposed it was dumb of me to give away so good a coat but I had felt sorry for the lad because he was a veteran.

Mollified, he walked out to the curb with me and wanted to know if he and his partner could give me a lift anywhere. I said they could and gave him Ruby Thiel's address.

Mason was the same type of cop as Carter, big and dumb, but honest. There are dozens like them on every force. When they let me out of the car, he said, "Don't feel bad about us picking up Jerry, Mr. Doyle. He's used to being in the can. We get him every other night or so for being drunk, or petty theft. He's kind of a character around town, you might say. He never did amount to much, and since he's come back from the service he's not worth the powder to blow him to hell. He gets a full disability pension, plenty enough to live on. But is he satisfied? No. He's all the time tapping around town with that white cane of his, making people feel sorry for him so they'll buy his cheap pencils, and picking up everything that isn't nailed down to the counters."

It was cold. I was cold. I felt like a sap. But there was nothing I could do about it. So I had made a mistake. So the blind lad was a petty chiseler. He had to do something to occupy his time. I had given him my coat of my own free will. I still didn't regret it.

Mason and Carter pulled away and left me standing on the curb. I walked on into the lobby and asked the blonde Circe if Miss Thiel had returned.

"Two hours ago," she told me. "I thought you were coming back at midnight."

I told her I had been detained.

I kept my hands in my pockets riding up to the fourth floor. She seemed disappointed but she did confide, "I told Miss Thiel that a *very* distinguished-looking, white-haired guy had asked for her and she seemed quite interested."

I said the white hair was premature.

"That's what I told Miss Thiel," she grinned. "That's why she was interested."

I told her someone ought to wash out her mind with soap, slipped her a buck so there would be no hard feelings, and walked down the hall toward the paneled white door she indicated.

I was making no progress—fast. And from here on in I would have to watch my step. The pot-bellied little chief of police hadn't been talking just to hear himself talk. Crooked or on the level, he was the law as far as Cobb Junction was concerned. He had swallowed Beamer's opinion of me whole. The first misstep I made would put me out of town.

Ruby Thiel proved to be small and dark, with soft black curls and a ready smile. If she had anything under her white silk hostess gown but what Mother Nature had grown there, I didn't know my feminine anatomy.

The apartment was a tramp's dream of heaven—soft rugs, dim lights, oversized white chairs and sofas and enough chrome around to run the Cadillac assembly line two months.

She held out a small hand dripping with diamonds. "You're Mr. Doyle, aren't you?" She spoke softly, with a slight drawl that sounded to me like Kentucky—which later turned out to be a good guess.

I was surprised she didn't suggest I take off my coat and ask if she could call me Tom. She was that fast a worker. I was impressed. There have been times in my life, before Sue and the twins appeared on my checking account horizon when—but why go into that?

I admitted my name, shook hands and walked on into the apartment. Miss Thiel followed at my heels, saying, "I hoped it was you when Mable said a distinguished-looking, white-haired gentleman had called. Mayn't I mix you a drink, Mr. Doyle?"

I said she could and she did. She mixed a rye-high, plenty strong. I sipped it, then got down to business. "Seeing you know my name, I presume you know why I am in town."

Perched on the arm of an overstuffed chair, one leg crossed over the other, she didn't try to be coy about it. "Yes, I do," she admitted. She reached for a cigarette and her hostess gown parted, revealing a goodly display of white calf.

"I see you have varicose veins," I told her. "Have you ever seen a doctor about it?"

She called me an unprintable name. It sounded strange coming from those rosebud lips. Then she grinned, but her grin was wry. "You're hard-boiled, aren't you, Doyle?"

I said there was a time and place for everything, and at the moment I was representing a man charged with murder I had reason to believe he hadn't committed, a man with less than five days to live.

She wanted to know what I expected her to do about it.

I said, "Tell the truth. Whose toes were Jackson and Reagan treading on?"

She pulled the wide-eyed baby act. "Why, no one's. Both Ernie and Larry were very much in love with me, you see. And I couldn't decide which one I loved the most. And—"

I butted in to ask her if she had gone to the movies very often during the 1935 to 1940 period.

Puzzled, she said, "Why yes, I suppose I did."

I said, "Then you remember how another so-called tough lad, Jimmy Cagney, used to smack his dames around, dames who lied to him."

We both stood up.

Breathing hard, she said, "You wouldn't dare."

I said she might be surprised. Her eyes suddenly venomous, she dug under the folds of her hostess gown and came up with a pearl-handled little .25 she had been wearing in a garter holster on the leg I hadn't seen. I slapped it out of her hand before she could squirt it at me, then slapped her lightly across the lips as I might have slapped one of the twins for flipping a spoonful of oatmeal at his brother. It had the same effect. It didn't hurt her physically. It hurt her feelings.

She sat down on the sofa and began to snivel.

I dropped the squirt gun into my pocket and sat down beside her. "Now let's start all over," I said. "Whose toes were Jackson and Reagan treading on?"

She nibbled at her lipstick.

"I know there is a Mr. Big," I continued. "He made a dumb mistake in phoning both Degano and me. I don't scare worth a damn and his phone call proves he does exist. I also know that you do most of his collecting. I imagine Shannon and Ricardo also gather in the sheaves. He had to cut them in to make his frame against Reagan stick. Now you go on from there."

She dried her eyes on the hem of her gown and asked me to get her a drink. I did. I was to be sorry I had. It gave her too much courage. With a stiff jolt under her navel she grew suddenly brave again.

"Why should I talk to you?" She rubbed her thumb and index fingers together. "What is there in it for me?"

"Nothing," I told her. "As far as I am concerned, you have collected your last dollar in Cobb Junction. But listen and record this, sister. Without your help I may not be able to clear up this mess in time to save Reagan. But now that I know he *was* framed, I'll spend every dime I have, and the next ten years of my life, if necessary, to prove it. And I'll see that you fry!"

The statement was strictly corn but it seemed to impress her. Her voice small, she said, "You sound as if you mean that."

I said I did.

She thought some more, then asked. "And if I do talk, what would happen to me—I mean, legally?"

I asked her if she had killed Jackson.

She said hotly that she had not.

"Then I will personally guarantee," I promised, "that you won't be charged with anything." I poured a little oil, "You're big-time stuff, honey. You don't belong in a rube town like this. Why not wash your hands? Why not take what you have in the kitty and move on to Chicago or New York?"

That did it. "All right, I'll talk," she decided. "I'll tell you who Mr. Big is—but only on one condition." She named it. "I'll make a deposition before any judge or lawyer that you name, the judge who tried Larry if you want me to. But after I make that deposition I want time to pack and get on a train before you do anything about it. I'll go straight to Springfield or Joliet, or any place you say. But I want at least a two-hour start before you blow the lid off Cobb Junction."

That sounded fair enough to me. I said so.

"Benson's the man you want," she told me. Her voice was bitter. "That small-time cop has been too big for his britches for some time now. I'll be glad to see him get what's coming to him. It was Benson who opened the town right under that old fuddy-duddy LaRue's nose. It was Benson who killed Jackson and framed Larry for the kill. He is Homicide in Cobb Junction. He also knows where most of the bodies are buried. Shannon and Ricardo were glad to climb on his bandwagon. It's been Benson all the way. It was Benson who killed Adler in a try for you."

I asked how he had known I was coming to town.

She said he had gotten word via the grapevine route from a punk named Jaferey, doing five to ten for grand larceny in Stateville, that I had been talking to Reagan. She imagined Jaferey, who had gotten into prison in the first place for not splitting his loot with Benson, had hoped Benson would spring him in return for the information. But it would seem, she said, that Jaferey had gotten into a jam trying to prevent another prisoner from tipping me, and he probably wouldn't talk now. To talk would be the same as pleading guilty to the murder of the other con. She believed his name was Bauer.

So far it was logical.

Ruby continued, "That mess at the station is proof of how dumb Benson really is. He let Tony Cass see him try to shoot you and Tony wouldn't scare. Tony demanded money, lots of it. So Benson let him hold some—for a time. You pointed out another dumb bull, his phoning both you and Degano. I tried to tell him at the time it was a bull, but he wouldn't listen to me."

Then she shut up and began to fold plaits in the skirt of her hostess gown.

I asked if she would be willing to put what she had told me on paper and sign it.

She said she would be. More, she believed both Shannon and Ricardo would talk once the balloon had gone up, "We all hate Benson's intestines," she told me. "But once we had gotten our fingers dirty, there was nothing to do but play ball."

I asked her if Benson had threatened the jurors sitting on the Reagan trial. She said she knew he had threatened Adler. "Benson had something on Adler," she said, "and he told the puff-belly if he didn't bring in a guilty verdict with no recommendation for mercy he would see to it that Adler wound up in one of his own coffins. And Adler wanted to live."

It sounded reasonable. Benson had been on the station platform. Benson had practically warned me to go easy, informing me he liked Cobb Junction as it was. He was in on all kills. Whenever murder became necessary he sat in the driver's seat. As head of local Homicide he was in a position to plant any needed clues and remove any embarrassing ones that might have been overlooked.

"Okay. I'll buy that," I told Ruby. "What was the name of the judge who presided at Reagan's trial?"

She said, "John Manners."

I asked if he was local. She said he was and I thumbed through the M's in the phone book until I found his telephone number. "You get some clothes on," I told her. "If Judge Manners won't come here, we'll go to him. I want him to hear your story. Then you can put it on paper and sign it."

She said that was all right with her.

I picked up the phone, gave the operator Judge Manners' number —then happened to glance in the big mirror over the fake fireplace while I waited for her to ring him.

Looking like a small, pleased black canary who had managed to swallow a cat, Ruby was smiling smugly at my back. She looked even more amused than Cass had looked at the station. For an instant I didn't get it. Then I knew. She had reason to smile. She had sold me a bill of goods. *Benson wasn't Mr. Big.* He was only the petty chiseler. I'd had him tabbed as from the start. She was playing me for a sucker. *Another smart frame was in progress, using me as a cat's paw.*

As I watched her, she got up from the sofa and waggled her hips to the bedroom door. I waited until she had opened it, then I dropped the receiver back in its cradle and turned and faced her.

She heard the click and looked back at me over her shoulder, her face as blank as a vestal virgin's pulling petals off the Vassar daisy chain. "What's the idea?" she asked. "I thought you were going to call Judge Manners."

"You damn near got away with it," I told her. "You would have if you hadn't begun to count your chickens before they hatched.

But you did. And they've come home to roost." I started across the living room toward her. "Now I want the truth this time."

She took a step as if to run into the bedroom, cried, "No!" sharply. Then she began to scream.

The report of a large-calibered gun fired in a small room buckets and reverberates. And the shots fired in the bedroom damn near shook the chandelier loose from the plaster. It did shake several pictures from the wall.

The girl clung with both hands to the jamb of the door for an instant, then, as if dusting the wood, bent sharply from the waist and slid down to the floor just as all the lights went out.

My own gun in my hand, I dropped to the floor expecting a second burst of gunfire. No more shots were fired. I inched across the rug on my belly and looked into the bedroom. An open window was a lighter blob of grey against the black. A cold wind skittered across the floor and whipped a wisp of the girl's hair in my face. It smelled sweet and alive.

I neither heard nor sensed the man behind me. Taking advantage of the momentary sensory blank when my ears had been roaring with gunfire and my eyes blinded by the sudden transition from light to dark, he had stepped over the body and into the room. The blow was totally unexpected. It caught me back of my right ear as accurately as if he had zeroed it in with the peep sight of a Springfield.

I felt the girl's body soft under mine as my left arm gave away. Then as consciousness faded out, I heard the voice of the lad who had called me on the phone. It sounded faint but sincere.

"I wish she hadn't smiled, Doyle. I wish you had believed her. I hoped you would. I hate to do this, believe me."

Then he bulls-eyed the back of my ear again and all consciousness blotted out.

CHAPTER FIVE

CAT IN THE NIGHT

IT WAS COLD. Blood was salty in my mouth, Somewhere, someone was pounding on a door and calling me by name. I fought back a wave of nausea and pushed myself to a sitting position. The lights were on again, but not for Ruby. They would never come on for her again. She had entertained one lover too many. The last one had been named Death.

The pounding on the door increased. "You, in there! Doyle, open up!" Carter called. "We know you're in there. What was all that shooting about?"

I looked for my gun. It was gone. But its almost identical twin was lying on the rug not far from my right hand. Three of the six chambers had been fired.

"Miss Thiel!" the elevator girl called shrilly. "Are you all right."

Then Mason said, "Hell, why bull around? Let's break the door down. The girl is positive the shots came from this apartment."

Without much hope, I wiped the gun of the fingerprints undoubtedly impressed on the butt and barrel while I had still been unconscious. I didn't need to be told the score. I knew it.

Mr. Big had been big-time clever. This one was pinned on me. I was on my way to join Reagan.

A heavy shoulder thudded against the door and Carter said, "Now, both together."

I walked to the window and looked out. A spidery steel fire escape led down into a black well. I was perhaps halfway down when I heard the lock tear loose from the wood. A moment later, Mable screamed, *"She's dead. He killed her. And he looked like such a nice man."*

Then there was pavement under my feet. I started to run and froze against the wall instead as one of the two detectives turned his flash down into the well. It turned out to be Mason. "He must have gone down the steel," he deduced. "Well, it's no skin off our noses. You want to call the station house or should I?"

The light traveled back up the wall. I flipped a mental coin and chose the alley instead of the street. Whatever I did I would have to do fast. Like most towns of its stripe, Cobb Junction had a code of its own. Within a few minutes the street would be lousy with cops and volunteers all eager to be the first to spot the dirty woman-killer.

Stumbling down the refuse-littered alley, I considered trying to muscle the truth out of either Shannon or Ricardo or both. But the odds there were too heavy against me. The news would reach the Regal Hotel before I could, and a score of outraged patrons would be on hand to help take me into 'custody.'

I decided that Simpson, the pawnbroker who had failed to find any record of Reagan having hocked his gun, was my best bet.

Simpson *had* to know who had gotten the gun out of pawn.

I stumbled over a garbage can, swore and stood envying a black alley cat picking his or her way daintily through the debris as I stood rubbing my shin. Then, as such things will happen, the whole thing was perfectly clear. *I knew who had framed Reagan. I knew who had shot Adler at the station. I knew who had kitted Ruby and left me to fry for his fun.* But knowing and proving what I thought I knew would be two different matters.

At the next street intersection a drunk was washing his hands against a telephone pole. I asked him if he knew where Simpson's pawnshop was. He said it was two blocks down the street but owlishly informed me he thought that it was closed. I asked if he knew where Simpson lived. He said he wasn't certain but he thought he lived in the flat over the hock shop.

I risked using the street to make better time. The crowd had thinned out some and a light snow was falling. I thought of my camels hair and swore. Along the two blocks to the pawnshop I had to pass my hotel. I debated briefly, then ducked into the package room entrance and walked two flights of fire steps up to my room to get the spare gun in my bag.

Nothing had been touched as far as I could see. I dropped the gun in my pocket and fingered the hole the first slug fired at the station had gouged into my bag. More light was beginning to dawn. If the slug hadn't gone through the bag, and it hadn't, it could well be I had proof that Reagan had been framed—in my own traveling bag.

I took it with me when I left and I didn't leave any too soon. The fire door had barely snicked shut behind me when the grilled gate of the elevator opened and a man's voice said, "That's Doyle's room there, Officer. Room 217." The Cobb Junction police weren't exactly stupid, just a trifle slow on the draw.

I wanted to talk to the switchboard operator, the one who had informed me gratis:

"Larry Feagan didn't kill Ernie Jackson, mister. They are electrocuting an innocent man. If you're working for Reagan you get to Ruby Thiel. She's the one who can tell you the truth."

But with the law already in the hotel I didn't dare to stop. I knew now that Benson wasn't Mr. Big. But he was a greedy moron and once he had me handcuffed and in one of the Cobb Junction station house's back rooms, I wouldn't have a snowball's chance in hell of talking sense to him. I never did find out who the operator was or why she had tried to tip me.

The cop sent to stake out my room was obviously a pavement pounder. There was no police car in front of the hotel. There was a taxi at the curb. I ducked out the package room entrance, tossed my bag in beside the driver, then opened the rear door.

He put his racing form away and asked if I wanted to go to the railroad station or the bus terminal.

I said I would settle for Simpson's pawnshop. Before he could tell me it was closed, I asked if he knew where Judge John Manners lived and if he wanted to make twenty dollars.

He answered yes to both questions and I passed a twenty through the open glass partition, telling him it was his if he would take the bag to Judge Manners, deliver it in person and tell him to hold it until further notice as it was connected with the Reagan case.

He wanted to know who he should say had sent it. I told him the name was John Doe and asked him if he had heard about the excitement up the street.

He kicked his coffee mill over and began to grind. "Yeah, I heard about it," he informed me. "I hear some guy has just knocked off Ruby Thiel." He didn't seem to be much interested. "But if you ask me, mister, she's had it coming for a long time."

Both Simpson's shop and the flat above it were dark. I didn't like the way the cabbie had looked at me when he pulled away. It was an even toss whether he would take the bag to Manners or drive directly to the police station. But either place was all right with me. All I wanted was to put the bag into official custody.

By striking a match I found out Simpson's first name was Roy. I considered ringing the bell, then walked up the short flight of stairs.

The door at the top of the stairs was cracked open and a thin frame of light showed around the edges. I dropped my hand in my pocket and rapped on the outer jamb.

There was no answer. I rapped a second time, pushed the door open and walked in. Simpson wasn't going to tell me anything. A big blond man with buck teeth, he had gone on ahead to join Ruby Thiel. He had only been dead a few minutes and there was still a trickle of blood oozing from the small brown hole between his eyes.

I had the whole set-up then. Mr. Big had made his pile. He was closing his books and getting out while the getting was still good. It stood to reason that Shannon and Ricardo would be next. With both Ruby and Simpson out of the way, they were the only ones left who could trip him.

I picked up the phone on the table, called the police station and asked to speak to the chief. LaRue was wide awake now and fairly sizzling.

"This is Tom Doyle," I told him. "I wish to report a homicide."

He damn near bit the mouthpiece off his phone. "Why, you kill-crazy veteran," he gave me sad sack Beamer's line, "I'm going to see you burn if it's the last thing that I ever do. I—" He broke off as his office door opened and a voice, probably, the desk sergeant's informed him:

"Hey, Chief. There's a taxi driver here who says a white-haired guy with no overcoat gave him twenty bucks to take this bag out to Judge Manners. He said he dropped him at Simpson's pawnshop."

LaRue came back on the phone being very coy about it. "Where are you phoning from, Doyle?" he asked me.

I told him, "Simpson's. It's his homicide I wish to report." I banged down the receiver and got out of there. I knew what I wanted to know. I had to contact the judge some other way.

I found a phone booth in a lunch room down the street. The main drag was lousy with sirens by the time I got my number, but no one paid any attention to me.

"My name is Doyle, Judge Manners," I told him when he answered. "I know this is a hell of a time to call you but I'm working on the Larry Reagan case." I played it cagey. "And I think I can prove false evidence and false testimony was introduced at his trial."

The old man backed up what Reagan had told him about him. "I wasn't satisfied with the outcome of that trial," he admitted. "But there was nothing I could do about it. But why call me up this time of morning?"

I said I hadn't time at the moment to explain but asked him if he would meet me at the Cobb Junction police station. "A man's life is at stake," I reminded him. "Reagan hasn't much time left."

He said promptly he would meet me at the station. "You are calling from there now?"

"No," I admitted, "I'm not." The sirens on the street had grown louder. "But don't worry about that. I'll be there by the time you get there."

There were three police cars parked in front of Simpson's when I reached the street again but no cordon had been thrown around the district and no street blocks had been set up. Even so, I doubted I would reach the Regal in time. I didn't. I was still a block away when the sirens began to wail again and the pack that had been sniffing around Simpson's roared by me to park in a squealing of brakes in front of the Regal Hotel. Cobb Junction was really jumping.

By the time I reached it the usual crowd had formed. I asked a man standing on the fringes what had happened.

"Two guys have been shot," he told me. "I hear some war veteran has gone nuts and is shooting up the town." He licked his chops. "That makes four murders tonight. Chief La Rue and Benson just stormed in. And brother, are they fuming!"

I said I could imagine, that four murders in one night were apt to give a town a bad name. He gave me a dirty look. I pushed on through the crowd into the hotel foyer. Ricardo's office door was open, and Benson and LaRue were scowling down at something on the floor.

The lobby was as crowded as the street. I ran my eyes over the crowd for the lad I was looking for. He wasn't difficult to spot. He was still wearing my camels hair coat. His white cane poised a few inches from the floor, he was begging a lad standing next to him to Jell him what had happened.

The lad told him Marty Shannon and Ricardo had been shot.

He gasped, "How awful. Who did it?"

The other lad shrugged. "They say some lad named Doyle."

As I watched, the blind lad tapped his way out of the crowd. He was carrying the battered case that held his stock in trade, but it was closed and the pencils and shoe strings he used as beggar bait were no longer on display.

I followed him out to the cab rank. Quite an argument ensued. He wanted to be driven to the railway station in time to make the 4:10 St. Louis train but the driver didn't want to leave the scene of excitement. "You meeting or taking the train, Jerry?" the cab driver wanted to know.

"Taking it," the blind lad told him. "I have to report at the hospital for my annual physical tomorrow morning at nine."

The driver said that was different, opened the door of his cab and I stepped into the picture by yelling "Copper!" for the first time in my life.

Mason materialized out of the crowd, yelled, "Hey! Someone tell the chief. It's Doyle!"

As agile as a mink, the blind lad tried to twist out of my grasp, so I poked the muzzle of my gun into his spine. "You almost made it, chum," I told him. "You were almost big-time but not quite. Now subside or I'll blow your spine in two."

He knew I meant it and subsided. In the red neon light of the Regal's sign his face was a sickly green.

Benson, a big gun in his fist, came charging out the door, stopped short when someone said, "He's got a gun in Jerry's back."

"Shoot him! Shoot him!" the blind lad screamed. "He's crazy."

Mason told me to put my gun away. I told him I would on one condition. He wanted to know what that was. "Open this guy's pencil case," I told him, "and show us what's inside."

Mason looked at Benson. Benson looked at the pot-bellied little chief. LaRue screamed. "Humor him. We can't afford any more killings." He shook his fist at me. "But I promise you, Doyle, you'll burn."

I asked if he would like a small side bet on that.

Putting the case on the walk, Mason fumbled with the lock and the lid popped open. There were no pencils or shoe strings in it. It was heaped with sheaves of bills, those I could see of large denomination. Squatted on his heels, Mason looked up at me, puzzled.

Their jaws gaping, Benson and LaRue crowded forward. I ignored them to tell Mason, "This is your Mr. Big. This is the lad who framed Reagan. He is also the lad who killed Adler down at the station tonight. A half-hour ago he killed Ruby. For your further information, he also killed Simpson, Ricardo and Shannon. There are undoubtedly others in the gang but those he wiped out tonight were the only ones who could put the finger on him as Mr. Big. And he didn't want that to happen. He had made his pile. He was willing to call it quits. But before he did quit he made certain there would be no one left to talk or demand a split."

The cab driver gasped, "Holy smokes. No wonder he wanted me to drive him to the station. He intended scramming on the 4:10."

The blind lad screamed, "Doyle's lying! It's none of your business how I got the money. I haven't killed anyone." Ignoring my gun in his back, he tore loose from my grasp and lashed around him with his cane. I gave way with the others until he stood alone in a cleared circle in the center of the walk.

I called to Mason, "Watch his cane. It's loaded!"

The blind lad whirled at the sound of my voice and leveled his cane at me. I stepped in and under it just in time to knock it up and deflect the slugs over the heads of the crowd.

A deadly silence followed. I broke it by twisting the gun-cane out of his hand and asking Benson, "Well, what do you want me to do? Wrap him up in cellophane?"

Judge Manners was small and grey and honest. He was also intelligent. Replacing the phone on which he had just called Stateville to ask the warden to tell Reagan the good news, he told me soberly, "You have done us a great service, Doyle." He looked at Benson and LaRue. "In more ways than one. But tell me this. Army doctors seldom make a mistake. If Jerry is blind, or even partially blind, how could he see well enough to perpetrate these murders we now know he committed?"

I said that would be something for the court's doctors to decide, but I doubted if his medical discharge was bona fide. "It could be any of several forms of partial blindness," I told him. "But I *know* he can see in the dark."

The judge called the medical turn.

"A cat tipped me to that," I told him. "He *had* to be able to see to knock me out as accurately as he did." Benson fingered the bills in the case. "Burny burn," I told him. "That money will have to be impounded pending disposition by the court as in the case of the four grand he planted on my client to make his case stand up."

The blind lad, whose last name it would seem was Phillips, cast oral aspersion on my mother's virtue.

I repeated what I had told him on the walk.

"You were big-time but not quite big enough, although I will admit I never saw a sweeter set-up. You and your pencils were welcome everywhere in town. You even had yourself thrown in the can from time to time to find out how things stood down here. However, if both Chief LaRue and Benson had been strictly honest you couldn't have gotten away with what you did."

LaRue protested shrilly, "I wanted to clean up the town. I—"

"You took your orders from Ruby," I interrupted him. "And some of your men—I don't know just which ones; that's up to a grand jury to find out—played dirty ball right along with you."

I told Manners the situation as I saw it. Others of the loose-knit gang may have had their suspicions, but Ruby Thiel was the only one who actually *knew* who Mr. Big was. Chief LaRue, along with Ricardo and Shannon and Simpson, had taken their orders from Ruby.

The blind lad sneered, "Then why did I kill them?"

"Because you couldn't be certain they didn't know, or at least suspect," I told him. "You couldn't take a chance. Other nitwits like Bauer, taking their orders from Ruby, had done your dirty work like stringing up that merchant who 'hanged himself.' But you killed Jackson and Adler and Cass and—"

Benson gasped, "Jerry killed Cass. Why?"

I said, "Because Cass saw him shoot Adler with his cane-gun. And he was greatly amused about learning who Mr. Big really was. So amused he got away with blackmail until Jerry got a chance to slip a knife into his back."

"Good Lord!" Benson said.

He gave LaRue a dirty look. He didn't seem shocked to find out his pot-bellied little chief was mixed up in the mess. He seemed more hurt to think he hadn't been getting a cut.

I told Judge Manners the story Ruby told me, substituting the name of Phillips for Benson. "But now that the situation is out in the open," I concluded, "it might be you can clean the town up."

He looked at LaRue. LaRue looked like he was about to break into tears.

"Cobb Junction will be cleaned up," Manners promised me grimly. He looked at my traveling bag standing on the desk beside the money case. "But about this traveling bag . . .?"

"That," I told him, "is exhibit A for the state. You should find a slug in there fired from Phillip's cane-gun that will match the slug in Adler and the two slugs the coroner took out of Ernie Jackson's body. Whether Phillips deliberately used Reagan's pawned gun I wouldn't know. That's something for you local boys to find out before you bring him to trial. Anyone know if he had a grudge against Reagan?"

Phillips answered my question, tight-lipped. "You're damned right I did. He married the girl I wanted and if you hadn't stuck your nose into the case he'd have burned in four more days." He peeled off his black glasses. "Okay. You have me. I know when I'm in a tight. My medical discharge was faked. I'm no more blind than you are." He took an aspirin box from his pocket and asked Benson if he could have a glass of water.

I started to butt in and didn't. The moron got him a glass of water. He took a pill from the box, popped it in his mouth and swallowed it. If it was aspirin, it was the first aspirin I'd ever seen come in capsule form.

Benson turned suddenly efficient. "Now start talking, you dirty killer," he roared.

Phillips ignored him to ask me, "What tipped you, Doyle?"

I told him a black alley cat and the fact that in his phone call attempting to scare me out of town he had stressed the words: *"the minute I laid eyes on you."*

"That was the reason for your call. You wanted to be certain I didn't suspect the blind man I had seen on the platform. A blind man obviously couldn't lay eyes on anyone."

"Well, it was fun while it lasted."

A green tinge spread over his face. He tried to keep his chin up and couldn't. It sagged until it rested on his chest.

Benson gasped, too late, "That pill. It wasn't aspirin."

"You must be a detective," I told him. "What correspondence school did you take from?"

They got a doc, the young lad I had seen on the station platform, and a stomach pump, but neither of them could do a thing for Phillips. He had taken the easy way out. By the time they started pumping he was explaining things to Ruby.

Then there was a lot more chitchat and phone calls and depositions as to this and that and it was seven o'clock in the morning when I wound up my part of the case. I shook hands with Judge Manners, making certain he had the address of my office. Then I walked over to the stretcher on which they had laid Phillips and peeled my camel's hair coat off the dead man.

Even in as bad a jam as he was, pot-bellied little LaRue was shocked. He wanted to know if I was so calloused to death I was willing to wear a coat a man had died in. I said I didn't see why I shouldn't. I had paid two hundred bucks for the coat and, besides, Phillips probably wouldn't need a coat where he was going.

Benson offered to drive me to the station. I think he wanted to be certain that I left town. As we parted, he admitted, "You're big-time, Doyle. You cleaned up a bad smell. You made suckers out us honest guys on the force." He stressed the word honest. "But for curiosity's sake, how much do you make on a case like this? How much did you soak Reagan?"

I told him I hadn't charged Reagan a dime and didn't intend to.

"In a pig's eye," he scoffed. Just then my train pulled into the station. "Well, good-bye and bad luck," he told me in farewell. "And if I never see you again it will be too soon."

I told him the same to him, and also the back of my hand. I was glad to see him go. I was glad to see my train pull in. I was even more pleased when it pulled out.

I'd had all I wanted of Cobb Junction. Besides, I wanted to look in the pockets of my camel's hair. It had looked quite bulky on Phillips, almost as if he had stuffed whatever he couldn't get into his case into my coat pockets. Was I surprised to find he had! There were eight fat sheaves of bills in all, totaling sixteen thousand dollars.

Did I keep it? What do you think? What would *you* have done—get off the train and go back and give it to Benson?

CRAWL OUT OF THAT COFFIN!

CHAPTER ONE

OVER MY DEAD BODY

IF I SAID THAT I WOULDN'T HAVE TAKEN THE CASE except that I needed the money, I would be lying. It got under my skin from the start although I knew I was in for trouble when I took it. You can seldom dig into a grave without disinterring a corpse. I had I an idea this one would smell. It did.

Sherry and I had been to see Maurice Evans in *Hamlet* and had dropped in at the Sherman House bar for a couple of drinks and a steak to take some of the culture out of our mouths, when the drunken little brunette planted herself in my lap and, peering into my face with alcoholic earnestness, recited:

"They bore him barefaced on the bier;
Hey no nonny, nonny, hey nonny;
And in his grave rained many a tear . . ."

I said, "The hell you say," and looked at Sherry. She gave me a raised-eyebrow look.

Before either of us could speak, the little brunette demanded: "Isn't that sad, Mr. Mercer?"

I said it was very sad, wondering how she knew my name, and hoping I didn't know her.

As if reading my mind, she added, "You don't know me, do you?"

I said I did not and she began to snivel. Here we go again, I thought. Sherry isn't red-haired for nothing. Me, I'm just an average guy. If a pretty dame talks to me in a bar I am liable to talk back. I have even had horses named Florence call me up. I tried to place the brunette. She looked a little like the twenty-six game girl at Matt's Place and a little like the new cashier at Tony's. But the diamond drops in her ears were real, her evening gown looked like Adrian, and you didn't buy the kind of perfume she was wearing in the dime store.

Hoisting the storm flags, Sherry said, "Now look here, Matt—"

Before she could go any further, the brunette turned in my lap and pointed a finger at her. "You stay out of thish." Then she cuddled up closer to me. "You're a nice man, aren't you, Mr. Mercer? And even if you don't know me you wouldn't want to see me in my bier, would you?"

"Of course not," I lied. "But if you'll get off my lap like a good girl and sit down in a chair I'll be glad to buy you a beer."

Sherry said over her dead body.

"Oh! Am I in your lap?" the brunette hiccupped. "Excuse me. I never sit in strange gentlemen's laps." She transferred to a chair with drunken dignity. "And I'll buy my own drink, thank you. I have money."

She dumped the contents of her evening bag on the table. There was a compact, comb, lipstick, handkerchief, cigarettes and matches. There were also two crumpled one-hundred-dollar bills.

I told Sherry I seemed to be in the wrong business. Still looking daggers at me, she said I seemed to be doing nicely.

The little brunette gulped what was left of my double rum, then ignored us to cup her chin in her palms and stare off into what would have been space if we hadn't been sitting just under the kettle drums. "Dead at twenty-one," she sniveled. "Alas, poor Yorick." So saying, she passed out on the table.

Her lips a thin line, Sherry wanted to know who she was. I told the truth. "So help me, honey, I don't know. To the best of my sober knowledge, I never saw her before."

She getting ready to call me a liar when Charlie Pierce threaded his way between the tables and stopped at ours. "Oh, here she is," he said. "I thought I might find her here."

"If you know her, take her away," I told him. "Here I am full of Shakespeare and culture, sitting here minding my own business, and what happens to me? A lady drunk."

A distinguished-looking man in his early fifties, Charlie is one of our better Chicago lawyers. By that I mean he has piled up enough in the tort and writ of habeas corpus business to leave the short corners and ambulance-chasing to lads on their way up. He laughed and sat down at our table, saying, "Every time I see you, Sherry, you are more beautiful than you were the last time."

She wasn't to be soft-soaped. "Who is that girl?" she demanded. "And how well does Matt know her?"

He laughed. "Oh. So that's how it is. Believe me, Sherry, to the best of my sober knowledge, Matt has never had the privilege of meeting the young lady before."

Sherry wanted to know what this 'sober knowledge' business was—a wolf lodge of some kind?

"I mean it," Pierce said. "I pointed Matt out to her during the intermission." He turned to me. "We were coming to see you in the morning on a matter of business and Betty must have slopped over while I stepped out into the foyer to make a phone call. Are you busy, Matt, or can you take a case for me?"

I lied that I was busy as hell, but seeing it was him I would see what I could do.

"There's good money in it," he said. He indicated the passed-out girl. "She's Betty D'Andrea."

The name didn't mean a thing to me. It did to Sherry. She gasped, *"The* Betty D'Andrea?"

Pierce nodded. "Right."

I asked Sherry who in hell Betty D'Andrea was.

She repeated, *"The* Betty D'Andrea, the heiress, the one in the society pages half the time. The girl who inherits half the D'Andrea money the day she is twenty-one."

"Oh," I said, "that Betty D'Andrea." Both the name and the girl were still Greek to me but there was some yarn connected with the name chasing around in the back of my mind. I tried to make it come forward and couldn't, I asked Pierce what she wanted with a private agency man.

"She doesn't want to die," he said simply. "Would you want to die if you were heir to fifteen million dollars?"

The girl's 'hey non nonny' business and her 'dead at twenty-one' began to make some sense. "No," I admitted, "I wouldn't. In fact I am worth considerably less than that amount of money, but the thought of dying and having Sherry marry some other mug to take care of my twins fills me with considerable abhorrence."

Sherry wrinkled her nose at Pierce. "Don't ask him how to spell it."

Pierce said, "I'm serious, Matt. Miss D'Andrea will be twenty-one the fourteenth of next month and while I know it has been some years since you have done personal bodyguard work, it will be worth one hundred dollars a day, all your expenses, and a bonus if Miss D'Andrea is still alive and can walk into the office of the law firm handling the estate on the fourteenth of next month."

Good pay for that type of work being twenty-five dollars a day, and a tot of lads willing to work for less, I asked him what the joker was. "What's the matter with her? Is she man-crazy, a dope, or a dipso?"

Pierce said to the best of his knowledge that her personal life was above reproach, she was not addicted to drugs, and this was the first time he had ever seen her drink to the point of intoxication. He added. "Not that I blame the poor kid. I'd probably be stiff as a board. You aren't familiar with the D'Andrea yarn, are you?"

I said a vague something connected with the name was buzzing around in the back of my mind but I hadn't been able to isolate it.

"The D'Andrea's don't live to be twenty-one," he told me. While I was considering that, he motioned our waiter to the table and told him to bring whatever we were drinking and a rum collins for himself.

The waiter looked at the passed-out girl.

"No. Nothing for her," Pierce said straight-faced. "Miss D'Andrea is driving."

It was quite a yarn he told. If you have been shaving for twenty or thirty years you may remember the start of the affair. It began back in the slit-skirt and gaslight era just before the First World War when a good cigar was a nickel, the best bonded bourbon fourteen dollars a case, and the butcher threw in a pound of country butter as lagniappe if you bought three pounds of twenty-cent sirloin steak.

The D'Andreas moved in the best social set, the smell of the tannery on which D'Andrea Senior had founded the family fortune having been removed from his money by liberal applications of giving to this and that and sending the offspring to Harvard and Wellesley. There were two sons and one daughter, Gene, Rene, and Renee, the last two perfect models of deportment but the oldest son and heir, Gene D'Andrea, being what was known in that day as "fast" and a "sporting man."

Rene and Renee married in their set and settled down. Gene, however, continued to haunt the race tracks, wear out shoe leather on bar rails, and have his name linked with some of the slightly soiled lilies of his day, until the elder D'Andrea publicly threatened to disinherit him unless he ceased his evil ways and conducted himself like a gentleman.

A new will, in fact, was already in preparation when both of the elder D'Andreas died suddenly and mysteriously one night in a fire that gutted their Indiana Avenue mansion, leaving the new will unsigned and the old one naming their beloved son, Gene D'Andrea, as sole executor, without bond, of their estate.

A family squabble, so Pierce said, immediately began, with the married son and daughter charging their unmarried brother with dilatory tactics in settling the estate, concealing valuable community assets, and transferring still others beyond the jurisdiction of the Cook County Probate Court.

He, however, continued his merry way untroubled, climaxing a madcap-career by marrying one Flora Fredric, a beautiful wench who was currently engaged in out-quivering the muscular contortions of Little Egypt at one of the local burlesque houses. Then, as if this wasn't sufficient to damn him in the eyes of the well-bred gentry of the day, on the night of March 28, 1915, during a poker game, on being accused of cheating, he shot to death a prominent and respectable merchant by the name of Harvey M. Bunting.

"This is better than *Hamlet,*" Sherry said. Pierce told her the best was still to come.

With the police close on his heels, Gene D'Andrea had fled Chicago with his beautiful chorus girl bride for the dubious sanctuary of the D'Andrea summer home in Michigan. Then with the local police pounding on the front door, he had promptly put a bullet through his own brain, but not before he had made a handwritten will by-passing his brother and sister and leaving the bulk of the D'Andrea money to any issue they might have, said money to be paid to them when they reached the age of twenty-one. And as a final, ironic gesture he had named his wife Flora to be executor without bond.

Sherry wanted to know if he had gotten away with it, and while Pierce was explaining some of the legal angles and suits and counter-suits the will had brought into being to the great delight of the legal profession, I remembered what I knew of the D'Andreas. It wasn't much. But the summer before, while touring the north Michigan country we, Sherry and the twins and I, had driven past the damnedest house I ever hope to see. It looked like something Rube Goldberg had dreamed up and discarded as too fantastic. There were at least two hundred rooms in it, all of different architectural persuasion and roof levels with wings running this way and that and bathroom fittings poking out where one might reasonably expect to see a door or a window. Nor had its owner finished with it, as a crew of men were busy roofing an obviously new wing.

I asked about it when I got gas in the next town and the service station attendant informed me it was the D'Andrea house, that old lady D'Andrea was a nut, with a firm belief that as long as she continued to expand her house she would never die. The house, to his knowledge he told me, had been under construction for twenty-eight years and he was personally acquainted with a man who had worked on it for eighteen.

I told Pierce that what he had been saying was very interesting, but I wanted to know what it had to do with the drunken brunette being willing to pay one hundred dollars a day and a bonus for a bodyguard.

He said, "She and her nineteen-year-old cousin Marvin are the last of the D'Andrea children."

I scoffed, "Don't tell me a screwball will like that stood up?"

He said it had. There had been a dozen court battles about it with fortunes spent on both sides, but Flora D'Andrea. the former chorus girl, had emerged from each one triumphant as the sole executor of the estate. Since then, the two other branches of the D'Andrea tribe had made spasmodic attempts to have her removed as incapable, but each time a court inspection of her books had proved that despite her passion for building, she had not only conserved the estate, but by shrewd market and real estate manipulations had increased it from five to thirty million dollars, the amount due to be divided between Betty and her cousin Marvin.

Nor had she been stingy with advances. The old lady had insisted that all children eligible to inherit under the will be raised in a manner fitting to their future stations in life and had on at least two occasions petitioned the court to advance sums ranging from payment for extra tutoring to the sixty thousand dollars she had insisted on spending on Betty D'Andrea's debut.

Sherry asked Pierce. "What do you mean, *all* children? I thought you said Betty and her cousin were the only heirs."

"Only *remaining* heirs," he told her. "Rene and Renee had, in all, seven children. The oldest child, a boy by the name of Georges, should have collected his share of the fortune back in 1935. But to date, and in answer to Matt's question why Betty is willing to pay one hundred dollars a day for protection, *none of the third D'Andrea generation have ever celebrated their twenty-first birthdays.*"

I felt a cold chill on my neck and it wasn't from any draft.

Pierce named the deceased heirs on his fingers. "On Renee's side of the family, Georges drowned while swimming at the D'Andrea estate two weeks before his twenty-first birthday. Charles died here, in Chicago, of a mysterious stomach complaint the night before he was to collect his share of the fortune. A girl named Madelaine was killed by a hit-and-run car shortly after she turned twenty. Rene's children fared no better. All of them were girls. Ann was killed by a prowler in the family home. Marcell was actually on her way to the lawyer's office when she disappeared."

"And the girl was never found?"

"No. Although from information in my possession the D'Andrea estate has spent well over two hundred thousand dollars in vain attempts to trace her. There is, I believe, a firm of private detectives still investigating her disappearance."

It was a honey of a case all right. I asked Pierce when he had to have an answer.

"Tonight. Right now," he told me. "If you don't want the case I'll have to get someone else." He laid his cards on the table. "I'm getting a sizable fee from Flora D'Andrea to see that Betty is alive to collect. I intend to see she is. And if it's money that's worrying you, that bonus I spoke of can go as high as ten thousand dollars."

I looked at Sherry. She was looking at the little brunette. "Poor scared little kid," she sympathized.

That settled it as far as I was concerned. "Okay. I'll take it," I told Pierce. "But only on one condition. Starting from right now until the morning of the 14th I want someone with the kid every minute of the night and day. I want them to eat with her, dress with her, sleep with her."

Sherry's eyes narrowed slightly.

I continued, "It being impossible for me to do so, I know just the girl op for the job. I've used her before and I'm willing to pay her salary out of my part of the take." I forestalled Pierce's objection. "Not that I won't be around. I will. But I also want to feel free to do a little digging into the background of the case, Marcell's disappearance and the deaths of Georges, Anna, Charles, et al. Is that okay with you?"

He said it was and I asked him to get Sherry another drink while I got Gwen Hayden on the phone. She was home and glad to get the work. I told her to pack a bag and come right down to the Sherman House. Then I went downstairs toward the men's room before going back to the table.

Two well-dressed huskies walked down the steps behind me but I paid no attention to them. I was to wish I had, later.

I walked on through the door and had just plugged the stopper into the wash basin when I realized I wasn't alone.

"Tough guy, huh?" someone said behind me.

I turned to see who had said it and a fist caught me between the eyes. A second and third fist followed before I could get up my guard. Then something that felt like a blackjack, and undoubtedly was, caught me in back of one ear and I lost all interest in the proceedings.

I came to sitting on the floor with my back against the wall. I got stiffly to my feet. Nothing seemed to be broken. My ring was still on my finger. My watch was still in my pocket. Nothing but my wallet was gone.

I looked at myself in a mirror. My eyes might color some later but right now they were only puffed. The lad who had handled the sap was an expert. He hadn't even broken the skin.

I doubted if robbery had been the motive. My ring cost three grand, slid easily on my finger, and diamonds are about as difficult to identify as cash. My watch was worth another hundred in almost any hock shop. Considering my recent conversation with Pierce, it was more likely the lads merely wanted to know more about me and had chosen, for reasons of their own, to use this rather unconventional manner. The contents of my wallet would tell them plenty.

I tried to remember what the two huskies who had followed me down the stairs looked like, and couldn't. Both had been big men but I doubted if I would know them if I saw them again.

I walked out into the ante-room and an alert-looking colored boy sprang to attention, a whisk broom in one hand. "Brush you off, sir?"

I gave him the change in my pocket but told him, "No thank you, son. It would seem two experts have attended to that little matter."

CHAPTER TWO

EXIT PADDY QUINN

ORNING WAS COLD AND GRAY. Exploring fingers of wind felt around the Loop corners, tugging and patting and flipping the skirts of the work-bound cuties. White-topped nylons were everywhere. But there was little howling being done. The rain that accompanied the wind was cold and when it wasn't beating into your face it dribbled down your neck off the building cornices and el structure. Jimmy, the morning barkeep in Matt's place, wanted to know what I was doing up so early. I told him I was working on a case and he scoffed, "Yair. I'll bet. You private eyes have it soft. You don't know what work is."

I admitted that could be so. But I could still feel the edge of the chair on which I had slept all night pressing into the small of my spine. It had transpired after Gwen Hayden's arrival that Betty D'Andrea's mother was dead, her father had married again, and the poor little rich girl was living alone in a smart but small furnished apartment on the drive. There being but one bed and one bedroom in it, and three in a bed being considered somewhat illegal since the Mormon Manifesto of 1890, I had gotten what sleep I could on an understaffed chair in the living room.

I asked Jimmy if Inspector Haig had been in. He said he had, so I bought a small fire for my stomach and went next door to the Detective Bureau.

I found Haig in the squadroom putting, the fear of God into a young punk who was suspected of being one of a juvenile mob who had killed a druggist during a hold-up. Haig wanted to know what brought me out on such a lousy morning. I told him I was working on a case and would like to check some of its back history with him when he had time,

When I mentioned the name D'Andrea, he grunted and told one of his squad to take the punk back to his cell. Then he walked into his office with me. "That's a screwball affair if there ever was one," Haig admitted. "Just what do you want to know?"

I told him I wanted to know what the department had on the case, and if any charges had ever been brought against anyone. He sent one of his boys for the file but there was little in it Pierce hadn't told me the night before.

His file consisted mainly of the autopsy report on Charles, the killing of Anna by a prowler, and the mysterious disappearance of Marcell. But there was nothing newer than 1940. And no one had ever been apprehended.

There was also mention made of Madelaine's death but it had officially been written off the books as an unsolved hit-and-run case in which the driver had never been apprehended. Georges having drowned In Michigan, there was nothing on him at all but a written notation by Haig that at the request of the boy's parents he had contacted the Michigan authorities by phone and they had assured him they were satisfied that the boy's death was accidental.

"But it's screwball just the same," Haig said. "Five kids dying or disappearing just before they turn twenty-one *can't* be coincidence. Such things just don't happen, Matt."

I said that was the way I felt about it. He wanted to know who had brought me into the case. I told him Pierce and why. Then I asked if he had ever met Flora D'Andrea, the executor of the estate.

Grinning, he said he had. "Innumerable times during the various investigations. Believe me, she made it tough for us." He sobered. "But if you are thinking of trying to tag the four deaths and Marcell's disappearance onto her, put it out of your mind. We worked on that angle for two months after Marcell's disappearance. And the old lady is positively in the clear. In that instance she was waiting in the office of the law firm handling the estate when Marcell left the house. In the others outside of Georges drowning, she wasn't within five hundred miles of the scene of the crime. In the second place she has no motive. The money doesn't go to her even if they all die."

I asked where it did go.

He said from the legal information he had, that was a moot question but it would undoubtedly revert to the original D'Andrea heirs, Rene and Renee.

Which left the case right where it had been all the time—up in the air.

I wrote down the name of Flora's lawyers—Prosper, Allen and McCready—and thanked Haig for his information. On my way out, I turned in the doorway to ask if he had known Gene D'Andrea, the original core of the boil.

"I did," Haig told me. "I was a rookie patrolman working out of the old Peking Station then. And Gene D'Andrea was an insufferable, arrogant young pup. After his parents died he used to boast in the levee bars that neither his sister nor brother would ever get a penny of the D'Andrea money."

I said it would seem that he had made good his boast and called Gwen Hayden from a pay phone in the hall. She said Betty was up and trying to eat breakfast, but that the heiress to fifteen million dollars had a peach of a hangover, remembered nothing of the night before, and had insisted on phoning Pierce to have Gwen's presence in the apartment explained. I told Gwen to keep her in the apartment if she could as I wanted to talk to her later that morning. Then I grabbed a cab over to LaSalle Street and the offices of Prosper, Allen and McCready.

I asked to see one of the partners and was ushered into Allen's office. A red-cheeked old man in his middle sixties, dripping respectability, he was kind enough to say he had heard of me and was pleased to learn I had been called into the case to protect the person of Betty D'Andrea, whom he called a very sweet child.

His firm, he said, had acted as Flora D'Andrea's attorneys for thirty years. As young men, the estate contest had been a Godsend to them. But in later years the constant court battles and wranglings had begun to wear on their nerves. He passed one hand over his eyes. Then there had been the fatalities. He, for one, would be pleased when the estate was finally divided between the two remaining heirs. He sounded tired,

I asked him to tell me something of Flora D'Andrea. He said she was a remarkable woman, typical of her class, attractive at fifty-three, and an excellent business woman, the D'Andrea fortune having swollen under her guidance from five to over thirty million dollars.

I asked what he meant by "typical of her class."

The old man's grin was almost boyish. "Well, Flora was a chorus girl. And she has never quite gotten over it." He repeated, "Even at fifty-three she is a most attractive woman and I have never been able to understand why she insists on spending nine-tenths of her time up in that lonely North Michigan county."

I said I had seen her house, and his grin widened.

"That house." He shrugged. "Well, I guess all of us are entitled to one weakness. And that monster of a house is Flora's. She is thoroughly convinced that the day she stops building, she'll die."

I asked him the same question I had asked Haig. He said by now the issue had become so confused he would hesitate to venture even a guess as to what would become of the D'Andrea money if both Betty and Marvin should die. "But let us hope that doesn't happen," he added.

As my last question, I asked if it was true that Flora D'Andrea had spent two hundred thousand dollars trying to trace Marcell. He said it was, and that from time to time he still got a bill and a report from a firm of investigators by the name of Gleason & Baily.

I thanked him for his time and left. Out on the street again I tried to figure my best move. There were two things I could do. I could go back to the apartment and pass the next seventeen days in pleasant chit-chat, never allowing Betty out of my sight except when she was sleeping. Or I could keep on moving, smelling into graves.

Seventeen days was a long time. The other heirs had undoubtedly been watched. Still, Georges had drowned; Charles had died of a mysterious stomach complaint; Madelaine had been killed by a hit and run car; Ann been killed by a prowler; and Marcell had disappeared. Death had found a way to get at them.

Rain dribbling down my neck, I considered Flora D'Andrea. Both Pierce and Allen were above suspicion, and both men had given Flora a clean bill. Both men seemingly liked her. But as the executor of the estate she was the core around which the whole thing revolved. I wanted to know more about her. Both men had mentioned the fact and seemed to accept it without question, but, while I was no judge of such matters, it seemed a trifle strange to me that a former muscle dancer should suddenly blossom forth with the type of financial brains that could build up the D'Andrea money as she had.

The more I thought about it the stranger it seemed to me. It was a starting point at least, and as far as I knew, a new one. Inspector Haig was no fool. There was no need for me to back-track over the ground he had, covered. Besides, that angle of the case was eight years old.

What I wanted was action. I got it.

By Inspector Haig's own admission he had been a rookie at the time that Gene D'Andrea had been haunting the levee. But back in 1915, or thereabouts, old Paddy Quinn, long since bumped off the force without a pension during one of Chicago's periodic reform waves, had been a Captain of Detectives. I bought a pint of bonded rye, whistled down another cab and gave the driver Quinn's address.

I had been at the West Side rooming house before to buy information from Quinn, and the witch of Endor who ran it knew me. A slattern with two missing front teeth, she hissed that Quinn was in his room and went back to whatever she was doing in the basement.

The place was bad enough when the weather was dry, but in the rain it smelled like the original sin, with variations. Someone was frying onions in one of the rooms. A couple was quarreling in another.

I climbed the moldy carpet to the second floor, making a mental vow never to take a crooked dollar, or at least be certain it couldn't be traced back to me. Paddy, they told me, had been quite a gay blade in his time and a high liver. But the reform wave that had swept him out of office had also washed out his bank account. The last time I had called to see him, he had been swamping in a bar.

A big hulk of a man with flesh hanging where the fat had been, he had failed a lot since I'd seen him last. It took him a little time to place me, but once he did he was cordial. "Come in. By all means come in, Mercer. I'm always glad to see an old friend."

His voice was still deep and rumbled like an old time actor's. He insisted I sit in the one chair and fumbling a pack of crumpled cigarettes from under the pillow, offered the package to me. I took one so as not to offend him. 1 knew he didn't have a dime. He had been strictly from larceny all his life. But the old man still had his pride and had to be handled, with kid gloves. "I'm in a jam again, Paddy," I told him, uncapping the bottle of rye. "And I thought maybe you could help me out with a little information."

His face lighted as he said he would be pleased to do what he could for me. I took a drink and handed him the bottle. As he drank I considered giving him a ten-spot for the information that I wanted, then tripled it in my mind. I would never miss the money. It would mean a lot to him. "Of course I'll pay for it," I continued. "That's only fair." I slipped three ten-dollar bills from my wallet and laid them on the battered dresser. "I don't know what we younger men would do without you, Paddy."

He licked his lips looking at the money. "As I said, I'll be pleased to help you, Mercer. What is it you want to know?"

"Everything you know about Flora D'Andrea," I told him. I nudged his mind. "You know, the burlesque muscle dancer who, married Gene D'Andrea, the rich young punk who shot that merchant in a poker game, then blew out his own brains."

"Oh, yes," Paddy nodded. "I remember it very distinctly. I was in charge of the case." He nipped at the bottle. "That was back in—hmm—1914 or '15. D'Andrea and his wife skipped out for Michigan." He snorted. "And very officious they were about it."

The remark didn't make sense to me. I asked who had been officious about what.

He told me, "The Michigan authorities. As I recall his name, it was Baily, an incompetent, damn little rube county sheriff and his deputy whose name I can't remember." He dramatized the scene. "There I was, hot on D'Andrea's heels and if the damned farmers hadn't jumped the gun and flushed the quarry I'd have taken him alive."

I tried to guide his mind back into the channels in which I wanted it. "A pretty girl, Flora, wasn't she? I imagine she had lots of lovers before she married Gene."

"She was popular," Paddy nodded. He chuckled. "There were a lot of gay blades of that day who were willing to pay plenty to have their name's changed to John Doe when the case broke in the papers."

I asked if the names of Prosper, Allen, McCready or Pierce had been among them.

He said, "I think Charlie Pierce squired her around for a while, although I wouldn't swear to it." He hit the bottle again. "That was so long ago. But if he did, he wasn't to be blamed. Flora was a pretty girl."

"But how was she for brains, Paddy?" I asked him.

He was taking a drink of whiskey and he almost blew it through his nose. When he had stopped choking he snorted, "Now that's a hell of a thing to ask a man about a muscle dancer when he has a mouthful of rye. She didn't have any brains. She was the kind of a dumb little blonde you had to tell to come in out of the rain. And I mean that literally. That's why she fell so hard for Gene. Not that he wasn't a good-looking devil. He was. Tall, dark and handsome, as they say nowadays. And as bad as he was good-looking."

I said Flora must have had a few brains to do what she had with the D'Andrea fortune.

"That," Quinn said, "is just what I'm getting at." He nipped at the bottle, then stared out the grimy window at the rain. "You know, Mercer," he told me finally, "I'm an old man now. About all I can do is think. And I've laid here many a night wondering about that case, about the way Gene drew his will, about none of the heirs ever living to be twenty-one."

Rain pelted at and dribbled down the window in spurts. A board creaked in the hall. The smell of frying onions grew stronger.

Quinn continued, "And the more I've thought about it, the more I have cope to the conclusion that there is a stranger in the wood-pile. It wasn't Flora's brains that kited the D'Andrea fortune up to its present fantastic sun. But I think I know whose brains are responsible. I tried to tell Haig my theory the time that last girl disappeared. But he was so damn fall of his own importance and so afraid I was going to try to borrow a ten-spot that he wouldn't even listen to me."

I added two tens to the three that I had put on the dresser. "I'm listening, Paddy."

He lowered his voice confidentially, but it still continued to boom. "Digest this point first," he told me. "Gene D'Andrea had no real right to any of the D'Andrea money in the first place. In the second place I don't think—"

Whatever he didn't think was lost in the creaking of the opened door. I instinctively reached for my gun but not in time to keep the gun in the doorway from pouring three shots into the old man's back.

I fired at the face I couldn't see but that I knew had to be back of the gun. I doubt if I even came close, though, for Paddy, rearing from the bed like a stricken stag, lunged into me and sent me spinning against the wall, with lead prickling holes in the faded paper by my head.

Out in the hall, some woman began to scream for the police. Then one of the big men who had slugged me at the Sherman the night before barged into the room and made a swipe at my head with his empty gun. That was a mistake on his part. I put two .38's through his stomach, dodged him as he fell and ran out into the hall to run smack into his partner with sufficient force to knock my gun from my hand.

But either he didn't know that, or he had had enough. Before I could recover the gun, he ran down the steps five at a time and, brushing the screaming slattern aside, raced out the front door.

I followed in hopes of getting a shot at him, but by the time I had reached the stoop he had disappeared into the rain. It would have been suicide to follow. I walked back into the rooming house to find the slattern already at the phone.

I took the receiver out of her hand, dialed Central Bureau, asked for Inspector Haig's extension and began the conversation by saying I wished to report a homicide.

Then I phoned Charlie Pierce. He wanted to know where I was calling from and how I was doing. I told him that could wait and asked him if he had ever kept company with Flora D'Andrea.

I expected him to lie. He didn't. "Why, yes, I did, Matt," he admitted. "That was one of the reasons she came to me about this matter concerning Betty." He chuckled. "In fact, I was paying my attentions to her, as we called it in those days, when Gene D'Andrea practically waltzed her out of my arms. Why? Why do you want to know?"

I hung up without bothering to answer and went back up stairs. Paddy was dead. The big hood I had shot was still alive, but dying. "It's your last chance if you want to talk, chum," I told him.

He said distinctly, "The dirty heel ran out on me," and died.

Haig arrived less than ten minutes later with a tail of reporters close behind him. "Now who would want to kill Paddy?" Haig asked. "The old man was almost eighty."

I said that was the reason he had been killed, his memory went back too far. "You wouldn't remember, would you, Inspector, some crackpot theory of Paddy's that he tried to tell you while you were investigating Marcell's disappearance?"

He said, "Hell no. That was eight years ago, Matt. And Paddy was full of theories. Why?"

I told him what Paddy had said, then gave him the old man's last words. Haig thought a moment and said he believed he could explain the first part of the statement. Several times during the various trials, Rene and Renee D'Andrea had attempted, unsuccessfully, to prove that Gene was an adopted child. He wanted to know if that helped me any.

It was to mean more later but it didn't mean anything then and I said so, adding that if we could identify the hood I had been forced to shoot it might help to clarify matters.

None of Haig's squad knew him. Neither did any of the reporters. He was a husky guy in his middle twenties. His clothes were expensive and well cut, but somehow he didn't have the city look that should have gone with the clothes. I looked at his hands. They were callused. If the sudden hunch that I had was correct, he wasn't too long away from a plow.

Ben Gandy of Haig's squad went through his clothes. "No labels and no laundry marks," he reported. "In fact, the only thing I find in his pockets outside of cigarettes and some change, is this."

He held up a familiar looking wallet and the reporters crowded closer. I took my wallet out of Candy's hand and checked its contents. There were eighty dollars more in it than I'd been carrying but otherwise its contents seemed to be intact.

"Don't get too eager," I told the boys. "I *know* that his name isn't Mercer."

CHAPTER THREE

GLEASON AND BAILY

TWELVE DAYS HAD PASSED. The big lad lay in the morgue still unidentified. Nor had his partner been found. He had seemingly disappeared into the same void of space that had swallowed up Marcell. Everyone concerned with the case was getting jumpier by the minute. I had proved to my own satisfaction that Charlie Pierce and the firm of Prosper, Allen & McCready were acting in good faith. My spine had a permanent ridge from sleeping on the understuffed chair. But I was no closer to a solution of the case than I had been on the night in the Sherman when Betty sat down on my lap.

She came out of the bedroom with Gwen, who was too heavily made up and had deep circles under her eyes. The kid was scared. She had reason to be.

She wanted to know if Jimmy had shown up yet.

I was still saying he hadn't when the doorbell rang. Gun in one hand I opened the door on the chain. It was Jimmy Mason with a corsage for each of the girls.

A nice punk about Betty's age whom she had met at college, he worked in an architect's office for peanuts but after an under-the-epidermis search of his background I had allowed him to drop in evenings to get her mind off of herself and, incidentally, make a fourth hand at bridge. The punk was obviously in love with her, and she with him. But being a well-bred young lady *she* couldn't propose. And I had a very good hunch he was sitting on his, "Will you be mine, darling," for two very good reasons, both of them being money. He hadn't a dime. She was heiress to fifteen million dollars.

If she lived to collect it. I made my nightly call to Sherry and said good night to the twins while the girls made little fluttering noises over their corsages.

Sherry wanted to know if I was certain I wasn't enjoying my work. I assured her that I wasn't, then herded my flock together.

The proposed gathering of the clan was strictly Haig's idea. He thought that if all concerned were to get together and kick the ball around a bit we might come up with something. It was as good an idea as any. God knows I hadn't made any progress.

Mason remarked as he helped Betty into her coat that he had noticed two uniformed men on the walk. I told him they also were Inspector Haig's idea. From now on, up to and including the morning of the fourteenth, Betty was to be under constant guard.

We met at Renee Moran's home on the South Side just north of the South Shore Country Club. A big, square stone house set well back from the drive on a wide lawn well dotted with bushes, it was class without climbing up into the confiscatory brackets. Moran was a prosperous South Side doctor, and D'Andrea money had never been anything but a heartache to him. It had cost him three of his children. Marvin, the only one left, a likeable kid in the sweat-shirt age met us at the door.

"Hi, sister grave-bait," he grinned at Betty.

She returned his grin, but feebly. Mason said he shouldn't talk like that. Betty's father and his new wife had arrived before us. Both of them seemed like nice folks. I had questioned both of them exhaustively several days before. Neither one stood to gain a penny. And Rene D'Andrea, like Moran, had lost two children, both of them girls.

"Chin up, sweetheart," he greeted his daughter. "We're going to lick this thing." She said she hoped so. So did I. And I wasn't thinking of the money angle, I like anyone with intestinal fortitude and Betty D'Andrea had it. Outside of the one night she'd slopped over she was taking the thing in her stride.

The living room was in the back of the house, overlooking what I imagined was the garden. Allen was sitting in one corner of it with Pierce, earnestly discussing whatever it is high-priced lawyers discuss in their off moments. Charlie was still a trifle provoked with me for the grilling I had put him through, but he offered to shake hands. "That is, on one condition," he qualified his offer. "Your admission you are convinced I am not a mass murderer and merely called you into the case to cover my back trail." "You cut a wide one," I told him. "I sure as hell thought I had something when Paddy Quinn said that you and Flora used to hold hands."

"We did," Pierce grinned. "I don't know where it might have led, but once Gene D'Andrea cut in I didn't have a chance. I don't know what Gene had, but whatever it was, it made women crazy about him."

There was the usual round of cocktails. I sipped Betty's before she drank it, much to her indignation. "Why, you don't think," she exclaimed, "that my own uncle and aunt would poison me?"

I said I was past the thinking stage. From here on I hoped to emulate the frog who, having fallen into the milk can, had to keep moving and churning around in the hope that he would make butter and be able to climb out.

Haig showed up at nine with a surprise. He said he had been in telephone contact that morning with Flora D'Andrea at Loon Lake and she had insisted on being at the get-together, qualifying her insistence only by her ability to charter a plane to fly her to Chicago.

I studied the faces of the family as he told us. Despite the thirty-year-old will contest all of them genuinely seemed to like "Auntie" Flora, as they called her.

Rene D'Andrea explained it to me. "The mess was Gene's making, not Flora's. And all the time the will has been in the courts, Flora has been most generous about making advances. Outside of what she has done for the children, time after time she has come to my personal financial rescue."

It sounded like appeasement to me, throw the dog a bone and he won't bark. But I didn't say so. I did ask him the same question I had asked his sister Renee: that is, if his brother Gene had been an adopted child.

He said he didn't know for certain. They had been raised as blood brothers and sister. And it wasn't until after Gene had committed suicide that someone had begun to circulate the rumor that Gene had been born out of wedlock to their father before he and their mother had married.

I asked if they had attempted to trace down the rumor. He said they had, without success. "But personally," he concluded, "I can't see what possible difference that could make."

The germ of an idea eating at my mind, I thought I could. I asked him if Gene had been cruel as a child.

Rene told me, "Gene was a veritable little devil, the kind that pulls wings off of flies, blows up toads with straws, and actually likes to drown puppies."

I checked the various notes I'd made and walked over to where Allen and Pierce were sitting. "What did you tell me," I asked

Allen, "was the name of that firm of private investigators who are still checking on Marcell's disappearance?"

He told me, "Gleason and Baily."

There it was. It had been in front of my nose all the time, ever since my conversation with Paddy. I had the whole thing then. I thought I knew what to do about it. But I couldn't run out on Betty, leaving her unprotected. Besides I wanted to see Auntie Flora.

I asked Allen if he remembered the firm's address offhand. He said he did not but would be glad to look it up in the morning and phone me the information. I walked out in the hall and checked the classified phone book. There was no Gleason and Baily listed.

"Phone Prosper, Allen & McCready in the morning," I advised Inspector Haig, "and get the address of a firm of alleged private investigators by the name of Gleason and Baily. You'll probably find they have desk room somewhere. And on one of the desks you should find the fingerprints of the big hood I killed at Perry's."

From then on, up to the almost-fatal payoff, the gathering was a bore as we exhumed the dead children one by one and their respective parents wept over them.

The Morans had been summering at Loon Lake when their oldest son Georges had died. It had happened early one morning. He had gone down to the lake alone, as was his custom, and had not returned. Two days later his body washed up on shore. There had been no evidence of foul play and the local coroner, a Doctor Gleason, had stamped the death as "accidental drowning."

I asked if they had been staying in the D'Andrea mansion.

Moran said they had not. "We were summering in one of the guest cottages on the grounds," he told me. "We were on the best of terms with Flora but she already had her building bug and the main house was impossible for the hammering."

That had been in 1935 and had been the last summer that any of them had spent at the lake.

Charles was dug up next. On the night before his twenty-first birthday his parents had given a party to celebrate his coming of age. Only the two families had been present. Shortly before ten, Moran senior had been called, erroneously as it transpired, to the bedside of a patient. Promptly at ten, Auntie Flora had called from Loon Lake to offer Charles her congratulations and advise him to spend his money wisely. A few minutes after ten, and before his father returned, he was dead. An autopsy disclosed he had died of some form of obscure poison believed to have been administered in powder form.

"He had a cut on his lip?" I asked Renee.

She looked at me, puzzled. "Why yes. Some stranger had picked an argument with Charles only that afternoon and punched him repeatedly in the mouth."

"And what time was it when the man from the telephone company came to check the trouble on the line?"

"He came while we were eating," Moran answered. "But how did you know? I haven't thought of him from that moment to this."

I looked at Haig. He looked sick. He spread his hands in a futile gesture. "No one told me about the repair man."

"The poison was sprinkled on the mouthpiece of the phone," I explained to Moran, and dug up Madelaine's body.

From what her father and mother told us I was inclined to believe her death was accidental. At least it could have been. Then we started in on Rene's children.

He looked old and worn and tired. All of the time we talked he fondled Betty's hand. His daughter Anna's death was definitely murder and listed as such in the police files. She had been alone in the family house and Rene and the girl's mother had returned from a late party to find their home looted of most of its valuables and their daughter dead on her bedroom floor, brutally slugged to death.

I asked Betty where she and her sister Marcell had been at the time. She said she had been ten years old, in bed asleep, and had heard nothing until she heard her mother scream. Her sister Marcell, nineteen, had been at a dance with a boy friend.

I asked where Auntie Flora had been and was informed she had been at Loon Lake.

"Surely, Mercer," Rene D'Andrea said, "you don't suspect Flora of complicity in these crimes?"

I told him my ancestors had been English and I followed the custom of English law in all matters concerning crime. To me every one was guilty until they had been proved innocent.

We took up Marcell's disappearance next. That one was really a honey. A high-spirited, strong-willed girl with a definite flair for writing advertising copy, she had left home when she was twenty and established her own apartment.

On the morning of her disappearance she had reported at nine o'clock at the advertising agency for which she was working, informing her immediate superior, however, that she was leaving at eleven o'clock to collect her share of God knows how many million dollars.

There had been a lot of good-natured joshing about it in the office, but she had left promptly at eleven. Someone had seen her in the elevator. Someone else had seen her cross the walk. Then she had stepped into a passing cab—and had never been seen again.

Rene blamed himself. He blamed his divorced wife. In the light of what had happened to Anna they should never have allowed Marcell to leave home. If he had escorted her personally to the office of Prosper, Allen & McCready—

"She would have been killed some other way," I told him. "Possibly shot down on the street. Our killer cut it pretty close that time."

"Our killer!" Haig said sharply. "Then you know who it is."

"Yes, I think I do," I told him.

Any further revelation was interrupted by the doorbell.

"That must be Auntie Flora," Marvin said hopefully. "I'll let her in."

He started for the door. Haig would have let him go. I stopped him halfway across the room. "Not without me, sonny."

"Gosh you're suspicious," he grinned.

I said in my line I had to be.

By the time we were halfway to the glass door we could see the caller wasn't a woman. It was a uniformed man. At least a man wearing a uniformed cap.

"Darn it," Marvin said disappointed. "It's only a Western Union boy. Shucks. That means Auntie Flora isn't coming. She probably couldn't charter a plane."

It was a good gag. It fooled me. My hand dropped away from my gun butt as the lad on the stoop pushed the button again and called, "Western Union," impatiently.

I opened the door and Marvin took the telegram.

"Sign here," the lad on the stoop said brusquely. But instead of a book he was holding a gun in his hand.

I admit it caught me off balance. Even so I didn't do badly. I caught the twin heir by the collar and yanked him around behind me, taking the burst of slugs intended for him through my left arm.

The messenger didn't wait to fire a second burst. He thought, for one thing, that he had gotten me. Besides, the grounds were lousy with Haig's men. He wasn't, or thought he wasn't, taking any chances. But as it turns out in most cases, quantity seldom replaces quality. One man could have stopped the would-be killer. But with heads popping up back of every other bush everyone, including myself, was afraid to fire at the fleeing man for fear of shooting someone else. I did throw two slugs at his heels as he darted across the parkway into the traffic on the drive but couldn't tell if I had hit him or not.

Then the criss-cross of cars on the drive blotted him from sight. Haig charged past me into the night and the things that he called his men would have had anyone less than an inspector on the carpet for language unbecoming an officer. But as one of them told him to his face:

"Now who in hell would expect a Western Union boy to turn out to be a killer?"

I turned back into the hall. Marvin, white-faced and trying hard not to cry, the way a kid of that age will, said, "Thank you, Mr. Mercer." He wasn't cocky now. And when his mother, weeping buckets herself, took him into her arms, he did bawl.

Haig came back grim-faced to report the would-be killer had gotten away and to ask if I had gotten a good look at him.

I said I had not. There was no light on the stoop and he'd worn the brim of his cap so cocked as to hide his eyes. "But don't let that worry you," I told Haig. "I know who he is."

I picked the telegram from the floor. It was post-dated Loon Lake and read:

> Sorry. Unable to charter a plane because of weather conditions. Am leaving in the morning and should arrive by noon. Meanwhile spare no expense to protect Betty and Marvin. Hire more private detectives if Inspector Haig thinks wise, I will foot all bills. All of my love.
>
>   Aunt Flora

Eating humble pie, Haig wanted to know if I thought the telegram was a fake. I said I doubted it although that would be easy to check. I said it was far more likely the would-be killer, knowing the approximate time of the arrival of the message, had slugged the messenger.

Charlie Pierce said I seemed to be calling my shots but asked how the killer had known that Marvin would answer the door. I admitted that one was beyond me but pointed out that if neither

Betty or Marvin had answered the door all that he had to do was deliver the telegram and no one would be the wiser.

Haig started to ask the question that was burning on his tongue but I shook my head at him.

Betty and young Mason had crowded into the hall with the others, Gwen Hayden close behind them with a small-calibered gun in one hand. Betty was the first to notice the blood on my shirt. "Those shots!" she cried. "They struck you!"

I unbuttoned my shirt and looked at my side. One of the slugs had nicked me slightly. "That's right," I agreed with her. I took off my coat and rolled up my sleeve to see what damage had been done to the cork-and-metal affair that Uncle Sam had given me to replace the flesh-and-blood affair the boys of the Briefly Rising Sun had considered expendable. None of the slags had struck a control. There was nothing wrong with my arm that I couldn't fix with a pair of pliers.

My most immediate concern was Betty. I had things that I wanted to do. But I had been hired to protect her. I couldn't be in two places at one time. I couldn't take her with me and I didn't dare to leave her for fear the killer, desperate now, might double back. So I thought up what seemed to me a logical solution.

Pointing at the poor little rich girl I told Haig, "Arrest that woman, Inspector. I accuse her of being an accessory before the fact of attempted murder."

Maybe there is such a charge. I wouldn't know.

In the dead silence that followed, Haig looked at me like I was crazy. Then, no lame brain, he saw what I was driving at.

"Right," he said shortly. "Get Miss D'Andrea's wrap. Miss Hayden. I am taking her down to the Bureau and locking her up on Mr. Mercer's charge."

That much was off of my mind. Haig would be able to hold her at least twenty-four hours without having to book her. She would be safe for that length of time. And a lot could happen in twenty-four hours. I intended it should.

Tears trickling down her cheeks, Betty's voice was that of an unjustly punished child. "But I haven't done a thing. Mr. Mercer, except what you've told me to do. And I *can't* be an accessory to anything. I haven't been out of yours or Miss Hayden's sight for two weeks."

"Don't give me that hey nonny stuff," I said gruffly.

Pierce swore, "The man is out of his mind."

Young Mason swore he was going to get a lawyer.

"There are two of them in the room," I pointed out. Then I walked Haig into a corner and he and I had a heart to heart talk on the subject of resurrection.

Spring hadn't gotten around to getting this far north as yet. Early morning was so cold the snow creaked under my feet and great patches of it still clung to the spreading branches of the first growth pine that rose high on both sides of the clearing.

From the slight knoll on which I stood, the D'Andrea monstrosity looked even more like a Rube Goldberg creation than it had the summer before. But studying it carefully, I could see it had been built on a plan carefully masked by the series of seemingly meaningless wings. It was, from the vantage at which I viewed it, a huge wooden spider web with the original D'Andrea home the core or the base of the maze.

Smoke rose from one of the chimneys of this inner core and I could see lights in the windows. Beyond the house proper was Loon Lake, a solidly frozen body of water perhaps three miles wide and five miles long. To the left of the house on a level plain, and also on the shore of the lake, I could see three hangars and tattered wind sock rising from what appeared to be a small private air field.

I considered going directly to the house but doubted if once I had left the hill I be able to find my way through the maze to the inner core. Besides I had several fish to fry and I wanted it to be known I was in town before I turned the fire under the griddle.

Small towns begin their days early. Most of the store windows were lighted. A dozen cars were parked at the curb. I drove directly to the Baily Hotel. A big frame affair it had been filled to capacity when Sherry and I had tried to get in but had, I imagined, few guests but traveling men during the winter months.

I asked for a room with bath, paid for it in advance and went into the coffee shop. A well-padded, middle-aged waitress was making fresh coffee in the steamer. I ordered coffee, sausages and hot cakes.

She took a loot at my clothes and asked me if I had been driving all night.

"No. I just drove up from Marquette," I told her. That much was true. I had flown from Chicago to Marquette. And if Paddy Quinn had found the Loon Lake authorities uncooperative, I hadn't had the same experience. At least not with the State Patrol.

It was one of their cars I was driving, or rather, a car belonging to one of them.

Over my coffee I asked the waitress if there was an airport in town.

"Yeah. Kind of a one," she informed me. "Old Doc Gleason's boy started one out at the lake last summer. It was supposed to be a flying school. But he never taught no one to fly that I know of. He spends most of his time flying Mrs. D'Andrea here and there or taking long jaunts with Sam Baily."

I said flying must be interesting and asked if he ever flew nights. Yawning, she told me he did. "He just came back from somewhere last night. At least I heard a plane about three o'clock this morning. You want syrup or sausage grease on your hot cakes?"

I said syrup would be fine. From where I sat I could see almost all one side of Loon Lake's main street. There was a Gleason movie house and the one-story bank on the corner featured the names of both Baily and Gleason in the gold leaf on its window. There was also a Baily dry goods store and a Gleason filling station.

When the waitress brought my hot cakes I pointed out the fact, suggesting that the Baily and Gleason families must have been among Loon Lake's first settlers.

Her smile was wry. "You don't know the half of it, Mister. Sheriff Baily and old Doc Gleason *are* Loon Lake. You should see homes they live in. And the way they act. Honest to goodness it makes you sick sometimes. You'd think they came over on the Mayflower with Pocahontas, or something."

A blue-eyed, elderly man with his overalls tucked into high-laced boots, and wearing a shabby blue-and-red mackinaw came in and, sitting down at the counter beside me, wiped his mustache with the back of his hand. "Just passing through, stranger?" he asked me.

He had a pearl-handled gun on one thigh and I had a fair idea he had a star pinned to his suspenders.

"No. I have some business in town," I told him. "My name is Mercer, Matt Mercer. And I've called to see Mrs. D'Andrea about a grave."

It didn't faze him. He merely said, "Oh," drank a cup of coffee and went back out into the cold.

"That's Joel Gray, the day constable," the friendly waitress told me. "He hates Sheriff Baily like sin on account of he should be sheriff but even his friends are afraid to vote for him on account of the sheriff having a mortgage on most of the farms in the county. But what did you mean you've called to see Mrs. D'Andrea about a grave? You selling tombstones?"

Before I could tell her I wasn't, a swarthy man wearing a soiled cook's cap poked his head in through the swinging door leading to the kitchen and called, "You're talking too much again, Mabel. What do you want to do? Get both of us fired?"

I paid my check, asked the room clerk for my key and went up and lay down on my bed with my gun convenient to my hand. It took about forty minutes for the news I was in town to reach the ears I wanted it to.

I don't know what I expected Baily to look like. Whatever it was, he wasn't it. A big man with flesh hanging where fat should be, he looked a little like Paddy Quinn. He also looked like a man who had carried too big a burden too far. What's more he hated my intestines. And the more that I looked at him the plainer it was why he should hate me.

"Excuse me for barging in like this," he apologized. "But the name Matt Mercer isn't too common and when I heard a man by that name was in town I wondered if you could be the Matt Mercer the Chicago papers have reported to be acting as Miss Betty D'Andrea's bodyguard?"

I said I was that Mercer.

He introduced himself as the local sheriff, but seemed at a loss just how to proceed from there. He finally asked outright what I was doing at Loon Lake. I told him the same thing I had told the constable. "I want to see Mrs. D'Andrea about a grave."

CHAPTER FOUR

THE HOUSE THAT
LOTS OF JACK BUILT

E KNEW WHAT I WAS TALKING ABOUT. I could tell by the way his fingers shook as he lighted a cigar. But he didn't know what to do about it. When he couldn't stall any longer he said, "That is a rather interesting statement, Mr. Mercer. Just what do you mean by it?"

I said I would prefer to explain that to Mrs. D'Andrea, but seeing he represented the law as far as Loon Lake was concerned I would be pleased to have him accompany me when I did talk to her.

He chewed that one over, shook his head and lied, "I'm afraid you are too deep for me. But I not only accept your offer; I insist on being present when you do talk to Mrs. D'Andrea. You—are alone?"

I said I was and he seemed vastly relieved.

"We'd best get going then," he said flatly. "It seems to me I heard someone say that Mrs. D'Andrea was flying to Chicago this morning. Come on. We'll use your car."

A thin man with a gray goatee was standing on the walk just outside of the hotel. Baily introduced him as Doctor Gleason. "His name is Mercer," he told the other man. "And he wants to see Flora D'Andrea."

"Oh. Is that so?" Gleason said. "Hmm. Funny. I was just on my way to get my car and drive out there. Mind if I ride with you, Sheriff?"

It was so patent it was funny,

"Not at all," Baily said. "But if it's okay with Mr. Mercer, I think we'll use his car." He got in back. Gleason slid in beside me and slammed the door.

I was glad to see Constable Gray watching us from a doorway. Somehow I didn't feel quite so alone.

As we got out of town. Baily leaned forward and said, "Mr. Mercer says he wants to see Flora about a grave."

"Well," Gleason said, "you don't say. Yours must be an interesting profession, Mr. Mercer."

I admitted I seldom had to take any great quantity of benzedrine tablets and asked if either of them had ever heard of a firm of private investigators in Chicago by the name of Gleason and Baily.

Both me straightened in their seats but said that they had not.

I left it there until we reached the house. Close up, it looked even worse than it did at a distance. Some of it had been painted and some had not. A group of blue-nosed carpenters were warming their hands at a fire they had built in an old oil drum.

One of them wanted to know if the sheriff knew where Mrs. D'Andrea wanted them to start in next. Baily said he did not but that he would speak to Mrs. D'Andrea and send word back to them. "Park right over there," he told me, "under that portico."

I parked where I was told and he led the way into what appeared to be a kitchen with a bathtub in the center of the floor. From there he had his choice of five doors. He chose one that led into a forty-foot ballroom that, in turn, opened into a bathroom from which a flight of stairs led up to another kitchen which, in turn, opened into a parlor complete with a mirrored wall.

None of the rooms was heated. None of them was furnished; The whole thing was jerrybuilt, and where the plaster had fallen off the walls I could see the outside through two-inch cracks in the siding.

The rest of the house was as bad. The damnedest things kept cropping up in the damnedest places. As if in explanation, Gleason told me, "Mrs. D'Andrea is slightly eccentric."

It was a masterpiece of understatement if I've ever heard one.

Then the character of the building changed. The inner wings were well and substantially built. After passing through perhaps fifty rooms we descended a flight of stairs, and Baily rapped on a closed door at the bottom. "It's Sheriff Baily, Mrs. D'Andrea," he called. "That private detective you had your Chicago lawyer hire to protect Betty wants to see you."

Flora opened the door in person and a gust of heat rushed out. The picture I had seen of her failed to do her justice. She looked closer to forty than fifty-five, and a young forty at that. Her hair was bleached, but artistically so, and she still bulged just enough in all of the proper places. She was dressed in a smart traveling suit and carrying a mink coat over one arm.

"What are you doing here, Mr. Mercer?" she asked, puzzled. "You are supposed to be guarding Betty." The fingers of one hand caught at her throat. "Don't tell me that something has happened to her?"

It was well done. If instead of marrying Gene D'Andrea she had left muscle dancing for the dramatic stage, I have no doubt she could have gone fat.

"No. Nothing has happened to Betty," I told her. "And nothing is going to happen to her."

"Oh I'm *so* glad," she said, relieved. "Gene's money has been nothing but a curse from the very day he died."

"Blew his brains out," Baily told me.

Gleason added, "Messiest thing I ever saw. I'll never forget how he looked in his coffin."

Baily grew dramatic. "There we were, hot after him, ready to arrest him for murder. He knew he didn't have a chance with us. So—"

"Yes. You told me before," I turned him off. "So he ups with his trusty .45 and took off for the promised land."

Baily looked at me sourly. I looked around the room. This wing of the house was both heated and furnished. The furniture alone had cost as much as my house and lot.

I sat down on the arm of a chair. "Look," I said, "there's no sense wasting time, I've come to see you about a grave."

It grew so still in the room that I could hear my arteries hardening.

She said, finally, "A grave?"

I nodded. "That's right." I included the others in the remark. "Look. Why stall around any longer? We are all adults, I hope. And I know the whole thing. I know why none of the D'Andrea heirs have ever lived to the ripe old age of twenty-one. I know how Gleason and Baily, here, came to own all of Loon Lake." I threw in the bait. "And I want in on the racket, see? Then ten thousand dollars Pierce offered me is peanuts. I want at least one hundred grand in cash, or when I leave here I am going to blow the whole thing to the State Patrol."

Breathing hard, Flora said, "The man is crazy."

"Out of his mind," Doctor Gleason agreed.

"Not by that hair on your chinny chin chin," I grinned at him. "I'm not as crazy as you are if you really think you can get away with murder. The old saws have a way of coming true. One of them is that murder will out. There is another to the effect that it takes brains to make big money. That was the first thing that tipped me. No muscle dancer ever lived who had the brains to run a few-million-dollar stake up to the present size of the D'Andrea fortune. You had to have help," I told Flora. I scowled at Gleason and Baily. "And both Sheriff Baily and Doctor Gleason seem to be excellent business men."

Both men seemed relieved rather than frightened by the left-handed compliment, but Baily shook his head. "You're barking up the wrong tree, Mercer. And I am afraid that your attempted shake-down has failed. Tom Gleason and I may be good small-town business men," he walked right into the trap, "but we know nothing what-so-ever about the stock market."

I swung on Flora. *"Who did advise you then?"*

She did her best to tear her handkerchief to shreds but couldn't seem to find any words in it.

"Flora," Gleason helped her out, "got the financial tips that helped her to build the D'Andrea fortune up to its present size from her spirit control. The same spirit control who warned her that if she ever ceased to expand her home she would meet with sudden misfortune."

I said that was quick thinking. "But now can you tell me this, Doctor Gleason? Or will we have to call the spirits in? How has it happened that despite the present size of the fortune and Mrs. D'Andrea's well-known generosity, none of Gene D'Andrea's heirs have ever come into their share?"

"Ah," Sheriff Baily said softly. "Now we come to the grave you spoke of."

"Five graves," I said coldly. "Georges', Charles', Madelaine's, Anna's, and Marcell's."

"Nonsense. Arrant nonsense," Doctor Gleason snorted. "Far too much has been made of that angle. Their deaths were purely coincidental."

"But convenient," I pointed out. "Even Inspector Haig of Chicago Homicide and Mrs. D'Andrea's own lawyers seem in doubt as to what would be the eventual disposition of the fortune should none of the heirs live to collect their share. But I will venture a layman's guess that, having done so well with it to date, the money would remain in Mrs. D'Andrea's control for at least the balance of her life."

She licked at her lips and the gesture somehow disgusted me. It reminded me of a buzzard feeding on carrion. However it turned out I wanted the whole thing over—and fast.

Slipping my gun from its holster and resting it on my knee I tried to force the issue. "I charge the three of you with the five murders. Now what are you going to do about it?"

A little of the gray left Baily's face as he dug up a small portion of courage somewhere. "Laugh at you," he said unsteadily. "The charge you make is absurd and can readily be disproved in any court of law. With the exception of Georges D'Andrea's death which was accidental, and so certified by Doctor Gleason as county coroner, not one of the three of us has been within hundreds of miles of the so-called crimes when they happened, and we can prove it."

I slapped my next one right into his teeth. "Can you also prove that your son, the one lying unclaimed in a drawer at the Chicago morgue, wasn't present at the time that Doctor Gleason's son shot Paddy Quinn and attempted to kill me?"

I had known he would break. He did. "Damn you, Mercer!" Baily screamed. "My boy was worth two of you."

"Then you should have raised him better," I said. "You shouldn't have allowed him to keep the company you did. Another very true old adage is that one rotten apple will spoil a barrel." I raised my voice. "All right. Let's get it over with. Come out, rotten apple! I don't know which door you are standing behind, but I do know you are listening to me. Come on out and join the party, Gene!"

In the silence that followed, the former muscle dancer began to cry. Her mink coat slipped unnoticed to the floor. Then, somewhere behind me, a door opened and a man's voice advised me, "Lay your gun carefully on the carpet, Mercer. Then kick it over toward Sheriff Baily and it could be that you will live a few minutes longer."

I did as I was told, then turned around on the arm of the chair.

A tall, well-dressed, handsome man with a thin, ascetic face and jet-black hair was regarding me gravely from the doorway. He was holding a long-barreled Colt in one hand and an automatic in the other. Behind him, also armed, was the young husky who had slugged me in the Sherman and run out on me at Paddy's.

I got up off the arm of the chair. "Welcome back to the land of the living, Lazarus. For a man who blew out his brains thirty-three years ago, you are looking remarkably well."

The supposedly dead Gene D'Andrea swore at me.

"Tch, tch, Gene," I reproved him. "Remember Auntie Flora is present."

He came into the room slowly, young Gleason at his heels. Still tearful, Flora wanted to know what they were going to do.

D'Andrea said he would think of something.

"It better be good," I needled. Before I could say more, the phone on the end table rang. He nodded Flora to it.

One palm over the mouthpiece, she reported, "It's the carpenters. They say they are finished with that wing and want to know what to do next."

He considered his answer, told her, "Tell them to go home. That phase of this thing is finished. And the fewer eyes there are around during the next few hours, the better for out purpose."

Baily shuddered violently. "No more killings, Gene. Please."

Flora told the carpenters to go home.

D'Andrea turned his eyes on Baily. They were gray and flat, unblinking. "What do you suggest?" he asked "Phoning the State Patrol?"

The once-fat sheriff shuddered even more violently. "I wish to God," he whimpered, "that I had never gotten into this."

"You should have thought of that thirty-three years ago," D'Andrea told him. His face and eyes were expressionless. His voice reminded me of Peter Lorre playing one of his suavely sinister characters. But Gene D'Andrea wasn't playing. He turned his flat eyes on me. "We'll have to kill you, of course. I'm sorry I didn't kill you last night. For a few moments I was hopeful I had."

I said, "You were the Western Union boy."

He nodded. "Yes. Time is running short, as far as Betty is concerned. I was going to announce the telegram was for her. But your being there spoiled that. You have spoiled quite a few things for me, Mercer. Everything was running so smoothly until you came into the case."

I asked if that was so why he had told Flora to commission Charlie Pierce to engage me.

"I didn't," he admitted. "We merely told him to engage a private detective and to spare no expense. There have been so many 'tragedies' among the D'Andrea heirs I thought it best that Flora have an unassailable cover. I thought I could outwit you. But I see now I made a mistake."

I told him it was one of the few mistakes he had made. It seemed to please him.

"I think I have been fairly clever," he admitted, "especially for a 'dead' man forced to depend on others for most of his leg work." His eyes moved back to Sheriff Daily's face. "Principally stupid oafs like you and your dead son." His eyes moved on to the Gleasons. "And on a pair of cowards like you."

Young Gleason flushed but said nothing.

I asked him what kind of a punk he was to let a fifty-five year old man get away with a remark like that—and those damned eyes came back to me.

"It is no use trying to stir up dissension among us, Mercer," D'Andrea told me. "We are in a bad spot. They all know it. They also know the only possible thing that can pull us through is my brains. You knew, or at least suspected, I was still alive when you came here. To how many persons did you entrust that suspicion?"

I told him the truth. "Two men. Inspector Haig of the Chicago Headquarters Homicide Squad and an Inspector Harry Gillman of the Michigan State Patrol."

"That makes our position difficult," he admitted. "Otherwise you could simply disappear." He smiled for the first time. "As Marcell did." Still holding the automatic leveled on my middle, he scratched his cheek thoughtfully with the long barrel of the Colt. "Nor, with Betty still alive and due to come into her inheritance in only a few hours, can we waste much time on you." He came to a decision. "No. It looks as if you and I are going to have to make a deal."

I was interested to know how much he would offer. It would be nice to know in moments I was scrambling for a living, and finding the scrambling hard, that I had once turned down a half-million-dollar bribe, "How much do you offer?" I asked him.

He said, "You insult my intelligence, Mercer. Give me some credit as a judge of men. You wouldn't cover for murder for ten times thirty million dollars. No. I was speaking of your children."

My children?

He left me sweating to turn to Flora. "It looks very much, my dear, as if I am going to have to depend on you to take care of Betty. I will describe the method and detail later. If you are clever about it, I doubt you will even be suspected. After all, you *are* her loving aunt. You advanced sixty thousand dollars for her debut."

The woman worshipped the heel. I could see it in her eyes. She said, "Whatever you say, Gene."

My throat was dry. I demanded. "What was that crack about my children?" He ignored me to tell young Gleason, "You will fly Flora to Chicago this morning just as we had planned. And you will take your father with you. You observed the routine of the Mercer family as you were instructed?"

"I did," the younger Gleason said. "Mercer's wife takes their twins to the pre-kindergarten school every afternoon at one o'clock. They stay there until four when she calls for them again."

I said, "You leave my kids out of this!" a mental picture of what Rene D'Andrea had told me flashing through my mind:

"Gene was a veritable little devil, the kind that pulls wings off of flies, blows up toads with straws, and actually likes to drown puppies."

D'Andrea continued to ignore me. "You will assist your son in getting the children and taking them to a spot I will designate," he informed Doctor Gleason. "And you will stay in that spot with them until you hear from me."

"No," the elder Gleason protested.

"But yes," the resurrected dead man insisted. "For years you and Sheriff Baily and your two sons have bled me. I have made you rich and a power in the community, all for a little favor you did for me many years ago. I would have hanged in those days. Today, if caught, I will go to the chair. But I can promise you if I do that you will both go with me."

Sheriff Baily whimpered there was no capital punishment in Michigan.

"Ah. True." D'Andrea smiled for the second time. "But all we did was conspire in Michigan. I committed the murders in Illinois."

"Lay off my twins," I told him. "I am a reasonable man. What kind of a deal do you want from me?"

He said, "In a few moments you will phone Inspector Haig of Homicide and Inspector Gillman that after a thorough investigation of the old D'Andrea mansion you are convinced you erred in believing me alive. Then you will remain here with me until your twins are in my hands. After that, what happens to them will be strictly up to you."

I asked how he hoped to waltz the twins out of their pre-kindergarten school.

"You are going to write a note to their teacher," he told me. "They should have a sample of your handwriting and when presented by a professional man of Doctor Gleason's appearance . . ."

I took a quick step toward him and he thumbed back the hammer of the Colt. "Or you can die right now," he continued, "secure in the knowledge that your children won't be very far behind you. And I assure you, Mercer, I am a man who keeps my promises."

I was beginning to see how he had built the D'Andrea fortune to its present size. The man was clever.

"Well, you seem to have it about sewed up," I admitted. "Just tell me this one thing, Gene."

His smile was patronizing. "What do you wish to know?"

I asked him, "Just how are Flora and the two Gleasons going to get from here to Chicago to kill Betty and kidnap my twins with the house surrounded by State Police? And just where are *you* going to hide?"

He turned to Sheriff Baily, livid, "You said when you phoned me that Mercer was alone and there wasn't a State Patrolman in town."

"There wasn't," I answered for Baily. "But if you think I am one of those private detectives you read about in books who go poking their heads into vipers' nests without a pit of their own to hiss in, you are crazy. At six o'clock this morning, an hour before I hit town, Inspector Gillman phoned Constable Gray to be on the look-out for me. And as soon as he saw us leave the hotel Gray was under instructions to phone the farmhouse where Inspector Gillman and a flock of his troopers were waiting."

His face a shade paler than the belly of a shark, the resurrected dead man trained both of his guns on me. But by then I was in motion, my hideout in my hand, blazing away at his knee-caps as I dove for the carpet.

He went down screaming and blasting at everything in sight. The younger Gleason, caught in the back by a slug just as he wrenched open a door, fell through it flat on his face. I felt two slugs pound my shoulder, hard. But I managed to get to my feet again and kick D'Andrea in the jaw.

The elder Gleason and Sheriff Baily wanted no part of hot lead. Both of them stood with their hands over their heads.

"You louse!" Flora screamed at me. "You've killed him! You've killed my Gene!"

But she wasn't screaming very loud. She had the fingers of both of her hands laced under her left breast, and as I watched, little trickles of what it takes began to paint her white fingers the same color as her nails.

I picked up all of the guns I could find, including two that I found on Baily, then sat down on the floor with my back against the wall, thinking what a hell of a way I had picked to make a living and hoping the boys wouldn't be too long in finding their way through the maze.

"It looks like we've lost," Baily whimpered.

"Yeah. So it does," I agreed.

Her fingers and nails one color now, the former muscle dancer who had loved not wisely but too well tried to kneel by the heel she had loved, and collapsed on top of him.

At least one part of her alleged metaphysical prognosis had come true. The day she had stopped building the wooden wet) around her spider, she had died, with a slug from one of his guns in her heart . . .

After leaving the doctor I had gone to for a check-up and a bit of fresh repacking, Sherry wanted to know if I was certain I felt strong enough to join the wake in Inspector Haig's office. I told her Charlie Pierce would be there and for an eleven-thousand, eight-hundred-dollar check I would cheerfully climb Mt. Whitney with the twins on my back.

She said I would look damned silly doing it but agreed it was a lot of money.

Pierce and Allen were both there, as well as Betty and Mason. The men all shook hands with me and Betty kissed me. "I think you are wonderful," she said.

"We won't keep you bit a minute, Matt," Haig told me. "Both Baily and Gleason have talked their heads off for hours. The story was just as you told it to me. When Paddy Quinn showed up with his warrant, they beat it out to the D'Andrea place and made a deal with Gene. For so much down and so much now and then they agreed to pass him off as a suicide. Facing the rope, it was a God-send to D'Andrea and he jumped at it . . .

"As deputy coroner, Gleason certified him as dead. He also saw that Paddy and the town folks didn't get too good a look at the body, just enough to convince them Gene was dead. But Paddy, so Baily says, has always been a sore spot with Gene. He was always afraid the old man, on thinking it over, would smell a rat, and he transferred his own fear to young Baily and Gleason who were taking up the leg work where their old men had left off. That's why they trailed you to Paddy's and shot him. They were afraid he had finally worked it out.

"And, of course, as you figured out, that crazy building was just a super hide-out for Gene. It would have been almost impossible for the police to ferret him out of the place—even if we had known he was alive."

Pierce said, "Gene *had* to be smart. He *had* to increase the fortune to support the drains on it. More, he knew what he was doing when he made that will. He knew he couldn't live in his tomb without money and he intended to see that none of the heirs he named would live to collect their allotted shares."

I asked if he had admitted the killings.

Haig said that so far D'Andrea had admitted nothing, his jaw being broken in two places. But Gleason and Baily had given them enough to work on and he was certain he could send D'Andrea to the chair if he never confessed. Haig said, "It was Gene who drowned Georges. It was Gene who poisoned the mouthpiece of the phone. He boasted to both Gleason and Baily that his own sister had seen him but had failed to recognize him in his repairman's outfit . . .

"Madelaine came next. She was easy. He ran her down with a car. He was the prowler who killed Anna. But both Baily and Gleason swear he would never say just what happened to Marcell."

"Once he started killing," Haig continued, "he couldn't stop. Once the money was out of Flora's hands he had no way of getting more. Then, too, he considered it *his* money."

That reminded me of what I had come for. I told Pierce to get busy writing me a check. He started to protest that the client who had commissioned him to engage me was dead, but Allen told him to keep his commitment and he would see the estate okayed it.

Haig scowled at the size of the check as Pierce handed it to him to hand to me. "I work almost two years for that much," he scowled.

Sherry scowled back at him. "Well, what do you want Matt to do, cry about it? After all he has twins to feed."

And then the clock on the wall struck midnight and old Mr. Allen got out of his chair and shook hands gravely with Betty. "Congratulations, my dear. And may your money bring you all the happiness in the world."

The first of the legitimate D'Andrea heirs had come under the wire a winner.

"Betty came over and kissed me again. "Thank you so much, Mr. Mercer." Then she went back and stood in front of Mason. "If you won't ask me, I'll ask you," she said softly. "Will you please marry me, Mr. Mason?"

All of us laughed but Mason. He couldn't laugh. The young punk had his mouth full and was acting like he enjoyed it. In fact he was still making up for lost time when Sherry and I left the office.

"It all just goes to show you," I told her, "what can come out of culture. If we hadn't gone to see *Hamlet* that night we wouldn't have had this check."

She said, "Darn the check," and I noticed that her eyes were wet. She glanced wistfully back into the office. "Am I still attractive to you, Matt? Do you still love me like that? I mean like when we were first married?"

I kissed her hard, right there in the hall. When I'd finished her eyes were shining.

"Yes. I guess you do," she told me.

MARRY THE SIXTH FOR MURDER!

CHAPTER ONE

LOST CORPSE

THERE WAS NOTHING MAGNETIC OR ROMANTIC about the great lover's voice over the phone. His words were blurred with a trace of hysteria behind them as he said: "I'm in a jam, a bad one, Slagle. Can you come right over? Please."

It was four o'clock in the morning. I started to hang up, and changed my mind. It was the "please" that stopped me. I hadn't known the word was in Steve Millet's vocabulary. I did ask if he was certain the matter couldn't wait for a few hours.

"I'm positive," he told me. "I—I think I've killed someone. But I can't talk about it over the phone."

I asked where he was calling from. He said his San Francisco Valley ranch. I promised I would get there as soon as I could and cradled the phone. Sally woke up while I was dressing and wanted to know where I thought I was going at four o'clock in the morning with it still raining as it was. I told her Steve Millet had phoned and it would seem he was in another jam.

She said, "Nothing trivial, I hope," lifted her lips to be kissed, then buried her face back in the pillow.

I kissed her, found my trenchcoat in the closet and sloshed on out to the garage, sorry I hadn't worn boots. Both the patio and path were ankle deep in water. It had been, so the newspapers said, the driest February in Southern California in sixteen years. But March was making like a lion, a wet one. It had begun to rain about noon the day before and since then the precipitation had been practically continuous.

It wasn't too bad in the hills, but along the floor of the valley the roads were running rim deep with water. Overnight, the storm drains and arroyos had been transformed into swift-flowing rivers with all the power of flash-floods behind them.

Twice I almost smacked into stalled cars. Once I almost got smacked. I was glad to see Millet's gates. They were well lighted and stood wide open. I drove in through a double row of dripping eucalyptus and almost into the rear end of Millet's unlighted six-teen-cylinder, custom-built foreign sport job.

The car was in keeping with the ranch. Both had cost plenty. Millet had sunk most of the take of three of his best pictures into fifteen acres of the most fertile soil in the valley. Old age insurance he called it. But to the best of my knowledge, in the ten years he had owned the ranch all he had raised on it was hell.

A big, good-looking heel in his late thirties, Millet was waiting for me on the loggia of the ranch house. He said, "Am I glad to see you!"

I looked past him at the lighted windows of the rumpus room. A typical between-pictures Millet hoe-down was in progress. From where I sat in the rain I could see a half-dozen feminine bit and extra players in various stages of acute alcoholism. I could also see Paul Glade, the gambler, two of his boys, and three other men I didn't know.

"Now, look," I told Millet. "If getting me out of bed at four o'clock on a morning like this is one of your drunken gags . . ."

He waded through the rain to poke his head in the window I'd rolled down. "It isn't. I swear it isn't, Johnny."

Before he could say any more a cute little red-haired trick who looked like a fugitive from a choir loft, but who was having trouble with the shoulder strap of a low-cut evening gown, staggered out onto the covered part of the loggia and wanted to know why Bunny—her name for him—was standing in the rain.

Millet said she should go back to the party like a good girl, mix him a drink and he would be with her in a few minutes. She staggered back into the rumpus room still having trouble with the strap.

Without getting out of my car I told Millet, "All right. Let's have it. What do you mean you *think* you've killed someone?"

The story, as he told it, wasn't pretty. It was typical Millet. Now don't get me wrong. There are a lot of nice lads in Hollywood. Nine out of ten of the big stars are ladies and gentlemen. They pay their taxes, marry, and live as normal a life as any of their fans. But Millet didn't belong in that category. He would have been a heel if he had been a plumber. And because he'd been born with a classic profile and an ability to read lines, he thought he owned Hollywood.

It seemed that his own party had begun boring him and the liquor supply to grow low. So he had gotten out his car and headed for a spot he knew of that sold stuff by the case after hours.

I asked, "Alone? That is, you were alone?"

He said he had been alone. He also had been driving too fast, as usual, when he had seen the girl and her dog. That had been just this side of the storm drain on Sepulveda. He had attempted to brake the car, but it had skidded—as far as he knew directly into the girl and her dog. At least, he had heard a scream.

I asked, "You didn't stop to find out if you did hit her?"

He whined, "I didn't dare to stop, Johnny. I had two cases of whiskey in the car, liquor on my breath, and two 502's on my ticket."

502 is drunken driving in Los Angeles.

"Besides," Millet continued, "if I get in another jam the chances are that Consolidated won't renew my contract next month." He breathed good rye in my face. "What am I going to do? What do you advise me to do?"

I lighted a cigarette while I thought it over. It was strictly business with me. Private eyes are a dime a dozen along the Sunset Strip and I couldn't keep meat on the table if it wasn't for the annual retainer Consolidated pays me to pry their bad girls and boys out of the minor jams that might affect their box-office value. But this wasn't a minor jam. By not stopping, Millet had aggravated a misdemeanor into a felony. And while the studio paid me to extend a helping hand, I knew what their reaction would be to this one.

"I'm afraid this is one you're going to have to face," I told Millet. I got out and looked at the grill of his car. There were no marks on the grill, but the right front fender was badly dented. He had hit something. "And the longer you put it off the worse it is going to be for you. Not even God's gift to women can get away with a hit-and-run charge."

He told me not to be sarcastic.

I said I wasn't being sarcastic, I was merely stating a fundamental fact. To be certain, however, I left him standing in the rain while I walked through the rumpus room into the living room to phone Saul Bliss, the head of Consolidated's legal staff. His reaction was what I expected.

"He'll have to face it, Johnny," Bliss told me. "We wouldn't crawl out on a limb like that for the biggest box-office draw we have, and we certainly won't do it for a has-been." He added a note of caution. "But before you have him report it, I would make certain, if I were you, that he did hit someone."

I said I had already figured on doing that and hung up. Paul Glade, the gambler, nasty as he always is when he is drinking, left off pawing a little brunette to get to his feet and stop me as I walked back through the rumpus room. "So Steve whined to you, did he?" he asked. He tapped my chest with his finger. "Well, get this and get it straight, Johnny. Not you or all of Consolidated is going to keep me from collecting my dough."

I said he was talking Greek to me and pushed on past him to the door where the red-haired girl, a highball glass in one hand, was peering out into the rain. "Why doesn't Bunny come in out of the rain?" she demanded.

I told her it was beyond me unless it was that he didn't have sense enough, and rejoined Millet who had crawled into my car. "Bliss says no dice," I told him. "You'll get the usual legal representation, but the studio isn't sticking out its neck. Bliss suggested, however, and I concur, that we make certain you did hit someone before you report it in."

The thought seemed to cheer him slightly. "Maybe I just imagined the impact. Maybe I didn't hit anyone."

From the looks of his right front fender he was kidding himself. But it was no skin off my nose. "We'll use your car," I told him. "We'll drive back to the storm drain first, then down to the Valley Station."

I slid in back of the wheel of his car before he could. My annual retainer from the studio didn't obligate me to ride with a madman. It was a nice job to drive. And economical. I'll bet he got at least four blocks to the gallon. As I tooled it through the drive I asked him, "You owe Glade any money?"

"A few dollars," he said sourly. "What's the matter? Has the studio decided I can't gamble now?"

It was on the tip of my tongue to tell him I had a fair idea the studio didn't much care what he did, which it wouldn't if it didn't intend to renew his contract. But he had enough grief for the moment so I let it go. "No. I just wondered," I told him. "Glade braced me when I went in to phone and said something about you owing him some dough."

He repeated, "A few dollars."

It was raining, if possible, harder than ever. There was little traffic on the road. Dawn and a silver-winged transport plane came over the foothills back of Burbank just as we reached the storm drain. The road itself was passable, but the wash was a roaring river. I pulled over to one side, being careful to keep two wheels on the pavement. There were no cops and no police cars at the drain which could mean any one of three things:

The body hadn't been discovered.

It had been discovered and taken away.

Millet hadn't seriously injured the girl and she had walked away under her own power.

But what a girl and her dog would be doing walking down Sepulveda in the middle of a cloud burst was more than I could figure out. "This where it happened?" I asked him.

He said it was. I got out of the car and looked around. The rain had washed out any traces of his skid. I couldn't see any body, or any sign a body had been there. But, on the other hand, if he had hit her hard enough to hurl the body into the open drain it was possible that it wouldn't be found for days. I went back to the car and asked him how fast he had been going. He told me, "Maybe sixty-five. Possibly seventy."

A truck splashed by going the other way. It was growing lighter now. I walked back to the edge of the drain for one last look. It was then I saw the dog, a little black and white terrier, lying on the edge of the drain. It was dead. A cheap, braided, leather leash, the kind you can buy in the dime store, trailed from the collar on its neck out into the water.

I climbed back of the wheel again and turned the car around telling Millet as I did so, "If there was a girl with a dog, you hit her all right. The dog is still there on the bank. What kind of a dog was it you thought you saw?"

He said it was a little black and white dog and I increased the speed of the car. He wanted to know where we were going. I told him to the Valley Station to report an accident. Glum, he wanted to know if there was any other way it could be handled and I told him that there wasn't. "Just don't blow your breath in the sergeant's face," I told him.

Kinley was on the desk at the Valley Station. He didn't think much of Millet. He had dispatched too many squads out to his ranch to quell incipient riots. I will say this for Millet. Once he was in the station he didn't whine. He told a straight-from-the-shoulder story, much as he had told it to me, with the exception that he told Kinley that after feeling the impact he had stopped his car, gotten out in the rain and looked around but could see no trace of either the girl or the dog. So, not knowing just what to do, he had phoned me for advice. Together we had returned to the scene of the accident. I had discovered a black and white dog on the edge of the storm drain and here he was.

Kinley was stumped for a while just how to book him, the squad he sent out to the scene finding the dog but no body. He decided finally to make it reckless driving, figuring I suppose he could always slap a hit-and-run against Millet when the girl's body was discovered. Instead of being grateful, Millet was cocky all the way back to the ranch, boasting how he had gotten out of that one, and how even when the girl's body was discovered they wouldn't be able to pin anything on him. "It was an accident, strictly an accident," he insisted. He crowed, "And Kinley never even smelled my breath."

Morning was full now. The rain had lessened somewhat and the side road leading to his ranch was heavy with the fragrance of orange blossoms. Somehow they made him think of the red-haired little chickadee who'd called him Bunny. As we pulled up in front of his loggia I asked him who she was.

He told me, "My fiancée."

So saying, he slipped a pint bottle from a side pocket of the car, tilted it to his lips, then sat holding it without offering me a drink. That was okay with me. I walked over to my own car, glancing into the rumpus room as I passed it. Glade and his boys were gone. So were the girls. At least none of them were in the rumpus room. It looked like all rumpus rooms after a brawl, littered with empty bottles and glasses and cigarette butts. It looked like all rumpus rooms with one exception.

That was the red-haired girl. Curled up on a battered redwood chaise lounge next to the window, an empty highball glass still in her hand, the troublesome shoulder strap forgotten, one bare white shoulder exposed, asleep with a half smile on her lips, she was still waiting for Bunny. She was a pretty kid, and a nice one, not more than seventeen or eighteen. I had no way of knowing where she had come from but she didn't belong where she was.

Millet had followed me to the window. Tilting the bottle again, he leered in through the glass. "Nice, eh?"

"I hope you choke," I told him.

I did. I wanted no more of the affair. I wanted no more of Millet. But before the murder-go-round that followed was finally stopped and the D.A. handed the brass ring to the proper party, I was to get plenty of Millet, the red-haired little chick, and a gawky young Lochinvar named Arnst Gary who rode in from Wewoka, Oklahoma.

CHAPTER TWO

CRY MURDER!

I
T WAS ONE O'CLOCK by the time I reached my office. It was still raining but not hard. I poured two ounces of prevention before opening my mail, and drank it looking out the window. I had spent most of the morning at the studio with Bliss. He told me frankly that as far as they were concerned Millet was washed up. It had nothing to do with the accident the night before. What with a half-dozen of the younger lads coming up the way they had, Millet's popularity with the bobbysoxers had receded with his hairline. Consolidated did not intend to renew his contract. He was to be so informed within the month. For the sake of the good of the industry as a whole, however, the studio wanted the affair of the night before soft-pedaled as much as possible.

I was kicking Millet around in my mind and admiring the trim underpinning of a brunette in a red transparent raincoat when Glade barged into the office accompanied by the pair of muscle-bound chimpanzees who bodyguarded him. "What did Millet want with you last night?" Glade began without preamble. "What were you doing at the ranch?"

I asked why he wanted to know and he said not to give him that stuff.

"Millet's in a jam of some kind," he accused.

I admitted that could be so, then asked him why, if he wanted information about Millet, he didn't go to the source.

He told me, "Because the damn fool took off for Las Vegas this morning with that little red-haired tramp he has been making a big play for."

When I asked him how he knew, he handed me a sheet of Millet's monogrammed stationery. Scrawled across it in Millet's writing was the message:

> Cherry and I leaving for Las Vegas to be married. Keep the home fires burning. Back in two or three days—I think.
>
> Millet

I handed it back to Glade saying I wasn't interested in Steve Millet's marital affairs. "No. Neither am I," he admitted candidly. "But I am interested in money. And what I want to be sure of is that Millet's contract with Consolidated is going to be renewed. Like the big, good-natured sap that I am, I let Steve get into me for almost fifty grand. And I want my money, see?"

"If anyone owed me fifty thousand dollars, I'd want it, too," I told him. In the light of the information that I had gotten from Bliss I could have added he was going to have a fat chance of collecting it. I asked instead why he had come to me.

He said, "Because you're Consolidated's troubleshooter. Every time one of their bad boys or girls get their pinkies dirty they have instructions to phone you. And I want to know why Millet phoned you last night."

I looked from him to his apes and, being allergic to having my face punched in, decided I didn't want any trouble with them. So I told him the story as I had it.

Glade seemed relieved. "That's it? That's all there was to it? He run down some dame in the rain, a thing that could happen easy to even a sober guy?"

I said that would seem to be it.

"Then I guess my dough's safe," he decided. "After all the other screwball stunts he's pulled the studio wouldn't refuse to renew his contract because of a little thing like that."

Glade turned on his heel and walked out, his apes lumbering after him, I poured another two ounces of prevention, glad I wasn't in Millet's shoes. Glade meant to collect his money. He would, one way or another.

There was nothing worth mentioning in the mail. I sorted the advertisements from the bills, then phoned the Valley Station. A crew had been searching the banks of the storm drain since morning but they hadn't found any body. They were beginning to think that Millet had imagined he'd hit someone. The lieutenant I talked to wanted to know if Millet had been drinking. I evaded the question by saying I hadn't been with him at the time, thanked him for his information, and hung up.

Then I did what I should have done in the first place. I called the Bureau of Missing Persons and asked for Flanery. "Yes. We had three calls last night," he told me. He listed them with their addresses. One was a Mrs. Grace, living in Alameda. One was a Bessie Small, with an address on Harvard Boulevard. The third was a Laura Jean Jones with a North Hollywood address. He had the description of each but none of them was listed as being accompanied by a small black and white terrier.

I called at the Grace home first. It turned out to be one of those things. Mrs. Grace answered the door in person, told me what she thought of the police and of any nitwitted husband who would call the Missing Person's Bureau merely because, unable to return home on account of the rain, she had stayed over night with a girl friend. It could be her story was true. All that mattered to me was the obvious fact that it hadn't been she whom Millet had catapulted into the storm drain.

Bessie Small was still missing. But she didn't own, and had never owned, a dog. In fact she disliked them intensely. And after talking to the slattern who said she was her mother it seemed at least probable to me that the girl had merely tired of an unpleasant home and had struck out on her own.

That left me with Laura-Jean Jones. Flanery had given me a phone number with that one. I called but got no answer. On a hunch I drove out Sunset to Sepulveda and cut through the canyon to the storm drain.

A city squad car was parked on the far side with a bored driver at the wheel. "Yeah. The boys have been searching all day," he told me. "But the chances are if she did go into the storm drain they won't be able to find her until the water recedes." He repeated, "If she *did* go into the drain. You never can tell what the movie folks will do for a little publicity."

He showed me an afternoon paper. There was a two-column cut of Millet and the little red-haired dame. Her name was Cherry Gamble, and while the story said she was an actress none of the pictures in which she had appeared was listed. It was more likely she was some little extra who had attracted Millet's eye and to whom he had promised stardom.

I felt sorry for her.

Ringing the cut of Millet and Cherry was a circle of pictures of his former wives, five to be exact.

The driver of the squad car told me, "Look at her. Then look at him." His neck muscles stood out like cords. "I tell you, mister, if a kid of mine ever married a heel like that I'd blister her backside until she couldn't stand the touch of scanties for a year."

I read on down the story. Out of courtesy to Consolidated's publicity department, and in return for a full-page ad puffing the studio's current feature picture, the accident angle of the yarn had been played down to a few sticks of type. Millet believed he had struck someone while driving in the rain that morning, it said, but the fact had not as yet been verified. He had, however, reported the accident and a charge of reckless driving had been filed against him.

No mention was made as to how the reporter had. learned of Millet's latest marital venture. I made a mental note to inquire into the fact and, leaving my car where it was, I walked on up the road to the nearest house. The lady who answered the bell said:

"Yes. As I told the other officer who inquired, I heard a scream about four o'clock this morning. In fact, I heard two screams, spaced perhaps thirty seconds apart."

That was interesting, if true. I asked her if she was positive that she had heard two screams. She said she was positive. She hadn't, however, seen anything or anyone. It had been raining too hard for her to see more than a few feet beyond her bedroom window.

I thanked her for the information and walked back to my car. If I remembered correctly, there was an all-night drive-in stand about a mile up the road.

I had remembered correctly. There were no car hops on duty who had been on duty the night before, I found out. And outside of my own bus and a couple of cars in back parked in an Employees Only zone, there was only one other car in the stand, a 1937 Studebaker. It was parked all by itself in a far corner.

I asked the counterman if it belonged to one of the help. He said it did not. "I don't know who it belongs to," he admitted. "It was there when I came on duty this morning. Why? You think we ought to call the cops about it? You think it's a stolen car?"

I went over and looked at it. It was a coupe in good condition. The driver's license and registration card weren't on the shaft of the wheel where they belonged, but the contents of the glove compartment obviously belonged to a woman. I found a discarded pancake compact, a box of loose powder, a pair of ladies' driving gloves about size five, some loose hairpins, an empty candy box and a' pair of expensive harlequin sun glasses.

I called the Valley Station again from the wall phone inside the stand and asked for Lieutenant Green, the lad who had wanted to know if Millet had been drinking. "I think I've found something that might interest you," I told him. "I think I have found the missing girl's car at the drive-in stand a mile south of the drain." I gave him the make and license number of the car. "At least I think it's worth your while to check it. If Millet *did* hit someone it stands to reason that she didn't drop out of the sky. She had to come from somewhere. But why was she walking her dog in the rain a mile from where she left her car is beyond me."

Green said the chances were it wasn't her car but he thanked me for my cooperation and said he would check on the car immediately. I bought a cheeseburger I didn't want, a cup of coffee I did, then got on my horse again.

The address on Saltillo proved to be an old-fashioned, square frame house set well back in a mass of rain-drenched shrubbery between two modern apartment houses. I parked my car at the curb and walked down a weed-grown path to a tired porch littered with yellowed shopping throw-aways and last years' campaign literature. The blinds were drawn. There was no name under the bell. The thin wail of a piccolo floating out of one of the open upper windows was the only sign the house wasn't unoccupied. I rang the bell and nothing happened so I banged the door. The uninterrupted wail of the piccolo was the only answer. I tried again and a voice over my head informed me:

"You'll have to go around to the side door and pound real hard. The old man claims he isn't, but he's deaf. A nice-looking old man like him. He should wear a hearing aid."

I stepped off the porch to see who was talking. It was a good-looking, middle-aged woman leaning on the sill of one of the second-floor windows of the apartment house next door.

"That is," she added, "if you are looking for Mr. Jones."

I asked her if he had a daughter by the name of Laura Jean. She said he did. She started to say something more, changed her mind and closed the window. I walked around to the side door and banged it as hard as I could without cracking the panel. The piccolo stopped this time and a few moments later, still holding the piccolo in one hand, Jones opened the door in person.

"Come in, son. Come in," he boomed before I could say a word. "If you wish to see Thaddeus Jones, come in."

He sounded like Senator Claghorn, but he seemed to mean it. A well-built old gentleman of perhaps sixty, he led the way into the shade-drawn living room. The inside of the house was a lot better than the outside. The furniture was old but in good taste. A film of dust covered it all.

Jones motioned me to a chair, then sat in one across from me, his head thrust slightly forward in the unconscious gesture of the slightly hard of hearing. "Yes? Yes?" he boomed.

I looked at him to see if he was kidding. He wasn't. It was just his way of speaking. I had seen his type before but only in motion pictures. He was one of the few men I have ever met who might be rightly termed a gentleman of the old school.

I said, "You reported your daughter Laura Jean missing last night."

"Oh. You're from the police," he said. "No. It wasn't last night," he corrected me. "It was this morning I became alarmed. You see, she didn't come home last night. Very unusual. Very. In fact it's never happened before. You have some news of her?"

I asked him what kind of a car she was driving. He thought a moment, told me, "I believe it was a Studebaker. Yes. I'm positive it was. She purchased it in Oklahoma City especially for the trip out here. But why do you inquire?"

I told him I had found a deserted 1937 Studebaker coupe at a drive-in stand on Sepulveda Boulevard and asked if he had known his daughter's destination when she had left home the evening before.

He said that he did not. "But you say the car is deserted?" He got up from his chair. "That means there has been an accident. Laura Jean is hurt?" His face was grey.

I said that was the fact I was trying to ascertain, then asked if his daughter had a dog.

"She has," he said promptly. "Snippy." He spread his palms. "A little black and white terrier about so large."

I gave it to him straight. "Then I am afraid there has been an accident. At least, one was reported about a mile from where your daughter's car was found." Without mentioning any names I described the storm drain and told him I had found a black and white terrier on the bank of it.

He said, "My God!" and sat back in the chair, one hand clutching at his heart. Then, fumbling a pill box from his vest pocket, he asked if I would please get him a glass of water. When he had washed down the pill with a swallow of it, he explained. "My heart. Sorry." He straightened in the chair with an effort. "But what in the name of time was Laura Jean doing walking Snippy in the rain on a lonely boulevard at four o'clock in the morning?"

Thinking of the woman who claimed to have heard two screams thirty seconds apart, I admitted, "That is a point that puzzles me. You say you don't know where your daughter intended to go or whom she intended to meet last night?"

He shook his head. "I do not."

I tried another tack. "Los Angeles isn't your home? You and your daughter moved here recently?"

"Fairly recently," he said. "About eight months ago."

"Why? That is, why did you move to L.A.?"

He said, "Laura Jean believed she could get into pictures."

"But she had no success."

"No," he admitted. "She did not."

I asked if he had a picture of her and he pointed to a picture of a compact brunette on the radio. She wasn't bad looking, nor was she particularly pretty. I had a vague impression I had seen her in the flesh at one time or another.

"All right. Now tell me this," I said. "What part of the country did you come from? And what gave your daughter the impression she could break into the picture racket?"

He told me the family home was in Oklahoma, that he had a small ranch not far from Wewoka, a ranch that had been in his family since Oklahoma had been Indian territory. He sat staring at the picture. "As to why we came to Hollywood, I've often wondered. Laura Jean wasn't happy here. She cried a great deal of the time, undoubtedly because of her failure to engage in the picture business."

I said, "Undoubtedly." A faint picture was forming in my mind but it was too nebulous to come through.

The old gentleman got up from his chair again. "But why do we sit here? Surely there must be *something* we can do."

I told him everything was being done that could be done and gave him a faint bone of hope to chew on. "We don't *know* that anything has happened to your daughter. She may have parked her car and gone somewhere with a friend. She did have a friend, a boy friend, here in Hollywood?"

"Yes," Jones admitted. "She did. He called for her several times, A disagreeable chap named Black, much too old for her for one thing." He began to pace the floor. "No gentleman for another."

I asked him to describe Black. His description was as vague as the faint picture in my mind. In his middle or late thirties, tall, dark, a wisp of a mustache, flashily dressed—you could have swung a canary feather on the corner of Hollywood and Vine and knocked down two dozen men of that description.

I thanked him for his information, told him that the police would undoubtedly contact him later that evening and asked if I could borrow the framed picture of Laura Jean. He said I could not but found and gave me a snapshot of her that was a reasonable likeness.

I left him still clutching the piccolo in one hand, a nice, futile, worried old gentleman.

I should have called it a day. I didn't. I was poking my nose into something I wasn't being paid to investigate. But the matter of the divided screams bothered me.

If Steve Millet had been driving between sixty-five and seventy miles an hour when he had skidded into the girl it was only natural she should scream. But why had she screamed again—thirty seconds later? Thirty seconds is a long time. Tick them off on your own timepiece.

CHAPTER THREE

FIRST BLOOD

NIGHT HAD FALLEN while I had been talking to the old man. I phoned Sally from the drug store on the next corner, told her I wouldn't be home for supper and to expect me when she saw me. She wanted to know if I was still working on the Millet affair. I said I was and she asked:

"But you're all right, Johnny?"

I said I was.

"And you know that I love you, more than anything on earth?"

I said I was surer of that than I was of salvation, and I blew a kiss into the phone. I dialed Bliss at the studio, failed to get him, finally reached him at his home. He said he had been trying to reach me at the office for an hour. "The police have found the girl's body," he told me. "And they have tentatively identified her by car keys found in the pocket of her jacket as a Laura Jean Jones of 41638 Saltillo Avenue, North Hollywood. had better buzz over there, Johnny, and see how the family is fixed. This thing can develop into a nasty stink. The police have added a hit-and-run and leaving the scene of an accident to the reckless driving charge. There's a warrant out on both charges for Millet now."

I said I had already seen the family, that it consisted of a gentlemanly old father, and that while he didn't seem to be rolling in money, I doubted very greatly if he could be bought off, if that was what was in Bliss' mind.

He said he was just thinking of the good of the industry as a whole. I said, "Yeah," and hung up. I was up to here with the whole picture business. Millet was washed up. He was a has-been. The studio didn't intend to renew his contract. But to avoid the bad publicity his arrest and conviction on a manslaughter charge would bring they were now willing to lay plenty on the line to prove it had been two other guys in his car, that in reality Kilroy had been driving, and Millet had been home all the time drinking orange soda pop and reading *Mother Carey's Chickens*. The police would do their best but by the time the high-priced studio lawyers got through kicking the case around, Millet would get off with a slap on the wrist, be free to raise more hell, drink more whiskey, and marry more eighteen-year-old girls.

Out on the street again I considered going back and telling the old man that Laura Jean's body had been found. I did drive by the house but there was a police cruiser parked in front so I knew that angle had been cared for.

I had bought a paper in the drug store. It had come off the press before the change of charges and the discovery of the body. It still headlined the great lover's romantic nuptials, and ranged around Millet's picture was the same circle of his former wives. The make-up man seemed to get a bang out of printing them.

I stopped at the Hitching Post and read the latest details over a double rye. The lucky bride, so the paper stated, had played several parts in pictures, which was a nice way of saying she walked on in a couple of mob scenes. Of more interest to me was the fact that her real name was Bessie Charles, that she came from Wewoka, Oklahoma, and that she had met Steve Millet in the same town two years before when he had been on location for Consolidated's masterpiece, *Indian Territory.*

I had forgotten he had starred in the picture. I bought another drink, then called Bliss again. "Before you can tell me I'm fired, I quit," I informed him. "This time I think I have Steve where I want him. And I'm going to nail his hide on a fence."

"Now look, Johnny," he protested. "Don't you do anything crazy. I'll have you blackballed out of every studio in Hollywood. You'll never make another dime in Southern California."

He was still sputtering when I hung up.

I paid for my drink, walked back to my car and froze as the muzzle of a gun dug into my spine. "Easy does it, Slagle," one of Glade's chimpanzees warned me. "You ain't got no cause to be sore and nothing ain't going to happen to you. All Paul wants is a little talk."

"Then why the gun invitation?" I asked him.

"Just so you won't refuse."

I got into my own car as directed and drove on out the Valley to Glade's Club, a low-slung grey convertible loafing along behind us. The club was back in the hills, just over the L.A. line. It cost Glade plenty to build it. It also brought him in plenty of money.

The bar was red leather and chrome. It was too early for the booths to be occupied, but a director and producer I knew were sopping it up at the bar. Both invited me to have a drink. I looked at the chimpanzee behind me and told them, "Later. Wait for me. I'm going to have a little talk with Paul."

Out of their hearing the chimp said, "Wise guy."

"Insurance," I corrected him. "It's a very nice thing to have. You ought to get yourself some."

Glade was waiting in his office. He got right down to business. "Cut it out, Johnny," he told me. "I know you have a grudge against Steve. I know you have been waiting a long time for a chance to pay him off. But take my advice, Johnny, and cut it out, understand?"

I asked what his interest in Millet was.

He told me, "Fifty grand. And if the studio doesn't renew his contract I haven't a chance of collecting. Does that make it clear?"

"No," I admitted frankly, "it doesn't. In the first place Millet's contract *isn't* going to be renewed. And if you have nosed around as much as I think you have this afternoon you know that. What's more, you haven't a snowball's chance in hell of stopping this thing. If you're thinking the same thing I am, so are the police. It would seem the lady in the white house near the storm drain talked to some officer before she talked to me."

Glade knew what I was talking about, but his reaction wasn't what I had expected. He seemed relieved. "Oh. I see." He took a packet of bills from his desk drawer and laid it on the blotter. "Look. Let's stop beating around the bush, Johnny. How would you and Sally like to climb into your car and spend three or four months in, well, lets say, Ensenada?"

"Starting when?" I asked him.

He pushed the packet across the desk. "Starting right now. There's ten thousand dollars for expenses."

I was tempted. Then I thought of the little red-haired chick and told him, "Sorry."

The thing was bigger than I had expected. I thought I had most of it now. But for the life of me I couldn't figure how Glade hoped to cash in.

He nodded to one of his chimps. I sidestepped but not quite fast enough. The barrel of his gun damn near tore off my ear. Through a fog of pain I heard the other chimp say, "He told a couple of guys at the bar to wait for him. He said he was going to have a talk with you."

"Well, he's having it," Glade said coldly. He nodded again and the second blow caught me fair. The last I heard was Glade saying, "Send Mabel and Gwen out to keep the two chumps company. In a half-hour they'll forget that they ever saw Slagle."

The room was small and plainly furnished, obviously a sleeping room for one of the help. As soon as I could stand on my feet, I tried the window. It was barred. The door wasn't any more use to me. It was both solid and locked. There was a wash bowl in one corner. I cleaned the blood off my face and out of my hair as best I could, then sat back on the bed.

I doubted if Glade intended to kill me or have me killed. He didn't like to play that rough. He was merely stalling for time, and my nosing around the way I had and putting two and two together was interfering with the horse he had backed between the shafts of Steve Millet's apple cart.

It had looked pretty simple to me after talking to Thaddeus Jones, figuring out the screams, and reading the night paper. Now I wasn't so certain. Glade was a heel but he wasn't petty. He didn't do anything for peanuts. There had to be money, big money, in this thing somewhere.

More, some time during the afternoon, he *had* to have talked to Millet, long distance to Las Vegas, most likely. On leaving the Hitching Post I had put the evening paper in my pocket. It was still there. I unfolded it, found the light switch and read the story again.

It would seem that even two years ago, when Bessie Charles had only been sixteen, Millet had recognized she had talent. He had suggested she come to Hollywood. Twelve months before, she had followed his advice. A casting director had changed her name to Cherry Gamble. She had been assigned no roles to date, outside of a couple of walk-ons, but had been content to study under Steve Millet's tutelage. Undoubtedly, as the bride of the great lover, he would insist she be featured in his next starring picture.

That was written by a man. I turned to a sob sister's account of the same affair. She called Cherry a Cinderella girl and stressed the fact she had been working in a five-and-ten-cent store when Millet had first been attracted by her beauty. In neither story could I find what had to be behind the whole affair—money, lots of it.

I sat listening to the music of the band. It came to me thin and faint, which meant the walls of the room were for all practical purposes sound-proofed. Yelling for nonexistent help wouldn't get me a thing but a sore throat and maybe another beating.

I found a cigarette and lit it. It tasted good.

It was still smoking when a key turned in the lock, the door opened, and one of Glade's two chimps came in. "Paul was worried about you," he admitted. "He don't want to hurt you, see. Why don't you play ball, take the dough and go south for a while, Slagle?"

I asked him if Paul had told him to tell me that, He said he had. "If it was me," he added, "I'd just conk you on the head, dig you a hole somewhere and let it go at that."

"That would solve about everything with the exception of the woman who heard the screams," I admitted. "What time does the plane of the happy bridal pair land?"

Caught off his mental balance he said, "Midnight," then crossed the room to the bed and cuffed me. "Wise guy, huh? You had to establish the fact Paul talked on the phone to Millet."

I rolled back as if to avoid the blow, doubled my knees up to my middle and gave him both feet in the stomach. His eyes agonized, he doubled up, his head hitting the side rail of the bed as he fell. To make certain he was comfortable I slipped his gun from his holster and smacked him as hard as he'd smacked me. Then, stuffing the gun in my belt, I locked the door behind me, dropped the key in my pocket, and walked down a short flight of stairs to a small false balcony that overlooked the main dining room of the club.

By the size of the crowd it was late. I saw perhaps two dozen people I knew, including Glade, immaculate in white tie and tails. He was standing beside the table of Glenda Glory, the movie columnist, laughing heartily at something she had said. Some call her the Sacred Cow of Hollywood. Myself, I think she's a pretty good scout. But that could be because of the break that she gave me and Sally. She could have made a Roman holiday of the affair but instead she allowed it to die a natural death. Glenda likes to be kowtowed to. Sure. What woman doesn't?

At the foot of the stairs I paused to allow a party of good-time Charlies, steered by a pair of Glades' pretty shills, to pass me and enter the gambling rooms. Then I headed straight for Glenda's table.

Glade opened and closed his mouth twice but didn't say anything. Glenda said, "Hello, Johnny. I see Millet has done it again."

I said, "So it would seem."

Glenda continued, "At least he had something to offer the others, but not this poor foolish child." Her shrewd eyes narrowed. "Anything new on that accident, Johnny?"

I looked at Glade as I told her. "Nothing that I know of so far. But there may be developments by morning I am almost certain there will be. I'll give you a buzz the minute that anything breaks."

She said, "You're a good boy, Johnny."

Glade didn't seem to think so. His eyes stabbing holes in my back, I walked through the bar and out into the parking lot. The attendant hadn't been warned not to let me have my car. I suppose they hadn't thought it would be necessary.

I tipped him a buck and left fast but not so fast I didn't see a car swing out into the road a scant thirty seconds behind me. Glade had managed to instruct his boys to gather me in again. I tore down the winding road too fast, then, reaching the floor of the valley, pulled off to one side, killed my lights and tugged the chimp's gun from my belt.

There were three lads in the pursuing car. They rounded the last bend and skidded to a stop thirty feet beyond me as they realized my tail lights had disappeared.

Resting the gun on the ledge of the door I put a slug into both of their back tires. Then, still without lights, I meshed my boat into gear and pulled around them with my foot pushing the peddle to the floor. By the time they woke up there was nothing they could do about it. At least they did nothing at the time.

I wanted to go to the Valley Station. I wanted to talk to Lieutenant Green before he served his warrants on Millet. If what I now believed to be true was fact, the police were still muddling along in the dark. Glade had been faster on the mental trigger than they.

He knew the set-up for what it was—murder. And unless Millet had confided in him, which wasn't likely, there was only one way he could have learned. After talking to me in my office and learning about the so-called accident, Glade had smelled both a rat and profit and had driven to the scene. It must have been Glade or one of his boys to whom the woman of whom I had inquired had told of the divided scream.

Only one angle still bothered me. That was motive. There had to be money, a lot of money in the set-up somewhere. In the hope of discovering who had it before Millet's return with his bride I turned off onto a muddy side street and drove to his ranch instead of to the station.

It was a mistake on my part. It caused me to foul up the case. And it damn near made Sally a widow.

CHAPTER FOUR

LOCHINVAR

IT HAD RAINED ON AND OFF ALL DAY. Now it was coming down in earnest. The sodden ground refused to absorb any more water and the low-lying fields on both sides of the road were shallow lakes. More, a high wind was blowing, and here and there a tall palm or eucalyptus had given up the struggle and was tilted precariously over the side road leading to the ranch. Millet's drive was even worse. Not far in from the gate a fallen eucalyptus completely blocked the drive,

I left my car and sloshed the rest of the way on foot. There were no lights in the main house, but from the feminine squeals issuing from the garage apartment of Uan, Millet's house boy, I judged that Uan was entertaining. Like master, like man.

I opened the front door with a key on my ring that I had been saving for some time. I was wet to the skin. My shoes were so sodden with water I made squashing sounds as I walked across Millet's big oriental rug to his desk. It was stuffed with bills but there were no letters or papers in it that were of any interest to me.

I tried the desk in his bedroom next. It was quite a room, wainscoted with mirrors and equipped with a specially built bed as large as the average bedroom. There were several letters to "Bunny" signed "Lovekin" in the desk but they all had L.A. postmarks and there was no mention of Wewoka or Laura Jean Jones in any of them. I tried a chest of drawers and a dresser with even less results. The hell of it was I didn't know what I was looking for.

I looked at my watch. It was a few minutes after nine. If the information I had tricked from Glade's chimp was correct I had three hours before Millet and his bride returned from Las Vegas. I doubted if Glade would reason that I would go to the ranch. It was as good a place to be out of the rain as any.

I found a phone in a concealed wall panel and tried to call Lieutenant Green but I could tell the line was dead as soon as I lifted the receiver. The line, as I recalled, paralleled the drive and the uprooted eucalyptus had undoubtedly taken it out.

I would have to drive to the station. Squooshing back down the corridor I poured myself a drink at the rumpus room bar and put a half-dollar on the wood where it couldn't be missed. I wasn't taking any favors from Steve Millet, not even a drink. I drank, looking in the back bar mirror and thinking of the description of Black that old Thaddeus Jones had given me.

The description fitted me as well as it did anyone else. I am the same age as Millet, too old to marry a bobbysoxer. I am also tall, dark, with a thin mustache. I have never claimed to be a gentleman. And while I don't drape the body in clothes as loud as some, mine aren't exactly Amish.

Thinking of clothes made me realize mine were wet and uncomfortable. I added another half-dollar to the one I had laid on the bar and, peeling off my coat and trenchcoat, hung them in front of the big electric heater in the wall. They were so wet they steamed. I bought a third drink and drank it, toasting my legs and back and having a hell of a swell time thinking about how much I hated Millet.

The three drinks and drying the surface of my clothes took maybe half an hour. I was just reaching for my coat to go out and get wet again when the pounding on the front door began. Tugging the hood's gun from my belt I walked to the window in my shirt sleeves.

In the light over the door I could see a husky youth using a fist as big as a ham to beat on the paneling. He was wearing frontier model dungarees with their cuffs and his feet stuffed into expensive-looking, high-heeled boots slightly run over on the outside corners of the heels. A worn, black leather windbreaker protected his upper body from the rain dripping off the peaked brim of a battered ten-gallon hat. Where his chin should be, there was chin and plenty of it. Whoever he was and whatever he wanted of Millet, he wasn't a Vine Street cowboy. He was the real McCoy.

I considered letting him knock until he gave up and went away. I was to wish I had. Instead, I went on into the front room, opened the door and asked him what he wanted.

He took one look at me and said, "Where is she?"

"Where is who?" I asked him.

He sneered, "A comedian, eh?" and using the ham with which he had been beating on the door he tried to punch my head off my shoulders, using my jaw as a point of contact.

If I hadn't rolled with the punch he might have done it. As it was, it rocked me so hard I forgot I had a gun in my hand until it was too late to use it. He wasn't missing a trick, though. He slashed my wrist with the heel of his hand and the gun fell to the carpet

"Where is she?" he repeated. He spoke, without raising his voice, in an urgent drawl. "No wonder she hasn't been writing to me lately. No wonder she said she might never come back to Wewoka. Well, she's going to! Understand?"

I thought I was beginning to. "Now, wait. You have me all wrong," I told the youngster. "I'm not Millet. My name is Slagle. And I don't like Millet any better than you seem to."

Not quite sold on me as yet, he picked the gun from the floor, his eyes never leaving my face. "If you're lying to me, if you are Millet, I'm going to beat your face in, mister," he informed me. "Bessie and I have been sweethearts since we were shirt-tail young 'uns, and no pitcher actor, great lover or not, is going to take her away from me!"

I said, "You are referring to Bessie Slater, the late Cherry Gamble, now Mrs. Steve Millet."

He decided to believe I wasn't Millet. "They aren't married yet, are they, mister? Bessie couldn't marry such a man. She isn't married to him, is she?"

I closed the front door, took him by the elbow and leading him into the rumpus room bought him a drink. "Now start at the beginning," I told him. "Just who are you and where did you come from."

He said his name was Arnst Gary and he had just gotten off the Oklahoma City-Los Angeles plane. According to his story, he had been in Wewoka that morning seeing about some fittings for a well he was wildcatting on his ranch, when the editor of the local paper who knew and liked him had called him in and showed him an A.P. dispatch right off the tape. Gary told me, "They wanted more information about Bessie. And it said she was going to be Steve Millet's sixth wife. That's all I needed to read. I got a plane as soon as I could and here I am." He went back into his theme song. "Where is she?"

I fished the paper from the pocket of my coat and handed it to him. He glanced at the picture of Cherry, skimmed through the article. Then, laying it down on the bar, he asked me, "Is there a regular airline to this Las Vegas or will I have to charter a plane?"

I said there was a regular flight to Las Vegas but according to information that I had, Millet and his bride were returning to Los Angeles by midnight.

He said, "Good, I came out here to kill him and his own house is as good a place as any."

I said that was pretty strong talk.

"I love Bessie," he said quietly. "And if I thought she would be happy with such a man, I wouldn't be here. But he won't make her happy." The big youth tapped the pictured circle of Millet's former wives. "His past record speaks for itself. He studded all over Oklahoma while he was making that picture down there two years ago." He seemed trying to convince himself. "Bessie doesn't really love him. She's just got Stardust in her eyes."

For as young a lad as he was he made a lot of sense. I asked if he knew Thaddeus Jones.

"He's Bessie's uncle," he said. "Laura Jean got the Hollywood bug about the same time that Bessie did and she and her father are out here somewhere."

"And he, Jones, is worth a lot of money?"

Gary shook his head. "No. The old man is too danged stubborn. What with the few cattle that he runs and a piece or two of town property that he rents he has just about enough to keep himself and Laura Jean." He added, "Not that he couldn't be worth a lot of money."

Before he could explain, the door of the rumpus room opened and Uan, backed by two uniformed Valley patrolmen that I didn't know, walked into the room. Both of the patrolmen had their guns drawn.

"See?" Uan hissed at the cops. "No friends of Mr. Millet. Just break in and drink his whiskey."

"I didn't break in," I told the cops. "And Uan knows who I am."

"Never see you before," the Filipino lied.

"So you didn't break in," one of the cops said to me. "Okay. Then how did you get in?"

I was damned if I was going to explain about the key. Besides, I wanted to see Lieutenant Green. "Okay. So I broke in," I agreed with him. "Take it easy," I cautioned Gary. "There is no use talking to these lame-brains. I could show them my credentials, but I don't intend to. I'll do my talking at the station."

He said, "To hell with that stuff. I didn't fly out here to get into any little trouble." Before either cop realized what he was about he had a long-barreled Colt pistol in his hand. "Now we're all even," he told them. He backed toward the rumpus room door, opened it with his left hand and, backing out into the rain, slammed it shut behind him.

Neither cop was a fool. They had no intention of playing hide-and-seek in the rain with a gun that size. One of them frisked me while the other one said sourly, "If the house boy hadn't been on the job you and your partner would probably have made a killing." He glanced at the furnishings of the room and I knew what he was thinking. His whole place hadn't cost him as much. "Come on. Get your coat on. We'll let you tell it to the lieutenant."

Green was friendly but cagey. He knew I didn't like Millet and he knew why. He listened to my story, drumming on his desk top with his fingers. "That's quite a yarn, Slagle," he said quietly. "Maybe you ought to be writing for the studios instead of keeping an eye on their bad boys and girls."

From the way he said it I knew he had been 'seen.' Nothing crooked. No outright graft, understand. But with all their power and money the studios are able to smooth the path for an ambitious man and sprinkle tacks in the road of anyone who doesn't see quite eye to eye with them.

He glanced at a notation on his pad. "Oh, by the way. I see you aren't working for Consolidated any more. In that case just what were you doing in Millet's rumpus room?"

I told the truth, "Buying a drink before I came over to see you."

"And your partner?"

I said he was no partner of mine.

Green smiled thinly. "No. That's right. The big punk with the old-fashioned dog leg just flew in from Oklahoma to talk to Millet about a dame, a mere thousand odd miles since morning."

"Planes now fly from L.A. to New York in less than seven hours," I reminded him.

He said, "Not commercial planes," got up from his desk and reached his slicker off its hook. "Let's go talk to the woman who heard the screams."

It was still raining, buckets. In the car I asked Green if he had as yet identified Laura Jean's boy friend, Mr. Black.

"No," he admitted. "Not yet. But from the old man's description you could be the lad. And hating Millet like you do I wouldn't put it past you to try to frame him for murder, Johnny."

There it was, cold turkey.

I said, "You're crazy. In the first place I never knew Laura Jean Jones existed until I called Flanery this morning and later talked to her father."

Green said, "But you knew right where her car was parked."

I pointed out it stood to reason she had to reach the scene of her death by some means of locomotion other than foot power. Then I said sourly, "Sure. Knowing exactly what hour Millet was going to run out of liquor this morning I tricked Laura Jean out to the drive-in stand, then walked her and her dog a mile through the rain, timing it exactly so we would reach the storm drain at the moment Millet did. Then I pushed her in front of his tar, drove thirty-two miles home and crawled into bed to wait for his call."

Green was fair about it. "Putting it that way, it doesn't make sense. Besides, the old man would have recognized you and said so. But the drivel you have been telling me doesn't make sense, either. As I see it, it's a straight manslaughter rap with no special onus on anyone's shoulders." His ambition showed in the dark. "I don't like Millet much better than you do. But the girl had no business walking down the road at three o'clock in the morning. She must have been out of her mind. And while I'm not excusing Millet, understand, visibility being what it is in a rain storm, what happened could have happened to anyone."

I made him sore by asking, "What are you bucking for, captain's bars? You should have made a better deal. I know of an inspector who remembers Bliss and Consolidated every night in his prayers."

He said sourly, "Go to hell. Remember, I can still slap a breaking-and-entering charge against you and it might just be I will."

I said just as sourly, "I've been charged with worse."

Despite the fact it was almost twelve o'clock, the house nearest to the storm drain was brightly lighted. The driver of our car turned up the lane, cascading a solid sheet of water over a flowering wild crab tree.

A thin-faced man in shirt sleeves with bright red knitted suspenders dangling in loops around his thighs answered Green's rap on the door. Behind him I could see the woman to whom I had spoken. Her face was flushed and, despite the hour and the fact she was wearing a bathrobe over a long silk nightgown, she was clutching a pouch-type leather purse tightly to her breast.

"My name is Green, Lieutenant Green, of the Valley Station," Green introduced himself. "And while I'm sorry to bother you this time of night, information has just come to me that you folks possess some information that might be valuable to our investigation of the accident that occurred down the road a little ways in the early hours of yesterday morning."

The thin-faced lad hitched his suspenders over his shoulders, a blank look on his face. "What accident?" he demanded. "Was there an accident down by the storm drain? Was that what the police car was doing down there all day?"

Green looked at me. I looked at the woman. "Remember me?" I asked her. "Remember the man you told you heard two screams spaced about thirty seconds apart?"

Her pouch purse still clutched to her breast, she shook her head. "I never saw you before," she lied. "And I know nothing about any screams. We went to bed early last night and I didn't wake up until eight o'clock this morning." She wet her lips with the tip of her tongue and appealed to her husband. "Isn't that right, John?"

He said flatly, "Yeah."

There was nothing I could do about it. Green apologized for disturbing them. Back in the car he said, "Wise guy."

"Yeah," I said. "A wise guy. Wise enough to know that if you had looked in that dame's purse you would probably have found the ten grand Glade tried to bribe me with."

CHAPTER FIVE

MIDNIGHT

DESPITE THE RAIN there was a good crowd at the airport to watch the great lover and his bride come in, most of them photogs and reporters and the working stiffs who dig up the dirt and chit-chat that the Louella Parsons, Hedda Hoppers, and Glenda Glorys publish in their columns. The studio had seen to that. Even though they intended to give Millet the air they meant to wring the last possible drop of publicity from his name and marital peccadillos.

From where I stood under the dripping eaves of a private hangar I could see Bliss talking earnestly to Lieutenant Green. From time to time Green shook his head stubbornly. Whatever it was Bliss was trying to sell him, undoubtedly about holding back the hit-and-run and suspicion of manslaughter warrants until morning, Green wasn't having any.

He wasn't too bad a Joe. He had proved that by releasing me on our return to the station. Uan hadn't been there to sign a complaint and Green said he was damned if he would. He was ambitious. Most good cops are. But he wasn't exactly a fool and the act of the couple who lived out by the storm drain hadn't been too convincing.

From where I stood it looked to me as if the whole affair was beginning to give Green indigestion. He was willing to play ball with Bliss. But bribery was still out. Green didn't want any dirt on his hands that a bar of soap wouldn't remove.

The big chartered plane bounced lightly, then taxied up the strip while the crowd surged past the barrier. I searched it for Arnst Gary. But if the young Lochinvar who had sworn he intended to kill Millet was part of the welcoming committee he had ditched his black leather windbreaker and his ten-gallon Stetson.

I did see Glade and the hood I had slugged at the club and made certain they didn't see me. I knew too much to suit them, that is, if

I was right in my assumption that Glade had stepped over the border this time. He had dirt on his hands that wouldn't wash off.

The bride was the first to appear. Smiling over a sheath of roses with stems almost as long as she was, she popped out of the door of the plane to be greeted by a fusillade of flash bulbs. Millet stepped out on the ramp behind her, a prop smile on his face. He was a handsome devil but his fingers trembled slightly as he lighted a cigarette and stared through the match flare at Glade. Then he saw Lieutenant Green and a scowl wiped the smile from his face.

I left the shelter of the hangar and walked slowly toward the crowd, half expecting to hear a shot any minute as the kid from Oklahoma made good his threat to kill Millet. But either I had misjudged his chin or something had detained him. Holding Cherry by one elbow, Millet walked down the ramp and was swallowed by the crowd.

When I reached it the camera men were concentrating on Cherry, giving her instructions about smiling, raising her skirt, etc.

It was cheese-cake in the rain, but it was good. They didn't need to tell her to smile. The kid was having the time of her life. Cinderella had made good. A kid from Wewoka, Oklahoma, had married the great lover. Lovekin had her Bunny.

I skirted the crowd to the edge of the shelter where Millet was arguing with Lieutenant Green. "This is a hell of a note," he was swearing. "A fine way for you to treat my bride. My God, man! We've just been married! Can't your warrants wait until morning?"

Green said, "No," but added that Millet could be admitted to bail on either warrant, and Bliss, somewhat unwillingly, agreed to accompany them to the Valley Station and post bond on both the manslaughter and hit-and-run charges. So saying, he immediately went into conference with Benny Thomas, the studio's public relations man, and Benny began to circulate among the working stiffs, spreading largess here and there as an inducement for them to play up the romantic angle and tone down the other.

Beaming again, Millet Slipped his hand under his bride's elbow and escorted her to Bliss' car. She was wearing a red, transparent raincoat with a hood. She looked like Little Red Riding Hood. The big bad wolf had her and she was very pleased about it. I doubted that she knew her cousin was dead.

I wanted a word, in fact several words, with Millet, but there was no use in my going to the station. I drove directly to the ranch, parked my car in someone's drive a quarter of a mile away and waded the rest of the distance on foot. Uan somehow had routed out a crew of men and cleared the drive. Every room in the house was lighted for the reception of its sixth bride. I wondered if Millet would carry her over the threshold.

On the chance that Glade might have detailed some of his boys to watch the house I kept well back in the trees. It still was raining but it didn't matter. I was as wet as I could be.

It wasn't more than forty minutes before Millet and his party arrived. It included the bride, Millet, Paul Glade, and his two chimpanzees. All went directly to the rumpus room after being welcomed by Uan. Cherry was no longer smiling. Her eyes were round and sad. Somewhere along the line she had learned that Laura Jean was dead.

Keeping well in the shadows, I moved up to the wall of the rumpus room and stood by an open window, listening.

"Don't take it so hard, kid," Millet was telling his bride. "I couldn't help it. Even Lieutenant Green admits that. It is just one of those things."

The kid was pretty but not so dumb. She wanted to know, "But what was Laura Jean doing walking down the middle of Sepulveda Boulevard with Snippy at three o' clock in the morning?"

Millet said, "There you have me."

Glade added, "She was probably meeting some guy. Maybe this guy named Black her father says she was playing around with."

I could see as well as hear. As Glade spoke the name Black he looked at Millet and the actor winced.

"Undoubtedly," he agreed. He filled a water tumbler half full of whiskey and handed it to Cherry. "Now you drink this like a good girl and go into our room and get ready for bed. I'll be with you in just a minute."

Blushing, she protested she couldn't drink so much whiskey but he insisted and she did as she was told. "Poor Laura Jean," she told Glade in parting. "She would have been so proud to know I'm married to Steve."

Millet patted a convenient curve. "Yeah. Sure. Now you run along. I'll be with you as soon as I have a few words with Mr. Glade about a business matter."

She started out the door, then turned back saying, "I wonder—"

"What?" Millet asked her.

She said, "If I shouldn't have told the police that Mr. Black wasn't the real name of Laura Jean's boy friend."

Millet's face turned ashen.

"What was his name?" Glade asked.

Her eyes wide, Cherry admitted, "1 don't know. She told me he was an actor, an important one. But just like Steve made me promise never to tell anyone we were engaged, he made Laura Jean promise not to tell even me who he really was until they were married."

Looking at the fingernails of his right hand, Glade said, "The fool! The damn fool! No, I don't think it will be necessary for you to tell the cops."

Millet filled the water tumbler with whiskey, drank half of it, then forced the rest on the girl. "Come on. Drink up," he said crisply. "A loving cup to a long and happy married life. Let the dead bury the dead."

She protested, "Steve," but drank it. "Poor Uncle Thaddeus," she added. "He's going to feel just terrible about this." She hiccupped. "And so do I. Poor Laura Jean."

Millet closed the door behind her, walked back to the bar and half filled the tumbler this time.

"Getting stinko isn't going to do you a bit of good," Glade warned him. "You've got to act, and act fast." Millet fingered the four half-dollars that I had laid on the bar and Glade continued, "Of course, if you don't care if Mr. Black goes to the chair, that, I suppose, is Mr. Black's own funeral." His face darkened "And mine." Glade crossed to Millet in three strides and grasped him by the coat front. "Now listen to me, you punk. In trying to collect the dough you owe me I've laid myself wide open to an accessory after the fact charge. And you're going to get me out of it. See? That's why I got you back here from Las Vegas. As I see it, there is only one thing that can trip you up. So listen. Here's what you're going to do."

I listened, all ears. But instead of giving Millet his instructions, Glade said, annoyed, "Close that damn window, will you, Tommy? There's a draft on the back of my neck."

Tommy closed the window. The ranch house was well built. The window casings fitted snugly. Glade continued to talk but I couldn't hear a word he was saying. I sloshed around to the rear of the house in the hope of finding an open window. The one I found was lighted and in Millet's bedroom. Cherry had slipped out of her clothes and into a sheer black nightgown. She had a pretty little body. She reminded me of Sally, as Sally had looked some ten years before. As I watched her she tried to renew her lipstick in the wall of mirrors. She was having trouble in focusing her eyes. And now that she was alone she didn't look too happy. Now that she had what she wanted, I knew what she was thinking. She was wondering if she wanted what she had.

I heard a car pull away from the front of the house and started to move on only to feel the cold, wet muzzle of a gun nuzzling into the slight hollow under my left ear.

"So you lied to me, did you?" the kid from Oklahoma hissed hoarsely. "You want Bessie for yourself. Well, neither of you are going to have her, understand? I've been waiting here in the rain for three hours to kill Millet. And I'm going to kill him just as soon as he walks in that door."

In every ointment there is usually one fly. Arnst Gary was the fly in mine. I hissed back, "Don't be a fool! You'd only go to the chair if you did. This thing is big. It's murder. Put that gun away and let me handle this."

He wanted to know what I was going to do.

I said I didn't know. I didn't. But I did know one thing. I had to get this yokel out of my hair before I could do anything. Backing from the window I turned and faced him. "Okay. If you're going to shoot Millet, let me out of here," I said.

His lips tightened. "No. You'd warn him."

I glanced sideways into the room Cherry was turning down the covers of her bridal bed and for some reason twin tears were trickling down her cheeks. "All right. Shoot him then," I whispered. "I don't like him any better than you do. Shoot him. There he is."

Gary turned his head sideways sharply, leaving his chin exposed. I put all that I had in the blow. It caught him flush on the chin. He grunted and collapsed in my arms just as Millet did enter the room. I took the gun from the youth's fingers, lowered him to the ground, and watched Millet.

He had a bottle and two glasses in his hands. He set the glasses and bottle on one of the tables by the bed, took off his coat and slipped the knot in his tie. I didn't get the move. I had expected something else.

"Well, here we are," he leered at Cherry.

Love making. Romance. The answer to a young girl's prayer. Two glasses, a bottle of whiskey, and "Well, here we are." And he got five thousand a week as the dream lover of millions of women.

Cherry sat on the edge of the bed, her hands folded in her lap. "Yes. Here we are," she said, sniffling.

He poured two shots in the glasses and wanted to know what she was bawling about. She told him, "Laura Jean. Oh, I do so wish it hadn't had to happen."

"So do I," he said sincerely.

He insisted she drink the whiskey. She did and he poured her another and another. It was obvious by then what he was about. He was trying to make her pass out.

Between drinks he petted her automatically and kissed her several times. But his mind wasn't on his business. On top of what she'd had in the rumpus room, the third drink did the trick. Her heavy lids dropped shut. She looked like a sleeping doll. He slipped her legs under the covers and pulled the sheet up to her chin.

Then he got heavily to his feet, retied his tie and put his coat back on. It was fairly clever at that. He was free now to go about his business. If the case ever reached a jury there weren't twelve men out of twelve thousand who would ever believe, after one look at Cherry, that any man *could* leave her on his wedding night. For her part, if she awakened in two or three hours, to find Millet beside her, she would never know he'd been gone. He had an almost perfect alibi for the next few hours.

The youth on the ground began to groan as he came to. I clamped a palm over his mouth, my eyes never leaving Millet. He took a pair of gloves from one of the dresser drawers and put them on. Then, reaching into his side coat pocket, he pulled out and examined a cheap nickeled revolver of the mail-order type. Satisfied it was fully loaded, he dropped it back into his pocket and, walking as if he were wearing a pair of divers' leaded shoes, turned out the light and left the bedroom.

I started around the house and the punk on the ground recovered full consciousness—violently. Cursing me hoarsely he wrapped his arms around my legs and tried to pull me to the ground on top of him. I told him not to be a damn fool, that Millet had gone and I had to follow him. The youth continued to try to wrestle me down. I could have slugged him with the barrel of his own gun. I didn't. As badly as I wanted to follow Millet I also wanted some information. I wanted the youth to explain what he had meant by his remark:

"No. The old man is too danged stubborn. What with the few cattle he runs and a piece or two of town property that he rents he

has just about enough to keep himself and Laura Jean. Not that he couldn't be worth a lot of money."

"Stop it, you fool!" I swore. "I'm on your side."

He wouldn't believe me until I had kicked him half unconscious. Then I hauled him to his feet and shining my flashlight in the window of the bedroom showed him that Cherry, or Bessie as he called her, was both alone and asleep.

Still dubious of my purpose he stumbled after me around to the front of the house. Millet's big car was still parked under the car port, but the black Ford coupe that had been standing next to it was gone and a pair of taillights were fading rapidly down the drive.

It would have taken too long to walk to my own car. I used Millet's imported job. I thought I knew where he was headed and, if possible, I wanted to get there before he did.

I prodded the kid from Oklahoma into the car with his own gun then handed it back to him as I tooled the big car out of the port and headed it down the drive. "Now start talking," I ordered him. "What did you mean by saying old Thaddeus Jones *could* be worth a lot of money."

Saltillo was hushed with the drugged sleep of early morning. There was no black Ford parked in front of 41638. I drove Millet's car around the block and parked it on the next street. Then, Gary at my heels, I cut through someone's yard to come at the place from the rear.

There was a dim light on the second floor in one of the front windows. I tried both doors. They were locked. A kitchen window, however, was open. I cut the screen with my knife and instructed the kid from Oklahoma to wait back of a clump of bushes from which he could see the side door. "As soon as anyone comes," I told him, "make like a whippoorwill."

He said whippoorwills were a woods bird and never frequented crowded cities.

I said that Millet wouldn't know that and crawled in through the window almost knocking over a pile of dirty dishes the old man had stacked in the sink. The body as far as I knew was still down at the morgue but there was a feeling of death in the house.

I slipped off my shoes and tiptoed up the stairs to the second floor. Then, remembering something I had forgotten, I tiptoed back and cracked open the side door to make things convenient for Millet.

Up on the second floor again, I tiptoed down the hall and looked in the front room. Jones was sitting in an easy chair staring off into space and rocking forward and back on the base of his spine the way some people do when their grief seems more than they can bear. From time to time he picked a framed picture from the table and stared at it instead of into space. It was the framed picture of his daughter.

I turned to find a room in which I could hide, reached for my gun—and changed my mind. The cheap little nickel-plated revolver leveled on my middle, Steve Millet was regarding me with alcoholic gravity.

"Wise guy," he said. "You thought you were going to burn me, didn't you, Johnny? You hated me badly enough to throw up your contract with Consolidated to try and get me. Well, you're not going to. I'm going to do what I came to do, then I'm going to let you have it, too."

I asked, stupidly, "How did you get in?"

He said, "Through the front door. I was standing out in front, you sap, when I saw my car drive by. Lucky I took the key from Laura Jean's purse. I had a hunch that I might need it."

I said, "You'll never be able to explain my body."

He had a cigarette in his lips. Twin spirals of smoke curled out his nostrils. His smile was thin. "Why should I attempt to explain it? I'm home in bed with my bride, remember? I married my sixth wife this morning." He motioned with his gun. "All right. Into the room with the old man. I want to get this over with."

Jones evidently hadn't heard us in the hall but he got to his feet as I backed in, directed by the gun in Millet's hand.

"Black. Mr. Black," he greeted Millet.

"Hi-ya," Millet said coldly.

Jones looked from him to me, then back at the gun in Millet's hand. "What does this mean?" he boomed. "Why are you pointing that gun at this policeman?" Anger darkened his face. "And what did you do to Laura Jean? Why did you leave her at that lonely spot? What was she doing walking in the rain at three o'clock in the morning?" He added, "Laura Jean is dead, you know."

"Yes," Millet said. "I know."

"You should know," I needled. "You killed her."

I doubt if the old man heard me but he read my lips. "He killed Laura Jean? Mr. Black killed Laura Jean? The police told me she'd been run down by some actor by the name of Millet."

"He is Millet," I told him.

"Millet? Black is Millet?" Jones puzzled.

Steve wasn't happy about what he had to do. I asked if I could smoke a cigarette. He said I could and I whistled the first few bars of *Over There* as I fished the pack from my pocket. He wanted to know what the idea was. "I'm making like a whippoorwill," I told him. I lighted the cigarette. "How are you going to do it, Steve? Shoot me first, then shoot the old man and put the fatal gun in his hand? That was the payoff in your picture *Crime on Tuesday*. Remember? That was the one in which Sally starred with you. And remember what happened to the villain? They waltzed him up to San Quentin and scorched the seat of his pants."

Murder wasn't Millet's forte. Blood flooding his jowls, he scowled at me. "Shut up. You're damn right I'm going to shoot you and I'm going to shoot you first."

"You waited too long," the kid from Oklahoma said from the hallway behind him. He nudged the base of Millet's spine with the muzzle of his dog leg. "Drop that gun, or don't. I'd just as soon you didn't. I flew over a thousand miles to kill you and I'd hate to spend all that money for nothing. Make up your mind."

"Arnst!" old man Jones gasped. "Arnst Gary! What are you doing here?"

Gary told him, "I came to take Bessie home where she and Laura Jean might better both have stayed." He repeated, "Drop that gun!"

His face a fish-belly white, the gun fell from Millet's nerveless fingers. Looking over his shoulder he asked Gary, "Who are you?"

"The man that Bessie should have married," the kid from Oklahoma told him. "The man she would have married if you hadn't turned her head with a lot of nonsense."

He started to say more when a window shot open next door and some woman began to scream: "Help! Police! Murder! Five men have just sneaked into Mr. Jones' house. Someone with a phone call the police! There is something terribly wrong next door!"

Gary and I made two. Millet made it three. His face apoplectic with anger, Paul Glade, followed by the chimp I had slugged out at his club, pounded up the stairs to complete the total. Both of them had guns in their hands. "You damn fool," he swore at Millet. "I was afraid something like this would happen. That's why I followed you. Shoot him! Shoot him, you fool, and let's get out of here!"

He dug his gun into Gary's back as he spoke.

"Pick it up," he continued to Millet. "Pick up your gun and shoot the old man. We'll take these other two with us when we leave."

Like Millet, murder wasn't his forte. Glade was a gambler. Before he knew what had happened the kid from Oklahoma spun on his heel, depressed the barrel of Glade's gun with his left hand and slapped him hard with the barrel of the gun in his right. Glade went down like a sack of wet markers.

At the same time I swung on the chimp. I hit him so hard the back of his head left a mark on the plaster but not before he had burned one into my shoulder. Then I turned back to Millet. With the panic of a frightened sheep he was dodging wild blows of the piccolo, forgetting he had a gun in his hand. The great romantic lover. I twisted the gun from his fingers and then stepped in to keep old Thaddeus Jones from clubbing him to death. The old man didn't know the whole score but he was nobody's fool. He wanted to kill Millet. He would have if I hadn't stopped him.

"Let the law do it," I told him.

Then everything grew hazy. I heard Gary say, "You're shot!" and the next thing I knew a police surgeon was bandaging my wound and Green was pacing around my prone body like Leo the M.G.M. lion.

"Can he talk?" he demanded of the surgeon.

I told him, "Fluently," sat up, and drank the beaker of whiskey that Jones squatted down on his haunches to offer me.

"Then talk!" Green demanded. "What the hell is this all about?"

I told him, "Murder."

Blood still trickling from a nasty cut on his forehead, Glade said, "The man is mad. Out of the kindness of my heart and in deepest sympathy for his grief I accompanied Mr. Millet here to see if Mr. Jones needed financial assistance. Having accidentally brought about the death of Mr. Jones' daughter, Steve naturally feels responsible."

"That's quick thinking, Paul," I admitted. "But you're bailing a sinking ship." Millet was trembling as if he had the ague. "Black and Millet are one and the same," I told Lieutenant Green. "And the reason he came here tonight was to kill the girl's father so he couldn't identify him."

Green mulled that over. "Then the girl's death—"

"Wasn't accidental," I told him. "He met her at that drive-in stand where you found her car, drove her to the storm drain, killed her deliberately, and threw her body into the water. You see there were *two* screams. One when she realized what he intended to do. The second when he did it."

Millet buried his face in his hands and moaned, "Oh, God!"

Green looked at Glade. "And Paul?"

"Paul, merely smelled money and climbed on the gravy train," I told him. "As much as I hate to admit it, all that you have on him is an accessory after the fact charge." I watched Millet shake and enjoyed it. "But with Steve now it's something different. You can book him for murder in the first degree."

Green puzzled, "But with everything to live for, why should he get himself into a mess like this?"

I said, "That's just the point. He didn't have everything to live for, at least those things, namely money, that are important to him. He's known he's been slipping for some time. He knew Consolidated didn't intend to renew his contract. He owed Paul fifty thousand dollars." I scowled at Millet. "But being a far-sighted heel he anticipated this two years ago and bent a bow, a bow with two strings to it. One named Laura Jean, the other her cousin, Bessie." I asked Thaddeus Jones. "How large a ranch have you?"

He said, "Not large. About five hundred acres."

"And there are oil wells on it?"

"No, sir," he boomed proudly, "there are not. I wouldn't have one of the stinking things on my place. I am a rancher, sir, as my father and his father were before me."

I winked at the kid from Oklahoma. "But there are oil wells around your ranch?"

Jones admitted indignantly, "They practically encircle me."

I addressed Arnst Gary. "You're from the same town, son. Tell Lieutenant Green what you told me driving over here."

The youth bent the brim of his Stetson into a sharper peak. "Well, it's common knowledge back home," he told Green, "that one of the biggest pools of oil in the state is under the Jones acreage." He grinned. "But no one had ever been able to talk reason to the old man, not even his own daughter. He says he has ample to live on and he intends to live and die a rancher."

I asked, "But the acreage is valuable, isn't it?"

"It is."

"And if wells were sunk on it, they might bring in how much a day?"

He shook his head. "There is no telling that. But even if oil dropped back to a dollar a barrel I'd say up to two thousand dollars a day clear profit."

"Okay. There it is," I told Green.

"I still don't get it," he admitted. "How did Millet hope to profit?"

The rest was guess-work on my part, but when Millet did break down and confess I wasn't too far from fact. I said he had probably hoped to marry Laura Jean but she couldn't make up her mind whether he wanted her or the fortune that would eventually come to her. Meanwhile he was also making love to Cherry as a second string to his bow. As the daughter of Jones' sister and the only other blood relation, she was next in line to inherit."

"Say, that's right," Gary said. "I never thought of that."

I don't believe he had. I continued by saying that pressed for money Millet had undoubtedly demanded that Laura Jean to come to some decision. Whether her answer was no or whether she somehow found out he was trying to ride two horses was something Millet would have to tell us. Whatever it was, he knew the game was up if she talked to her cousin. So he made the early morning tryst with her, deliberately killed her, threw her body in the drain, and then drove home and phoned me.

But to make certain that Cherry didn't back out when she learned what happened, he married her before she knew. Green knew almost as much about the rest of it as I did. Worrying about his fifty grand, Glade had gone to the scene of the murder and learned as I had learned about the screams. Scenting big money in blackmail if nothing else he had contacted Millet in Las Vegas by phone and demanded to be cut in oft whatever was cooking.

The police surgeon broke in then to say, "You've talked enough."

And that was okay with me. I had said all that I needed to say. Green asked me to keep myself on tap and left with his three prisoners. I had another shot with the old man; then I asked the kid from Oklahoma if he would drive me back in Millet's car to where I was parked.

He said he would, and did.

The rain had stopped. As far as I could see the Valley was a carpet of green and blossoms. As I transferred to my own car he cleared his throat and said, "I don't aim to thank you for what you've done for me. I don't know rightly how I could. But, well, seeing as you seem to know a little something about women I—I would like a piece of advice."

I knew what was on his mind. "Take Millet's car back where we got it," I told him. "Then go in and talk to Bessie. Bust in a window or kick a door down if you have to. No," I corrected myself. I took Sally's key to Millet's front door from my key ring and handed it to him. I'd had my use of it. "No," I repeated. "Use the front door. Don't try to soften the story. Don't try to make it tougher than it was Just tell it as it happened."

He thanked me for the key but made no motion to take his foot from my running board. His heart was in his words. "You think in time she'll grow to care for me again?"

"I'm positive," I told him. "And I'll tell you how I know. The same thing happened to another lad about ten years ago. Steve Millet married his girl right out from under his nose. And in a way it was worse with him. He had to eat his heart out for two years before she realized she'd made a mistake, divorced Steve and married him." I hesitated, told him, "That was her key I just gave you."

"Oh," he said. "Oh, I see." He took his foot off the running board.

I stopped at the big gas station on the corner of Van Nuys and Ventura, told them to fill up my tank and check the oil and called Sally while I waited.

"I'm on my way home," I told her.

She said, "Oh, honey, I've been so worried."

She meant it. Her voice had that little catch to it that can make a man's eyes, smart.

"There's been quite some trouble," I admitted. "But Steve Millet is done for, finished."

There was no hesitation. She said, "I'm glad." Her voice was almost harsh, but concern crept back into it as she added, "But you're all right, Johnny? You're okay?"

I was tired. I was hungry. My shoulder was giving me hell. But I was telling the truth when I, told her, "I feel fine. Just fine. Put on a pot of coffee, sweetheart. I'll be there in fifteen minutes."

NOTHING TO WORRY ABOUT

IF THERE WERE ANY LETTERS of fire on Assistant State's Attorney Brad Sorrel's broad and distinguished brow they were invisible to his fellow passengers in the lighted cabin of the Washington-Chicago plane, as it circled the Cicero Airport at fifteen minutes to midnight. The stewardess, appraising his broad shoulders, greying temples and hearty laughter, considered the woman to whom he was returning very fortunate indeed. His seatmate had found him intelligent and sympathetic.

At no time during the flight, or during the hours preceding it, had there been anything in Sorrel's voice or demeanor to which anyone could point and say, "I knew it at the time. He was nervous. He couldn't concentrate. His conversation was forced. He talked and acted like a man about to kill his wife."

It was no sudden decision on Sorrel's part. He had considered killing Frances, often. Only a firm respect for the law that he, himself, represented had deterred him. He had, in the name of the state, asked for, and been given, the lives of too many men, to be careless with his own. Intolerable as his marital situation had become it was preferable to facing a jury whom he had lost the right to challenge.

The No Smoking and Please Fasten Your Seat Belt panels over the door of the pilot's compartment blinked on. The lights of the field rushed up to meet the plane.

This is it, Sorrel thought. *In twenty minutes, thirty at the most, Frances will be dead. Poor soul.*

His seat mate wound up the telling of the involved argument and verbal slug-fest in which he had just engaged with the Office Of Price Administration. Sorrel gave him one half of his mind, sympathizing hugely, assuring him he had been right, that it couldn't last forever, and agreeing that it seemed that private business was headed for a boom.

The other half of his mind considered the thing that he had to do. It would not be pleasant. In his search for a solution to his problem he had inspected, weighed, and judged, the none too many means by which murder could be done. The alleged clever methods—accidental death, suicide, death by misadventure—he had rejected almost immediately. They left too many loopholes for failure. Few of them ever succeeded. There was a reason. No matter how brilliant a killer might be he was seldom, if ever, a match for the combined technical, executive, and judicial branches of the law.

Crime detection, trial, and judgment had become akin to an exact science.

The art of killing, the three M's, means, method, motive, had changed little in the known history of man. To take a life one still had to shoot, knife, drown, strike, strangle, or poison the party of the unwanted part. And, as with most basic refinements to the art of living, the first known method of murder used—that of striking the party to be removed with whatever object came first to hand— was still the most difficult of detection, providing of course that the party who did the striking could maintain a reasonable plea of being elsewhere at the time.

It was, after mature consideration, that method that Sorrel had chosen. He had even chosen his weapon, one of the heavy cut-glass candlesticks that stood on Frances' dressing table.

"Murphy. J. P. Murphy is the name," his seatmate identified himself. He shook Sorrel's hand vigorously. "It's been a pleasure to meet you, Prosecutor. And if you do decide to enter the senatorial race, as I've seen hinted at in the papers, you can count on my vote as certain."

Sorrel's hearty laugh filled the plane. "Thanks. I'll remember that, Murphy."

His only luggage was his brief case. The stewardess insisted on getting it down from the rack for him. He tucked a forbidden bill in the breast pocket of her uniform. "Nice trip," he smiled. "And thanks."

"Thank *you,* Mr. Sorrel!" She beamed. One met such few really nice men. Most tipping hands brushed or hovered, seeking a partial return on their investment.

Sorrel stood in the open door of the plane a moment, sniffing the night air. The fine weather was still holding. It was neither too hot nor too cold.

He descended the steps and lifted a hand in greeting to the pilot as he passed the nose of the plane. He did so habitually on his not infrequent trips. There must be no departure from the norm, no errors of omission or commission, no nervously spilled milk in which the bacteria of suspicion might breed.

He, John Sorrel, assistant state's attorney, was returning from Washington with nothing on his mind but the successful conclusion of the business that had taken him there. He wasn't nervous. He felt fine. He assured himself that he did.

In the doorway of the terminal Murphy touched his arm. "I'm taking a cab to the Loop. If you'd like to share it, Sorrel—"

"Thanks, no," Sorrel said. "My car should be waiting." He managed to edge his words with the proper amount of innuendo without being vulgar. "You see I—well, I'm not going directly home."

The other man winked. "I—see."

They parted after shaking hands again. He was, Sorrel realized, running the risk of being slightly too clever. But the more people who knew, or who thought they knew, that he had gone directly from the plane to Evelyn's apartment the stronger would be his alibi.

He had never kept their affair a secret. He doubted that any prosecutor, judge, or jury—if it should come to that—would question so embarrassing an alibi as a husband's being forced to admit that, while his wife had been killed, he had been with another woman, railing against the deceased, because she had refused to divorce him.

Despite the lateness of the hour the terminal was crowded. He saw three or four men whom he knew and nodded cordially to as he passed through the terminal.

Jackson was waiting behind the wheel of a department car. Sorrel tossed his case into the back seat and slid in beside him. "So you got my wire."

"And why not?" Jackson asked. "You wanna go home, the office, or—" He left the question open.

Sorrel sighed. "Home, I suppose. But let's drop by the Eldorado first."

"I figured that," Jackson said.

Sorrel rode, the night wind cool on his cheeks, eager to be done with what he had to do, wishing that Frances had been reasonable. If she had been, if she had been willing to divorce him, none of this would have to be.

In front of the building he told Jackson, "I won't be long, I think."

Jackson fished in his vest pocket for a toothpick, found one. "Take your time."

He meant it. He liked Sorrel. He liked Evelyn, too. For all of her good looks she was a lady. Frances Sorrel wasn't, what with her calling a spade a dirty shovel and her drinking and her fighting—she was no wife for a man who soon might be a senator. Although, at that, he reflected, he had heard someone say that she had worked like a dog for the money that had put Sorrel through law school, and she had always sworn she hadn't started to drink and chase until he had gone lace curtain Irish on her.

Under the marquee of the building the colored doorman grinned whitely at Sorrel. "Glad to see you back, Mister Smith. Been missin' you for a week now."

Sorrel creased a five dollar bill and slipped it into his hand. "I've been in Washington saving the nation."

The doorman chuckled, hugely amused. "He say he been in Washington savin' the nation," he confided to Jackson.

Jackson continued to pick at his teeth. "Yair."

Inside the lobby, Sorrel paused briefly, suddenly short of breath. This was murder. He, John Sorrel, an assistant state's attorney who would have been state's attorney had it not been for his wife, and who was being considered by the party as a senatorial candidate, was proposing to steal into his own home by stealth and remove the sole obstacle who stood in the path of his political success.

That angle would not enter the case, however. It would not be considered a motive. None of the powers-that-were had ever mentioned Frances. But he knew. There was the feminine vote to consider. And what with things as they were the party couldn't afford to take a chance. Frances' scenes were too well known. She drank. She cursed. She was unfaithful. Not that he had ever been so fortunate as to obtain proof that would stand in a court of law.

He closed his eyes and saw his wife as he had seen her, fat, slovenly dressed, her face puffed with drink, during the last public scene that she had made. That had been in the lobby of the Chalmer's House, before a delighted ring of onlookers.

"Sure I'm drunk. An' I'm a tramp," she had taunted while he had tried vainly to hush her. "An' don't you tell me to shut up. Wash a hell. I'm human. The trouble with you is that you've got too big for your bed. You're one of them whitened seple-curs like Father Ryan wash always talking about." She had turned to the crowd, her voice suddenly gin-throaty, maudlin tears spilling down her cheeks. "I'm not good enough for him any more. Me, who put him through school, who loved him when he didn't have a dime." She had attempted to embrace him. "Cansha understand? I still love you, Johnny." The tears had dried as abruptly as they had come. "An' I'll shee you in hell before I'll let some painted young tart make a bigger fool of you than you are. Now go ahead an' hit me. I dare you to, you blankety blankety blank."

Sorrel opened his eyes, his moment of weakness gone. There was only the one thing to do But at least in one respect she was wrong. He was very human. He wanted to feel Evelyn's arms soft and cool around his neck, hear her assure him again that some day everything would be all right, if only they were patient.

His jaw muscles tightening, he opened the door of the self-service elevator and punched the twelfth floor button. He was finished with being patient. He had been patient for ten years. It was not his fault, it was her own fault, that Frances had not grown with him. One thing he knew. He could no longer stand the sight or sound or touch of her.

Tonight must end it.

In front of Evelyn's door he slipped his key from his pocket, paused at the realization that if he saw her now he would make her a party to his crime. More, she would attempt to dissuade him. It was best that she know nothing about it, until the affair was over.

Light streamed out from under her door. Her radio was playing softly. He could hear the sound of movement, a drawer being opened and closed. It was enough to know that she was home, that she had received his wire and was waiting. Good girl. Evelyn was a brick. Whatever happened, he could count on her.

He descended to the second floor, left die elevator and walked down the service stairs and out of the side door. The coupe was parked where he had left it. His one fear had been that he might find it stripped.

The motor started easily. He glanced at his watch in the dash light. Five of the thirty minutes that he had allotted himself were gone. Driving at forty miles an hour, the three miles he had to travel would take him two minutes each way. It was fifteen minutes of one. Allow even six more minutes for mishaps and he still had plenty of time to do what he had to do and be back in Evelyn's apartment within a half hour from the time that he had left Jackson. At one fifteen he would phone down to the doorman and ask him to have Jackson bring up his brief case and the bottle of rye it contained.

He had no fear that Frances would not be at home. His telegram had stated that his plane was arriving at midnight. Clinging to the tattered remnants of their marriage she always made it a practice to be home and more or less sober whenever he returned.

"You'll never catch me that way," she had told him once. "I'm a good wife to you, Johnny, see? And I'm willing to be a better one if you would only let me. Why can't we start all over?"

There were a dozen answers to that one, the best of which was Evelyn. The two women had never met. Frances knew that she existed, that was all. That was enough.

As he slowed for the intersection at 63rd Street, Sorrel smiled wryly at a suggestion that Evelyn, intrigued by the fact that they had never met, had made.

"We know she's not true to you, Johnny," she had pointed out. "She has no right to point a finger. She doesn't know me. So, why can't I strike up a drinking acquaintance with her, or take a job as her maid, or something, and get some concrete proof that would stand in a divorce court?"

Sorrel had refused to hear of it. Frances was shrewd. A scene between the two was unthinkable. Frances fought as they fought in back of the yards, where both of them had been born—for keeps. Then, too, a sense of guilt had assailed him. His own hands were not clean. He, and he alone, was responsible for Frances' infidelities. She had a warm, impetuous, nature. She was merely reaching out for the love that he denied her. He had told Evelyn at the time that whatever was done, he would do. He was keeping his word now.

There were few cars on 63rd Street. There were none on the darker residential street onto which he turned. He drove for another quarter mile and parked a half a block and across the street from his home.

There were lights in both the kitchen and in Frances' bedroom. The shades of the bedroom were drawn, but, as he watched, a vague figure crossed the room, too far back of the shade to seem more than a passing shadow.

His eyes felt suddenly hot and strained. His throat contracted. His mouth was dry. His hands felt cold and clammy on the wheel. He sat a moment longer, wondering at himself, revolted by the thing he had come to do. This was murder. This was what other men had done for reasons no better than his own and he, in his smug superiority, safe in the law's ivory tower, had thundered against them and denounced them as cool-blooded conniving scoundrels.

He stepped from the car with an effort and crossed the street. He had come a long way in his climb up—he intended to go still further. With Frances dead and Evelyn beside him, there was no goal to which he might not aspire.

He stopped under a spreading elm tree in the yard and cursed his shaking hands. There was no reason to be afraid. The law would never touch him. He had planned too well. There would be no insurance angle. Frances had none. His only gain would be peace of mind and that wasn't considered a motive for murder. A few of the boys in his own office might suspect him but no one would be able to prove a thing.

Frances' failings were well known. She had come home drunk. She had left the door unlocked. A night prowler had entered and killed her. No one would be more surprised and shocked than he when he returned with Jackson an hour from now and found her—dead.

He slipped his key in the front door. The inner bolt was shot and it refused to open. He considered ringing the bell and killing her in the hall. He decided to stay, as far as possible, with his original plan. There was no convenient weapon in the hall. A single scream would shatter the stillness of the sleeping street. What he had to do must be done in silence.

The back door leading into the kitchen was open but the screen door was locked. He , slipped on a pair of gloves and fumbled m one corner of the porch where he had remembered seeing a rusty ice pick. His luck was holding. The pick was there. He probed it through the screen and lifted the hook from its eye.

The door open he waited, listening, hearing nothing. There was a half emptied bottle of milk, a clouded glass, and the remains of a peanut butter sandwich on the kitchen table.

Frances, he decided, was playing the sober and repentant wife this time.

Believe me, John. I love you. I'll stop drinking. I'll do anything you say. You're all that matters to me. Why can't we start all over?

He had heard it so many times that he could play the record by heart. He noted that the kitchen shade was up. Anyone entering the kitchen would be visible from the darkened windows of the house next door. Sweat beading on his forehead, he slipped in a hand before him and snapped the switch, thankful that he had noticed the shade in time. It was the little things of murder that sent men to the chair.

The darkness magnified his strain. His mouth grew even dryer. He heard, or thought he heard, the pounding of his heart. He had to force himself to cross the kitchen, feeling his way along the wall to the rear stairs,

Now he could hear sounds in the bedroom. She seemed to be opening and closing drawers, probably in search of one of the bottles she was always hiding from herself.

He crossed the dark hall toward the closed bedroom door and his weight caused a board to creak. The light in the bedroom went out and the door opened. They stood only feet apart in the black hallway, aware of each other but unable to see.

The blood, Sorrel thought suddenly. *It will splatter. I'll be covered with blood. Damn it! Why didn't I think of that!"*

Then he realized he still was clutching the rusted ice pick in his hand. It was as good a weapon as any, better than most. Murder Incorporated had used them as the chief tool of their trade. An ice pick had been used in the case of the State versus Manny Capper. The sweat on his brow turned cold. Manny had gone to the chair.

Galvanized by his own terror, crying put hoarsely, Sorrel sprang forward. His groping hand felt teeth in time to clamp his palm over the welling scream. It died still-born as he plunged the pick in his hand repeatedly into the yielding flesh. The body he held ceased squirming and sagged limply. He allowed it to fall to the floor, relieved to be rid of it.

The ice pick fell from his nerveless hand. He tried to fumble a match from his pocket and could not. His hands were shaking too badly. Afraid of the dark, afraid of the woman whom he had killed, he squatted beside the body and felt for a pulse with the back of his wrist, where flesh gaped between glove and coat cuff. There was no pulse. It was over, done with, *finis.* He was free.

He crept back down the stairs and out through the kitchen to the porch. Then he remembered the pick. It would have no fingerprints on it. He considered returning for it and his stomach rebelled.

So there were no fingerprints on the death weapon. So what? Most house prowlers with the sense of gnats wore gloves. It was nothing for him to worry over.

He walked silently, unseen, back to his car and examined his gloves in the dash light. One was slightly splattered with blood but there seemed to be none on the cuffs of his suit. All that remained to be done was to rid himself of the gloves.

It was over, done. He was free. There was nothing to stop him now, nothing to stop the boys from running him for whatever office they pleased. Frances had made her last scene. He was young, under forty. His new life was just beginning.

As he drove the horror of the thing that he had been forced to do left him. He wanted to sing, to yell, to shout to the stars that he was free. He contented himself with a grin.

It had been a relatively simple matter, after all. He wadded the gloves into a ball and tossed them out the car window. They could not be traced to him. There was nothing to tie him to the murder but the fact that he and Frances were married. Back at the Eldorado he parked the coupe in the same space it had occupied before and glanced at his watch, before switching off the lights. It was eleven minutes past one. He was four minutes ahead of schedule.

He expended them by walking to the corner and peering around it cautiously. The doorman and Jackson were deep in some discussion. Satisfied that he had not been missed, he entered the side door.

Telling Evelyn would take some doing. She would be horrified at first, but she was quickwitted enough to realize that no other course had been open to him. It didn't matter now. All that mattered was that the thing was done.

His throat and mouth were normal again. In the bright light of the cage he could see no bloodstains on his suit. He had been fortunate. He was whistling softly, almost cheerfully, as he inserted his key in the door.

~ ~ ~ ~ ~

The radio was still playing softly. A bottle of his best scotch beside her, Frances was sitting in one of Evelyn's easy chairs. "I knew you'd come here first," she said. "What's a matter? Was your plane late?"

He stared at her open-mouthed, screams he was unable to utter tearing at his throat.

"You poor damn fool," his wife continued. "Why didn't you let me meet her? Why didn't you make me realize what a swell kid she really was? Why didn't you tell me that the boys wanted to run you for senator? You should have known me better, John. You're my man. You always will be. No tramp was goin' to take you from me. But a sweet kid like that is another matter." She fluffed at her frowsy hair. "I feel kind of honored like."

Sorrel managed to gasp one word, "Evelyn—"

Frances nipped at the Scotch. "Oh, you didn't know. Well, she showed at the house his morning and gave me a song and dance about being a maid out of work, her with fingernails that long." She laughed, shortly. "So I hired her and I pumped her. She's probably goin' through all my things right low, spyin' on me." Frances picked an oblong scrap of yellow paper from the table. "She never even got a chance to see her telegram because I copped her key from her purse and come over here shortly after I got the telegram that you sent me. Mine was all right. But after I read this one I kinda wondered." She read it aloud, " 'Sweetheart. Be in your apartment at twelve tonight. Don't leave it for any reason. And don't let anyone in but me. This is important, more important than you realize.' "

His voice sounding strange to himself, Sorrel asked. "You—knew?"

Frances Sorrel smiled thinly. "I know you," she admitted. "But don't worry. Think nothing of it. As long as your plane was late, you've got nothing to worry about."

DANCE WITH THE DEATH-HOUSE DOLL

CHAPTER ONE

YOUR PICK OF MURDER

IT WAS THE FIRST TIME I had ever been in a prison. I didn't like it. The warden's secretary started to tell me to go peddle my papers, looked at the triple bank of ribbons on my chest, and changed his mind.

"You earn those, Sergeant?" he demanded.

I told him that I hadn't found them in cracker-jack boxes and repeated my request.

"And you don't know the girl?"

I told him the truth. I had never even seen a picture of her. All I was doing was carrying out Johnny's last request. Until I had gone to her former address that morning, I hadn't the least idea that she was in prison, let alone in the death house, slated to burn for murder.

He said, "It sounds screwy to me. But I'll see what the warden says."

He went into the inner office. I walked to the window. The square-jawed man in the battered hat, who had ridden down with me on the train, was talking to one of the guards on the wall. I imagined that he had picked me up at the girl's apartment. That had been about ten that morning.

The warden came to his office door. "Harris tells me that your name is Duval—Sergeant Mike Duval."

I said that was right.

"And you want to see Mona Ambler?"

That wasn't strictly the truth. There was more to it than that. But I wasn't going to talk—my only interest in the girl was keeping the promise I had made to Johnny. And that they knew.

"Yes," I said. I wondered what kind of a run-around this was.

The warden considered a moment, then invited me into his office and offered me a chair. "Suppose you tell me all about it, Sergeant."

There wasn't much to tell. I told them what there was. Johnny was my kid brother. He had met the girl on his last leave in the

States. They had been married, planning big things, like kids do. But they hadn't had much time. His leave had been canceled. In Sicily, he had gotten a letter from her asking how about a dependent's allowance.

"This was how long ago?" the warden asked.

"The letter came about six months ago," I told him. "But Johnny hasn't been in the States for over a year and a half." He nodded, and I added, "The letter said she had had a boy."

He built a temple of his fingers. "So?"

"So Johnny got killed in the landing at Anzio. But before he died, he asked if I'd take care of her and the kid. I said I would."

The secretary said that it was the damnedest thing he had ever heard of—that no mention of a child had been made at her trial. I couldn't figure that, but I let it go.

The warden's name was Kane. He suggested, "Suppose we go see Mona."

He led the way down a long, narrow, stone corridor that smelled of antiseptic. Every two hundred feet or so, a guard had to open steel doors to let us through. While we were crossing a large stone yard toward a little separate building, he asked if I was familiar with the case.

I told him I wasn't. The girl—even her name—meant nothing to me.

"She's earned the chair, Sergeant," he said. "She lured a poor stupe of a wholesale jeweler up to her hotel room and shot him in cold blood."

A matron opened the door of a small office. When Kane told her what we wanted, she said she would get the girl. "But I don't care how many confessions she signed," the matron added, "that girl never killed anyone."

Kane looked at his nails and said nothing.

I don't know what I expected. But the girl who came in wasn't it. She didn't look like a killer to me. She looked like a scared little kid wearing her mother's old-fashioned gold earrings.

"This is Sergeant Mike Duval, Johnny Duval's brother," the warden introduced me. "Johnny died in the landing at Anzio. The sergeant has brought back his last request—he wants to take care of the child. There was a child?"

She winced as if he had slapped her. When she spoke, her voice was low and throaty. "Yes. There was a child. There *is* a child," she added.

He wanted to know where it was and she told him that it was none of his business.

I cut in then and told her that she didn't need to worry, that I'd see the kid was taken care of for life. All she had to do was name her lawyer and I'd make the arrangements with him.

She looked at me and seemed to quiet down.

"Let's get on with it," I suggested. "I've only got five days leave. I've got to be back in New York on the twelfth."

I asked her her lawyer's name and address—and the kid's. She gave them to me. She asked a little about Johnny and I told her. She cried a little, and when it was over, I stood holding her hand like a fool. She looked at me and said suddenly, "Since Johnny went away, I'd forgotten guys like you still existed." And then she added with a smile, "Funny-face."

I'd put the last lad who had called me that in the station hospital. But the way that she said it, I didn't mind it a bit. I have a funny face. And she still didn't look like a killer.

Then the warden suggested we'd better go.

I asked her if there was anything I could do for her. She told me that there wasn't.

"Just—just think of me once in a while," she smiled.

Then she began to bawl in the matron's arms and the warden walked me out of there. He kept saying, "Don't let her get you. She's no good. The state proved it at her trial."

I told him what I had thought before and he asked didn't I know there was a war on. "All she wanted from your brother was a dependency allotment."

He started naming names, then, in connection with the state's case against her, and one stuck in my craw—that of Joe LaFanti— I had read it in the papers a long time ago, when he had been picked up by the cops and charged with one racket or another.

We shook hands in his office and I thanked him for being as helpful as he had. He said to think nothing of it, and I was out in front of the prison again, climbing into the taxi I had waiting. The square-jawed lad in the battered hat was still waiting, too.

I called over to him and told him that if he intended to tail me back to Chicago, he might as well climb into the cab with me and split expenses as far as the station in Joliet.

He pretended that he didn't hear me. And that was all right with me. I was to wish a little later that I had walked over and busted him in the jaw. When I tried to do it at Central Bureau, he had too many cops around him.

I rode back in the smoker all the way, and it was a hell of a
thing—I kept seeing Mona the girl all the way, and thinking how
little and white and frightened she had looked when I had left her
bawling in the matron's arms.

I was still thinking about her when I walked through the train
gates into the LaSalle Street Station in Chicago and the big lad
tapped me on the shoulder.

"Sergeant Duval?"

I said that was my name. He said that his name was Diamond,
of the headquarters homicide squad and he wondered if I would
mind answering a few questions he wanted to ask.

"Concerning what?" I asked.

He told me, "Murder."

There were eight big lads in the squad room, including the gent
in the battered felt hat.

He thought he was a choirmaster. "Now you're going to sing,
and sing loud," he told me. He ran his finger across my campaign
ribbons and medal bars. "Those don't mean a thing to us. You can
buy 'em in any hock shop. Start talking, phoney. What was the big
gag about getting to see Mona Ambler?"

I told him the truth. He laughed, "Don't give us that heifer dust.
You just used that yarn about the kid as a stall to get in and talk to
her. Where did she plant the rocks? What's LaFanti's latest stunt
to save her?"

I said I didn't know, that I didn't know LaFanti.

They all laughed heartily at that. I insisted it was the truth and
the lad in the battered felt clipped me with a sap so hard that the
whiskey veins stood out in his face and I bounced off the wall,
"Start singing, stooge," he ordered.

I tried to get back at him but there were too many cops between
us. Every time I'd belt one off his feet, two more would step up.
They had me on, the floor and were working on my face when a
slim, blond, middle-aged man wearing nose glasses walked into
the squad room and asked what was going on. I found out later his
name was Olson and he was the First Assistant State's Attorney.

The guys who had been working on my face got up. Nobody
answered him.

"I'm waiting, Captain Corson," Olson said.

The big lad in the battered felt was Corson. "Look. You run
your office. I'll run mine," he told Olson. "LaFanti's up to something. I spotted it this morning when this musical comedy soldier

showed up at Mona's old apartment. He laid it on too thick, see? As if anyone didn't know where she was. The case has been in all the papers for two months."

Olson asked me how about it? I told him that outside of the Stars and Stripes, newspapers had been scarce on the beachhead at Anzio. He asked for my travel orders, read them and handed them back saying, "I can't begin to tell you how sorry I am that this happened, Duval. And as for you," he looked at Corson, "I wouldn't be surprised if this means your shield. It just so happens that the sergeant's bars and ribbons aren't phoney."

Corson's face turned grey. He was forty-eight or forty-nine, I knew he was thinking of his pension. "How was I to know?" he asked, stiff-lipped. "I never saw a guy with three banks of ribbons before, outside of General MacArthur."

"You have now," Olson told him.

He said that I could use his office if I wanted to wash up and brush my uniform. I wanted to, and I did. When I looked halfway G.I. again, I lighted a cigarette and asked Olson if he would mind telling me the story. He asked if I meant about Mona, I told him I did.

He said, "There isn't a lot to tell. We've had her listed as La-Fanti's girl for almost six months now. But outside of paying for a lawyer, he hasn't lifted a finger, so far as we can tell, to save her. That's what stirred Corson's bile. You see, LaFanti has always boasted that his political in is so strong that nobody connected with him would ever burn."

I asked him how long Mona had to live. He told me five days. He also said that they were expecting a last minute move by La-Fanti to save her, although the Governor had sworn that he would refuse to reprieve her or commute her sentence.

I asked why the state was so anxious to burn her. He told me. It wasn't pretty. She and a diamond salesman by the name of Stein had gotten drunk together. At least Stein had gotten drunk. Some time during the night, after he had passed out, she had put a .38 to his head and blown his brains out. No one had heard the shot but the coroner set the approximate time at four o'clock in the morning. She had made two outside phone calls after that but the police had been unable to trace them, as there was a new girl on the switchboard and she had neglected to write them down. At seven Mona had called the desk and told them to send for the police. When homicide had gotten there, she had been crying in a chair and some two hundred thousand dollars worth of diamonds that were known to have been in Stein's possession had disappeared. Her prints were on the murder gun. The diamonds had never been found. She had confessed she killed Stein.

"Your brother picked a hell of a dame to fall in love with," he concluded. "If you'd come to me first, I could have told you that, as a side-line, she made a racket of marrying soldiers and then dunning them for a dependent's allowance. The Feds were after her when we got her."

I thanked him for his time and trouble. He wanted to know if there was anything more he could tell me. I told him he'd said enough and got the hell out of there. My face was hot. No wonder Corson had thought I was a phoney.

"Think of me once in a while."

I swore.

I started north up State Street. Somebody said, behind me, "Going our way, Sergeant?"

I started to turn and a gun barrel swathed in a coat pocket bored into my spine.

"Which way are you going?" I asked.

The invisible lad with the gun prodded me towards a big car parked at the curb. There were two hoods in front. A big, smooth-shaven, good-looking lad with a smile as oily as his hair was holding down tire back seat.

"Does it matter, Sergeant?" he smiled. "Get in. I want to talk to you. My name is LaFanti."

I hesitated and he turned off the smile like a light.

"Get in," he said coldly. "Get in, or we'll plug you right here on the street.

I got into the car.

CHAPTER TWO

SOBS IN THE DARK

LAFANTI'S APARTMENT WAS SOMETHING. It wasn't far from the Loop, on the lake-front. It occupied the whole top floor of the building. The high-beamed studio living room had a big stone fireplace at one end and a balcony at the other. French windows opened out onto a landscaped terrace. The Drive was twenty-eight floors below.

"You like it?" he asked me.

"It's quite a foxhole," I admitted.

One of the hoods, a blond Polack lad by the name of Hymie, chuckled, "He's okay, huh, Joe?"

LaFanti told him to shut up. A gun punk whom he called Gordan opened a portable bar and began to slop whiskey into highball glasses. LaFanti asked if I wanted a drink. I admitted that I could use one. There had been plenty of wine where I'd come from, but Old Grandad had been rare.

Hymie asked how I liked the Army, I told him fine. One of the other lads said that he'd tried to get into the Marines but they had turned him down on account of his record.

When I had finished my drink, LaFanti suggested, "Now suppose you tell me all about it."

I asked if he meant about Mona. He said he did, so I told him what I had told the warden and Olson. I said I didn't see why the kid should suffer for something that was not his fault. I also told him what both Captain Corson and Olson had said about him.

He said, "Pay no attention to those guys. They'd give an arm apiece to hang a bad rap on me, soldier. They're jealous, see?"

I didn't, but I said I did.

Gordan poured another drink. LaFanti said, "Now that we've got that out of our way, let's quit stalling, Sergeant, and get down to cases. The dame shot off her mouth, of course?"

I told him, "She didn't say a dozen words, outside of giving me her lawyer's name and address so I could fix it about making an allotment and leaving my insurance to the kid."

He asked if I expected him to believe something as crude as that.

I told him it was the truth.

"Why lie to me, Sergeant?" he asked. "I know dames—and I've been lied to by experts." He took a wallet from his pocket and began to count out bills on the arm of his chair. "But because you didn't crack to either Olson or Corson, I'm willing to do right by you. Say when."

I told him he was talking over my head.

"What did I tell you?" Gordan asked. "All small town punks are would-be sharpers. He's going to stick you for plenty. Then I wouldn't trust him twenty feet."

Hymie suggested that maybe I was leveling. They all laughed at that, LaFanti laughing from the corner of his mouth. "Okay. How much?" he demanded.

I wanted to know how much for what.

The lad who had wanted to join the Marines said, "The guy is smart. He's making the mountain come to Mohammed."

LaFanti drummed on the arm of his chair a minute. "What did you do before you got into the Army, Sergeant?"

I told him I had worked in a garage and he wanted to know how I'd like to buy it. I said that would be fine but that I doubted if I ever could, it being a pretty fair-sized garage and having the Ford-agency, besides.

"You can buy it if you'll keep your mouth shut," he told me. "I'll lay the money on the line with any lawyer you name. Or I'll put it up in escrow with your home-town bank. All you have to do is keep your mouth shut for five more days about what that screwy dame in the death house told you."

I couldn't think of anything she'd told me that I hadn't already told him, outside of her saying that she hadn't known that men like me still existed. And she had been wrong on that score. A lot of men are homely. And a lot of lads have red hair. All of us Duvals have.

I told him I didn't know what he was talking about and he got ugly. "Okay. If you want it that way," he said, "I guess it can be arranged." He nodded to the would-be Marine. "Soften him up a bit, Tommy."

The hood walked over to where I was sitting and threw a hard right at my head. I rolled with the punch, brought up my knees to my chest and gave him both feet in the belly so hard that he went through the fireplace screen into the big stone fireplace.

"You hadn't ought to have told him to punch me," I told LaFanti. "I don't want anything from you guys. All that I want is out of here."

Gordan slipped a sap from his hip pocket and looked at me thoughtfully.

"You'd better just keep on looking," I warned him.

LaFanti got to his feet. His face was ugly.

"Think it over, Joe," Hymie warned him. "Don't get us in no deeper. This guy ain't a punk. If he doesn't show on schedule the whole damn United States Army is going to be looking for him."

LaFanti said, "Yeah," sourly. "That's the reason I tried to buy him off. But we can arrange the other if we have to. There are always accidents. Maybe he could go swimming and drown." He walked across the room away from me. When he turned back he was holding a long-barreled .38. I could tell by the way he held it that he knew how to use it.

"Okay. Let's have it, Duval," he said. "Start talking. What lies did she tell about me? And where did she stash the ice?"

Tommy crawled out of the fireplace. Right then he would have made a hell of a looking Marine. "Let me shoot the son," he begged.

LaFanti waved him to one side. "I said, start talking, Sergeant. I'm through handling you with gloves."

I told him he was nuts. The girl hadn't told me a thing.

"I get it now," he said. "No wonder you didn't tell Corson. You're figuring on keeping the ice for yourself and holding the other over my head as a club."

Both he and the lad with the sap took a couple of steps toward me. Tommy and Hymie drew their guns. I wished I knew what he wanted to know. But I didn't. So I backed a few steps and knocked over a little end table.

A picture in a silver frame fell face up on the floor. It looked like Mona—and it didn't. In the picture she could have been a pin-up girl by Varga. She was all lines and glitter and flame. No wonder Johnny had been crazy about her. But the death house had done things. She wasn't glittering now. She was a meek, scared kid. Somehow I liked her better.

When I had backed as far as I could, I told LaFanti, "I don't know what I'm supposed to know, or what Mona is supposed to have told me. But if you're figuring on taking me, come on."

LaFanti said, "Don't mark him up if you can help it."

Tommy and Hymie came first. I cow-kicked one and broke the other's arm. They went down and out of the picture, but not for long. Gordan was tougher. He danced in, swiped me with his gun barrel, and danced back before I could land a blow.

I picked up the end table and threw it in his face. Before he could get it out of his eyes, I slugged him with the side of my hand just above his kidneys. He went down screaming that he was maimed for life.

LaFanti backed up a few feet.

"You're good," he admitted.

So was he. I tried every trick I'd learned in dirty fighting. He blocked them with barroom counters. Guys who live in fourteen-room apartments and drive V-16 Cadillacs usually know their trades, and he knew his.

He packed me into the wall and I tried to knee him. He caught my knee and we went to the floor. Gordan was back on his feet. So were Tommy and Hymie. First I rode him, then he rode me, his three hoods hovering like buzzards and slapping at my head with their guns whenever I showed on top.

I couldn't take much of that. I didn't. There was a *whoosh* as one of them landed a gun barrel on the back of my skull and the whole damn apartment blew up.

For a moment I thought I was back at Anzio. I buried my nose in the carpet. Then the flares began to die out and someone asked, "You don't suppose the guy was leveling? You don't suppose that the dame didn't talk?"

"Hell no," LaFanti grunted. "Unless we get rid of the guy, we won't be safe until after they pull that switch."

I opened my eyes and Gordan said, "Look out! He's coming to!"

LaFanti walked over beside me. "Go back to sleep, punk," he said.

To make certain that I did, he kicked me in the jaw.

It was night when I came to again. Even that high up, I could hear the lake swishing against the rock breakwater. I was lying on a bed. I wasn't tied. I figured that they were afraid that a rope might mark my wrists. And the Feds would be suspicious wherever I was found.

I lay looking at the ceiling through the dark and wondering how many of them were still in the apartment and what my best move would be.

It was then I heard the girl crying. It wasn't loud. And she wasn't really crying. Her breath sucked in jerkily and died in sobs, as if she had been crying a long time, and were tired. I tried to place the sound and couldn't. She could be in one of the rooms, or in an apartment on one of the lower floors.

Then I heard her say, "Oh, my God," and I knew she was in the apartment.

I got off the bed and walked to the door. I expected it to be locked. It wasn't. I cracked it and looked out. Gordan and Tommy were sprawled in easy chairs reading the evening papers. No one else seemed to be in the room. I went back to the bed and sat down. The girl was crying harder now. I wondered who she was. I wondered what LaFanti and his crowd thought Mona had told me.

"Unless we get rid of this guy, we won't be safe until after they pull that switch."

I remembered LaFanti saying that and it didn't make sense to me. Johnny had been the quick one in our family. I always get things the hard way. All I could think of was getting out of the joint and maybe going and talking to Olson. He probably could put it together.

Outside of a few sore spots and bruises, I felt pretty good. I walked back to the door. The two hoods were still reading their papers.

As I watched them, Tommy said suddenly, "There'll be hell to pay when he doesn't show."

Gordan got up from his chair like his kidneys were still hurting and uncorked a fresh bottle of rye. "So what? No one saw him get into the car. He can't be traced to us."

Both of them took a drink and began to talk. I slipped out into the room and tiptoed across the carpet. It was like walking through grass. The pile came halfway tip my shoes. I wanted Tommy's gun. It was lying on an end table beside him.

They heard me before I could get it. Tommy swore and his hand streaked for the gun. I got it before he did. And I was through fooling around. I poked the barrel of it into his mouth and he spat out teeth like beans. Then he tried to gag—and couldn't. I'd pulled the trigger.

Whimpering, Gordan threw a slug at me. The lead went wide by inches. I could see by his eyes he was thinking of the hole in Tommy's head. Before he could trigger again, I scooped up the rye bottle and smashed it across his face. He went down howling and clawing the glass from his eyes.

I gave him the boots to make sure that he'd stay where he was. Then I got out of there,

The elevator cage was waiting at the floor. The pimply-faced kid who ran it was peering through the grille.

He wanted to know if those were shots that he'd heard. I told him they were and not to let anyone in until I came back with the cops.

He looked at me as if I was crazy. "But that's Joe LaFanti's apartment," he protested.

I asked him if he was telling me.

I thought I would be back with the law in minutes. It was closer to an hour. Captain Corson paced Olson's office, damning all red tape.

Olson refused to be hurried. He insisted, "We want LaFanti, yes. But we want him right this time. And getting him right means warrants."

He had four of them when we started: Search, kidnapping, felonious assault and assault with a deadly weapon with intent to kill.

Once we were started, we went fast. I rode with Olson and Corson in a squad car. There were four more cars behind us, one of them filled with reporters. I asked Olson what he thought La-Fanti had been afraid of that Mona would tell me.

He said it was hard to say. Corson said he was willing to bet that LaFanti had killed Stein himself and that Mona was covering for him.

"But that doesn't make sense," Olson said. "In the first place, LaFanti had an alibi. In the second place, nobody like Mona would go to the chair for any man."

I expected to see a crowd outside the building. There wasn't. The same pimply-faced kid was running the elevator. He looked right through me like he didn't see me.

Corson asked him if anybody had gone up since I left and he said, "Naw. Nobody's gone up since the blonde about three this afternoon."

Olson looked at him sharply but said nothing. We squeezed into the cage like K-rations. One of the reporters wanted to know what Olson was charging LaFanti with and he gave them the list.

They wanted to know if he thought he could make it stick. He said he was going to try.

The door was closed. Corson banged on it with his gun. LaFanti was home. He opened the door the length of the safety chain and growled, "So what do you want, copper?"

He'd changed to a dressing gown and slippers since I'd seen him last. "Remember me?" I asked.

"Open up," Olson said. "This is a pinch, LaFanti. We're coming in."

The big hood shook his head. "Oh, no. I know my rights. No one comes in without a warrant."

"We have one," Olson said. He read it to him through the crack.

LaFanti hesitated, closed the door, and slipped the safety chain. When he opened the door again, he said, "Let's talk right here."

"The hell you say!" Corson growled.

He pushed by him into the living room. LaFanti wanted to know what he was charged with. One of the reporters told him kidnapping and attempted murder.

"Now I know it's a gag," he grinned.

I repeated, "Remember me?"

He looked at me and shook his head. "No. I can't say that I do. What's the gripe with you, soldier?"

I said, "I'll gripe you!" and swung a hard right to his jaw.

He let it slide off a forearm and asked Olson, "What's eating on this guy? What's the matter? Is he crazy?"

I said, "You never saw me before, I suppose? You and three of your lads didn't snatch me. You didn't bring me up here and offer to buy me a garage if I'd keep my mouth shut about what Mona told me this morning. And when I refused, you and your three hoods didn't beat me unconscious. You weren't planning to dump me in the lake. You—"

I realized that everyone was staring at me and I ran down like an unwound clock. Lumping it all together, it *did* sound screwy as hell. There wasn't a sign of anything wrong in the apartment.

I looked over at Olson. He asked, "Where are the lads you say you killed?"

LaFanti puzzled, "Killed?"

I pushed past him into the room. There were no bodies on the floor. There was no blood. There was no sign of a fight. Even the end table that I had thrown in Gordan's face was standing, unbroken, by a chair, supporting a half-filled bottle of rye.

"They were there," I insisted. "Right there on the floor. I left them bleeding like pigs."

Corson knelt down and felt the rug, then smelled it.

"So?" Olson asked.

"Not on this rug," Corson told him. His men fanned out to search the apartment.

LaFanti crossed to a door. "If you don't mind, just pass this one room by."

"That's the room," I told Olson, "that I came to in. I lay in there for half an hour listening to some dame crying."

LaFanti grinned, "The guy is nuts. I—"

I pushed him aside and opened the door. A young blonde was sitting on the bed putting on her shoes. If she had been crying she didn't show it.

She looked at the mob in the living room and gasped, "Joe! What is this, LaSalle Street Station?"

I shut the door and LaFanti grinned, "You still think that's the same room, soldier? Or have you got your apartments mixed?"

Corson asked, "How long has she been here?"

The blonde heard him and called through the door, "Tell him it's none of his damn business. Joe."

One of the reporters repeated what the elevator boy had said. " 'Naw. Nobody's gone up since the blonde about three this afternoon'."

LaFanti walked over to Olson and began to talk earnestly, in a low voice, I caught the words, "battle fatigue—war neuroses. They sounded funny as hell coming from a punk like Joe LaFanti but Olson didn't seem to think so. He was listening thoughtfully, nodding his head and not looking at me,

Corson continued to prowl the apartment. I saw him pick up something small and white, gaze at it thoughtfully a moment, then drop it into one of his vest pockets.

I began to edge toward the door, and stopped, staring at the picture of Mona in the silver frame, remembering something that Johnny had told me. I had the whole picture now, even if some of the pieces were missing.

On the ether side of the room, Olson was asking, dryly, "And you're willing to swear that he wasn't up here at all this afternoon?"

"I swear," LaFanti lied. "Ask the elevator boy. Ask anyone in the building. Until he walked in with you fellows, I never saw him before."

"And Tommy and Gordan?"

"They're down at our place in the Dunes." He nodded across the room. "After all, when a man has company—"

Corson figured my move just as I reached tile hall door and called, "Hold it, Mike!"

I whipped out the gun that I had taken from Tommy and leveled it. "In a garrison cap," I told him, "All I want to know from you, is this. If a lad is committed to the psycho-ward in this man's town, how long does it take to put him through the mill?"

He told me four or five days.

I said, "Thanks. That's all that I needed to know."

I slipped out the door and closed it behind me.

LaFanti tugged the door open, shouting, "Stop him. The man is crazy!"

I put a slug through the lobe of his left ear. He shut the door.

The elevator punk gaped at me, open-mouthed. "So help me, Sergeant—" he began.

I told him to shut up and take me down. I had a hell of a lot to do and not much time in which to do it. More, I had felt a damn sight safer in Anzio than I did in Chicago.

They *had* to kill me now. I knew. And while they didn't know what had tipped me, they *knew* that I knew.

CHAPTER THREE

LADY BE DEAD TO ME

THERE WAS NO ONE in the lobby of the hotel where Mona had formerly had an apartment but a little old rheumy-eyed clerk. I took a twenty from my money belt and laid it on the counter. "That's yours for the right answers to three questions," I told him.

He wanted to know what they were.

I asked, "Who was Mona's best girl friend? What beauty shop did she go to? Where did she used to live before she came to Chicago?"

He said, "A mousy little dame by the name of Clara. The shop across the street. Pierre, South Dakota."

I told him the bill was his.

The Beauty Shoppe across the street was closed but there was a light in the back room. A well-built, middle-aged, red-haired woman answered my pounding on the door.

"I'm afraid someone's steered you wrong, soldier," she smiled. "This isn't that kind of a Shoppe."

I told her that all I wanted was some information. She considered my question and shook her head.

"No. Come to think of it, she didn't."

I asked if she knew her right name. She told me she thought it was Jones. "I know her right first name was Mary. Why? What's all this to you, soldier?"

"It could be a lot," I told her.

I thanked her and got on my horse. The radios should be squawking now. They were. There was a prowl car parked on the next corner. One lad was yawning behind the wheel while his partner sneaked a beer. The car radio was blatting:

Five-feet eleven. One hundred and eighty pounds. Red hair. Broken nose. Blue eyes. When last seen he was in uniform. Tech sergeant's rating. He is wearing a triple bank of campaign

ribbons and medal bars. He is armed. Handle this man carefully . . .

I waited in a store doorway until the other cop came out of the
tavern and the prowl car pulled away. They might want to handle
me carefully, but nobody wanted to be as careful as I.

The tavern on the corner was as good as any. I took my bars
from shirt and ripped the chevrons from sleeve. The thread ends
gave me some, trouble. When I was satisfied I walked into the bar
and bought a beer. I also asked the barman would he mind if I
used his phone booth to make a long distance call.

He said that was what it was there for and gave me change for
my five in quarters, grinning, "You ought to fall for some dame
that lives closer, soldier."

I said I was working on it and went into the booth and asked
long distance to connect me with the Pierre operator. She wanted
to know who I wanted to talk to in Pierre and I told her I didn't
know. She said there would be a charge and I said that would be
all right. Then I waited.

When I got through to the girl in Pierre, I asked her to connect
me with anyone in town who might know a Mary Jones who had
left there about eight years ago. She said she would connect me
with the editor of the local paper, who knew everyone in town. He
didn't know the Jones family very well, but he did know what I
wanted to know. I thanked him and hung up

I bought another beer and caught the barman looking at my
chest, then at my sleeve. I looked in the back-bar mirror. I wasn't
fooling anyone. My ribbons and chevrons were in my pocket but
you could see their outline on my tunic where the Italian sun
hadn't faded the goods.

He walked into the back room. I scrammed and whistled down a
cruising cab. At first I just told him to roll. Then I gave him the
address of the south-side nursing home where Johnny's kid had
been placed, according to Mona. I doubted that they would think
of looking for me there.

The driver was full of misinformation. He told me all about
myself. I was a shell-shocked looney. Every cop and M.P. and
Shore Patrol in town was looking for me. I had tried to kill Joe
LaFanti because he had been nice to my brother's girl—as if one
more guy in her life had mattered.

I pulled the old one about Chicago not being as big as New York or London, but I didn't laugh. All I could think of was that scared little kid in the death house telling me about Johnny . . .

Funny-face. On a hunch I had the cab wait half a block from the nursing home and told him I wouldn't be long.

The lady who answered my ring was nice but firm about it. She said it was after ten o'clock and that if I wanted to see one of the children I would have to come back in the morning.

I gambled she didn't listen to police calls and told her who I was. That made everything different.

"Of course, Sergeant Duval," she smiled. "Come in."

The kid was in a crib on the second floor. And he was Johnny's. He had the same red hair and blue eyes. More, he wasn't asleep. When he saw me he smiled and kinda burped.

I told the nurse, "Look. He's laughing."

She patted him till he did it again, and said it was only colic— but it looked like a laugh to me and I felt pretty good about it. He was Johnny's kid, sure. But legally he was going to be mine. Or was he? It was time for me to get on my horse again.

I told the lady that as soon as I got back to the outfit I'd make arrangements through my C.O. with the O.D.B. to send her an allotment for his keep, but meanwhile, did they need any money?

She said no, that his board had been paid for six months in advance by the friend of his mother's who had brought him, along with a satchel of three-cornered pants, on the morning Stein had been killed.

I asked her what time was this and she told me about five in the morning.

That rang a bell. I asked could I see the satchel and she didn't see why not, but they hadn't been able so far to use any of the things. It seemed each baby had a locker. She opened Johnny's and handed me one of those rubberized canvas duffle bags like you can buy in most any drug store. It still was packed with little shirts, and dresses and diapers.

"The shirts and dresses we can use," she told me, "when he grows into them. But we have a diaper service."

She went to quiet a kid that had woken up. I felt the bottom of the bag. It was too thick by half an inch and the rubberized lining on the bottom had been pulled loose at the corners and glued back. I had the last two pieces of the picture, *I knew why the girl in La-Fanti's apartment had been crying. I also knew where the Stein diamonds were.*

The crying kid had woken up the others. They all were bawling now, including Johnny. I put the bag back in his locker. It was a lot safer there than with me.

Out on the street again, I could hear a police siren helling. I walked back to my cab and asked the hacker if he'd ever had a fare to Joe LaFanti's place down in the Dunes.

He said he had, that it was just the other side of Miller and that he had hauled a state senator down there once. I said, "Okay. Let's go." He wanted to know if I meant to the Dunes and when I said I did he looked at me hard and I knew that he recognized me.

The siren cut out abruptly. The green lights of a squad car rounded the corner and coasted past us to brake in front of the nursing home. "Make a U-turn," I told the hacker. He gaped from me to the squad car, goggle-eyed. Two of the lads had gone up to the door. Two more were standing in the street looking back at the cab.

"Gees! I can't do it, Duval," he whimpered. "They'll shoot. Those guys are looking for you."

I showed him Tommy's gun and he changed his mind.

Down the street, the two lads who had gone to the door were running back to the squad car, yelling at the driver to turn around. The prowl swung in a sharp turn, pulled up over the curb and pinned the cab with his spotlight Then lead began to hammer the cab. I shot out the spot and put a slug through their right front tire.

"Now roll!" I ordered my driver. He pushed the gas to the floorboards, saying, "You'll be sorry."

"I can't help it," I snarled at him. "My war neuroses are driving me nuts."

The lodge was low and rambling, built in a hollow between two dunes, about a hundred yards from the road. Sand had drifted over the lane leading in. There were lights in the big front room and one in the back of the house.

I paid off the hacker at the road. He took the money but said he'd wait. He said, when he thought it over, I didn't act too crazy to him. I probably had a right to be sore at LaFanti, on Johnny's account. Besides, his cab was full of bullet holes and he'd probably get hell when he checked in, if he didn't get arrested.

I walked across the sand to the house. There was a moon, but clouds hid it most of the time. When I get close to the house, I crawled.

There was a big screened porch across the front of the living room. The screen door was unhooked I eased inside and looked in through the windows.

Several hard-faced gents I didn't know were playing cards. Gordan sat in a chair, his face wrapped up like a mummy's, not saying anything. Hymie, his arm in a sling, was pacing up and down like a yardbird on his first tour of guard duty. He kept saying, "Why doesn't Joe come? What the hell are we going to do if the law busts in and wants to talk to Tommy?"

One of the lads playing cards said not to worry about the law, but that he, for one, would feel better when they got rid of the stiffs.

Another lad wanted to know what they were waiting for. Hymie told him, "Joe."

Gordan groaned, "Damn Joe LaFanti. And damn Stein and his diamonds."

I crawled around to the back of the house. A big colored boy in a white chef's cap was snoring in the kitchen. I walked in past him to the hall.

The joint had cost LaFanti money. The kitchen was as big as a house and there were enough rooms for a hotel. I looked in five before I found them. The room was dark except for moonlight.

Tommy was lying on an Indian rag, wrapped in a sheet. A couple of sashweights were wired to his ankles. I unwrapped him enough to get at his pockets. When I found the spare clip for his gun I felt better.

The girl lay watching me from the bed. Her wrists and her ankles were tied. Her eyes were swollen from crying. She tried to talk and couldn't. Her lips were plastered with tape. I felt the lobe of the ear nearest me, then I sat down on the bed beside her and asked her had she killed Stein.

She shook her head.

I asked her could she prove it on anyone else.

She shook her head again and began to cry. That brought the situation back to snafu—normal, and well fouled up. I cut the ropes on her wrists and ankles. She eased the tape from her lips. The first thing she said was, "They're going to kill me."

I nodded, "Yeah. I figured that." Then I lighted a cigarette while I figured my best move. It was a mistake. She saw my face in the flare of the match and screamed: "Johnny!"

The chef in the kitchen woke up and wanted to know, "What the hell—?"

I tried to shut the girl up and couldn't. She was hysterical. "They told me you were dead," she screamed. "They told me you were dead!"

Feet pounded down the hall, I kicked the glass and sash out of the window, picked the girl off the bed, and dove for the outside just as the room door opened. A slug whistled past my ear. Another one burned my side. The girl kept right on screaming,

When I rounded the corner of the house, the colored boy was starting out the kitchen door. He saw me and changed his mind. He stepped back in and slammed the door. Hymie yanked it open and flipped a third shot at me. I stopped and threw one back. He sagged against the jamb, then slid down it to the floor. I was sorry it had to happen. But still, he would have made a lousy Marine,

No one else tried to stop us. Either they weren't in it as deep as the others or they figured like Gordan did, and waited to damn Joe LaFanti and Stein and his diamonds.

The hacker was waiting a few feet from his cab. He had the engine running and a tire tool in one hand. "You okay?" he asked me.

I said I was and put the girl into the cab. He wanted to know who she was and I said that he should ask her. He did. But she couldn't tell him a thing. She'd fainted.

The morning was hot and steamy. The prison was still asleep as we pulled up in front of the warden's office. But Kane and Olson were waiting. So were Captain Corson and LaFanti.

I hoped I hadn't made a mistake in phoning them to meet us. The girl's story sounded screwy as hell to me. I didn't see how we could prove it.

Olson smiled at me, thinly. "You seem to have made quite a night of it, Sergeant."

I told him I'd spent nights I'd enjoyed more.

The girl didn't look at LaFanti, He didn't look at her. She just sat down in a chair and began to cry. Her cheekbones were flushed. Her cheeks had sunken in. The tape and the crying she had done had played hell with her makeup. She wasn't pretty any more.

Olson polished his eyeglasses. "So?"

I looked at Warden Kane. "She'll be here in a moment," he told me.

Corson turned his back like he had to cough. He didn't. He was shifting his shoulder holster so he could get at his gun in a hurry.

I took Tommy's gun from my belt and laid it on the Warden's desk. Then the matron, came in with Mona.

She wasn't a scared kid any more. She was a woman. Her hair wasn't hanging in braids. It was done up on the top of her head, She had what it took to fill out a grey prison gown and make it a Paris creation. Her eyes were shining and she was holding her chin high. But when she saw the girl in the chair it began to quiver.

Then they were crying in each other's arms.

Olson wanted to know what the hell. I told him, "You convicted the wrong girl. It seems there are two Jones girls, just like there were two Duval boys."

Warden Kane said that he didn't get it. I told him it was a long story and maybe LaFanti would explain. He told me to go to hell, so I asked Mona what was her name.

She told me Clara Jones.

"I'm Mona," the other girl said. "But I didn't kill Stein."

"Can you prove this?" Olson asked.

She said she couldn't. Her story wasn't pretty. She had gotten Stein drunk. She had clipped him in an alley. And during the night Tommy and Gordan had brought him into her room and LaFanti was shaking her and telling her that she'd burn unless she gave him the diamonds. They had searched the room but hadn't found them. Then LaFanti and his boys had left. Frightened sober she had phoned her sister, Clara, who had only arrived in town some days before.

Olson studied the two girls. Both were about five feet two. Both had long black hair. Both were built like Varga girls. Both had blue eyes and fair skin. But the resemblance stopped right there. Mona looked like herself. Clara looked like Mona might have looked at one time.

Olson wanted to know if the relationship had been established. I told him not legally, but that if he would check with Pierre, South Dakota, he could establish it without any trouble.

Corson admitted, unwillingly, that maybe the original pinch had been a bull on his part. His thick neck got red. "But the dame *said* she was Mona. And she stood mute, which is the same-like as pleading guilty."

Olson recalled that there being no previous arrest or conviction there had been no fingerprints to compare.

Clara took up the story. That was the part I'd been afraid of—it was bound to sound thin. People didn't stick out their necks that way. Or, did they? Would I have done the same thing for Johnny?

Clara had come to the hotel. She had believed Mona's story. Between them they had figured out what had seemed at the time a logical means of procedure. Mona knew all the ropes. She had the diamonds to trade for the truth. If Clara would take her place for a few hours, she thought that she could make a deal with LaFanti. What neither girl realized at the time was the fact that this was something that not even LaFanti's political drag could get him out of. This was murder. It was either his neck or Mona's.

And then I thought of the kid, and I could sort of see Clara doing it.

Mona had left the apartment with the diamonds. She had picked up the kid at the apartment and had delivered him to the south-side nursing home, posing as a friend of herself.

Corson wanted to know why.

"Because I was afraid Joe would snatch him," she told him. "But he didn't. He snatched me instead. He's kept me locked up in his apartment ever since. He *wanted* Clara to burn."

"Why?" Kane asked.

I told him the answer to that. "Because LaFanti knew that once somebody had burned, the law wouldn't dare to admit that it had made a mistake by reopening the case. Meanwhile he could work on Mona and maybe make her tell him where she had stashed the diamonds."

LaFanti sneered, "And I suppose you know where they are?"

I told him, "Sure. They're under Johnny's pants, in the bag Mona took to the nursing home."

Corson said that he would be damned. LaFanti wanted to know if I expected a sane judge and jury to believe a yarn like that.

There was a long silence. Then Olson sighed, "As much as I dislike to, I'm afraid that I must say that the story is pretty fantastic. Naturally such a gross miscarriage of justice could not take place without collusion, fraudulent cooperation, of the State's Attorney's Office."

This was it. I looked at Corson and said, "Naturally. Why don't you take down your hair, Olson, and admit that you are not only LaFanti's political drag, but also his silent partner?"

It turned so still I could hear my heart beat.

I picked up Tommy's gun, still watching Corson. "You don't get me in a cell," I told them. "And it won't wash off this time. You've got your hands too dirty. The thing LaFanti was afraid of was that Clara might have told me the truth when I saw her yesterday—"

Olson shook his head. "The man is a mental case! That story of his being in LaFanti's apartment yesterday afternoon was another pipe dream."

Corson's neck turned red. All the time I had been sniping with a carbine, he'd sat back with a .45 in his hand, "No. It wasn't a pipe dream," he said. The red spread into his face. "Look. Just who the hell do you guys think you are that you can pull the wool over a cop's eyes who was investigating homicides when you were wearing rubber pants?" He stabbed a finger at LaFanti. "Duval wasn't in your apartment yesterday afternoon? He didn't kill Tommy and damn near kill Phil Gordan?"

"He did not," LaFanti said thickly.

Colson took a tooth from his vest pocket. "Then where did this tooth come from that he blew out of Tommy's mouth? And why did the Acme cleaners replace your rug between six and seven last night while Olson was stalling like hell to give you time to clean up and get Mona and the stiffs out, by insisting we needed warrants? And how could a punk elevator boy, making twenty dollars a week, suddenly buy a convertible Caddy coupe for two grand, second hand? It couldn't be because he was lying, like that blonde, could it, Joe?"

LaFanti turned as white as Olson. "You can't prove a thing."

"I think I can," Corson said. "As soon as Duval called me, I called the Indiana state cops and had them check on your place in the Dunes. Everyone was gone but Hymie and Tommy and Gordan. Hymie and Tommy weren't talking. Duval had seen to that But Gordan sang like a canary."

He told the story that Gordan had told. LaFanti, Hymie, Tommy, and Gordan had been keeping an eye on Stein. They'd seen Mona clip him, but when they'd looked for the diamonds at her place, they hadn't found them. They thought Mona hadn't got them and tried to strong-arm the information on them out of Stein. Stein fought and LaFanti shot him. They planted him in Mona's room, partly to clear themselves, partly to force her to come across with the stones, if she had them.

LaFanti screamed, "I've an alibi."

"Yeah, sure," Corson said. "You were supposed to be talking to Olson."

LaFanti shot twice through his pocket. I missed him but Corson didn't. The hood reached up a palm as if to say nix, then he followed his hand to the floor.

"How about you, Olson?" Corson asked.

Olson said he would prefer a judge and jury. To prove it he held up his hands.

Then I realized that Clara was crying. "She's hurt! He shot her," she cried.

Corson walked over to Mona and knelt beside her. "He get you bad, kid?" he asked gruffly.

She didn't answer him. She couldn't.

I wondered a little what she would say to Johnny—she was smiling a little, so maybe they were talking over the old times, when he'd been home. Whatever she'd become since, she'd been okay then—and Johnny had lived in a few glass houses himself, so he wasn't much of a hand at throwing rocks.

Clara buried her face in my tunic.

Corson cleared his throat, hard. "Just tell me this, Duval? How did you know were *two* girls?"

"Johnny told me," I told him, "A jeweler in Palermo wanted to sell him some antique earrings for his girl. But he said that she couldn't wear 'em because her ears weren't pierced." I tugged Clara's old fashioned eardrops. "And Clara's are."

Then Corson bellowed at Kane and asked what was he staring at and why wasn't he phoning the governor on account of I only had three days of my leave left and I had things to attend to. So after a while they said that we could go about our business.

DEAD—AS IN MACKEREL!

AS IF I DIDN'T HAVE ENOUGH on my mind, the hearing on the renewal of my license was being held in one of the courtrooms on the fourth floor of the City Hall. I had no business being there. I didn't want to be there. I should have been pacing up and down the corridor outside the maternity ward of the hospital waiting for Doc Hanley to come out and tell me if it was a boy or a girl and how Sue was. I still think I should have gotten some consideration. After all, it was the first time that I had ever been a father.

The hearing was uncalled for. It was also very informal. Beamer called me a crook, a conniving private shamus with no regard for the law, a blot on the city's escutcheon, a kill-crazy veteran, and a suborner of evidence.

I called him a lot of things. Then I took off my coat and, State's Attorney or not, offered to push his teeth down his throat. I meant to. I would have. But I didn't get a chance. Two bailiffs stopped me before I could get to him and Judge Green banged the bench so hard he broke his gavel.

I expected Green to fine me for contempt. He didn't. Maybe his contempt was greater than mine. I wouldn't know.

From a strictly legal angle, Beamer had a case. I had been calling my shots the way I saw them. On the other hand, Lieutenant Nobby of Homicide, Captain Gleason of Morals, and old Inspector Jensen of the Narcotic Squad, all testified that while some of my methods might not be in strict accord with the letter of the law, they were effective, and that while I might have short-cut a few legal corners I had always co-operated whole-heartedly with their departments.

Don't tell me that it doesn't pay to stand in with the boys in blue. They can make you or break you. I know.

As a result of their testimony, my license was renewed. Judge Green beamed at me over his bifocals and told me to go and sin no more. Even State's Attorney Beamer offered to shake hands and call it quits but I told him to put it in his hat. In my eleven years with inter-Ocean and my two years on my own I've seen some sad sacks in public office, but we the people picked ourselves something when we voted him queen of the mayhem.

Out in the corridor, Harry Nobby was all ears to know if it was a boy or a girl and how was Sue. I told him that I was mildly interested myself and called the hospital from the City Sealer's office.

I didn't get much. Some dumb cluck at the hospital switchboard, with her mind on the Armed Forces and her eyes on somebody else's chart, told me that for an old lady of seventy-two Mrs. Doyle was doing as well as could be expected, that the X-ray had shown no malignant growth, and that she was scheduled to go on the table at eight o'clock the next morning.

Before I could ask if she hadn't made a mistake in her Doyles she snapped her gum in my ear and hung up. I said to hell with it and told Nobby I'd call from the office on my way to the hospital.

He wished me luck, told me to calm down, and pulled the old one about he had heard that they seldom lost a father.

I told him I'd heard that one before and that I wasn't excited.

He said, "That's fine."

I pulled my right glove onto my left hand, stuck the wrong end of my cigar in my mouth, and cut across Randolph Street to the office to pick up the flowers and the candy that I'd bought for Sue.

Max got up from the mourner's bench in the outer office and wanted to know if we were still in business.

I said we were and told Mable to get the hospital on the phone. "I may be a father," I told her, "and here I don't even know it."

"Maybe," Max said, "you ought to hire a good detective."

I gave him a dirty look and walked on into my office. The phone was already ringing. "Now, look, honey," I told the girl at the hospital switchboard. "Let's be lace-curtain Irish this time. Let's not just get any old Doyle's room. Let's us both concentrate. I want to talk to Mrs. Tom Doyle. Catch on? T as in trinitrotoluene. O as in Oedipus. M as in make like Mickey Rooney."

"I will connect you with her room," she trilled.

I knew that Sue was probably sore because I wasn't there, so as soon as I heard her receiver lift I did a little trilling of my own. "Hello, honey. This is the papa bird calling."

"Yah?" a male voice answered. "Well, this are the yanitor and yust what do you want me to do about it? Build you a nest, you cuckoo?"

I told him to go to hell and hung up. And that's when the dame in the mink coat came in.

I waved her out of the office. "Go away. I'm not seeing anyone today."

"That's what Mable and I both told her," Max said gloomily.

"He'll see me," the girl in the mink coat said. She closed the door in Max's face and came in and sat down.

I told Mable to try the hospital again and took a quick look at my would-be client. She was worth looking at. Her mink coat was worth at least five grand. She was young, not more than twenty-two or twenty-three. Her voice was low and throaty. More, I had a hazy recollection of having seen her somewhere before.

"Look. I'm awfully sorry, Miss," I began, "but—"

"Babies cost money," she said flatly. She opened her purse and laid five crisp one-hundred dollar bills on my desk. "And five hundred dollars will buy a lot of three-cornered panties."

I flicked the bills with my fingernail. "For what?"

"Five minutes' conversation," she bargained. "There will be more if you think I—that is, this girl I want to tell you about, let's call her Miss Z, needs a bodyguard."

"In other words," I said, "you wish to state a hypothetical case."

She said, "Come again?"

I quoted Funk and Wagnalls: " 'Hypothesis: A state of things assumed as a basis of reasoning, experiment, or investigation; loosely and generally, an unsupported or ill-supported theory, guess, or conjecture.' "

She shook her head. "This isn't any guesswork on my part." She corrected herself again.

"I mean, on the part of Miss Z. There is an old goat who wants to leave her two hundred thousand dollars in his will. But Miss Z is afraid of two things."

I picked up the five hundred dollars. "Give."

"One," she continued, "she is afraid that his relatives may try to do away with her when they find out about the will. Two, she's afraid they will go to court after he dies and try to have the will busted."

I made a Leaning Tower of Pisa of my fingers. "And you, that is, Miss Z, would pay how much to have this bequest go through unprotested and unchallenged?"

She said, promptly, "Ten per cent."

"Don't bother with the hospital right now," I told Mable over the inter-office annunciator. "I've just picked up a college education for Junior."

"Harvard or Vassar?" she wanted to know.

I told her not to be impertinent and flipped the switch.

"That is," the girl in the mink coat continued, "Miss Z will pay ten per cent provided she's still alive when the will comes out of probate."

I agreed, "Provided. How did you happen to come to me?"

She shrugged. "Mr. X suggested it. Besides," she added, smiling, "I've heard that your fees are high, but you go all the way out for your clients."

"You and the State's Attorney," I said sourly. I had a hunch to tell her to take her case and peddle it somewhere else. But I didn't. "All right. Let's get down to facts," I suggested. "Who wants to leave you two hundred grand in his will, and why?"

She took a deep breath. "You aren't going to believe me. Jim didn't."

I wanted to know who Jim was.

"That's none of your business," she told me. "And Jim's all wet. This money is being left to me because I'm a sweet little girl who reminds Mr. X of his dead daughter."

I lifted my eyebrows at that one.

"Believe it or not," she said flatly. "That's the truth. I never saw Mr. X until two weeks ago when he was waiting outside of, well, where I work, one night."

I took a drink from the office bottle on that one, then offered it to her. I expected her to refuse. She didn't. She took a man-sized swig from the neck and wiped her cupid's bow on the back of her hand.

"Believe it or not," she repeated. "He doesn't want a thing of me. All he wants is to leave me this money. He's already added a codicil to his will and shown it to me. And what I want to know is—"

"Yes—?"

"Can that codicil be made foolproof?"

I told her that I thought it could. "This Mr. X would be willing to go into court and tell a judge that he is making this bequest in his right mind and of his own free will?"

She said that she thought he would.

I told her, "Then I'll have the young lawyer down the hall draw up a petition stating that the testator fears that his relatives will seek to break his will on the grounds that you mentioned before, and that while still in a position to testify the testator wishes to appear before the court and have a declaratory judgment made attesting to the codicil."

She said that it sounded complicated.

I admitted I wasn't a lawyer and I might have the legal terms all mixed up but that I knew such a thing could be done because I had read of a similar case in the newspapers recently. An old lady had wanted to leave her money to her chauffeur. "Now about the relatives?" I asked. "How many of them are there and how close are they?"

She said that she only knew of four: two nephews, a niece and a brother.

"And you think they'll try to break the will?"

She began to cry. "I know so. One of the nephews is as bad as Jim. He thinks—" she blew her nose on a wisp of lace, "well, you know what he thinks. He came to my hotel last night and made an awful scene." she sniffed. "And this afternoon, just before I came here—"

I interrupted her. "You live at what hotel?"

She named a near north-side hotel that wasn't in the same league with her coat.

"Okay. Let's get the legal angle taken care of first," I told her. I wanted to get it on paper, get her out of the office, and be on my way. "Ask Max to step down the hall and see if young Hanson is busy," I told Mable. "If he isn't, I want to see him, right away." Then, struck by a sudden thought, I asked the girl, "How old is this Mr. X?"

The question seemed to cheer her. "He's listed in *Who's Who* as eighty-three."

I uncapped my fountain pen. "Fine. Now let's forget this Miss Z and Mr. X stuff and get down to cases. Who—?"

"I wonder, please," she asked, "if I could have another drink. It's the excitement or something, I guess. I don't feel so hot."

Her voice sounded faint and faraway. The corners of her mouth were twisted. Her eyes looked suddenly sunken and strained. I said, "Of course," and pushed the bottle across the desk. She leaned forward in her chair to reach for it and continued on to the floor with a little moan.

By the time I could get around the desk she was lying on her face, one arm extended above her head. I thought she had fainted, so I turned her on her back and opened her coat to give her air.

The only thing that she was wearing under the five-thousand-dollar mink, outside of her shoes and stockings, was a wide white dancer's belt, a bra, and a few silver spangles pasted or glued on her flesh.

More, she hadn't fainted. She was dead. Her body had stopped twitching. Her face was beginning to turn blue.

Max came in with Hanson at his heels. Max wanted to know, "What did you do to the dame?"

I told him I hadn't done a thing, that she had just said that she didn't feel so hot and had pitched out of the chair on her face.

Mable wanted to know if I wanted her to call Lieutenant Nobby and I told her yes.

Hanson didn't say anything. He did raise his eyebrows. I knew what he was thinking. And I knew what Beamer would think.

Max had walked around where he could see. "The face is unfamiliar. But I recognize the torso."

I asked him who she was,

Hanson seemed surprised. "You mean you don't know?"

I told him I didn't, and he told me that the dead girl was Dolly Adoree, the strip-tease lovely from the Lyric burlesque house around the corner.

That made everything wonderful. The more I thought about it, the more fantastic her story sounded. I could see the headlines— Strip Teaser Dies Mysteriously In Office Of Sleuth. Sue would love that.

Max shook his head gloomily. "Boy, is she dead! I never seen a deader dame. What are you going to tell Beamer?"

I picked my hat off the desk. "To hell with Beamer. What am I going to tell Sue?"

Mable wanted to know where I was going. I told her to tell Nobby that I'd be right back, and walked around the corner to the Lyric.

It was a typical five-a-day grind house. A dingy alley-way led back to the stage door. The doorman was a dried-up little old man, the type that everyone calls Pop. I creased a five-dollar bill lengthwise and asked him what he knew about Dolly Adoree's love-life.

He leered at me: "She's a nifty number, Mister. But you're too late. She's taken."

I wanted to know by whom.

He looked at the bill and drooled, then looked at me and shook his head. "You'd better ask someone else, copper. I should wind up in an alley for a lousy five-dollar bill?"

I said that was up to him and pushed on in backstage before he could stop me. It smelled of cheap perfume and powdered flesh.

The picture had just ended. On the other side of the asbestos the candy butchers were giving the Frozen Sweets hell. The chorines had begun to drift upstairs for the opening number of the second show. I asked a little redhead where I would find the stage manager, and she pointed out a heavy-set man in his shirt sleeves standing by the light board.

I walked over and told him who I was. He took a dead stogie from his mouth and looked up from a racing form long enough to ask what I thought that made him.

I said, "A chump, unless you dig the wax out of your ears and listen. Dolly's dead."

His eyes had a tendency to bulge. They popped. "You aren't kidding me, mister?"

"I never saw a deader dame," I repeated Max's obit.

After the first shock, it didn't seem to surprise him much. He sucked at a back molar, said, "So Dolly finally got it, eh? I could have told her it would happen." He wanted to know the details, if she was stabbed, or shot, or what, and where it had happened.

I told him that could wait. "Right now, I want to see her dressing room. And I also want to know who was the last person here to see her."

He led the way downstairs. His name was Kovak, spelled with two K's, and he guessed he was the last person who had seen Dolly, unless it had been Pop or one of the girls. "She slipped out right after the first show," he explained. "I ast her wouldn't she be cold with only her coat on over her dancing costume. But she told me no. She said she was only going around the corner—had some business to attend to."

"She told you what it was?"

Kovak shook his head. "Not me. She wouldn't tell me the time of day since that new boyfriend of hers give her that mink coat." He spat and put two thick fingers together. "And believe it or not, mister, her and me used to be like that."

I let the boyfriend angle ride for the time being. There was nothing unusual about the dressing room. There was the usual mirror framed with light bulbs. The make-up shelf was littered with foundation and liner sticks and rouge pots and bottles of whitening. There was also a bottle of gin on the shelf. Her street dress was hanging on a hook.

"About this boy friend—?" I asked Kovak.

He looked at his watch, poked his head out the dressing-room door and bellowed, "Okay. Let's go, youse dames. Places." He turned back to me, saying, "I gotta go now. But if there's anything that I can do to help you or the cops, Doyle—"

I took him by the shirt-front. "You can tell me her boyfriend's name."

He looked frightened. But he wasn't afraid of me. He seemed to be debating something. "How did she die?" he asked me.

I told him I didn't know but that I imagined that she had been fed a delayed poison of some kind, probably one of the cyanides.

He said there was nothing delayed about cyanide. I agreed but pointed out that it could have been put in a capsule.

He thought that over, nodded. "Yeah. Maybe you've got something there." His heavy face twisted in a scowl as he came to some decision. "Why that dirty son-of-a-gun. Okay. I'll talk, Doyle. Now this is just guesswork on my part, see. I only caught one glimpse of the guy. But I think—"

He stopped short as the lights dimmed down and blacked out entirely. "Damn that crummy electrician," he exploded. If I've told him once, I've told him a hundred times that when he pulls the house lights, he shouldn't—"

There was a quick step in the hall. A pencil streak of orange spat at the place where I knew Kovak was standing. The blast of a heavy gun rocked the dressing room, and glass shattered somewhere behind me.

A second and third shot followed he first. Kovak made a mewing noise in his throat, stumbled against me, and went limp in my arms.

I stepped back and let him fall, my own gun in my hand. I couldn't see or hear a thing. My ears were still ringing. But the gunman was still there, I knew.

I felt sideways on the shelf for a jar or something I could throw. My fingers closed on a rouge pot but I didn't get to throw it. *There were two of them, not one, and one of them was in the dressing room, behind me. I could feel his hot breath on my neck.*

I spun on my heel, shooting as I turned. I didn't hit a thing, but he did. The barrel of his gun connected with my skull.

I stood swaying, out on my feet but conscious. Somewhere dames were screaming.

"Stay out of this, understand, Doyle!" a cold voice cut through the fog. "You're over your head, see? And what's more, you keep your trap shut about what Dolly told you."

"C'mon. C'mon!" a second voice urged from the hall.

The screaming of the dames grew louder. It was the chorines up on-stage, screaming for the cops. I took a chance, balled a fist and threw it. It slid along flesh and bone and skinned my knuckles.

"A tough guy, eh?" the voice said. "Okay. Take it, sucker!"

A gun exploded in my face and all the screaming stopped.

When I came to, the lights were on again. I was lying on my back on the dressing-room floor, rimmed in by a circle of broad-toed black shoes. By rolling over on my side and holding my head in both hands I managed to get my eyes as high as a pair of grey tweed trousers, and followed them up to Harry Nobby's face.

He wasn't smiling.

Beamer was standing beside him. He looked as pleased as a G.I. on Saipan doing bunk fatigue with a Varga girl in his arms. "Kinda stubbed your toe this time, didn't you, Doyle? " he asked.

No one offered to help me up. By holding on to the shelf I managed to get to my feet and uncork the bottle of gin. I drank, looking into what was left of seven years of bad luck for someone. My face was speckled with powder burns. The slug that had knocked me out had seared a nasty burn across one temple.

"Durable Doyle," Beamer purred. "All right. Whenever you're ready."

I turned around and asked him what he meant. He pointed to Kovak's body and wanted to know if I thought that he thought that the pixies had killed him.

"Let's have it, Tom," Nobby said.

I gave them the story straight, from the time that the girl had walked into the office. It sounded fantastic as hell.

Nobby chewed it over. A big, bluff, red-faced man, he had been on the force enough years to know that the incredible often happened.

Beamer demanded, "And you expect *me* to believe that?" He highlighted what I had told him. "A mysterious Mr. X, you don't know his name, wanted to leave a burlesque strip-teaser two hundred thousand dollars. She promptly falls dead in your office. You come over here to see what you can see and two mysterious men pop out of nowhere and attack you."

I said that about summed it up.

"The hell it does," Beamer said. He picked a small vitamin-pill bottle from a heap of things that the fingerprint boys had already dusted and classified, unscrewed the cap, took out a capsule and squashed it between his fingers. It reeked of crushed peach-pits. "This is what you were after, wasn't it, Doyle?"

He was over my head and I said so.

Lieutenant Nobby indicated Kovak with his thumb. "I tell Beamer it sounds screwy to me, but Beamer thinks you killed him."

I wanted to know why I should kill a man that I didn't know from Adam.

Beamer shook a bony finger in my face. "I'll tell you why. Because you're an opportunist. And as soon as the girl died, you realized that the poison was undoubtedly somewhere here in her dressing room. So, without even waiting for Harry's squad, you clipped over here to get it, intending to turn the heat on whoever it was who killed her. But Kovak caught you prowling and you shot him!"

"In other words, I had my mind on blackmail."

"You did."

I hit him so hard that he caromed off the coroner, who was just coming in the door, into Marty Eagles of the *Times-Tribune*. He got up dripping claret and spitting threats.

Nobby rubbed the palm of his hand across his jowl. "You shouldn't have ought to have done that, Tom," he informed me.

I asked him if he thought I had killed Kovak. All he would say was that it looked peculiar. Then I demanded to talk to the doorman, and Nobby sent one of his boys to get him. Pop came in, working his toothless jaw on the stem of a stinking corncob pipe.

I asked him who the two lads were who had come in after I had. The old man looked surprised and said that no one had. "I wasn't supposed to let him in," he told Beamer. He made a gesture with his palm. "But he pushed me, like that, out of his way."

Beamer had talked to him before. "After attempting to question you concerning the dead girl's boyfriend?"

"Yeah. That's right," Pop answered.

Beamer asked if I admitted that much. I said I did. I also said that I had offered Pop a five-dollar bill if he would tell me the dead girl's boyfriend's name, but that he'd turned it down, saying he was afraid that if he told me he'd wind up in an alley.

Nobby asked the old man if he'd said that.

Pop denied it indignantly. "Naw," he said. "He's just making that up in his head."

I told Nobby that he was lying and asked him if he knew any local hood by the name of Jim. He said that he knew several and which one did I mean. I admitted I didn't know, but shortly before the girl had died she had told me that Jim, whoever he was, wouldn't believe that Mr. X wanted to leave her two hundred thousand dollars just because she was a sweet little girl who reminded him of his dead daughter.

"Stuff!" Beamer snorted. "I don't believe a word you've said. And I'm holding you for the Grand Jury."

"Charged with killing Novak?"

He said that was correct.

"He caught me snooping and we shot it out?"

"That's it."

I walked over the end of the shelf where the tech boys had stacked the brass they had picked up alongside of my gun.

"Then perhaps, just so they don't get hell from their city editors," I told Beamer, "you'll explain to the newspaper boys what happened to the gun that Kovak used on me. And while you're at it, you'd better tell them just how in hell I managed to shoot a .45 cartridge out of a .38 Police Positive and eject brass all over the floor."

Several of the news boys whooped. Layton of the tech squad said it couldn't be done. Nobby felt for his sap and looked thoughtfully at Pop. Beamer, gagging on his bile, admitted that maybe he'd been hasty.

I picked my hat off the floor, pointing out, "Which all goes to prove that you never want to count your Doyles before they're jugged."

Beamer went down fighting. "But the case doesn't make sense! Why was the dame poisoned? Why was Kovak killed? Who slugged you? And why would any old goat want to leave a cheap strip-teaser two hundred thousand dollars?"

I started to tell him that if he knew *all* the answers he could probably get on the Quiz Kids program, changed my mind and admitted, "I wouldn't know the answers to questions one, two, and three. But as for four, maybe he doesn't like his relatives."

I was to find out later that I'd scored a bull's-eye with that one. But right then I wasn't interested. I was thinking of Sue. As I started out the door Nobby asked where I was going.

"To the hospital," I told him. "Remember? I'm about to be a papa bird."

Beamer snorted. "That's nothing to be proud of. Even monkeys reproduce."

I turned back and shook his hand. "Right on the nose," I assured him. "You're living proof."

The street lights had come on by the time I reached the street, and a cold rain had begun to fall. Despite the glib talk I had given Beamer, I didn't feel so hot. The lad with the gun, whoever he was, hadn't been kidding. And he wasn't any novice. Unless I cracked this thing, quick, I was living on borrowed time. I didn't know a thing—and at the same time I knew too much.

Max was waiting at the mouth of the theater alley-way, studying a life-sized color cut-out of Dolly. "It isn't fair," he complained. "All of them curves for the worms." He added, as an afterthought, "They wouldn't let me come in."

I told him that he hadn't missed a thing and asked if Mable had gotten in touch with Sue to explain why I'd been delayed. He said he didn't know, having followed Lieutenant Nobby and State's Attorney Beamer as soon as they had started for the Lyric.

"You look like hell," he told me. "And Sue isn't going to like it. Maybe you'll frighten the baby."

I said that Sue hadn't married me for my looks and that the kid would have to get used to me sooner or later.

There were two things I could do. I could drop the case, or go on. And the dead girl had given me five hundred dollars. She had come to me because she'd heard I stood in back of my clients.

"Give me your gun," I told Max. "Now here's what I want you to do." I described Pop to him. "Strike up an acquaintance with him. Stay with him. Get him stiff. Find out Dolly's boyfriend's last name."

"On the swindle sheet?" he asked hopefully.

"And I hope you choke," I told him. I wanted another drink so bad I could taste it. But I knew that if I showed at the hospital with liquor on my breath, Sue would swear I'd been drunk.

I whistled at a cab. It swished on past on the wet pavement. I walked on up to the corner, bought a paper, then walked across State to Wabash and on to Michigan without having a bit of luck.

When you don't want a cab, they haunt you. As soon as it starts to sprinkle, they all go underground. The street was jammed with home-bound office workers. I had no way of telling if I was being tailed.

The paper got soaked. I threw it away after glancing at the headline. Jo-Jo McGurn, the tough hood, who had shot his way out of Alcatraz, was still featured. I hadn't made the black ink as yet.

On the corner of Michigan, Corrigan, the white-haired old sergeant of roundsmen, recognized me and wanted to know if it was wet enough to suit me. I said it was, started to walk on, and then turned back. If any lad knew the Loop, it was Corrigan. He's walked it for thirty-five years. And, after all, the field was limited. "Look," I asked him. "What old Chicago buck of eighty-three with a penchant for chorus girls is famous enough to have made *Who's Who?*"

"Faith," Corrigan grinned, "and any old buck of eighty-three who—"

"It's not what you think," I stopped him. "But this lad is rolling in money. And he's got a brother, a niece, and a nephew."

Corrigan thought a moment, shook his head. "It's hard to say offhand, me not knowing the extent of their relations. But it could be old Max Siegal the corporation lawyer, Phil Curry the architect, or mayhap old Judge Jensen. All of them are past eighty. All of them have money. All of them have looked at the girls in their day."

I wrapped a ten around a cigar and stuck it in his raincoat pocket.

"God bless you, son," he beamed, "for being so thoughtful of an old man."

Thoughtful. I almost took the ten back. The white-haired old grafter had more apartment buildings than I had rent receipts. I cut across to the Library.

The librarian looked at me as if she wondered if I could read, but she got me a copy of *Who's Who*. Curry fitted the bill exactly. He was eighty-three years old. And while there was no mention of a niece or nephew, he did have a brother, Thomas. He was listed as living on Ohio a few blocks from the lake. Moreover, he fitted in with what I knew. Either a lawyer or a judge would have known that he could have gotten a declaratory judgment.

Outside again, I fought my way into a cab that happened to hesitate and gave the driver the Ohio Street address. "And don't pull your flag," I warned him. "I'm going on to the Stuyvesant and I'll make it worth your while."

The house was old but well-kept, sandwiched in between a hotel and an apartment building. An over-buxom blonde in her mid-

dle thirties and gold silk lounging pajamas answered the doorbell.
I could smell good Scotch, and lots of it, as she asked me what I
wanted.

I said I wanted to see Mr. Curry, Mr. Phillip Curry.

A man's voice in one of the rooms off the hall wanted to know
who it was and she repeated what I'd said.

"Well, he can't see him," the voice said. The speaker followed
it into the hall. He was a plump, dissipated man with receding hair
and flabby dewlaps. You see his type at ringside tables in every
sucker trap. He motioned at me like I was one of the help. "Go
away, my man, go away."

I stepped into the hall instead and closed the door behind me.
The blonde giggled drunkenly, "Isn't he forshful, Henry?" She
tried to focus her eyes on my face as she informed me, "I'm very
fond of good-looking forshful men."

Henry called her a five-letter word.

"Look," I told him. "I'm not here to argue with drunks or nym-
phos. I'm here to see Mr. Phillip Curry. Just tell him that Dolly
Adoree sent me."

He stepped back as if I had slapped him, and I knew I'd hit the
jackpot.

"What about Miss Adoree?" he wanted to know.

Before I could say anything, the blonde informed me, "She's
nothing but a tramp, a dirty little tramp whoosh trying to steal our
money." She was drunk, but she knew what she was saying. Her
eyes glittered dangerously. "But she isn't goin' to do it. We'll
fight her in the courtsh. We'll see her in hell firsh. And whash
more, Henry's told her so."

If it was an act, it was a good one. "That's fine. In fact that's
just dandy," I told Henry. "Because you see, she's dead. She was
murdered this afternoon."

His mouth gaped open. His face turned a dirty grey.

"Murdered? Who was murdered this afternoon?" a thin voice
asked from the landing of the stairs.

Phillip Curry might have been eighty-three, but he was well pre-
served. His hair was perfectly white, but his color was good and
while his face was slightly veined it had none of the parchment
appearance of great age. His black broadcloth suit was well cut.
He was wearing a stiff stand-up wing collar. I hadn't seen one in
ten years. He looked like money in the bank.

"I'm Phillip Curry," he introduced himself, offering to shake hands. "I don't believe I caught your name."

I told him.

"Oh, yes." His blue eyes twinkled. "Tom Doyle. The young man who doesn't see eye to eye with State's Attorney Beamer. I've been expecting you to call. Then Dolly's seen you?"

I told him she was dead.

"Dead?" he repeated, incredulously.

The blonde started to say something and Henry told her to shut up.

Phillip Curry studied the younger man thoughtfully. "My brother's boy, Henry Curry," he said. He indicated the blonde. "And my sister's daughter, Jane." He passed his fingers across his eyes, bewildered. *"You say that Dolly is dead?"*

I said yes. He led the way into a wood-paneled library. The blonde and Henry tagged along, the blonde sing-songing, "I'm glad thash she'sh dead," between hiccups.

I may have been in screwier households, but I don't remember when. Curry pointed to a decanter of Scotch and lighted a long, thin cigar. Once he had gotten it through his head that the girl was really gone, I liked the way he accepted the fact.

"Now tell me all about it," he said simply.

When I had finished my story the blonde repeated that she was glad. Henry looked more frightened than ever. Curry asked me, "Then as yet the police don't know the identity of Dolly's mysterious Mr. X?"

I said no, expecting the old, hush-hush. But Curry had what it took. He reached for the phone on the desk, asked the operator to connect him with Central Bureau, then turned to me and asked to whom I thought he had better speak.

I told him Homicide.

His face a fish-belly white, the younger Curry protested, "No. Don't call the police! Don't get us involved in this mess!"

"And why not?" Curry asked. "I have nothing to hide, and nothing of which to be ashamed. I was very fond of Dolly." He hesitated briefly, licking at his thin lips. "And I think I can assure you, Henry," he added quietly, "that whoever is responsible for her death is going to the electric chair."

The younger man buried his face in his hands and muttered, "I didn't kill her. I didn't."

He seemed to be trying to reassure himself. The blonde began to cry.

Curry got his number. While he was talking to Lieutenant Nobby, I told Henry, "You may or may not know it, but you're on the well-known spot. Dolly told me you threatened her last night."

"We had a scene," he admitted.

"And you were in her dressing room this afternoon?"

He shook his head vehemently. "I was not."

"But I was," the blonde admitted. She had sobered considerably. "And I told that little tramp just what I thought of her. Uncle Phil had no right to leave her all that money. It belongs to Henry and me. It was left to us in trust."

I said I wasn't interested in the financial aspect of the case. Curry held out the phone and said that Lieutenant Nobby would like to speak with me.

"Nice going, Tom," Nobby boomed. "We'll be right out. Will you be there when we get there?"

I told him I didn't think so, that I was still on my way to the hospital, but that after I'd seen Sue I'd be back and to wait for me.

Curry was concerned. He wanted to know if someone in my family was ill. I told him not exactly, but that I was momentarily expecting to have a child,

The blonde sniggered nastily.

"That is, my wife Sue is expecting a child," I corrected. I picked up my hat from the sofa and fired one parting shot. "Your interest in the dead girl, of course, Mr. Curry, was strictly platonic."

He assured me that was so.

"You just wanted to leave her the two hundred thousand dollars because she reminded you of your own dead daughter."

He said that was also true.

"Then perhaps you can tell me this." I fingered the bruise on my cheek. "What was her boyfriend's last name? All I know is that his first name is Jim, but I'm very anxious to contact him."

Curry expressed surprise. His smile was rather wry. "You have me there, Doyle," he admitted. "I didn't even know she had a boyfriend."

The blonde said something about there being no fool like an old one.

Henry walked with me to the door. "Don't let the old man fool you," he whispered hoarsely. "He looks and talks like a saint. But he isn't."

I said that was interesting.

He expounded, "It was our money, Jane's and mine, that he was willing to that girl. And I'm glad she's dead." His voice rose shrilly. "I'm glad, understand."

I lighted a cigarette in the open door. "If anything," I asked him, "just what do you do for a living?"

He admitted he hadn't worked for some time, but when he did work he was a chemical engineer. I thought of the capsule that Beamer had crushed under my nose. It wouldn't take much of a chemical engineer to combine cyanogen with a metallic element and come out with cyanide.

In my book he was guilty as hell. He had motive. He had threatened the girl. He had access to the means of murder. But he wasn't the lad who had slugged me in Dolly's dressing room. And from where I stood, the case against him was *too* good.

I gave him the usual line about if I was him I wouldn't try to leave town, and walked down the steps through the rain. The hell with it, I thought. Let the cops figure it out. By putting Nobby on the trail I've earned my five hundred bucks.

That was what I thought. The cab was still waiting at the curb, the driver slouched over the wheel.

"Let's roll, Bud," I told him.

He reached around to open the door, but instead of stepping in, I stepped back, my right hand in my topcoat pocket. *He might be a cab driver. But he wasn't the one who had been piloting the hack when I'd told him to wait.*

"Don't try it, Doyle," a cold voice from the back seat warned. "There are two guns on you. Take your hand out of your pocket!"

I said, "The hell with that."

Shooting through my pocket, I threw four slugs at the voice, but I'd forgotten about the driver. He leaned out of the cab and conked me with a tire-iron. He was good with the iron, damn good. Before I could spray one his way he hit me a second time and my knees began to sag. I took a couple of steps toward the stairs with the hazy idea of holing up. But I didn't make it by twenty feet. The third step that I took, the wet pavement came up and kissed me.

The matting on which I was lying was coarse and smelled of onions. I had a dark-brown taste in my mouth, but it wasn't booze. It was blood that had trickled down from my skull and dried on my cheeks and lips. I opened my eyes and for all of the good it did I might as well have kept them closed. It was so dark I couldn't have seen my right hand in front of my face even if it hadn't been securely lashed to my left, behind my back.

I tried moving my feet. I wasn't going anywhere. My ankles were not only tied, they were also tied *to* something.

Not too far away, I could see the lighted outline of a door. As my head began to clear I could hear a murmur of voices. Two men seemed to be arguing about something.

I heard the words *money, scram,* and *dead,* distinctly.

While I was trying to puzzle them out, the door opened and a man came into the room. He closed the door too quickly for me to see his face, but I could see that I was in a warehouse loft of some kind. At least that explained away the onions.

"You awake, Doyle?" he wanted to know.

I said I was, trying to place the voice.

"I'm a son-of-a-gun," he admitted. "You're a hard man to kill."

He sounded Italian to me. I said, "It's practically impossible, Giuseppi. And if you know what's good for you, you'll untie my hands and feet right quick."

He showed me what he thought of that by trying to kick in my ribs. "Beeg mouths," he informed me. "That's what all coppers are."

I placed the voice. He was the lad who had urged, "C'mon" in Dolly's dressing room. I chanced another flank attack. "Scram. Beat it, Giuseppi. I don't do business with punks. Tell Jim I want to see him."

He thought that one over a moment, then kicked me. "Never you min' about Jim. You talk to me. What was you doing in that house on Ohio, huh?"

I told him I was selling magazines, and he went to work on my ribs in earnest. "You're just asking for it, sucker. C'mon now. Come clean. The old geek who lives in that house is the sap who wanted to leave all that money to Dolly, huh?"

I thought that one over a moment. Curry had already admitted his identity to Harry Nobby. Harry would tell the boys. It would be in all the morning papers. I wasn't giving away a thing and perhaps if I strung along I could smell out the connection. "Yeah, he's the man," I admitted.

"How much *you* clip him for?"

"You're way over my head," I told him. "I don't know what you're talking about."

"I betcha," he jeered, and was gone.

You figure it out. I couldn't. The more I thought it over, the less sense it made. The argument in the other room resumed. Then, somewhere in the building, a heavy door opened and slammed. A moment later a third voice broke in on the duet: "The joint's still swarming with cops, but they're thinning out. Just before I left they threw young Curry in a squad car."

Someone asked, "Yeah?"

"Yeah," the newcomer chuckled. "One of the harness bulls told me that they found his fingerprints on that bottle of vitamin pills that killed her."

Then the voices went into a huddle. I couldn't hear a thing. The heavy door opened and closed again. The light still burned in the other room but no one said anything, and no one moved.

I inched back on the sacking and jerked my feet. It damn near tore the skin off my ankles, but something gave. I hoped it wasn't bone.

When the roaring in my ears died down I tried it again and my shoes slipped off, the rope slipping off with them.

I waited for my head to clear, then tiptoed to the door and peered in through the largest crack. There was a lad lying on a cot, but either I hadn't made much noise or he was a sound sleeper. I took a mental inventory of my pockets. I didn't carry a knife. The only thing I could think of that might help me was my lighter. It took almost an hour to get it. When I did get it, it wouldn't light.

I lost my head; dropped it, cursing, on the floor and kicked it. It banged the door like a shot.

I waited for the lad on the cot to come in. I waited for five minutes. Then I looked through the crack again. He hadn't moved. I jockeyed the door open and walked in. He had a good reason for not moving. He was dead.

There was an empty whisky bottle on the table. I smashed off the neck and sawed at the rope on my wrists with the glass, meanwhile trying to figure the lad on the cot. I was dumb not to get it sooner. He was the lad in the cab who had told me to take my hand out of my pocket. And I'd put all four shots where I'd aimed them.

When my wrists were free I washed off the blood as best I could at a stained sink in one corner, got my shoes, then gave the lad on the cot a once-over. His pals had been there before me.

The big outer door that I had heard slam was locked. I smashed a window and crawled through it. Then, struck by a sudden thought, I crawled in again and went back for another look at the dead hood on the cot. My slugs hadn't left much of his face, but I thought I knew who he was. At least a part of the picture was beginning to make sense.

I wanted to get in touch with Lieutenant Nobby, but I wanted to see Max first. The night elevator man said that Max had staggered upstairs about two. He also wanted to know did her husband come home or did a truck run over me. I looked at the mirror in the cage. I looked like hell. I hadn't washed half the blood off. My right temple was a mangy purple. One of my eyes was swollen almost shut. A second-hand man wouldn't have given me four-bits for my clothes.

"I suppose after Guadalcanal and all them other places that you fought, Mr. Doyle," the night man said sagely as he let me off on my floor, "Chicago seems pretty tame to you, huh?"

I gave him a dirty look and walked on into the office. Max was snoring on the mourner's bench. He reeked of whisky and instead of turning off the light he'd spread a morning paper over his eyes. Jo-Jo McGurn wasn't in it with me. I'd made the black print all right, and so had Dolly. The streamer read: DARING DANCER DIES IN DETECTIVE'S OFFICE.

Underneath the headline was a picture of myself in uniform and a larger picture of Dolly Adoree in not much of anything. The lead was a masterpiece of innuendo. The way that first edition had it, the girl had practically died in my arms, to which she had fled from the unwelcome advances of an elderly suitor who had wanted to trifle with her honor for a million dollars. It hinted I knew her pretty well.

I sat down at Mable's desk, plugged in a line and called the hospital. They wouldn't ring Sue's room that time of morning, but they did connect me with the night nurse.

"This is Tom Doyle," I told her. "And I wonder if you'd please tell me if—"

She broke in crisply. "I don't believe that I care to talk to you, Mr. Doyle. And I might also inform you that Mrs. Doyle has seen the morning papers."

I told her that was what I had been afraid of, but that I could explain. "And I'd be very grateful to you," I told her, "if you'd tell me—"

There was a click on the other end. Max sat up on the bench, shedding papers. "A boy or a girl?" he demanded.

"I'll be damned if I know," I admitted.

I took the suit and shirt and spare accessories I always keep in the office out of the closet, laid them on my desk, stripped down to my shorts and washed more carefully this time, meanwhile satisfying Max's curiosity. "How about you?" I asked him. "You find out what I wanted to know?"

"Did I?" he hiccuped. He gave me an elbow-by-elbow description of the glassware that he and Pop had hoisted, holding back the snapper for the climax. "Of course," he concluded, "Pop didn't come right out and spill the name. But he was filthy with hush-hush dough and I'm willing to bet you twenty bucks that Dolly's mysterious boyfriend Jim is really—"

I called the name before he could. He looked at me resentfully and wanted to know how I did it.

I looked at my face in the mirror. "The hard way," I assured him.

Sergeant Cooper in Nobby's office said that Harry was there, but he couldn't come to the phone at the moment as he and State's Attorney Beamer were very busy interrogating a Mr. Henry Curry. I said that was a very high-class name for beating the hell out of a guy, and had young Curry broken yet?

Cooper said, "Not yet. But we've got him dead to rights, Tom. We've got a dozen witnesses from her hotel who heard him threaten to kill her if she didn't give the old man the gate. He admits he's a chemical engineer. And the lab boys found his fingerprints all over that phony bottle of vitamin pills that killed her."

I asked him if he'd give Lieutenant Nobby a message and he said okay. "Then ask Harry this," I told him. *"Ask him, if he was a dame who had just had her life threatened by some lug, if he would swallow a vitamin capsule that the lad who had threatened him gave him?"*

Max got a bottle from the cabinet, saying that called for a drink. "So it was Jim all the time?" he asked me. "He was jealous of the dame on account of old man Curry. He knew that young Curry had threatened her. So, somehow, he gets Henry's fingerprints on the bottle, gives the bottle to the dame and, trusting him, she takes one."

I buckled on my holster, slipped a fresh gun in the slot and admitted he had a good theory with a few exceptions. In the first place the lad we had known as Jim would have been more likely to shoot a two-timing dame than he would have been to poison her. In the second place she hadn't been frightened of Jim or she would have told me so. In the third place the buxom blonde niece of old Curry had practically admitted to me that she had been the last of the Currys to see Dolly.

Max puzzled, "You mean you think the dame killed her?"

"No," I told him. "I don't. But I want to talk to the dame. And I want to talk to her right now."

Two or three doors off State Street, the Melshire Bar was still going full blast behind drawn blinds. Back in one of the areaways, a milkman was rattling bottles. A few hackers were congregated at the cab stand on the corner. But most of Ohio Street still slept.

I parked Max's car across the street and studied the windows of the Curry house. The first floor was blacked out, but there was a light in one of the front rooms on the second floor.

We crossed the street and I tried the door. It was locked, but not for long. Max is handy that way. He was also nervous. "I can see why Beamer don't like you," he whispered once we were inside. "What we are now committing is illegal entry. We could get five years for this."

I told him to worry about it, that was what I paid him a salary for, and tiptoed up the stairs. The lighted room was the one I wanted. The door was unlocked. I walked in with Max at my heels and closed the door quietly behind us.

The blonde, still wearing the gold silk lounging pajamas, was lying on the bed, a pinch-bottle of Scotch and a glass convenient to her hand. At first I thought she'd passed out. And she had. But she wasn't coming to.

"Boy. She's dead as a mackerel," Max said in the hushed tone that most folks use when speaking of the dead. Both of his hands behind his back, he sniffed at the uncorked bottle of Scotch and added, sagely, "Suicide, via the cyanide route."

I read the note beside the bottle. It was addressed To Whom It May Concern, and read:

I, Jane Curry, in my right mind, but deeply contrite over the thing that I and Henry have done, do, with the last of my dying strength, confess that it was Henry and I who poisoned Dolly Adoree. Henry procured the cyanide and prepared the fatal capsules. I staged a scene with her in her dressing room at the Lyric Theater and managed to exchange the prepared bottle for a similar bottle of vitamin capsules. We were fools not to think of the fingerprint angle. Our motive in poisoning her was, of course, an attempt to save for ourselves the two hundred thousand dollars that Uncle Phillip intended to leave her . . .

Max reached for the bottle of Scotch from force of habit, stopped just In time. "Boy. What do you think of that?"

I said that I thought it proved she had a lot of "dying strength."

"You mean it's a phony?" he gasped.

"It's phony as hell," I snorted.

Then I whirled toward the door—too late. A slim hand had cracked it open, reached in and switched out the light. Somewhere in the house a man screamed in pain or terror. From the darkness of the hallway Giuseppi said wearily, "I'm a son-of-a-gun, so help me, Doyle. When you was a little bambino your mother dropped you on the head, huh? You ain't got the sense to let well enough alone."

I put two slugs through the crack in the door. He cursed me in Italian. Then the whole damn house erupted. Feet pounded on the stairs. Someone in the hallway yelled, "Kill 'em!"

Slugs were criss-crossing the room by now. One of them punched out a window. I yelled for Max to get down and he asked what did I think he was doing.

I fired the last slug in my gun, then rolled close to the door for protection while I fumbled for a fresh clip. Before I could get one out of my pocket, Giuseppi and two other hoods rushed in.

I jerked Giuseppi's feet out from under him and his head smacked into the baseboard with the crunch of a rotten melon. His gun dropped from his hand but before I could pick it up one of the other hoods stepped on my fingers, shooting at the white of my face and missing it by inches.

Then Max threw the bottle of Scotch. It caught the lad in the throat. He stepped back, cursing, flipping a shot at Max. But by that time I had the gun. I jammed it into his guts and told him to hold everything.

But a prowl-car siren was wailing now. He made a break for the door instead. I shot for the back of his knees but Max, wrestling the third hood for his gun, slammed into me, threw me off balance and I got him in the small of the spine instead.

"'Don't kill him!" I shouted at Max.

He didn't hear me. He had twisted the gun from the third hood's hand and as the hood reached the top of the stairs Max nailed him in the back of his head. The hood fell the rest of the way downstairs, into the arms of the prowl-car cops who had been parked out in front of the Melshire listening to the music.

I found the hall lights and turned them on. There were hoods splattered all over the hall. McGinnis, one of the cops out of the East Chicago Avenue Station, knew me. "What the hell gives here, Doyle?"

I told him, "Murder!" I also told him to put in a call for Harry Nobby and State's Attorney Beamer.

The second cop, it turned out later his name was Durkin, wasn't so sold on the idea of taking orders from me. He came up the stairs three steps at a time and yelled for me to give him my gun.

I told him he could damn' well try and take it. I was boiling. *I knew who had killed the stripper. I knew who had killed the blonde. But the four lads who could prove what I knew were dead.*

Then he yelled I should give him my gun and no more foolishness. I bounced a short left off his jaw. Max caught him as he fell. "Well, it was a nice job while it lasted," he observed.

I said to hell with that and went in search of old man Curry. I found him in his bedroom in about the condition I had expected. There was blood smeared all over his face.

"Three hoodlums broke in here and shot me," he groaned.

I wanted to know why. He said he didn't know, that he had never seen any of the men before. His watch and some change and a ring and his wallet were piled in a little heap on the dresser.

McGinnis came in just then and said, "An attempted robbery, eh?"

I asked Curry if he knew that his niece Jane had committed suicide. He said that he did not and began to cry, saying that it was all his fault.

By the time we got him quieted down and out in the hall, the joint was filled with cops and Harry Nobby and State's Attorney B earner were coming up the stairs wagging a tail of reporters, and Durkin was busy whispering in Beamer's ear.

"This," Beamer shook his fist at me, "is the last straw." He looked at the stiffs and shuddered. "No matter what the excuse, there is absolutely no need for this sort of carnage. It gives the City a bad name."

Nobby identified Giuseppi as Frank Aleo, a West Coast hood and one of McGurn's old mob. He didn't know the other two.

Old Phillip Curry tried to explain things to Beamer. "You don't understand, Mr. State's Attorney. If it hadn't been for Mr. Doyle I might have been dead by now. These men broke into my home to rob me."

I let Beamer get that digested, then I told him, "Just in case you're interested, there's another stiff in the room to your right."

We all crowded into the room and Beamer read the note. When he had finished his bad temper was gone. "What did I tell you?" he crowed at the reporters. "Henry Curry is guilty as sin." He tapped the note. "She admits that they overlooked the fingerprint angle."

Fingerprint angle. I don't know how I could have missed it. I was so grateful to Beamer that I could have kissed him on both cheeks and hardly gagged at all.

Beamer looked at old man Curry, cleared his throat importantly, and continued to the reporters, "And you may tell the public in your next editions that no matter how highly placed, nor what wealthy connections he may have, I pledge my solemn oath of office that Henry Curry will go to the electric chair for the murder of poor little Dolly Adoree."

I said I doubted if a hock-shop would give him very much without better security and that if his oath of office was contingent on Henry Curry going to the chair I doubted if he'd ever redeem it.

Red-faced, he wanted to know what I meant.

I asked him, "How badly smeared were Henry Curry's prints?"

He said they weren't smeared at all. "They were very distinct and clean."

"And his and Dolly's fingerprints were the only prints on the bottle?"

He said that was correct.

"Then tell me this," I said, pointing to the dead blonde. "Why didn't she smudge the other prints or leave prints of her own when she exchanged the bottle?"

Beamer explained that she had thought of that and had been very careful.

I hooted. "And then she takes cyanide, *leaving a suicide note saying that she and Henry had been fools not to think of the fingerprint angle.*"

The reporters crowded closer.

Beamer sneered, " I suppose, as usual, that you have *another* angle."

"You're damn right I have," I told him. I told Harry Nobby, "I'm telling this to you, not to Beamer. And you take the credit. I've got mine. It all began with Dolly Adoree."

Beamer continued to needle. "How interesting."

"Keep it up, chump," I warned him. "You may be the State's Attorney to the electorate, but you're only a sad sack to me. And one more yip out of you and I'll bounce you off another wall."

Beamer started a hot comeback and changed his mind. He knew I'd do it. I continued, "Of course, I haven't got the facts. This is partially guesswork. But I know the motive was money. And I think we can safely say that Dolly's death was really an insurance murder."

Beamer looked superior.

Harry Nobby was worried. "I'm afraid you've muffed this one, Tom," he said. "We checked that angle. And Dolly didn't have a dime's worth of insurance."

"No," I agreed. "I don't suppose she did. But I'll bet you a hundred dollars to a dime that both Jane and Henry Curry had plenty." I looked at old Phillip Curry. "Is that correct?"

The old man wet his lips. "Why, yes. I believe that they were insured."

I let the room grow still, then I pulled the pin out of the potato masher that I had put together, tossed it into old Curry's lap and blew the whole case to hell. "You know damn well they were insured. *And you killed Dotty Adoree for their insurance!*"

"He's crazy! The man is insane!" Curry screamed.

Beamer puzzled, "He killed Dolly for *their* insurance. That doesn't make sense to me."

"It would if you had the brains of a gnat," I told him. "It was the perfect murder plot, but it's blown up in his face."

He protested, "But why should a man leave a girl two hundred thousand dollars and then kill her?"

I shook my head. "There never was any two hundred thousand dollars, at least not for a long time. That was a lot of heifer-dust, a come-on. Curry merely *told* Dolly he was leaving her the money. He never actually gave her a dime. How do I know he's broke? I don't. I'm just guessing," I admitted. "But homes this size usually have servants." I wrote my name in the dust on a table.

"Both Jane and Henry told me earlier in the evening that the money was really theirs, that it had been left to them in trust. A rich man would have turned it over. But Curry couldn't. He was broke. What's more, he was desperate for money. So he figured himself out a scheme that was damn' near perfect. If it had worked, he would have been rid of both Jane and Henry's claims, and he'd have had their insurance to boot What's more, it would have worked if it hadn't been for me and a certain boyfriend of Dolly's."

"Take it step by step, Tom," Nobby suggested.

I boiled it down to A-B-Cs. "Curry went to Dolly, his prospective victim. He told her that she reminded him of his own dear dead daughter and that he wanted to leave her two hundred thousand dollars in his will. Naturally she was thrilled. Naturally Jane and Henry weren't. They were sore as hell, just as Curry had known they would be."

Beamer clung to The State versus Henry Curry. "Young Curry *did* threaten to kill the girl."

"Sure he did," I agreed. "The old man figured on that. He also figured that when Polly died, the finger would be on Henry. And it was. You've been sweating him all night. You're still convinced of his guilt. What's more, if Homicide had waltzed in here and found Jane dead with that suicide note beside her, you'd have accepted it at face value, burned Henry, and the old man would have been sitting in the clear counting their insurance and laughing at us all."

"You—you're crazy," the old man accused again.

"He poisoned both girls?" Nobby asked.

"He did," I told him. "And he'd have gotten away with it if it hadn't been for Dolly's boyfriend, Jim. Jim followed her to my office. He overheard a part of our conversation. But he didn't hear all she told me and he was afraid that she might have tipped me. That's why he tailed me back to the Lyric and took a pot-shot at me. That's why he killed Kovak. He was afraid Kovak knew who he was and for reasons of his own he didn't want to appear in the case. Why he bribed Pop instead of killing him, I don't know. I do know that he trailed me here to the house because he *knew* who had given Dolly that bottle of vitamin capsules."

Nobby asked, "And Henry's fingerprints—?"

"Planted by the old man, of course," I told him. "That wouldn't be hard to do. Henry looks like the type of a lad who would take vitamins. All old Curry had to do was snitch the bottle, dump out what was in it, and put in the cyanide pills."

"But this—Jim," Nobby persisted. "What did he intend to do?"

I said I imagined that he intended to kill Curry, but his plans had been interrupted. "By the time I came to in the warehouse," I explained, "Jim had lost all interest in killing the old man." I looked out at the dead hoods in the hall. "So had his gang. They figured to shake him down instead. That's what they were doing when Max and I got here. He probably offered to whack the insurance to save his hide. But I gummed that up by spotting Jane's note as a fake. After that there was nothing they could do but knock us off. So, they had their try for us, and missed."

"I'll buy that," Nobby said. "That sounds."

I tightened one last nut in the chair. "Curry's mussed himself up a bit to indicate a struggle, but if you'll wash that blood off his face I think you'll find he's not hurt very bad.

"Off-hand," I asked Curry, "how much were they insured for, Phillip?"

"Fifty thousand apiece," he began. Then he realized what he had said and began to curse me.

The reporters made a dash for the phone. I got there first. "Not on this one," I told them. "I'm calling the hospital."

I gave the operator the number of the Stuyvesant just as Beamer touched my arm.

"If you'd clear up one point, Doyle—"

I said I would be pleased to and he indicated the stiffs on the stairs. "Just which one of those is Jim, the missing boyfriend?"

I told him that none of them was, that Jim was lying on a cot in an old warehouse on Quincy near the river. He wanted to know if I was certain. I said I was. Then he wanted to know how I knew that he was still there. I told him that I knew damn well he was still there because he was very dead from me having shot him four times in the face.

Reamer's face grew red again. "You're a good operative, Doyle," he admitted. "But you are also a killer, and it has to stop. Therefore I'm going to make an issue of this boyfriend's death and book you for manslaughter."

I said that was all right with me, and asked the operator couldn't she get the hospital. She said she was waiting for a line, so many, folks calling that time of morning to find out how their dear ones were.

Beamer counted them on his fingers. "Four men dead. And what did you get out of it, Doyle? A measly five hundred dollars."

I asked him didn't he mean five thousand, five hundred dollars?

Beamer said he did not, that it was his impression that Miss Adoree had only given me a five-hundred-dollar retainer.

I said that was correct but that there happened to be a five-thousand dead-or-alive reward on Dolly's boyfriend, his right name being Jim all right, but him being much better known among the Police Positive trade as Jo-Jo McGurn, the goon who had shot his way out of Alcatraz.

Nobby whooped so loud he choked and had to go look for a bottle of rye. I didn't bother to look at Beamer because the gum-snapper was back on the wire saying sweetly, "Good morning, Stuyvesant Hospital."

"This is Tom Doyle again," I told her. "You know, Lace Curtain Doyle. Now be a good girl and let the janitor sleep."

I took a deep breath and when I heard Sue say hello I let it all out in a rush. "Look, honey. I'm sorry as hell. I'm crazy about you. I adore you. But I got stuck on a big case and I just couldn't get there. Now be a sweet mama bird and tell the papa bird if the little nestling is going to wear pants or a skirt."

Sue was swell about it. "Which would the papa bird rather have?" she asked.

I said that it didn't matter.

"Well, we've a nestful," she admitted. "One of each."

"It's twins!" I yelled at Nobby.

Beamer said, "You would."

"Remind me to give you a loaded cigar," I told him. And by keeping the siren wide open and plowing through all the red lights, we made the hospital in five minutes flat.

RAMBLE HOUSE's

HARRY STEPHEN KEELER WEBWORK MYSTERIES

(RH) indicates the title is available ONLY in the RAMBLE HOUSE edition

The Ace of Spades Murder
The Affair of the Bottled Deuce (RH)
The Amazing Web
The Barking Clock
Behind That Mask
The Book with the Orange Leaves
The Bottle with the Green Wax Seal
The Box from Japan
The Case of the Canny Killer
The Case of the Crazy Corpse (RH)
The Case of the Flying Hands (RH)
The Case of the Ivory Arrow
The Case of the Jeweled Ragpicker
The Case of the Lavender Gripsack
The Case of the Mysterious Moll
The Case of the 16 Beans
The Case of the Transparent Nude (RH)
The Case of the Transposed Legs
The Case of the Two-Headed Idiot (RH)
The Case of the Two Strange Ladies
The Circus Stealers (RH)
Cleopatra's Tears
A Copy of Beowulf (RH)
The Crimson Cube (RH)
The Face of the Man From Saturn
Find the Clock
The Five Silver Buddhas
The 4th King
The Gallows Waits, My Lord! (RH)
The Green Jade Hand
Finger! Finger!
Hangman's Nights (RH)
I, Chameleon (RH)
I Killed Lincoln at 10:13! (RH)
The Iron Ring
The Man Who Changed His Skin (RH)
The Man with the Crimson Box
The Man with the Magic Eardrums
The Man with the Wooden Spectacles
The Marceau Case
The Matilda Hunter Murder
The Monocled Monster

The Murder of London Lew
The Murdered Mathematician
The Mysterious Card (RH)
The Mysterious Ivory Ball of Wong Shing Li (RH)
The Mystery of the Fiddling Cracksman
The Peacock Fan
The Photo of Lady X (RH)
The Portrait of Jirjohn Cobb
Report on Vanessa Hewstone (RH)
Riddle of the Travelling Skull
Riddle of the Wooden Parrakeet (RH)
The Scarlet Mummy (RH)
The Search for X-Y-Z
The Sharkskin Book
Sing Sing Nights
The Six From Nowhere (RH)
The Skull of the Waltzing Clown
The Spectacles of Mr. Cagliostro
Stand By—London Calling!
The Steeltown Strangler
The Stolen Gravestone (RH)
Strange Journey (RH)
The Strange Will
The Straw Hat Murders (RH)
The Street of 1000 Eyes (RH)
Thieves' Nights
Three Novellos (RH)
The Tiger Snake
The Trap (RH)
Vagabond Nights (Defrauded Yeggman)
Vagabond Nights 2 (10 Hours)
The Vanishing Gold Truck
The Voice of the Seven Sparrows
The Washington Square Enigma
When Thief Meets Thief
The White Circle (RH)
The Wonderful Scheme of Mr. Christopher Thorne
X. Jones—of Scotland Yard
Y. Cheung, Business Detective

Keeler Related Works

A To Izzard: A Harry Stephen Keeler Companion by Fender Tucker — Articles and stories about Harry, by Harry, and in his style. Included is a compleat bibliography.

Wild About Harry: Reviews of Keeler Novels — Edited by Richard Polt & Fender Tucker — 22 reviews of works by Harry Stephen Keeler from *Keeler News*. A perfect introduction to the author.

The Keeler Keyhole Collection: Annotated newsletter rants from Harry Stephen Keeler, edited by Francis M. Nevins. Over 400 pages of incredibly personal Keeleriana.

Fakealoo — Pastiches of the style of Harry Stephen Keeler by selected demented members of the HSK Society. Updated every year with the new winner.

RAMBLE HOUSE's OTHER LOONS

The End of It All and Other Stories — Ed Gorman's latest short story collection

Six Dancing Tuatara Press Books — *Beast or Man?* by Sean M'Guire; *The Whistling Ancestors* by Richard E. Goddard; *The Shadow on the House, Sorcerer's Chessmen* and *The Wizard of Berner's Abbey* by Mark Hansom, *The Trail of the Cloven Hoof* by Arlton Eadie and *The Border Line* by Walter S. Masterman. With introductions by John Pelan. Many more to come!

Death Leaves No Card — One of the most unusual murdered-in-the-tub mysteries you'll ever read. By Miles Burton.

The Dumpling — Political murder from 1907 by Coulson Kernahan

Victims & Villains — Intriguing Sherlockiana from Derham Groves

Ultra-Boiled — 23 gut-wrenching tales by our Man in Brooklyn, Gary Lovisi. Yow!

Shadows' Edge — Two early novels by Wade Wright: *Shadows Don't Bleed* and *The Sharp Edge*.

Evidence in Blue — 1938 mystery by E. Charles Vivian

The Case of the Little Green Men — Mack Reynolds wrote this love song to sci-fi fans back in 1951 and it's now back in print.

Hell Fire and **Savage Highway** — Two new hard-boiled novels by Jack Moskovitz, who developed his style writing sleaze back in the 70s. No one writes like Jack.

Researching American-Made Toy Soldiers — A 276-page collection of a lifetime of articles by toy soldier expert Richard O'Brien

Strands of the Web: Short Stories of Harry Stephen Keeler — Edited and Introduced by Fred Cleaver

Through the Looking Glass — Lewis Carroll wrote it; Gavin L. O'Keefe illustrated it.

The Sam McCain Novels — Ed Gorman's terrific series includes *The Day the Music Died, Wake Up Little Susie* and *Will You Still Love Me Tomorrow?*

A Shot Rang Out — Three decades of reviews from Jon Breen

Mysterious Martin, the Master of Murder — Two versions of a strange 1912 novel by Tod Robbins about a man who writes books that can kill.

Dago Red — 22 tales of dark suspense by Bill Pronzini

Two Robert Randisi Novels — *No Exit to Brooklyn* and *The Dead of Brooklyn*. The first two Nick Delvecchio novels.

The Night Remembers — A 1991 Jack Walsh mystery from Ed Gorman

Rough Cut & New, Improved Murder — Ed Gorman's first two novels

Hollywood Dreams — A novel of the Depression by Richard O'Brien

Seven Gelett Burgess Novels — *The Master of Mysteries, The White Cat, Two O'Clock Courage, Ladies in Boxes, Find the Woman, The Heart Line, The Picaroons*

The Organ Reader — A huge compilation of just about everything published in the 1971-1972 radical bay-area newspaper, *THE ORGAN*.

A Clear Path to Cross — Sharon Knowles short mystery stories by Ed Lynskey

Old Times' Sake — Short stories by James Reasoner from Mike Shayne Magazine

Freaks and Fantasies — Eerie tales by Tod Robbins, collaborator of Tod Browning on the film FREAKS.

Seven Jim Harmon Double Novels — *Vixen Hollow/Celluloid Scandal, The Man Who Made Maniacs/Silent Siren, Ape Rape/Wanton Witch, Sex Burns Like Fire/Twist Session, Sudden Lust/Passion Strip, Sin Unlimited/Harlot Master, Twilight Girls/Sex Institution*. Written in the early 60s.

Marblehead: A Novel of H.P. Lovecraft — A long-lost masterpiece from Richard A. Lupoff. Published for the first time!

The Compleat Ova Hamlet — Parodies of SF authors by Richard A. Lupoff – A brand new edition with more stories and more illustrations by Trina Robbins.

The Secret Adventures of Sherlock Holmes — Three Sherlockian pastiches by the Brooklyn author/publisher, Gary Lovisi.

The Universal Holmes — Richard A. Lupoff's 2007 collection of five Holmesian pastiches and a recipe for giant rat stew.

Four Joel Townsley Rogers Novels — By the author of *The Red Right Hand: Once In a Red Moon, Lady With the Dice, The Stopped Clock, Never Leave My Bed*

Two Joel Townsley Rogers Story Collections — Night of Horror and Killing Time

Twenty Norman Berrow Novels — *The Bishop's Sword, Ghost House, Don't Go Out After Dark, Claws of the Cougar, The Smokers of Hashish, The Secret Dancer, Don't Jump Mr. Boland!, The Footprints of Satan, Fingers for Ransom, The Three Tiers of Fantasy, The Spaniard's Thumb, The Eleventh Plague, Words Have Wings, One Thrilling Night, The Lady's in Danger, It Howls at Night, The Terror in the Fog, Oil Under the Window, Murder in the Melody, The Singing Room*

The N. R. De Mexico Novels — Robert Bragg presents *Marijuana Girl, Madman on a Drum, Private Chauffeur* in one volume.

Four Chelsea Quinn Yarbro Novels featuring Charlie Moon — *Ogilvie, Tallant and Moon, Music When the Sweet Voice Dies, Poisonous Fruit* and *Dead Mice*

Five Walter S. Masterman Mysteries — *The Green Toad, The Flying Beast, The Yellow Mistletoe, The Wrong Verdict* and *The Perjured Alibi*. Fantastic impossible plots.

Two Hake Talbot Novels — *Rim of the Pit, The Hangman's Handyman.* Classic locked room mysteries.

Two Alexander Laing Novels — *The Motives of Nicholas Holtz* and *Dr. Scarlett*, stories of medical mayhem and intrigue from the 30s.

Four David Hume Novels — *Corpses Never Argue, Cemetery First Stop, Make Way for the Mourners, Eternity Here I Come,* and more to come.

Three Wade Wright Novels — *Echo of Fear, Death At Nostalgia Street* and *It Leads to Murder,* with more to come!

Eight Rupert Penny Novels — *Policeman's Holiday, Policeman's Evidence, Lucky Policeman, Policeman in Armour, Sealed Room Murder, Sweet Poison, The Talkative Policeman, She had to Have Gas* and *Cut and Run* (by Martin Tanner.)

Five Jack Mann Novels — Strange murder in the English countryside. *Gees' First Case, Nightmare Farm, Grey Shapes, The Ninth Life, The Glass Too Many.*

Seven Max Afford Novels — *Owl of Darkness, Death's Mannikins, Blood on His Hands, The Dead Are Blind, The Sheep and the Wolves, Sinners in Paradise* and *Two Locked Room Mysteries and a Ripping Yarn* by one of Australia's finest novelists.

Five Joseph Shallit Novels — *The Case of the Billion Dollar Body, Lady Don't Die on My Doorstep, Kiss the Killer, Yell Bloody Murder, Take Your Last Look.* One of America's best 50's authors.

Two Crimson Clown Novels — By Johnston McCulley, author of the Zorro novels, *The Crimson Clown* and *The Crimson Clown Again.*

The Best of 10-Story Book — edited by Chris Mikul, over 35 stories from the literary magazine Harry Stephen Keeler edited.

A Young Man's Heart — A forgotten early classic by Cornell Woolrich

The Anthony Boucher Chronicles — edited by Francis M. Nevins
Book reviews by Anthony Boucher written for the *San Francisco Chronicle,* 1942 – 1947. Essential and fascinating reading.

Muddled Mind: Complete Works of Ed Wood, Jr. — David Hayes and Hayden Davis deconstruct the life and works of a mad genius.

Gadsby — A lipogram (a novel without the letter E). Ernest Vincent Wright's last work, published in 1939 right before his death.

My First Time: The One Experience You Never Forget — Michael Birchwood — 64 true first-person narratives of how they lost it.

A Roland Daniel Double: The Signal and The Return of Wu Fang — Classic thrillers from the 30s

Murder in Shawnee — Two novels of the Alleghenies by John Douglas: *Shawnee Alley Fire* and *Haunts.*

Deep Space and other Stories — A collection of SF gems by Richard A. Lupoff

Blood Moon — The first of the Robert Payne series by Ed Gorman

The Time Armada — Fox B. Holden's 1953 SF gem.

Black River Falls — Suspense from the master, Ed Gorman

Sideslip — 1968 SF masterpiece by Ted White and Dave Van Arnam

The Triune Man — Mindscrambling science fiction from Richard A. Lupoff

Detective Duff Unravels It — Episodic mysteries by Harvey O'Higgins

Automaton — Brilliant treatise on robotics: 1928-style! By H. Stafford Hatfield

The Incredible Adventures of Rowland Hern — Rousing 1928 impossible crimes by Nicholas Olde.

Slammer Days — Two full-length prison memoirs: *Men into Beasts* (1952) by George Sylvester Viereck and *Home Away From Home* (1962) by Jack Woodford

Murder in Black and White — 1931 classic tennis whodunit by Evelyn Elder

Killer's Caress — Cary Moran's 1936 hardboiled thriller

The Golden Dagger — 1951 Scotland Yard yarn by E. R. Punshon

A Smell of Smoke — 1951 English countryside thriller by Miles Burton

Ruled By Radio — 1925 futuristic novel by Robert L. Hadfield & Frank E. Farncombe

Murder in Silk — A 1937 Yellow Peril novel of the silk trade by Ralph Trevor

The Case of the Withered Hand — 1936 potboiler by John G. Brandon

Finger-prints Never Lie — A 1939 classic detective novel by John G. Brandon

Inclination to Murder — 1966 thriller by New Zealand's Harriet Hunter

Invaders from the Dark — Classic werewolf tale from Greye La Spina

Fatal Accident — Murder by automobile, a 1936 mystery by Cecil M. Wills

The Devil Drives — A prison and lost treasure novel by Virgil Markham

Dr. Odin — Douglas Newton's 1933 potboiler comes back to life.

The Chinese Jar Mystery — Murder in the manor by John Stephen Strange, 1934

The Julius Caesar Murder Case — A classic 1935 re-telling of the assassination by Wallace Irwin that's much more fun than the Shakespeare version

West Texas War and Other Western Stories — by Gary Lovisi

The Contested Earth and Other SF Stories — A never-before published space opera and seven short stories by Jim Harmon.

Tales of the Macabre and Ordinary — Modern twisted horror by Chris Mikul, author of the *Bizarrism* series.

The Gold Star Line — Seaboard adventure from L.T. Reade and Robert Eustace.

The Werewolf vs the Vampire Woman — Hard to believe ultraviolence by either Arthur M. Scarm or Arthur M. Scram.

Black Hogan Strikes Again — Australia's Peter Renwick pens a tale of the outback.

Don Diablo: Book of a Lost Film — Two-volume treatment of a western by Paul Landres, with diagrams. Intro by Francis M. Nevins.

The Charlie Chaplin Murder Mystery — Movie hijinks by Wes D. Gehring

The Koky Comics — A collection of all of the 1978-1981 Sunday and daily comic strips by Richard O'Brien and Mort Gerberg, in two volumes.

Suzy — Another collection of comic strips from Richard O'Brien and Bob Vojtko

Dime Novels: Ramble House's 10-Cent Books — *Knife in the Dark* by Robert Leslie Bellem, *Hot Lead* and *Song of Death* by Ed Earl Repp, *A Hashish House in New York* by H.H. Kane, and five more.

Blood in a Snap — The *Finnegan's Wake* of the 21st century, by Jim Weiler

Stakeout on Millennium Drive — Award-winning Indianapolis Noir — Ian Woollen.

Dope Tales #1 — Two dope-riddled classics; *Dope Runners* by Gerald Grantham and *Death Takes the Joystick* by Phillip Condé.

Dope Tales #2 — Two more narco-classics; *The Invisible Hand* by Rex Dark and *The Smokers of Hashish* by Norman Berrow.

Dope Tales #3 — Two enchanting novels of opium by the master, Sax Rohmer. *Dope* and *The Yellow Claw.*

Tenebrae — Ernest G. Henham's 1898 horror tale brought back.

The Singular Problem of the Stygian House-Boat — Two classic tales by John Kendrick Bangs about the denizens of Hades.

Tiresias — Psychotic modern horror novel by Jonathan M. Sweet.

The One After Snelling — Kickass modern noir from Richard O'Brien.

The Sign of the Scorpion — 1935 Edmund Snell tale of oriental evil.

The House of the Vampire — 1907 poetic thriller by George S. Viereck.

An Angel in the Street — Modern hardboiled noir by Peter Genovese.

The Devil's Mistress — Scottish gothic tale by J. W. Brodie-Innes.

The Lord of Terror — 1925 mystery with master-criminal, Fantômas.

The Lady of the Terraces — 1925 adventure by E. Charles Vivian.

My Deadly Angel — 1955 Cold War drama by John Chelton.

Prose Bowl — Futuristic satire — Bill Pronzini & Barry N. Malzberg .

Satan's Den Exposed — True crime in Truth or Consequences New Mexico — Award-winning journalism by the *Desert Journal.*

The Amorous Intrigues & Adventures of Aaron Burr — by Anonymous — Hot historical action.

I Stole $16,000,000 — A true story by cracksman Herbert E. Wilson.

The Black Dark Murders — Vintage 50s college murder yarn by Milt Ozaki, writing as Robert O. Saber.

Sex Slave — Potboiler of lust in the days of Cleopatra — Dion Leclerq.

You'll Die Laughing — Bruce Elliott's 1945 novel of murder at a practical joker's English countryside manor.

The Private Journal & Diary of John H. Surratt — The memoirs of the man who conspired to assassinate President Lincoln.

Dead Man Talks Too Much — Hollywood boozer by Weed Dickenson

Red Light — History of legal prostitution in Shreveport Louisiana by Eric Brock. Includes wonderful photos of the houses and the ladies.

A Snark Selection — Lewis Carroll's *The Hunting of the Snark* with two Snarkian chapters by Harry Stephen Keeler — Illustrated by Gavin L. O'Keefe.

Ripped from the Headlines! — The Jack the Ripper story as told in the newspaper articles in the *New York* and *London Times.*

Geronimo — S. M. Barrett's 1905 autobiography of a noble American.

The White Peril in the Far East — Sidney Lewis Gulick's 1905 indictment of the West and assurance that Japan would never attack the U.S.

The Compleat Calhoon — All of Fender Tucker's works: Includes *Totah Six-Pack, Weed, Women and Song* and *Tales from the Tower,* plus a CD of all of his songs.

Totah Six-Pack — Just Fender Tucker's six tales about Farmington in one sleek volume.

RAMBLE HOUSE
Fender Tucker, Prop.   Gavin L. O'Keefe, Graphics
www.ramblehouse.com   fender@ramblehouse.com
228-826-1783   10329 Sheephead Drive, Vancleave MS 39565

www.ingramcontent.com/pod-product-compliance
Lightning Source LLC
Chambersburg PA
CBHW030350020726
47493CB00003B/764